VALKYRIES

BOOK TWO

all through
the blood

VALKYRIES

BOOK TWO

all through
the blood

a novel

JERI MASSI

MOODY PUBLISHERS
CHICAGO

All Scripture quotations are taken from the King James Version.

Library of Congress Cataloging-in-Publication Data

Massi, Jeri.
    Valkyries / Jeri Massi.
        p. cm.
    Summary: In the 1970s, behavior and family problems send
Tracey to a Catholic boarding school, where she struggles to
explore and practice her new-found belief in the Bible and
Protestantism.
    ISBN 0-8024-1514-8 (bk. 2)
    [1. Christian life--Fiction. 2. Catholic schools--Fiction.
3. Conversion--Fiction. 4. Family problems--Fiction.
5. Schools--Fiction. 6. Protestantism--History--Fiction.
7. Catholic Church--Fiction.] I. Massi, Jeri. Some through
the fire. II. Title.

PZ7.M423855 Val 2003
[Fic]--dc21
                                                    2002010667

1 3 5 7 9 10 8 6 4 2

Printed in the United States of America

To All Good Valkyries and True

PART ONE

JUNIOR YEAR

O N E

T he New England sun burned on the faded black-
top under the basketball hoop. Tracey Jacamuzzi's
feet felt hot as she expertly weaved back and forth,
changing hands with the ball as her shorter opponent
tried to reach in and snatch it away from her.

"Come on, Dibbles. Play like you've got arms, not
flippers." Tracey grinned as she took a fake step and
then went the other way to dodge around her friend
and get inside the key.

"But I'm trying out for the Dolphins." Dibbles
blocked her motion, though she couldn't get the ball
away. Her humor, Tracey realized, had not left her.

Weary of scrambling so fast in the hot sun, Tracey
pivoted and jumped, straight up, out of range of Dibbles's
short arms. The orange ball arced through the air and
looked like it would go in, but it hit the rim and
bounced off.

"Aha! Aaaagh!" Dibbles shouted. This was her
ploy to distract Tracey from catching the rebound.
"Kee-yiii!" They raced to catch it.

From behind Dibbles, Tracey jumped again and plucked the ball out of the air before Dibbles could reach it. Tracey stopped, rested the ball against her hip, and held up a hand to signal a time-out. Both girls relaxed and straightened.

"Better?" Dibbles asked.

"First of all, the Dolphins are a baseball team," Tracey said.

The short, slightly round girl made a wry face. "They're a football team, Coach Jacamuzzi."

"Oops. Well, no Dolphins for you. Just Valkyries. I think your blocking is terrific." Dibbles brightened. "And your shooting is great, too. But you've really got a disadvantage on getting rebounds." Tracey hesitated as she thought through that day's practice. "And you could do better on taking the ball away, Dib. You get right up against me on my blind side, and then somehow miss the ball. Get your eye on it first, then try to steal it. Don't reach and look at the same time. Mark the target first. Then snatch the ball away real quick."

Debbie Dibbley nodded. If she made the team, she would be the shortest girl ever to play for the Valkyries. The height disadvantage was significant, but she had terrific talent.

After just an hour, both girls were red-faced and drenched with sweat. One of the nuns came out on the steps of the residence hall and waved her arms to tell them their time was up. With the advent of this August heat wave, their afternoon practices had been limited to an hour. The restriction frustrated Dibbles.

"Maybe we should try the gym," she said.

"Mr. Szymansky chained the doors," Tracey told

her. "He says it's off-limits until they're finished with the floors, and he means it."

Dibbles let out her breath, and for once her perpetual good humor seemed to leave her.

"Come on." Tracey rolled the ball off her hip and thrust it at Dibbles. "Let's go to the hideout and recuperate. We can play after dinner."

The campus buildings of the Sanctuary of Mary and Joseph Convent and School for Girls were not air-conditioned. The dwindling number of summer residents searched out cool spots for retreat and comfort during the long afternoons.

The coolest place on campus was the empty dining hall, sheltered by several magnificent old trees. There were screened windows left open in the outer hallways, so anybody who opened all the dining room doors let in a refreshing cross breeze that never diminished. In the late summer months, when the campus was almost deserted, the main dining room became a private haven not invaded by the nuns or staff during the day.

The silent, breezy room of empty tables was an even better retreat if you went into the kitchen and helped yourself to the ice cream stored away in deep, round cardboard barrels in the steel freezers.

Tracey had been a resident student at Mary and Joseph—otherwise known as MoJoe—for two uninterrupted years, including all vacations and holidays, so she had worked out most of the secrets of the buildings for herself. But she was willing to share her knowledge, especially with her basketball protégée.

They stopped in the kitchen first and equipped themselves with one bowl each of Howard Johnson's chocolate chip ice cream. Then they sat down in the straight-backed chairs at the end of one of the long rows of tables.

The two girls could not have been more different. Tracey was the classic basketball player: tall and thin, with long feet and long hands. Dibbles topped the tape at five foot two, and even after scrambling all over the court for months to acquire the skills to make the team, she retained an elfin roundness. With dark hair that emphasized the stark whiteness of her fair skin, a round face, and two button-shaped blue eyes accented by quirky eyebrows and a turned-up nose, she looked like a cartoon character, or a clown.

And yet, Tracey thought as she watched Dibbles plow into the mountain of ice cream, once Dibbles got onto the basketball court, she quickly dropped most of her offbeat humor.

In the half-court games they had played over the summer with the other boarders and with a few of the staff, Tracey had quickly recognized that the short girl had a lot of talent, in spite of her difficulties in protecting the basket on defense. When it came to offense, Tracey could keep control of the ball in tight places, but Dibbles could take the ball where there were no openings. Huffing, face red, blue eyes snapping with intensity, she snaked into impossible places; and if she could not shoot, she snaked out again. She rolled right around the taller players, including Tracey, and shot or passed off before she could be trapped or blocked. Debbie Dibbley, Tracey thought, could roll tighter than an Ace bandage. Then, in the next instant, she would be laughing or clowning around. She never seemed to take anything seriously; but here it was, two days after summer school had ended, and—

instead of choosing the freedom of going home immediately—Dibbles was staying on for the rest of the
week to hone her basketball skills.

The dining room was quiet except for the breeze
ruffling through the open doors from the outer hallways. During the school year, this room was the scene
of girls milling around or busily eating and talking. It
was the place where deals and meetings were arranged,
where people plotted revenge against "narcs," and
where Sister Mary—the school's acting principal—
sometimes arranged to humiliate girls, as Tracey knew
to her own pain. But now there was only a dim hush
and a refreshing breeze, as though the dining room had
to recover from the school year with a few weeks of
rest.

"So you think I got the stuff?" Dibbles suddenly
asked in her singsongy voice.

"I can't believe CPR ever cut you from the team
last year," Tracey told her. "You're a lot better than
most of our second-string. If you keep working at it, I
think you could get on first-string this year."

"My looks go against me," Dibbles said, still
singsongy. "Sometimes we glamorous types are under-
appreciated for our other skills."

"Yeah, that could be a real problem." Tracey glanced
at her, taking a quick survey. "There's just not enough
of you, Dibbles. That's what fools people."

"Oh, there's plenty of me. It's just in the wrong di-
mensions. I'm quite densely packed." Dibbles lifted her
spoon to emphasize the point. "If somebody could figure out a way to stretch it all out, I could be as tall as
you and not lose a thing."

From the depths of the kitchen, they heard an

13

outer door close. Then a man's voice called, "Who's in here?"

"Oh, rats," Tracey muttered.

"Hung by our own petard!" Dibbles gasped. She glanced up at Tracey with a grin. "Cheer up, Jac. Now I get to see you suffer for your faith."

"In here, Father!" Tracey called.

"What is a petard, anyway?" Dibbles asked. She added in a low voice, "Just tell him CPR said we could."

"No, I'm not going to lie," Tracey whispered.

In a moment, the silhouette of the slender Father Williams, more often called Father Bing because of his resemblance to Bing Crosby, appeared among the countertops of the kitchen through the open double doors. He hurriedly negotiated his way around the cabinets and came toward them.

"A soiree!" he exclaimed, his voice disappointed. "And I wasn't invited?"

Tracey and Dibbles instantly grasped that they were not in trouble.

"You can join us, but only if you promise to referee the scrimmage tonight," Tracey said.

"It's a deal. I'll be right back." He hurried away to get his share of ice cream.

"How do you like that?" Tracey whispered. With Sister Mary's absence and the campus temporarily under the lax and generous control of Father Bing, she had not expected to get into real trouble for having a private bowl of ice cream. But she had expected that he would end the practice.

"Oh, Jac, Father Bing always lets you do what you want," Dibbles said in a low voice.

Tracey frowned and shot a sharp glance at her friend. "I'm not anybody's favorite!"

"It doesn't have anything to do with being his favorite, Jac. It's because you're stuck here all summer, and he feels bad for you. He's a softhearted guy."

"Well, maybe."

Actually, Tracey thought, the summer had not been all that bad. There were a few other basketball hopefuls around during summer school, and Sister Patricia Rose, the basketball coach and gym teacher known as CPR, had stayed for a few weeks. She would doff her habit and scrimmage with them on most evenings. Even Father Bing played now and then.

The impromptu half-court games had been fun. Tracey certainly felt a lot more accepted and at ease with everybody than she had yet felt at MoJoe. Part of the happiness, of course, was that Sister Mary had disappeared for the entire summer.

Father Bing returned with his ice cream and joined them at the long, quiet table, and the talk turned to safe subjects.

During the rest of August, a great quiet settled over the campus. Dibbles returned home for three and a half weeks, promising to practice every day on her own. Tracey knew that she would.

The days were uneventful, and Tracey enjoyed an austere happiness in being master of her own time, in studying and reading, and in practicing basketball by herself. MoJoe had given her discipline and purpose, even when she was lonely.

But the sorrow that was forever a part of MoJoe was no longer a sorrow she could forget about, especially with the new school year bearing down on her. The balance of constant control—endless, often meaningless, discipline; ugly uniforms; locker raids; high-pressure academics—was all carefully maintained and always would be. Tracey was on her way to the top of the pile, but she knew she was just as much a prisoner as anybody way down at the bottom. No one here was allowed to be happy for very long.

The only moments of forgetfulness she enjoyed were the afternoon and late evening sessions with the three-volume book that she thought was the most important Christian book in the entire world, *The History of Protestantism* by the Reverend J. A. Wylie. Dibbles thought it funny that Tracey would pore over the pages of tiny print and stilted woodcut drawings. But there was great comfort in reading Wylie, and Tracey could not be laughed away from him. Her only trouble with Wylie was that he wrote about Christians as though they had already conquered their sins, and she had not conquered hers.

Maddie Murdoch, a Protestant woman who volunteered at MoJoe, had said that there were times when you were utterly cast on God. When you saw your own weakness and knew there was nothing you could do; He had to do it for you. God didn't seem to be doing it for Tracey. Yet she couldn't even justify getting mad at God for betraying her, because she had betrayed Him first. She knew that her individual sins were confessed and forgiven, but it was what she was that frightened her: implacable, violent, hypocritical, and unfaithful. God could forgive the actions, but what about the person behind them who perpetrated such things?

When Tracey's thoughts became too dark, there was always the comfort of the basketball court. Maddie

Murdoch had also shown up several times during the summer. The memory of her advice about God was never far from Tracey's mind. She wondered what other questions she might ask Maddie to prompt more of such answers—answers that stuck with her.

Tracey devised the exact questions she wanted to ask—like, what, precisely, does forgiveness entail? Does it mean you'd get a chance to undo the things you'd done? She planned to ask that question without revealing how much the answer meant to her. Already in their short acquaintance, she had shocked and horrified Mrs. Murdoch more than once. She didn't want to do that again.

It was so much easier to be friends with Liz Lukas, the captain of the basketball team and Tracey's best friend and mentor. Liz had no expectations except that Tracey be nice and agreeable. When it came to religion and God, Liz didn't believe anything, or so she claimed. She was the exact sort of person that Tracey's former pastor had warned her not to be friends with. But Liz was the best friend anybody could have.

Tracey got a letter—the last letter of the summer, Liz promised—announcing that her friend would be returning sometime in the middle of the month, "just as soon as I can convince you-know-who that they've had enough of family togetherness." Tracey wondered what Liz's relationship with her parents was really like. It was hard to picture Liz not getting along with anybody. She was so calm and cool, so in charge of herself and every situation.

The days passed, each one marked by Tracey's long vigils on the lawn, watching in hope of Liz's return. She carefully hid her precious Wylie books in a closet on the unused fourth floor of the main hall. They were a secret possession that nobody could take from her. No one must ever know where they were hidden. Soon enough, when Tracey met Sister St. Gerard in religion class with fresh ammo, they would all want to know what she had been reading and where she had gotten it.

T W O

The ringing of the telephone out in the hallway was such an unusual sound that Tracey jumped as she came up the stairs one day from her solitary basketball practice. But the moment of startlement passed, and she raced to get it, expecting Liz's hearty greeting.

"Yes, yes!" she exclaimed, ready to let out a whoop at the sound of her friend's voice.

"Tracey, is that you?"

A new surprise, and the barest feeling of disappointment, caught her off guard. "Oh, hi, Mom."

"Well," her mother said, trying to sound light—and her effort at lightness sent a warning to Tracey—"that's a new way to answer the phone. How are you, honey?"

"Fine, Mom, how are you?" Tracey asked.

"We're fine. I was worried. I haven't gotten a letter from you since June, Tracey."

"I . . . I guess I keep meaning to write," Tracey began. "It's just so hard with everything going on—I didn't know it had been so long—"

"Well, honey, I thought I might come up to see you this weekend," her mom said.

Tracey paused, and then she said, "Does Dad know?"

"I really don't care if your father knows or not, dear. He can't make me believe that my oldest daughter is dead and gone. That's what he's tried, you know."

Tracey knew it perfectly well. She'd known, once her father had made up his mind to ban her from the family, that she was considered not only as if she had died, but as if she had never been born. Yet hearing such a thing from her mother drove the pain home more sharply than it had hit in the entire two years since she'd been sent away. It hurt, for a moment, as much as it had that first day when she had come to MoJoe and had felt so utterly alone. She caught her breath with a single gulp.

"Yeah, I know," she said.

"Well, his days of absolute rule are over," her mother said. "I'll be up Friday night."

"Sure," Tracey told her.

"I really can't wait to see you, honey. We have a lot to talk about."

"Yeah," Tracey said. She hung up without remembering to say good-bye.

A lot to talk about was right. She wasn't so dumb that she didn't know what they were going to talk about: divorce. And maybe, if her mom thought Tracey was the same dumb kid who had left home two years ago, she would even venture something about that sap, Jim. Something about meeting him a few weeks ago, and they were planning to date. Some lie that a cheap woman would tell her cheap, naive kid and figure the dumb kid would swallow.

Tracey wondered at how the years before she had become a Christian had been filled with such naïveté, and the two years since had been the years when she'd grown up. She'd learned the ways of the world and all that was cheap while sitting incarcerated at MoJoe. One thing Wylie had shown her: Whether it was enacted on the grand scales of European kings and popes, or whether it was a small drama that took place in the kitchen, the stairway, and the halls of a single home or the beds of one hotel, adultery always went with lies, and pretty soon violence would have its part. Adultery, lies, and violence were the same whether they were performed by kings or paupers. But somehow, it seemed that the kings and popes got away with their sins and held onto that same aura of grandeur, while the little people like her own mother were made cheap.

But really, it was all cheap. Let her mother and Lucrezia Borgia trade places—they'd be identical in reversed roles. And Tracey, in a palace or a dorm room, was the one walked on. Peasants still got slaughtered every day—they just went by different names and wore different clothes.

The boarding students always left stuff behind when they vacated for the summer. Tracey walked up the halls and went through drawers until she found the remains of an old, stale pack of cigarettes. She lit one and blew out a plume of smoke. For a moment she wondered why she should return to the role her mother had assigned her: dumb Tracey. Then she shrugged the thought off. True, she was a basketball star and made good grades—dean's list each semester. But that wasn't the Tracey her mother knew. And Tracey didn't have the strength to be proving something that her mother wouldn't even notice. This visit had one purpose: to tell her about the divorce and recruit her aid.

I've hurt a lot of people, she told the Lord. *I've done a lot of bad things, and I know it. But if You even listen to my prayers anymore—this one may shock you—please, don't let her take me home. Don't let me go where I'll hurt the rest of them, or where she can use me against my dad. Oh, Lord, You know what he did to me, but I don't want to go to court and testify against him. I can't do it.*

She pulled a long draw on the cigarette and held it in until her vision hazed over. Then she expelled it sharply and staggered a little, driving away the thoughts of what might come. Divorces could be really ugly, and she expected her parents' divorce to be one of the worst. Her father was a man to avenge himself. And her mother, she suspected, would try to make use of every weapon possible. Tracey's testimony would be weapon enough for anybody. *God, help me,* she thought again before she took another drag so long that it nearly made her sick. Then she put it out of her mind.

As it turned out, the announcement of the divorce was not as bad as Tracey had feared.

Her mother came up on Friday night. They kissed, and then she took Tracey out for dinner, though she made some comment about not having as much money as she'd once had.

For not having money, she took Tracey to a nice enough restaurant. Their talk was safe—which made Tracey realize that her suspicions were correct. The big news was coming. Normally, her mother would be quick to comment on, apologize for, or defend every-thing that had passed. But now she behaved as though none of it had ever happened. She was waiting for the moment to spring the big news, and that waiting was the worst part of the night for Tracey.

They had dessert, and still her mother said nothing about it. They got into the car and headed back for campus, and even then her mother said nothing. Tracey felt angry, impatient.

But as her mother parked in the darkness in front of the hall, she said, with a graveness that was appropriate and yet, in some ways, almost funny in its solemnity, "There's something I have to tell you, Tracey."

Tracey steeled herself, kept her face impassive, and asked, "What's wrong?"

While her mother spoke, she wrestled between playing the role of the innocent or throwing it all back at her mother—a tempting thought. She could tell her that she'd known all along, that there was reason to think that her father's violence was provoked by her mother's own adultery.

Tracey clamped down on these thoughts. She didn't have a single tie to the world now that the ties to her family were so badly cut.

When her mother finished, all Tracey said was, "Am I supposed to come home now?"

"Your father has agreed to continue paying for your education here," her mother told her. "He said he doesn't want to see you."

"It figures," Tracey said. "This religion thing really bugs him."

"If it comes to a custody battle, you may have to go to court to—"

"I'll never testify against either of you," Tracey said.

"You don't have anything to say about me!" her mother said, surprised.

"You can tell Dad for me, Mom," Tracey told her, "I won't testify against either one of you. If he wants to get custody of me, he might try to make me take the stand and say whatever he can get me to say, but I won't do it."

Her mother looked pensive. No doubt, Tracey thought, she was weighing out the advantages and disadvantages of Tracey's position.

At last her mother said, "Well, he doesn't want custody of you, Tracey, not if your beliefs stay this way. He's promised to take the other children from me, and I plan to fight him. You won't help me? Your father is a powerful man."

"It's wrong to testify against a parent," Tracey said. "I can't do it for whatever reason." As she said it, she realized that it might not always be wrong to testify against a parent. If her father were ever to hurt any of the others as he had hurt her, she would feel just as bound to testify against him as she now felt bound not to. But she didn't retract her statement. All her mother needed to know was that—as things now stood, anyway—Tracey could not testify. The Bible demanded honor to parents, and getting caught up in a divorce trial seemed almost as cheap and shoddy as the divorce itself, or the adultery that had provoked it.

"All right," her mother said. "But you can come home now. You can live with me. I . . . I have an apartment picked out, and I'll be moving in a couple of weeks."

"You aren't keeping the house?" Tracey asked, surprised.

"One of us has to move out for the proceedings to begin," she said. "As your father refuses to, I've decided to move out."

Tracey wondered how in the world her mother could afford such a thing, but she decided against asking.

The rest of their conversation was taken up with details of how a divorce worked, and at last her mother did tell her about Jim, a man she had "just met."

Tracey listened in silence and then said, "It's almost lights-out, Mom. I better go in now."

Her mother looked disappointed, as though expecting Tracey to ask more about this mystery man, but she said, "All right, dear. I have to get back. You take care of yourself. Remember, you can come home anytime you want now."

"Sure, thanks," Tracey said.

THREE

All Tracey really wanted was to get away from her mother, the car, and everything. She desperately hoped that Liz would be back now, back on this very day when she needed her so badly. She sprinted through the first floor of the hall and up to her room and found—to her surprise—that luggage had been left there.

"Liz!" she exclaimed out loud. But her friend wasn't anywhere upstairs. Tracey checked the luggage and the beds and found no note—nothing. She grabbed a jacket and ran down the stairs again, flipping on lights as she went so Liz would know she had come looking for her.

It didn't seem likely that Liz would be out on the grounds anywhere, now that it was dark. Tracey made for the gym. Liz probably had gone looking for her there.

But the gym was dark. As Tracey turned from it in disappointment and some anger, her eyes caught a brief flash of light from the farthest side of the school grounds, way, way over at the edge of the woods.

Not very hopeful, and a little frightened at what might be over there, she nonetheless went to explore. As she neared the place where she thought she'd seen the light, she almost gave up her search. Then the light reappeared for a second. She jogged closer and heard suppressed giggling and laughter. Girls' laughter.

Silent in the darkness, she edged closer to the woods and took a few tentative steps into the deeper darkness under the trees.

Again the sound of muffled laughter carried through the branches and twigs. Mindful of the thick carpet of old leaves from previous autumns, Tracey crept closer until she saw the silhouettes of three girls. The light switched on again, and she caught a glimpse of Liz struggling to get a bottle of wine open.

"Liz," Tracey said. The light switched off, and there was a sound of scuffling, as people prepared to run. Despair seized her. "Liz!" she cried.

"Wait, I know her," Liz whispered to someone. Footsteps, sounding unsteady as they rustled through the leaves, came toward her. The flashlight beamed in her face.

"Tracey, let's go up to the hall," Liz said. She threw an arm around Tracey, obviously trying to guide her away.

"Cool it," Tracey told her. "You havin' a party?"

"It was ending," Liz said. "Just ending."

"Come on," Tracey said, determined to see what was going on.

"No big party," Liz insisted. "Come up to the hall."

Tracey stopped and looked her friend in the eye. "No big party?" she asked. She took the bottle of wine from Liz's other hand. "This isn't empty yet."

Liz looked abashed.

"S'almost empty," she said.

"We can work on it," Tracey told her. She put the bottle to her lips and tipped it up. "Boone's Farm, right?"

"Hey, Liz, come on," a voice called in a hoarse whisper.

"Here we come," Tracey called back. She looked at Liz. "Why don't you introduce me to your friends?"

"OK," Liz said after a moment. She guided Tracey back to a small clearing by the side of a tiny rivulet of water that the girls at MoJoe called the stream.

Two strangers sat on the ground. "Who's this?" one of them asked.

"Tracey Jacamuzzi," Tracey told them. "You guys MoJoes?"

"I met them at the train station," Liz said, her words a little slower than usual. She had her eyes on Tracey, and Tracey, mindful of her friend's wariness and concern, tipped up the bottle again for a long drink.

"Hope you don't mind if I crash your party," she said.

"Jac—" Liz began, taking hold of the bottle.

"Would you cool it?" Tracey demanded. Her eyes met Liz's. "I'm a big girl, Liz. I can handle it, OK? You wouldn't believe what I can handle!"

Their eyes locked in the dimness. After a moment Liz said, "Sure. I know that. I just want a drink. It's my turn."

Tracey pushed the bottle at her.

Donna and Linda, who were not MoJoes, had struck up a quick friendship with Liz on the train.

28

They were catching the midnight train to Boston and were passing the evening in the most companionable way they could with their temporary friend. They gave Tracey cigarettes and kept the two remaining bottles of wine going around.

Afterward, Tracey had no memory of what they had talked about. She had one impression that never left her of trying to stagger back to the dorm with Liz and throwing up several times on the way, and it seemed that she was crying too. But she could never be sure if it really happened or if it was just a dream.

Morning was no dream. The light through the window sent a pain into Tracey's head that traveled in a thin but unbreakable line all the way down into her stomach. She rolled over to the edge of the bed and found the trash can right by the bed. Liz must have set it there. She threw up into it.

The act of vomiting, instead of easing her misery, increased it. The throbbing in her temples got a lot worse, and something in her stomach rebelled against throwing up again right away. She rolled back on the bed and groaned. A cold sweat lay on her forehead.

"You all right?" Liz asked, suddenly at her side.

"Shhh, shhh, quiet, Liz," Tracey whispered. "Oh, my—" She rolled over again and threw up into the trash can. This time, Liz's big hand caught her forehead and held her head up. Then Liz helped her lie back on the bed.

Tracey forced her eyes open a slit. Liz looked really sick too. The sight of her haggard face made Tracey feel worse instead of better.

"I got ice," Liz said in a thick, though quiet, voice.

"Heating pad," Tracey begged.

Liz staggered away and found her heating pad.

Tracey woke up again around noon. The trash can by her bed had been emptied and rinsed out. Liz sat on the floor, her back against the opposite bunk and her head on her knees, her arms wrapped tightly around them. Tracey dared to pull her face out of the heating pad. She carefully eased herself up in the bed.

Liz looked up. "Coffee?" she asked.

"Yeah," Tracey said. Her mouth felt like it was filled with cotton or sand.

Liz brought her aspirin, and she washed it down with a little water. She managed to get her legs swung over the edge of the bed.

"I'll get toast," Liz said. Tracey meant to ask her where in the world she would get toast, but the question took too much effort. She put her strength into getting up and getting into the shower.

By the time she got back from the shower, the coffee was ready in Liz's Poly-Perk. Tracey poured a cup of it, black and strong, and took a tentative sip. The first sip washed all the cotton and sand away. After a few more sips, she managed to find the strength to put on some jeans and a T-shirt. Liz returned with a plate of dry toast.

"I got it from the kitchen," she told Tracey.

"There aren't any toasters down there."

"I made it in one of the ovens. I just helped myself to what I could find."

Tracey nodded and sat down on the edge of the bed. She silently ate the toast and finished the coffee. Without a word, Liz filled up her cup for her again, and at last Tracey said, "Welcome back."

"Why in the world did you drink so much?" Liz asked.

"Seemed like the appropriate thing at the time," Tracey told her.

"Tracey—"

"Liz, would you cut it out? Why is it OK for you to drink and not me? Did you think you could come back and ignore me, and not have me try to get into whatever you were doing?"

"It's not that way, Jac," Liz said wearily.

"Well, what way is it?" Tracey asked. She could see that Liz's feelings were genuinely hurt by her tone.

"Jac," Liz said, "those girls just wanted a safe place to get smashed. I was trying to shake them. But when I got back here, I saw that you weren't around. So I said OK, we would drink together. I thought you'd get mad," she admitted. "But I couldn't find you to get you to help me get rid of them."

"OK," Tracey said, only half believing the story.

"The last thing I thought was that you'd get drunk too," Liz said.

"Why not?" Tracey asked. "Who cares?"

"You told me about the divorce," Liz said.

Tracey stopped. Then she said, subdued, "I didn't get drunk because my parents are getting divorced."

Liz said, in a lower voice, "I need you, Jac. I need you right now. Don't get mad at me. And don't get drunk."

Tracey straightened up and took a second look at Liz. "What's wrong?"

"Give your religion a little more time," Liz said. "I need you, Tracey. I need you to . . . to be the way you've always been."

Tracey slid off the bed to get a better look at Liz's face. Liz looked at her.

"What's happened?" Tracey asked. "Good heavens, Liz, what's wrong?" A new thought struck her. "Your folks aren't splitting too, are they?"

Liz almost smiled. "No."

Tracey crossed the space between them and set down the cup. "Well, what is it, then?"

"I can't tell you . . . it's really bad. . . . It's too bad to say—" To Tracey's horror, Liz began to cry. "Jac, it's too bad to say. Oh, heaven help me, why did it happen?"

Tracey grabbed her. "Liz!"

Liz Lukas—the unmovable, unstoppable—broke down and cried as heartily and helplessly as Tracey at her worst had ever cried.

Helpless herself, Tracey kept her arms around Liz, but she had the idea that Liz, even then, wanted to be left alone in her misery. But she couldn't leave her.

After a long time, as Liz brought her sobbing back under control, Tracey steeled herself to make a commitment that frightened her a little. "Whatever it is," she told Liz, "no matter how bad it is, Liz, you can tell me. I won't condemn you. I won't hate you. I'll find some way to help you. I won't tell the nuns."

Liz's laugh was full of such tiredness and helplessness that it lacked the warmth of a real laugh. It frightened Tracey. "The nuns!" Liz exclaimed. "The nuns know—the worst of it, anyway."

She looked up at Tracey. "Pray for me, Jac. And don't get mad at me. If it seems like I'm chickening out or something, don't get mad at me."

"I won't," Tracey promised. "Liz, you're my best friend."

Liz nodded wearily.

"If you can't tell me," Tracey said, "can you tell Maddie Murdoch? You want me to call her for you?"

"No, babe," Liz said. "Maddie Murdoch couldn't hack this. Sometimes you're right when you talk about her that way. She couldn't handle it; I don't think she could even comprehend why—" She stopped.

"OK," Tracey said. She took her arm away from Liz, aware of how much Liz disliked sentimental things. But she stayed by her, and they drank their coffee in silence.

F O U R

It was now Liz's turn to be tortured at night with bad dreams and long wakeful sessions. She took it all with a stoicism that shamed Tracey. When Tracey had been struggling with grief last year, it had shown in her every line, but Liz's troubles were invisible to the whole world, except for Tracey.

At first, Liz's basketball skills seemed to be suffering, but as the last days of summer ran out, she began to pick up. Students came drifting back, and the games of half-court were as spirited as any Tracey had seen.

But every now and then—like when Liz was in the act of pulling a rebound away from somebody—she stopped and let it go by, let the other person get the ball. Tracey's eyes were on her in every spare moment, and Liz always looked back at her at such times, when her confidence slipped, and Tracey alone saw that the blonde girl was struggling against the pleasures of the game that she felt she should not have.

"You're losing some of that cocksureness of yours, Miss Lukas," Father Bing told Liz one evening as he stood on the sidelines of the outside court and watched a few of them play.

"It'll come back," Liz promised. She shot a look at Tracey, who said nothing.

"Hope you're not slowing down in your old age," he added with a slight laugh.

"Not a bit," Liz said, with a countering laugh. "Come on out here and play for a few points if you think so." The challenge was so typical of her that he shook off his momentary doubt and let her be.

As the days hurried by, Liz was obviously working at her game, concentrating on the plays and her skills. Even Tracey couldn't tell, by the time school started, that Liz had other things to think of when she was playing ball. But at night her preoccupation was apparent. Time after time, Liz's calls woke Tracey up. "Stop her! Stop her! Somebody take it away!" she would cry—always a command or a plea for someone to be stopped.

"Liz," Tracey called softly one night, the night before classes started. "Liz!"

The outcries abruptly stopped, and Liz opened her eyes. Tracey left her bunk and sat on the floor by Liz's bed. "It's me, Tracey."

"I know," Liz said.

"Liz, we're going to get roommates tomorrow," Tracey told her. "We can't hide it forever. Can't you tell me what's happened?"

"No," Liz said. She turned her head to look at Tracey in the dimness. "No."

"Look," Tracey pleaded, "I know I'm not much of a Christian, Liz. I know that. But I do know that anybody can come to Christ and be forgiven. Nobody has to go to hell for sins. If you can't tell me, tell Him. If you can't say you're sorry to anybody down here, say it to Him. If you repent, if—"

"No," Liz said, but not angrily. "No, Jac. Just pray for me. OK?"

"Come on, Liz—"

"Just pray for me. I just want to forget."

"You can pray!" Tracey pleaded.

"No, He'll want me to tell them I did it. I can't. I can't!"

"If you're this sorry—"

"It would be better to be dead. Oh, Jac, this place is hell. It can't get worse than this. I hate this place so much—" Liz broke down into sobs of weakness and grief. "Just pray for me, for just one night of peace. If I could only sleep—"

Tracey took a course she'd never dared before. She didn't know how she had the courage. Maybe desperation, more than anything, did it for her.

"Oh, Lord," she said. "We know that we're sinners. We've done some really bad things—worse than we can admit to other people. But You know everything. Lord, don't leave us now."

She was surprised to feel Liz's arm go around her neck. Liz cried harder, into her pillow.

"God, have mercy on us both," Tracey added. "We're at the end of our ways. We're in all kinds of prisons here in this one place. What will we do, Lord, if You don't help us?"

She was so tired that she wasn't sure when her prayer sank from words to a whisper, then to thoughts, and finally to sleep. But her sleep was punctuated with

dreams of praying for help and with her audible mur-
murings for mercy.

Morning found Tracey still on her knees alongside
the bed, her head on the edge of the pillow. She woke
up with a crick in her neck, but she forgot about it at
the sight of Liz's empty bed. It was almost time for the
morning bell. Tracey jumped up and almost fell down
again. Both her legs were asleep. She caught the upper
bunk's steel frame and pulled herself up. As soon as she
could, she ran to the window, pulling on socks and
clothes as she went.

The campus glistened under a faint morning dew.
Spiderwebs sparkled here and there among the shrubs
and hedges. Liz and another woman were walking together on the hockey field, heads bent in conversation. It took Tracey a minute to realize that the woman
was Maddie Murdoch.

She pulled on the rest of her uniform—now that
classes were starting, the dress code was in effect
again—and ran out the door, buttoning up the vio-
lently pink blouse that marked her as a junior.

By the time she got out the front doors, Liz was
alone on the walk, and Maddie's car was retreating toward the gate.

"You talk to her?" Tracey asked.

"Asked her some questions," Liz said quietly. She
looked at Tracey. "I might have asked you, I know. But
you were asleep at last—I didn't want to wake you up."

"Maddie knows a lot more about . . . God, and
everything, than I do," Tracey said. "Did she help
you?"

"I only asked her questions," Liz said again. She
looked down. "Maybe it's not as bad as I thought. I . . .

I don't know. Let's go back inside. I don't want Mary or St. Bernard knowing I talked to Maddie."

They went inside again.

By breakfast time, Liz was dressed in the gold blouse of a senior. The new color seemed to please her—at least, her mood seemed better that morning. Tracey hoped things were getting back to normal. Maybe the new school year and basketball season would restore her friend.

F I V E

There was only one cuts list during basketball try-outs that year. Though many girls had come out for the first practice, one hour with the likes of Liz, Tracey, and Scooter had driven most of the hopefuls away. None of the previous year's first-string had graduated, and Peggy had come back a better player. Sister Patricia Rose's surprise and pleasure at Peggy's improvement was second only to her surprise at Debbie Dibbley.

She was much more frank in congratulating Dibbles on her skills than she had ever been with Tracey, and Tracey was surprised at feeling some resentment as she watched CPR walk off the court arm in arm with Tracey's former protégée.

"Are those the horns of jealousy I see?" Liz asked in a low, incredulous voice.

The comment shocked the envy out of Tracey. She looked at Liz.

Liz grinned. "Come on, Jac. The little kid is good, but she's not as good as you. Not by a mile."

"It's not that," Tracey said. "It's just that CPR's never acted so high about me. I don't know. She picks odd favorites."

"Safe favorites," Liz reminded her. "That's all you need—to have the coach make you her pet. CPR wouldn't do it if you were her kid sister. It would make you a perfect tool in Mary's hands. And it would make CPR a perfect tool too."

Tracey let the ball in her arm drop to the ground, and she dribbled it a few times in a slow, thoughtful way. "Sometimes, Liz, I just wish I could be special to someone. To anyone."

"Hey, you're special enough," Liz said as she deftly flipped the ball to herself and took up the dribble.

"Well, people notice me, that's for sure."

She knew that resentment would kill team spirit. Besides, it was completely unjust to resent Dibbles's good fortune in being in the lineup for the team and moving so quickly into CPR's affections. Dibbles was as unwitting about capturing favor as she was about most things. She just bumbled on her way, and good things happened to her. It took a few days, but Tracey managed to submerge whatever envy she felt in her own determination to play well. The resentment fell away, but the sight of CPR's obvious attention and praise to every good pass or shot from Dibbles never failed to sting Tracey.

The beginning of basketball practices had a good effect on Liz. She slept better, and it was easier for her to concentrate on her studies if the hour after dinner was spent in the gym. Tracey hoped that whatever had been bothering her was now waning.

Tracey's classes included Algebra II, English Literature from 1066 to the Renaissance, European history, biology, and a philosophy course taught by Sister St. Gerard—or St. Bernard, as the students nicknamed her. Their first philosophy assignment was to read *Man's Search for Meaning* by Victor Frankl. Tracey used Liz's old copy. Liz had shrugged off the book, but to Tracey, who had already learned about moral light from Wylie, Frankl's story of who survived in a concentration camp and who didn't made perfect sense. She only half understood Kierkegaardian psychology, and St. Bernard's lectures on existentialism didn't clear things up for her much. But she came away from the book much impressed by how important it was for Christians to plainly live their faith and plainly speak it. Being the salt of the earth meant not only converting others, but also preserving society and politics from the excesses and corruptions of things like Nazism and fascism.

She had started the school year more than ready to resume her old arguments with St. Bernard, but now she found herself listening more and talking less. There was no doubt that ultimately their forays into Plato, reality, Aristotle, and decorum were going to wend their way back into the Catholic Church being the mother church, and all that. But for the time being, it seemed crucial for Tracey to listen to what St. Bernard was saying. If St. Bernard had dreaded another class with Tracey, she soon dropped her guardedness when Tracey's hand went up in class. Tracey began to see in St. Bernard the marks of an excellent teacher— clear delivery, interesting, and pertinent. And Tracey sensed that St. Bernard was pleased with Tracey's keen interest in this new subject. She was flattered, no doubt—for St. Bernard had a huge streak of conceit—but she was also pleased with Tracey as any genuine teacher is pleased with a genuine student.

In her new pursuit of philosophy, Tracey nearly forgot about Liz's troubles. Liz herself acted normal most of the time. Most of their conversations were about the upcoming basketball season, and physics lab had lately taken up much of Liz's spare time.

October came in, breezy and cool at night, but still warm with the last lingering warmth of a mild New England autumn. The trees that bordered the campus slowly turned colors for about a week, then suddenly blazed up all at once, showing off the last of their glory in one huge effort. Frosts began at night.

One Saturday afternoon, Liz and Tracey spent about an hour shooting baskets on the outside court. Then they hastily returned to the hall to take advantage of the afternoon lull on the wiring to make coffee and eat the last of the summer's Tastykakes before the season began.

The girls' rooms upstairs were nearly deserted at four o'clock on a Saturday afternoon. Most of the freshmen and sophomores had gone on the school bus to the library, and everybody else was taking advantage of the school library, the laundry machines downstairs, or the loveliness of the afternoon for walks on the lawn.

"That hook shot of yours is really coming," Liz said as they came up the narrow steps to their third-floor room. She was interrupted by a loud thump. The walls of the stairwell vibrated.

"Was that a sonic boom?" Tracey asked.

They came up around the corner and saw two girls

standing at the other end of the hall, one very tall and the other short. It was Scooter and one of the freshman girls.

"Hey!" Liz yelled, and she ran down the hall. Tracey, not understanding, quickly followed.

As they got closer, she saw the angry, bitter look on Scooter's face. The look drove an arrow of memory into Tracey's heart, and she saw in an instant that Scooter—however nice she might be to fellow team members—had not changed all that much.

Liz shoved Scooter away from the new girl, an act that surprised Tracey. Violence, to Liz, was such a last resort that she usually didn't even consider it.

"What are you doing?" Scooter exclaimed.

"What are you doing?" Liz retorted.

"You all right?" Tracey asked the freshman, who was wearing her uniform and green blouse even though it was Saturday and she was upstairs.

The girl, who was as short as Dibbles and a little heavier, nodded. Tracey realized that the thump had come from Scooter knocking the younger girl into the wall.

"Go on, play the heroes," Scooter said. "Ask her where she's been."

"You tell us, lady detective," Liz returned.

"Down to Mary's office, that's where, making her report!" Scooter said.

"For crying out loud!" Tracey told her. "Mary hasn't had time to do anything yet. Would you cool it?" She looked at the new girl. "Mary hassling you?" she asked.

"She said she wanted to get to know me," the girl said. "I . . . I thought everybody talked with her—"

"You're a liar!" Scooter exclaimed.

"Shut up!" Liz yelled.

"What'd you tell her?" Tracey asked.

"Nothing."

"Come on, you didn't go down there like a hung dog. What'd you talk about?" Liz asked.

"She asked me about my parents and where I was from, and I told her. And she asked if I'd tried out for basketball—"

"Yeah, you of all people!" Scooter snapped. "And you thought she was serious?"

"Would you cool it, Scooter?" Tracey asked. She turned to the freshman. "What's your name—Donna?" It was on her name tag.

"Yes," the girl said.

"Mary wants to know all about a lot of things, but don't let her rook you into anything. Next time she calls you in, don't talk with her, whatever you do."

"She's already reporting to Mary about the team, can't you see that?" Scooter asked.

"Oh, you dope! What team?" Liz exclaimed. "The cuts list isn't even out yet!"

"She's got narc written all over her."

"I won't talk with her again!" the new girl promised. "I swear I won't!"

"Yeah, well, you're safe now," Scooter began. "But these two can't be with you—"

She was cut off in midsentence when Liz punched her. It was a well-thrown roundhouse delivered with a swing from Liz's hip and knee.

The crack of the blow mixed with a strangled gulp from Scooter as her mouth slammed shut. She hit the wall and fell over, blood coming from her mouth.

Tracey and the freshman girl stared at Liz, shocked.

Liz, as cool as ever, swore at Scooter. "That's the last time you threaten anybody around here," she added. She turned to the new girl. "As long as you stay away from Mary, you can bring all your troubles to me."

The new girl ran away as soon as they let her go.

Tracey stooped down to get under Scooter, who was bent over against the wall.

"Man alive, Liz, she's bitten her tongue something awful," Tracey said.

Blind with tears of pain, Scooter would have jumped away from Tracey, but Tracey said, "I won't hurt you, Scooter. Let me get you to your room."

She got under Scooter's arm and felt Scooter start to cry, outraged tears of both shame and pain. It was odd that Tracey had once wanted to see such tears inflicted on Scooter, but now that it had happened, she only felt a little sick and very sorry for her.

With a great effort, Tracey steadied her voice and said, "Would you please get some ice from the kitchen, Liz?"

For the first time since Tracey had known her, Liz seemed torn or twisted with rage and anguish. She looked ready to say no, but Tracey said, "Just get some ice, Liz. I'll stay with her until she's OK."

Her face a study in anger, Liz wordlessly strode away. Tracey helped Scooter to her room. With Liz's departure, Scooter broke out into sobs, each one puffing out blood onto Tracey's sweatshirt, which she had worn back from the outside ball game. The rules dictated that she change to her uniform at the gym before returning, but now she was glad she had let the rule slide that day.

"How's your tongue?" Tracey asked. She had heard the snap of Scooter's teeth, and she knew that her tongue must have been bitten hard. "Should I get you to one of the nuns?"

Scooter shook her head to indicate that it wasn't severed or badly injured. Still, it must have been terribly painful.

Liz returned carrying a basin with a few ice cubes in the bottom, set it down at Tracey's side, and left the room without a word.

Tracey made Scooter lie down on her side and gave her an ice cube to suck on. She went through the desk drawers until she found some aspirin, and by then Scooter could take them. Tracey followed the aspirin with ice water and told Scooter to swish it around in her mouth. She found a small bucket in the room, the type the girls used to carry their things down to the shower, and gave it to Scooter for a spittoon.

She went down to the kitchen for more ice and came back up unnoticed, the basin full this time.

Scooter could finally talk. "She didn't have to hit me," she said.

Tracey handed her the refilled glass of ice water. "You hit that kid, didn't you?"

"Pushed her," Scooter admitted.

"Yeah, and let the wall hit her," Tracey said.

"I was just trying to scare her away from Mary," Scooter exclaimed. Tracey could distinguish the sound of a swollen tongue behind the hurried words.

"The more you talk, the more you're going to use your tongue, and the more it's going to hurt," she advised the older girl. "Look, I was really surprised too when Liz hit you. You better keep off her bad side, Scooter. Something's been bothering her for a few weeks. But you don't have to boss around these freshmen."

"Narcs!" Scooter exclaimed, being brief in consideration of her tongue.

"Oh, who cares about narcs. There's always going to be narcs!" Tracey said. She was tempted to add that she herself had been unjustly accused of being a narc once, and had suffered for it—at Scooter's own hands. But she restrained herself. It would be too much like gloating, what with Scooter sitting there, punched. "All you do is drive them right to Mary when you pick on them," she said. "They get scared and run to Mary to protect them. It just keeps the whole cycle going." She turned to Scooter. "When Liz decides to start punching, nobody can stop her. I'm her best friend, and I'm telling you that. So you'd better leave the new kids alone."

She got up and gathered the pillows in the room for Scooter to lie on more comfortably as she sucked on the ice. "I better go," Tracey said at last. She looked at Scooter. "You gonna tell Mary?"

Scooter shook her head.

"Thanks," Tracey said. She left the room to go find Liz.

Liz was in the room when Tracey returned. The tall blonde girl lay across her bed, her chin resting on her folded arms.

Without speaking, Tracey took off the stained sweatshirt and put on her slip and blouse to get ready for the evening meal. "Coffee made?" she finally asked.

"I'll get it," Liz said, not looking at her as she got up and found the coffeepot in one of the overhead cabinets.

She left the room to get water, and Tracey put on her uniform and took out a clean pair of blue socks. As she sat down on the edge of her bed to put them on, Liz returned and glanced at her for the first time. "How is she?"

"Tongue's sore," Tracey replied. "But she didn't bite it through."

"A buzz saw wouldn't sever that tongue."

Tracey didn't answer. She turned her attention to getting her socks on, and after a moment's pause, Liz put the coffee in the filter, inserted it into the pot, and started the coffee perking.

After a long silence, the older girl said, "I really shocked you, didn't I?"

"At the moment," Tracey said.

"I meant to punch her, but not that hard—" Liz began.

Tracey glanced at her and then looked down. "I'm not the one to judge you for violence, Liz—not me, of all people. That'd really be the pot calling the kettle black, wouldn't it?"

Her soft answer seemed to ease some of Liz's defensiveness. Liz came over to Tracey's side of the bed and stooped down.

Tracey looked at her.

"I didn't even know I was going to hit her until I did it, Trace," Liz said, for once not using her favorite nickname for Tracey. "Suddenly she was against the wall, and I was surprised too, but I wasn't sorry. I'm only sorry I hurt her so much. But I swear I'd still hit her if it happened all over again."

"Liz," Tracey said, startled and suddenly sorrowful at her friend's truculence, "why? Why hit her? We'd stopped her already. We'd already convinced that kid not to run to Mary but to run to us for help."

Liz got up and went to get their coffee mugs. She didn't answer Tracey's question, and Tracey didn't ask again. She only stood up and said, "Well, Scooter told me she won't tell Mary. But, Liz, you can bet everybody else is going to know about it."

"Maybe that's the best thing," Liz said without turning around. "I'm tired of this narc thing. Let the little kids run to Mary—they never tell her anything important. We can pick 'em out the first day of school. They never find out anything." She put sugar and coffee creamer into their cups. Her back still to Tracey,

49

she added, "We're Valkyries, aren't we? Why should we beat up on little kids who don't have any friends? If we took care of them, they'd drop Mary pretty quick, don't you think?"

"When you say 'we,' do you mean you and me, or the basketball team, or the whole school?" Tracey asked.

"I mean whoever wants to be a Valkyrie," Liz said.

The coffee finished perking. Liz poured Tracey's coffee first and handed her the steaming mug.

"Look," Tracey said, "everybody thought I was a narc, and you helped me, Liz. I think you saved my life. I don't know what I would have done if you hadn't saved me." She took the cup.

Liz's face went the wrong way for a second, but with an act of will she regained her composure and said, pouring her own coffee, "It was a smart thing I did, for all of us."

Tracey changed the subject, sensing that Liz needed time to think over all that had passed.

She was satisfied, after dinner, when Liz went to see Scooter. The matter seemed resolved, and Tracey thought their peaceful routine would continue as it had before.

There was talk on the hall that Liz had punched Scooter for bullying a freshman. In the showers that night, as Tracey heard snatches of conversation passing back and forth among the rubber curtains, she got the idea that Liz's incredible train of glory had been increased, not diminished, by her recklessness. Already the girls were retelling what had happened to fit their interpretations of what kind of person Liz was and what kind of person Scooter was.

In a popularity contest with anybody in the whole

school, Liz would have come out first. The echoes of her mousetrap trick on Sister Mary were still ringing in the halls. Tracey was glad her friend was immune to the scorn of their peers, but she felt sorry for Scooter. Scooter was neither the ballplayer nor the person that Liz was.

She suddenly realized that in some ways, both she and Scooter were seconds to Liz—second in ability, second in notoriety. And though Tracey would never be Liz's equal, she seemed to rise with every ascent Liz made, while somehow Scooter got pushed further down. Was it an illusion, Tracey wondered. But it couldn't be. Her classmates regarded her more highly every time Liz scored a triumph on the court, or succeeded with an ingenious prank, or won admiration with her open, carefree friendliness. Yet Tracey's only claim to popularity was that she had been befriended by Liz. Liz had even taught her to play basketball, so anything she accomplished on the court had to be attributed to Liz's expert coaching and patience. Nobody knew as well as Tracey what a good coach Liz had been.

Tracey did not mind the undeserved favor; she knew that she would have loved Liz's friendship with or without the popularity, and with or without basketball. But she wondered why she should keep gaining and Scooter should keep losing.

She pondered the odd balance between Scooter and herself for a while as she lay in bed that night. The soft sound of Liz's breathing in the lower bunk against the wall let Tracey know that her friend was all right. Sleep came at last.

She awoke much later, startled by some strange movement in the room. After a moment, she realized that someone was standing in front of the closed door.

"Who's there?" she whispered sharply.

There was no answer, and Tracey jumped out of bed. The figure at the door turned to her and collapsed, partly against the door and partly against the closet next to it.

"Help me get out," she whispered. "Get me out of here."

"Liz!" Tracey exclaimed, so sharply that their two roommates woke up. "Liz, wake up!"

Liz did seem to wake up, but she said again, "Tracey, they've taken the doorknob away. Get it open. Get it open."

Without a word, Tracey found the knob, turned it, and opened the door, letting in the light from the hallway. Liz gave a gasp of relief and opened the door all the way. "I've got to get out of here. I can't stay in that bed another second. It's a prison—a trap—I'm going outside."

Tracey grabbed Liz's arm. "Are you crazy? Going outside?"

"I can't stay in here. I can't stay in here."

Tracey sighed and looked back at the two freshmen, sitting up in their top bunks. She turned to Liz. "Get some clothes on, at least. I'll come with you."

The night was clear, cool, and starless, and the grounds were only faintly illuminated by the outside lights around the gate and under the statues of Mary, Joseph, and Francis of Assisi.

"It feels good out here," Liz said after they'd walked down the flagstone path past the retirees' wing. Their footsteps on the flagstone reminded Tracey of the many walks she'd taken with Sister James. For a moment her mind turned back to that friendship and all the warmth and wisdom Sister James had shown her. Tracey could not do as much for Liz, except be there with her, even now, at three in the morning.

"You all right?" Liz asked.

"Sure," Tracey said. "Did you want to walk all the way to the end of the hockey field?"

"Let's go to that stream we found," Liz said.

"Sure," Tracey said.

They found their way with no difficulty. At first, Tracey kept listening for trespassers in the woods or on the field, but Liz seemed to be feeling better, more relaxed. When they reached the tiny rivulet of water, they sat down.

"We should have brought Cokes or coffee or something," Tracey said.

"I don't feel hungry," Liz said.

Tracey looked at her. "Were you having a nightmare?"

"One after another."

"Liz," Tracey said, "I promise you, as your friend, as a ballplayer, as a Christian, and as a Valkyrie, that whatever happened this past summer, I will not tell anyone." She realized as she said it that she had made a rather foolish promise. If Liz had done something truly immoral, the weight of the secret might break both of them. But she shrugged off the worry. It was hard to believe Liz had done anything really bad. It seemed more likely that something bad had been done to her.

"Tell me this," Liz said. "What do you think about what Scooter was doing today? Threatening that kid, knocking her into the wall and all?"

"You know I hate that," Tracey said. "I was as mad

as you at first. I wouldn't have let her hit Donna again. But Scooter knew that. That's why I never had to hit her—because she didn't dare push me."

"She was saying she'd get her again when we weren't around," Liz reminded her. "That was when I hit her, I guess—when I realized she wasn't really going to stop. I don't know. It just happened so fast."

"It was sudden, all right," Tracey agreed.

"But that's what they did to you," Liz said. "They ganged up on you when they realized you'd fight back. How'd that make you feel, Jac?"

Tracey looked down, her face aflame from the memory of the attack in the hedge her freshman year. She had not thought about it for a long time.

"I'll tell you the truth, Liz," she said at last. "I think I must know how women feel who get raped. I looked up and there were those faces, and they were going to make me be in pain. Team up and hurt me. And there was nothing I could do. It was even worse than—" She almost said, "when my dad knocked me down the stairs," but she stopped. Instead, she said, "They did it to other people too. They did it to Sandra Kean, and Sandra doesn't have any sports or religion to get her through something like that." Tracey stopped and looked up, a new thought driving away the memory of her shame. "Hey, Sandra's not here this semester, is she? I haven't seen her around."

Liz said nothing.

"Poor kid," Tracey added to herself.

They were both silent for a long time. Tracey was getting ready to ask Liz if they could go back to bed, when Liz said, "Sandra Kean's never coming back, Jac." She looked at Tracey.

"What do you mean?" Tracey asked. "Have you seen her?"

"You promised not to tell," Liz reminded her.

"I promise," Tracey said.

"She killed herself this summer."

For a moment, the night stood still. Then Tracey said, "How do you know that?"

"She's from Vermont. Not far from the cabins where my family stays. I saw her a couple times before she—I asked her once or twice to come on out and let me teach her how to shoot some hoops, but she always stayed away from me. Then matriculation notices went out—I got mine the first of August. And she killed herself that night."

The link between the MoJoe matriculation notice and Sandra Kean's suicide seemed likely to Tracey, who had known her own share of vast misery at the school. "Sleeping pills?" she heard herself ask.

"No," Liz said with a hint of irony in her voice. "Took her dad's handgun and put it in her mouth and pulled the trigger."

A sudden wave of nausea swept over Tracey. She pulled her knees up quickly and leaned against them. "Lord, help us," she whispered. It had crossed her mind that the suicide might have been just a ploy, Sandra's way of looking for pity—that maybe she had OD'd accidentally on sleeping pills, not meaning to go all the way.

Liz read the thoughts. "She meant it, and she did it," Liz said. "You all right?"

When Tracey straightened up, she could feel that all the blood had drained out of her face. She looked at Liz. "Is that what's been bothering you so much, Liz?"

Liz lowered her eyes and gave a slight dip of her head.

"It's like Sandra and I were the same person for a while," Tracey said. "The same things were done to us both. I tried to make friends with her our freshman year."

"I know," Liz said. "I tried to be nice to her too."

"Why are you blaming yourself?" Tracey asked. "I know you tried to help her. You did help me, Liz. I meant it today when I said you'd saved my life. My parents don't love me, all the girls hated me. I was so alone. I might have done the same thing as Sandra. But you saved me, and you tried to save her too."

"Jac," Liz said, "I burned the film."

"The what?" Tracey asked.

"I burned *Green Dolphin Street,*" Liz told her. "And Sandra took the rap for it."

Tracey pushed aside her surprise at finding out that Liz had been responsible for last year's most audacious prank. Sandra had confessed to burning the film in a bid for popularity with the other girls, but Sister Mary had seen through her lie and punished her for it. No one had ever found out who the real culprit was. "Liz, you didn't make her take the rap for that. She just got it into her head to say she'd done it."

"I could have helped her," Liz insisted. "I could have stepped in at the end of all that rigmarole and said she'd been my lookout. But I let her get stung for it. I never did help her."

"Nobody would have believed you, Liz!" Tracey insisted.

"They believe me because I'm Liz Lukas!" she exclaimed, and Tracey stopped her arguments. It was true.

If Liz had said that Sandra had been her lookout, that would have become the official story among the girls.

"If I'd never burned the stupid film, none of this would have happened," Liz said. "But I was so high over that mousetrap trick. I just had to do one more."

"Well, it wasn't right to burn the film," Tracey agreed. "But things went wrong for Sandra Kean from her first day in this place. You can't say that one bad thing made her commit suicide. And you never forced her to go down and confess. Liz, Sandra was so out of touch with reality. I know she was desperate, and desperately lonely. But do you really think you caused her suicide? She was so unplugged she never even realized that you and I would have helped her."

Liz kept her eyes down, not answering.

"I can tell you from experience," Tracey said, "that what Scooter and Susan and those other four did to me was a lot worse than whatever else happened to either me or Sandra. That might have been the big thing that hung over her and made her do it. Or knowing that Mary was waiting for her. Have you ever thought about what it's like to try to break away from her? And Sandra Kean was putty in Mary's hands."

Liz looked at her, her hope restored somewhat.

"What you did was wrong," Tracey told her, "but I don't think it caused Sandra to kill herself."

"I don't know—" Liz said.

"Maybe we'll never rationalize it away," Tracey said. "But, Liz, I know that sins can be forgiven, even if they can't be undone."

"That's what Maddie told me," Liz said, her tone indicating that she already knew what Tracey was ready to say.

"I'm not a very good Christian," Tracey told her. "I've messed up more things than I can count. But I'd still rather be a Christian than not be one."

"I don't know, Jac. Seems like the God who so loved the world and all that wouldn't leave us in a place like this," Liz said. "I think He's out there, but I guess I think that all that stuff about the cross and God among men is just something His public relations department came up with. He doesn't seem all that good to me."

Their conversation by the stream did not make Liz a Christian, but it did seem to ease her mind about Sandra Kean's suicide.

Tracey was amazed at herself for the odd mix of feelings the news had evoked. She felt some regret for not having approached Sandra more often. And yet, there had been so little progress made—none, really— it seemed that anything she might have tried would have been a failure. Her words to Liz had rung with a truth that even she had not guessed until that moment: Sandra had not really been plugged into reality. She had tried far-fetched things to win acceptance— like taking the blame for the spectacular film burning —but she had never been willing to take the normal, everyday kind of risks that acceptance entailed: being friendly and open and normal with people.

Tracey also realized that the deck had been stacked against Sandra from the beginning. Her parents had conveniently gotten rid of her by sending her off to boarding school, and Sister Mary had offered an easy but high-priced friendship. Mary had picked her out first thing: plain, overweight, frightened, and lonely. What a natural to be a narc. That had signed the death warrant for any chance that Sandra would have a normal introduction (if there were such a thing) to life at MoJoe. In the end, it may have been the thing that signed the death warrant for Sandra herself.

Tracey had always believed that suicide was immoral, and that every person who committed suicide was fully responsible for the act. Now she began to think the question over again, with surprising results.

She had dreaded Sister Mary, perhaps despised her actions, certainly disliked her. But now a new feeling nearly overwhelmed her whenever she saw Sister Mary: not anger, though she certainly felt that, but something wholly new, best described by words like *loathing* and *disgust*. Tracey felt a strong desire, not to fight the dragon in its lair, but to squash the spider behind the refrigerator.

The other odd thing was that Sandra's suicide drove Tracey back to praying again. She didn't know why. But her prayers were now prayers for all of them, not just herself. And for the first time, she prayed against people. Judgment itself she left in the Lord's hands, but she begged Him not to forget the injustices done to Sandra Kean. Whatever else Sandra had been, she had been only sixteen, hounded all her life, frightened, and alone. Tracey sharply felt the oneness she had mentioned to Liz; it was as though, for a while, she and Sandra had been the same person. So the tragedy of the girl's death stayed with her much longer than even Liz suspected.

The cuts list came out. Peggy and Dibbles had

made the team, though Peggy was still second-string, much to her disappointment. Tracey was shocked to find her own name directly under Liz's, starred.

"Looks like you're alternate captain," Liz said with a grin.

"Are you sure?" Tracey asked. "Maybe CPR'll tell us who's captain and who's alternate when we get together today."

"Nuts, Jac! You're alternate!" Liz exclaimed with a laugh. "See the asterisk by your name? That's what it means."

"Man, what was CPR thinking?" Tracey asked, taking the list into her hands.

"Right thoughts," Liz answered. Tracey looked up to see Scooter striding across the grass, away from the gym. Once again, Tracey had ascended and Scooter had descended.

Their first practice that evening was spirited. Tracey had always thought that the team was very good, but their quick, sure passes and the confidence with which they scrimmaged and used last year's plays made her think that they were better in this first session than they had looked in last year's final game.

Liz must have thought the same thing. After practice she hopped piggyback onto Tracey and let out a whoop as Tracey quickly steadied herself. "Championship for sure this year!" Liz cried. Everybody else cheered, and CPR only smiled instead of reproving Liz for premature hopes.

When Father Williams showed up for the second practice, CPR, instead of beginning on the new plays, had them scrimmage again. He watched from the sidelines, impressed, and then went up to the balcony where he could smoke his pipe without disturbing them.

After the scrimmage, CPR asked Father Williams if he'd like to say anything to the team. "Well, girls," he began, as they stood in a sweaty group around him, "I think you've worked very hard to get where you are this season." He glanced at CPR. "I think you all deserve new uniforms—and new warm-up suits. How's that sound?"

They applauded, and Liz gave a fierce whistle of approval through her teeth.

"You win that championship," Father Bing promised, "and I'll see to it that we all get some special treats. How's that?"

"You bet!" Tracey exclaimed.

As they ran into the locker room, leaving him in the gym conferring with CPR, Liz nudged Tracey. "We only get new uniforms either right before the championships or when he's sure we're going there."

"Man, I hope we do!" Tracey exclaimed fervently.

"I think it looks sure this time," Liz told her. "Didn't I tell you that Dibbles could play good with a little training?"

The new warm-ups came in two sets. One was black, with white piping and white collars, and the other was white with black piping and black collars. The team would look impressive when they came out onto the floor to drill in a checkerboard pattern of black and white.

The uniforms were black with white trim, but the shields were crimson.

In keeping with tradition, the Valkyries' first game was against St. Bede's. Tracey felt a little let down because she knew they would win easily, which they did. She was also startled to find herself disappointed that Maddie Murdoch had not come to the game. Mrs. Murdoch was a real estate agent with flexible hours, but sometimes she had to miss the home games in order to get time off for the away games. She had a chauffeur's license and always drove the team bus.

There was some controversy at the first game about who would carry the banner. Scooter insisted that Tracey and Liz should do it together, since they were captain and alternate, and that she should take the Valkyrie armor. Tracey resisted this.

"The seniors gave the armor to me last year," she reminded Scooter. "Not because I was or wasn't alternate, but because they thought I was like a Valkyrie."

"We're all Valkyries," Scooter retorted.

"Oh, yeah?" Liz asked.

Dibbles, usually so easygoing and quick with a joke, said, "It's Tracey's armor, Scooter. But look at it this way—if you carry the banner, maybe everybody will think you're alternate anyway."

In the end, CPR had to be called in to settle the argument.

"The captain always carries the banner," she said. "I've always picked the person on the team who was closest in size to the captain to carry the other side of the banner. That could be either Tracey or Scooter. And since the girls wanted Tracey to wear the armor, at least for this year, she'll wear the armor and Scooter will carry the second staff of the banner."

Tracey fitted the shield onto her arm while the banner was brought to the locker room and unfurled. Liz and Scooter charged out with it, to the accompaniment of a trumpet fanfare from Sister Theresa and one of the seniors. Immediately on their heels, Tracey charged out, sword up, to duck under the banner and then run in front of the MoJoe girls, waving the sword and clanging it against the shield. They cheered like she'd never heard them before: "Tracey! Tracey!" chanted the younger girls, and then the shout of "Jac! Jac! Jac!" drowned them out, coming from the older girls who were more familiar with her nickname.

The cheering changed as the next girl ran out and under the banner. Tracey hurried to the sidelines to ditch the armor with CPR. She took her place about three people down from Liz when the school song began. She put her hand over her heart and looked up at Liz, who returned the look as they began to sing.

> For strength the black, for truth the white,
> Our colors we hold dear.
> Let strength and truth abide in us
> In every heart sincere.

The first verse decided Tracey. She could not stop Sister Mary from buttonholing kids, but she could do her best to stop the older girls from harassing the younger ones who couldn't or didn't fit in.

EIGHT

The away game against St. Anthony's promised the team better competition, and this year there were few worries about losing. St. Anthony's had a tradition of good players—girls who were scouted for college teams, in fact—but the disciplined, hard-driving plays of the MoJoes had consistently kept them a few points ahead of their rivals.

Maddie drove to the game, and Tracey was so glad to see her that she stopped too long to talk on the top step as she was climbing aboard the bus.

"Yo, Jac, let's go!" Liz exclaimed from behind her, while she was trying to tell Maddie about the philosophy class. "The game starts at five, you know."

"Sorry," Tracey said, surprised to find herself genuinely embarrassed. She hurried back to a seat, her face red.

"Man," Liz exclaimed as she flopped down into the seat next to Tracey. "I'm glad you and Maddie are pals now, but don't go overboard."

"Sorry," Tracey said briefly, flustered at how apparent her gladness to see Maddie had been. Liz shot her a look, saw her red cheeks and said, "Oh, well, it's not that big a deal." She changed the subject.

Tracy could tell that the Valkyries' opening fanfare impressed their opponents. St. Anthony's was a school keen on spirit. Even though the sight of Sister Theresa and her young protégée playing trumpets was kind of funny, in Tracey's mind, the overall effect of the trumpets, the armor, the arrangement of the girls in their warm-up suits, and the school song made quite a show, however brief. Tracey noticed one or two of the nuns from St. Anthony's taking some quick notes. She got the idea that next time they played St. Anthony's, the school would have a production of its own.

Most of the players from the previous year were still on the St. Anthony's team, but the team used only a couple of simple plays that Liz, Tracey, and Scooter could easily anticipate. Even Dibbles, who was new on first-string, caught on pretty quickly to the way the St. Anthony's guards would try to get around her when they came down the court.

But the St. Anthony's guards didn't seem quite prepared for this short, funny-looking white girl who could scurry and scramble with the ball, her short legs pumping like pistons, her face quickly becoming scarlet from the exertion. One thing about Dibbles—she was so funny-looking that it was hard to take her seriously.

But there she was, passing off to Tracey and switching off with Liz right into the key to get the pass back and make a basket. Dibbles's extreme mobility no longer surprised Tracey. What did surprise her that night were the three times Dibbles shot from outside the key and sank the ball.

"You never told me you guys worked on that," Liz yelled to Tracey as they watched the ball swoosh through the net on the second of these long-distance throws.

"We never did," Tracey told her as they hurried back to play defense.

Dibbles's abilities were refreshing, but it was still up to the forwards and center to carry the offense. Intent on the game as always, Liz and Tracey didn't have time to count baskets and assists. They worked together well. Often Liz didn't have to signal Tracey into place, or let her know which play to use for getting into the key. Sometimes they seemed to move as though with one mind. As soon as Liz went up to shoot, Tracey went up to rebound, often putting in rim shots with a smoothness that won applause from the MoJoes and even some praise from the other team.

The Valkyries carried the game that night with a ten-point spread. The second-string played through most of the second and third quarters.

It was the record keeper who told Tracey that she'd been second highest scorer that night, right behind Liz.

"That's great," Liz told her as they went out to the bus later. "You were second highest last game too."

"Kind of surprising," Tracey said.

"Not to me," Liz told her. In a lower voice, she added, "I told you that you'd be better than Scooter someday."

But Tracey wondered if she and Liz were leaving Scooter out of some of their plays. Scooter knew what to do, but she didn't work with either of them with the same smoothness Liz and Tracey had together.

"Will you stay up here and keep me company?" Maddie asked Tracey as they climbed aboard the bus.

"Sure," Tracey said.

"I hate to be a party pooper," Liz said, "but I'm going back to get some z's."

"That was quite a game," Maddie said as the other girls came up the steps.

Tracey didn't want to talk about basketball. She had waited and waited to talk with Maddie about some of her questions.

"Can I ask you something?" she asked.

"Anything, dear," Maddie told her.

"You used to be Catholic, right?"

"Indeed," Maddie said. She looked at Tracey in the rearview mirror.

"What changed you?" Tracey asked.

"My, that's rather a story," Maddie said. "Are you sure you want to hear it?"

"Yes," Tracey said. "That is, if you want to tell it."

"No, I don't mind at all telling what the Lord's done for me," Maddie said. As CPR came aboard and nodded at her, she swung the door closed and started the engine.

"I was born near Dublin," she said as she pulled out, "and I was very 'bold,' as people used to say. My family came to America when I was twelve, and I was already very old for my age. Not with boys at all, because my father was so strict, but I'd studied out how Lauren Bacall looked when she smoked. I could imitate her pretty well, and I knew how to mix drinks— all sorts of useful things for a young lady."

"I would hardly have thought that of you," Tracey said.

"Hey Maddie, how long to McDonald's?" Liz bawled from the back.

"Twenty minutes, dear," Maddie called back.

"Thank you!"

"Well, my parents were very strict," Maddie said. "And I think that my own morals were much higher than I supposed—anyway, my moral expectations were. I married just out of high school, and my husband and I were cut from the same cloth. I put him through college, and we quickly explored socialism together and went through a short time as Communist Party members—"

"You're kidding!" Tracey exclaimed.

"I was very pro the Irish Reunification," Maddie added, "and he looked into that and supported it. Patsy and Beth Ann were born, and I didn't work. I was in favor of women's liberation; but as I said, even though my moral theories were rather loose, my moral expectations were higher. I advocated bra-burning and free love and felt that marriage was an outdated mechanism to force on people who were not able to cope with it—yet I remained a housewife, dressed very modestly, would not use profanity around my daughters, and remained faithful to my husband. Although I said I was an atheist, I still went to Mass on holidays, gave money to the church when the priest came around, and made a novena for Beth Ann when she was very sick with colic and couldn't rest."

"It sounds like you never really believed all the things you said you believed," Tracey ventured.

"Well, dear, I thought I believed them. And what was worse, I believed the very worst things in them. For one thing, I knew I wasn't an atheist, but I was so sure that God was not good—not my idea of good,

69

anyway—it was much more convenient to say He wasn't even real. And though I worked very hard to make my marriage work, I resented it that anybody should tell me I absolutely had to stay married if my husband should turn out bad. Nothing in those days bothered me as much as people using words like *couldn't* and *shouldn't*."

"Was there pot back in those days?" Tracey asked, wondering if Maddie had ever smoked it.

Maddie laughed. "No—well, not accessible for white, middle-class people. Vietnam was just a name that popped up every now and then because the French were trying to maintain order there. And there were beatniks back then, but not hippies. Oh, no, Tracey, my views were very radical, and I was proud of them—as proud as I had been that I could ape Lauren Bacall. But in practice, I looked just like any other middle-class housewife. I had an Irish accent, that's all."

"So what happened?" Tracey asked.

"The girls were in high school, and I began to feel very left out of things. My husband was working quite a bit. It began to seem as though life had gotten away from me. I wanted to go back to school, and I did start taking business courses. But it was hard on the girls for me to be gone so much and to be so busy. You see, I had always been there."

"Yes, I see," Tracey said. She saw better than Maddie did, in fact—guessing that Maddie had been the kind of mother who had probably waited on her kids hand and foot.

"Then I discovered that my husband was having an affair," Maddie said, "with a much younger woman.

70

We had advocated free love and things like that, but I suppose matters of honesty had never much occurred to him. He had never even hinted that there was another woman. When I confronted him, he simply asked me if I wanted a divorce. There was no apology and no indication that he would give her up and come back to me. I left it up to him, and he chose divorce."

"I'm really sorry," Tracey said. She wanted to tell Maddie that the same thing was happening in her family, but she didn't know how to change the subject. Then Maddie continued the story.

"After he left me, I had the care of the girls to think of. He was very generous financially, and I was able to finish school at night. But by day, it was very tiresome to sit around the house and see that he was never coming back. I felt very used and wronged. So I turned back to the church. And that went on very nearly a year.

"And then one day, some people from another church came and knocked on my door. At first I was silly enough to try to give them money. But then I found out that they had come to talk with me about religion. Somehow, most people resent that, but I rather admired them. They were very nice, and so I asked them in and gave them tea, and we talked about God, and I explained to them what I believed."

"They must have argued with you all day," Tracey said. "I bet they'd never met a socialist-IRA-atheist Roman Catholic before."

Maddie let out a clear laugh, appreciating the description of herself. "No, dear," she said. "They left me with a tract and a little pamphlet titled, 'I Made Mary Cry.' I read the pamphlet first. It had been written by a

71

man who had converted from Roman Catholicism. His words were so tender—it made me think and feel things about God that I had never felt before. I kept wondering if God would really be concerned about people as much as the man said. Certainly I knew that there were problems in the Roman Catholic Church. I had never realized that God Himself might not need an official sort of church at all.

"You see," she admitted in a lower voice, "I had hated the *couldn'ts* and *shouldn'ts* so much that I had been very keen on finding a social order that would ban them—and that would have been the worst thing of all. That's what radical thought is, the demand to be allowed to tell everybody that they must not be allowed to be moral."

Tracey had never thought of it that way, but with sudden realization she saw through the veneers of communism and other radical ideas. They weren't, as they claimed, societies working for the common good. Rather, they were societies forced to work for the ideology's concept of the common good. And Christianity itself, so very moral, could never advance through social orders or political systems, because it could not be forced on people. With a sudden flash of understanding, Tracey understood why Roman Catholicism had its incredible superstructure of rituals, vestments, sacraments, feast days, and artifices. It was a man-made system trying to force people into its concept of holiness: dictatorial, tyrannical, and not so very unlike communism in respect to its centralization and its claim to absolute authority. But only God could make people holy. The moment religion stopped being an action of God in a human being, it became a monster.

Tracey might have said something, but Maddie continued her story. "I read the tract and then called the church and asked when they had services. A day later one of the women from the church called me and asked me to a women's Bible study that they had on Tuesday mornings. I went, and the women were just as clear as the men about what they believed. I was very impressed with them. They all seemed so sure, and not only sure, they were *so assured*, if you know what I mean.

"I came and came for weeks, and got to know several of them. It was rather a long process for me. I had joined so many movements and belonged to so many things that when the real thing hit me, I dragged my feet. But you can resist the Spirit of God for only so long. And He would have me be His, so at last I could resist no further. I became a Christian."

"But not your daughters?" Tracey asked.

"No," Maddie said. "It was just one more movement to them—more pieces of mail on the kitchen counter, more meetings to go to. I did try to speak to them about it, but I'm afraid I've rather spoiled my daughters and ruined my credibility with them. They're used to not believing what I believe."

"And then you started helping out at MoJoe?" Tracey asked.

"After Patsy started college. I thought I might be of some use. You see, at first Father Williams let me have a Bible study with the girls. That didn't last many years. But it seemed that most of the girls who came to me—well, they had needs to be looked after. I thought I might still be of some use, if only by my presence."

Tracey recalled her grief on the day Sister Lucy had

been taken away from the retirees' wing. "Boy, you've sure helped me," she said in a low voice, half forgetting that Maddie was right there. She didn't see Maddie's quick look at her in the rearview mirror.

NINE

So Maddie was giving you her life story?" Liz asked that night after study time had ended.

Tracey, who was already in her bunk with her Bible open, glanced at Liz. "You heard us?"

"Only a little."

"Maddie had her wild side, that's for sure," Tracey said. "Did you know she used to be a communist?"

"No kidding." Liz flipped her pen onto the desktop and stood up to get changed for bed. Then she said, "CPR was sitting a few seats behind you, but I think she was plugged in to everything you guys talked about."

"You think she doesn't like it?" Tracey asked.

Liz shot her a wry look. "Well, Jac, this is a Catholic school."

"Does CPR know about Sandra Kean?" Tracey asked.

Liz nodded. "All the nuns know, baby. And I think they know I know too. They don't want it spread around—at least, Mary doesn't."

Tracey closed the Bible and rolled onto her back, putting her hands behind her head. "Something tells me CPR won't stop Maddie from talking with either me or you, Liz. Something tells me CPR's bugged by a lot of things."

Liz leaned against the top bunk and looked down at her. "CPR's never cut you any slack before, Jac. I think she's cool in some ways. But in other ways, she's a part of the system here."

"She let me pray that one time," Tracey reminded her. "And if she was rough on me last year, I think it might have been because Mary was riding her case, trying to keep me from getting an edge just because I'm good at basketball. Let's not forget Sister Mary."

Liz let out a brief laugh and walked away to get her nightgown. "No, let's not forget Sister Mary, the commandant." She changed quickly, and as she pulled the nightgown over her head, she asked, "What's the news from home? You haven't talked about it much."

"Nothing much, except now my mom says she can't afford to send me much money," Tracey told her. "I still have about fifty bucks, but I think it's belt-tightening time."

"You going to stay with her over Christmas?" Liz asked.

"Not if I can help it."

Liz glanced at her again. "Might be nice to go home for once, Jac."

"That's not home," Tracey said. "Just a lot of lies, and some strange guy who I'm supposed to treat like my dad—who I'm supposed to like? No way."

"She might make you come home."

"If I come home, they both have to behave while

I'm there," Tracey reminded her. "You know, carry on the game that they just met. I bet they let me stay here if I want to."

There were more new plays to be learned that season. One that CPR developed was a switch between guards and forwards. Dibbles and the other guard would bring the ball down, pass off to the forwards, and switch off with them, regaining the ball as they came into the key. From inside the key they passed back to the forwards, who were now outside the key, usually at the top. The forward who had the ball would shoot from out there.

Scooter was better at the long-distance shots than Tracey was, but the play was so surprising to other teams that either forward was usually open and had enough time to aim and sink the ball. They could vary the play several ways. One safeguard was to have the forward who didn't get the pass go back in to rebound with Liz in case the shooter missed.

They tried the play in the game against St. Agnes and found that it worked well enough to guarantee them a good lead early in the game. The second-string was able to maintain the lead in the second half.

"You know," Liz said after the game as they headed for the showers, "when I saw that we were playing both St. A's before Christmas, my heart went into my feet. Now I'm really glad. Most of the hard work is over."

"Just Lady of the Valley," Tracey reminded her. "We play them after Christmas."

"We might have a bad night and lose," Liz admitted. "But something tells me we're going all the way this year, Jac."

It certainly looked that way in every game up to

Christmas vacation. CPR was more relaxed and jolly than Tracey had ever seen her, and Father Williams showed up often to watch practices and to offer comments and praise after the games.

The winning season provided Tracey with the excuse she needed to avoid going home at Christmas. In a carefully worded letter to her mother, she explained that the team had enjoyed a winning season so far and was in line to go to the play-offs. In her new role as alternate captain, she preferred the chance to stay at the school over Christmas and practice every day instead of having to come to a new apartment and risk not having a basketball court at hand.

"If this were my first Christmas away from home, it would be harder to ask to stay," she concluded her letter. "But now that I'm used to it, and now that there's a reason to be here and try to get what we've all been working for, I'd like to stay and practice as hard as I can. Liz Lukas will be coming back early, and I suppose some of the other girls will too, if their parents let them. Our coach, CPR, will be back a week early, and she and I can work together until the others return."

Tracey had always kept her mother apprised of the progress of the basketball team, but her mother had never answered or even addressed the subject. Tracey knew her mother well enough to know that she cared nothing at all for sports—for girls in sports, anyway—and the steady stream of basketball reports, as well as her daughter's ascent to the first-string and to team alternate, captured her attention about as much as reports of snow in Siberia.

At Tracey's request, which provoked a long-distance

phone call, her mother did require more details before giving in. But she gave in.

"If this is what you want," she told Tracey before hanging up. "If this basketball thing really means this much to you, to not come home to your family, then all right."

Tracey got the idea that her mother's feelings or pride or something had been hurt, or at least rebuffed. But in the end, Tracey's request to stay would be less expensive for her mother, and it was clear that money was a big concern to her mother these days. She sent Tracey forty dollars and told her to pick out the presents she would like best. Tracey stowed the money for future away-game dinners.

T E N

Christmas came in with a whirl of snow on the very first day of vacation.

Tracey had been honest with her mother in reporting that many of the players would be returning early to get in extra practices. But the first days of vacation she spent alone as, one after another, most of the sisters left campus to visit their families over the holiday. She practiced in the mornings and afternoons, intent on making long shots from the top of the key or from just outside its perimeter.

Memories of Sister James, Sister Lucy, and Sandra Kean bothered her most when she was alone and when it was vacation time. Lately, some thoughts of Sister James had returned with a new sweetness. But not when she was alone, and not at Christmas. She had to consciously push away the thoughts as she worked. The best thing to do was move, move, move, and when Tracey's memories became painful, she gave up the long shots in order to drive the ball up the court and try unsuccessfully to dunk it. That kind of action drove every thought away and gave her mind a temporary rest.

In the evenings and at rest, she returned to Wylie, digging the books out of their hiding place up on the fourth floor. He came back like an old and welcome friend.

So far that year, St. Bernard had hardly touched on Catholic doctrine, so there had been no opportunity for Tracey to make the clear presentation against the Roman Catholic Church that she had wanted to make. Instead, she had learned about Plato's cave and optimism and Hegel and Kierkegaard. After Christmas her class was scheduled to do readings on Nietzsche and Carlyle and to discuss heroes, supermen, and nihilism. Tracey found philosophy class fascinating, but even she knew enough to understand that they were all playing with dynamite. The same ideas that were the basis for twentieth-century philanthropy had also planted the seeds for Nazism.

It was an unusual thing for Tracey to be grateful for a nun's guidance, but St. Bernard really did give her students a Judeo-Christian perspective on the man-made philosophies that had rocked the world from the mid-1800s to the present. St. Bernard was of Lithuanian descent, as were many of the sisters at MoJoe. One and all, they despised communism and everything that bred communism. St. Bernard herself, who could never be provoked or tricked into declaring whether the Bible was or was not the inspired Word of God, disavowed communism and socialism by saying, first and foremost, that these philosophies violated the scriptural teachings on the nature of man.

Despite Tracey's enjoyment of the class, she felt

relieved to leave hard and controversial readings behind and immerse herself again in Wylie's stories and
explanations.

The days leading up to Christmas passed almost
unnoticed. But Christmas itself, as always, hit Tracey
with a stark loneliness that even hard practice could
not drive away. She spent forty-five minutes in the
gym that morning, trying unsuccessfully to make some
progress in her shooting before she gave it up for the
day. There didn't seem anything to do but go back to
her room and try to read or maybe sleep away the unhappy day. She packed up the basketballs, pulled her
coat on, and locked up the gym before trudging back
up to the hall.

Maddie Murdoch's car was parked behind the bicycle shed, and Tracey stopped long enough to glance
toward the retirees' wing. She was almost tempted to
go down; just to see Maddie's familiar face would have
been enough, maybe, to offset all of the unhappiness
that the retirees' wing could call up in her. Then she
decided against it. Maddie would be busy helping out
and would likely only spare her a minute or two before
being pressed into service again, "carrying things
round." It wasn't fair to take her away from the lonely
old women in the wing.

Resolutely, Tracey turned back to go to the hall.
She stopped short when she saw Maddie just returning
from there.

"There you are!" Maddie exclaimed pleasantly as
she neared Tracey. "I was just looking for you—I'd finally thought to go down to the gym and was just on
my way. Merry Christmas, dear."

"Thank you," Tracey said. "I thought you'd be down there." She nodded toward the retirees' wing.

"I went around earlier," Maddie told her. "But I have to hurry home. I'm having a couple from my church over for a small dinner. Would you like to come?"

The invitation sent a thrill of hope into Tracey, but then she hesitated. She had a faint idea that people like the Murphys would be coming to see Maddie—people who could not understand her and whom she could not understand. An unexpected shyness came over her, and she thought to refuse—and yet, she was so lonely—

"Maybe you'd like to come over now," Maddie said kindly. "You could help me get ready, and then I'll run you back for your supper here, if you like."

"I'd like that," Tracey said, relieved. "That's awfully nice of you."

Maddie smiled. "We'd better hurry, though."

Tracey did hurry. She ran up to her room to throw off her gym clothes, douse herself in baby powder, and change into a clean skirt and blouse.

"A new record for changing!" Maddie exclaimed as Tracey came running down the steps to the front room of the hall. "I didn't mean for you to hurt yourself try-ing, dear."

"I didn't," Tracey promised. She met Maddie's eyes and smiled at her joke before pushing the door open with her back to let them out.

"How sweet you look," Maddie said suddenly. "You don't often smile."

The comment startled Tracey. "I don't?"

"Don't let my noticing stop you, though," Maddie

said, smiling in her turn, but with a sudden tenderness, as though she regretted her comment. They started out to the car.

Tracey glanced down and felt the familiar blush of embarrassment coming up her face. She'd never thought much about people noticing her face, or wondered how she looked to them or what they thought of her smile. But no matter how much Maddie liked it, Tracey couldn't smile, now that she was thinking about it, nor could she force one onto her face just for the effect. She regretted not being able to. "It . . . it comes and goes," she stammered.

They climbed into the car. Maddie changed the subject.

ELEVEN

Aside from one centerpiece made up of a basket of pinecones, a tall and narrow red candle in a gold candlestick holder, and a family Bible opened to Luke chapter two, Maddie's neat house was not decorated for Christmas. Tracey supposed that religious beliefs had prevented her from decorating, but Maddie's reasons were more practical.

"When the girls spend the holidays with their father, I find it much easier not to lug around a huge tree," she said as she took Tracey's coat and hung it up. "Well, there are endless vegetables to chop and a small bird to prepare. Which would you like to try?"

Panic seized Tracey. "I don't know anything about cooking—" she began.

"Well, I'll show you, dear, and don't worry. Neither you nor I could likely ruin vegetables. Come into the kitchen, and I'll find you an apron."

Maddie had not been kidding when she'd asked Tracey to come over and help. The Irish woman's preparations seemed, to Tracey, highly intricate. Yet Maddie, unlike Tracey's mother, remained master of herself and of the kitchen throughout the long process. Tracey tensed several times—like when the rice for pudding boiled over on the stove—but Maddie retained her sense of humor. Tracey began to relax.

It looked like quite a spread for these visitors, whoever they were: a string-bean casserole, a squash casserole, the small turkey and its stuffing, mashed potatoes to come, two different kinds of bread that Maddie had set to rise, rice pudding made with golden raisins that Maddie called sultanas, and all kinds of pies that Maddie had made the night before. She intended to serve the pies in a way Tracey had never seen before—with custard and whipped cream.

The whipped cream was in a bowl.

"Why'd you put it in a bowl?" Tracey asked.

Maddie looked at her blankly. "Well, dear, how else does a person put whipped cream on the table?"

"Well, we always just squirted it out of the can back in the kitchen," Tracey told her. "And brought the desserts to the table with the whipped cream on them."

"Do you really think that shaving foam in a can is whipped cream?" Maddie asked, half teasing and half surprised.

"Isn't it?" Tracey asked.

"Of course not. It's absolutely fake."

"Well . . ." Tracey hesitated. "What is whipped cream, then?"

"It's cream, dear. Whipped over and over," Maddie told her.

"Cream? Like milk?"

"Haven't you ever seen the cartons in the store labeled heavy cream?" Maddie asked her.

"Those little things?" Tracey asked, looking at the big bowl of whipped cream. "How many went into that?"

"One," Maddie told her. "Dear, I'll cut you a piece of pie myself, and you put this whipped cream on it and see if it doesn't taste altogether better than anything you've had before."

But Tracey stopped her. "No, Maddie, don't mess up a pie before dinner. I can have a piece tomorrow— or later." She glanced at Maddie with a smile. "We've worked so hard on this, I'd like to think of it all looking perfect when you serve it."

As Tracey looked at Maddie, she felt that same shyness coming back over her. She'd spoken lightly enough of helping Maddie prepare dinner, but the truth was, Tracey didn't know her way around the kitchen, nor did she understand the deep, almost religious reverence that Maddie had for hospitality. And she knew that her ignorance must be visible to Maddie. Like not knowing what real whipped cream was.

"Won't you reconsider and stay, dear?" Maddie asked her.

"You know, Maddie—" Tracey said suddenly. She looked right into Maddie Murdoch's eyes. "If you really knew me, you wouldn't like me. You wouldn't bother with being so nice to me if . . . if you knew me." In spite of herself, her face flamed red, and she felt her eyes moisten suddenly.

Maddie's face lost its look of good-natured teasing. A seriousness that almost frightened Tracey replaced the look.

"Why, Tracey," she said, "why shouldn't I like you?"

"Because I'm so bad," Tracey blurted. "And I don't just mean about that fight you saw."

Maddie looked down, then up at her again. "We're all bad when it comes right down to it, dear. I thought you knew that. Our righteousness comes from Christ."

"But I've been bad since I became a Christian—a real Christian," Tracey told her. "I think I've sinned worse in the last three years than I ever did before."

"Or maybe, before you trusted Christ, you sinned in ignorance," Maddie told her. "Never thinking much of your sins. Whereas now you think of them much more, and you take them more seriously."

Maddie's answer disarmed Tracey. She had never thought of it that way. There might be some truth in the statement, yet Tracey's side was also true.

"It's wrong to get drunk," she conceded, "but don't you think it's worse when a person does know better? Because I've been drunk since I got saved, Maddie. And I've smoked too. And there's other things—worse things than those things." And she stopped. Maddie had seen the violence.

"I think that drunkenness is a very serious sin, Tracey," Maddie said. "I wouldn't play that down a bit. But it's not my place to judge you for a sin that has been judged already and for which I can see you're repentant. Come into the living room a moment, dear."

Tracey obeyed her, and Maddie went to find her Bible. She brought it back to Tracey as she quickly leafed through it. "There are two concepts in the New Testament that bear on how we live," she told Tracey. "Even in Paul's day, many Christians tried as hard as they could to be good. They felt they ought to live up to God's standard of goodness."

"That's right, isn't it?" Tracey asked. "That's how I felt."

"I suppose, because it comes from a new and earnest love of God, that this feeling is right in some ways," Maddie told her. "But then, the impetus that continues to fire it is an underlying belief that we can be good if we try hard enough."

"Can't we?" Tracey asked. "Isn't that why Christ died for us?"

"Yes, dear. Christ died for us, and so now we can be good," Maddie assured her. "Which is telling the beginning of the story and telling the end of the story, but leaving out the whole middle part."

"I don't get it," Tracey said.

"Look at this," Maddie said, pointing to an underlined passage. She read it aloud: "'If righteousness come by the law, then Christ is dead in vain.'"

"I know that we have to be declared righteous by the blood of Christ," Tracey told her, a little annoyed in spite of herself. "It's the living part that I have trouble with."

"You can't be declared righteous by grace and then live righteously by works, Tracey," Maddie said with a slight sternness that checked Tracey's irritation. "It's all one or all the other. Living by works or living by grace."

"Well, how do we live by grace?" Tracey asked.

"Read Galatians carefully," Maddie told her. "And then read Ephesians. The truth is, we have a positional righteousness that comes from grace. That's the first concept, and it's called justification. We're righteous simply because God declares us to be righteous. The second concept is our conditional righteousness. It's called sanctification, and it also comes entirely of grace. That's the righteousness that God bears out in our lives, working through our consciences and our desires."

"How?" Tracey asked her.

"Through faith, Tracey. And this is how: When Christ died, He knew you. He set His love on you then, not so much on the day that you believed in Him, as you suppose. He put you in Himself, and when He died, you died in Him. When He rose, you were in Him then too, resurrected to new life. Now He sits at the right hand of God, and you're there too. Have you ever stopped to think about Ephesians chapter one? 'Blessed be the God and Father of our Lord Jesus Christ, who hath blessed us with all spiritual blessings in heavenly places in Christ.'"

Tracey had hardly ever paid attention to the first few verses of any of the Epistles. They had seemed to her like ordinary salutations. "No, I never thought about it," Tracey said.

"It means that we are blessed in the heavenlies, in Christ. In God's sight, we are as worthy as Christ to receive His blessings. And we are forever exempt from His condemnation. The Lord might chastise us, but that's to bring us back to Himself."

Maddie returned to Galatians and read aloud, "'I am crucified with Christ: nevertheless I live, yet not I, but Christ liveth in me: and the life which I now live in the flesh I live by the faith of the Son of God, who loved me, and gave himself for me.'"

"So that means—" Tracey said, hesitating. It was all so new that she wasn't sure what it meant.

"It means that as we reckon ourselves dead in Him, which we are, and risen to a new life in Him, a new nature is given to us—the resurrection nature, the nature born of God. But it's all by faith. As we are given the faith to reckon our sinful selves killed in Christ and our resurrected selves risen in Him, we have the power to live righteous lives."

"And never sin?" Tracey asked.

Maddie shook her head. "Nobody has a perfect faith," she told Tracey. "But we have a perfect God, and we wear a perfect righteousness." She closed the Bible. "And that," she said, "is why I'm nice to you." She smiled. "You and I are in Christ."

"But what about my sins, Maddie?" Tracey asked her. "They were really committed. I really hurt some people. Other people saw me drunk."

"I think you should read Galatians and Ephesians," Maddie told her. "And sometime soon, we'll have to talk about God's sovereignty. He lets us fall into some sins to teach us things, dear. Very often, to teach us how much we depend on Him and not on ourselves. But don't be worried or afraid. You've never yet done anything that's taken the God of heaven by surprise or undone Him."

It was time to go, and there was no time for them to sit in the car at MoJoe and talk further. Maddie had to get back for her company and her dinner. But she surprised Tracey with a kiss on the cheek as Tracey was getting out of the car. "Don't be so afraid of the God who loves you," she told Tracey. "And don't be afraid of me. Merry Christmas, dear."

TWELVE

Liz came back to find a more sober, yet somehow more tranquil, Tracey.

"Hey!" she exclaimed as she came through the door of their room and saw Tracey seated on the floor with her Bible open. "Come back from the mountain, Moses! Give me my Christmas present!"

Tracey, awakened from her train of thought, looked up and smiled. "Santa Claus brought you coal." She reached under the bed and pulled out the clumsily wrapped care package she had made for Liz. These days, it was hard to get presents as nice as she had once been able to afford. If Maddie had not kindly offered to bake some things, Tracey's present would have been slim indeed.

Liz was genuinely pleased. "Whoa! Look at this! All kinds of goodies! Confess, Jacamuzzi! You can't make petit fours. Where'd you get 'em?"

"Maddie Murdoch," Tracey said, with a nod to acknowledge the correctness in Liz's accusation.

"I got you a coupon book," Liz said, tossing a thin

package at her. Tracey opened it, and four index cards fell out. Each one was covered with pasted-on magazine pictures of food, and they were all labeled: "You got a dinner date with the Wonder Polack."

Tracey looked up at her. "Thanks. I know I can use these."

"So how was your Christmas?" Liz asked. She glanced at the Bible, which had several passages underlined. "I was right," she said. "You been to the mountain—with Maddie Murdoch leading the way, huh?"

"What makes you so sure Maddie pointed out any mountains to me?" Tracey asked.

"Look, Jac, I'm no Catholic, but I really like Mother Teresa," Liz said. "And I'm no fundamentalist, but I like Maddie Murdoch too. You don't have to be a Christian to see real, deep-down holiness."

Tracey sighed and then said, "I've been really messed up about a lot of doctrines, Liz. I was so keen on what was wrong with Catholicism, I never bothered to study out real biblical doctrines, instead of so much denominational stuff."

"Maddie clear some things up for you?"

"She's trying to. And I'm trying to understand, but it's hard. And then I get so uptight about it, I think I almost choke myself." She glanced at Liz. "Like, maybe I keep yelling so loud for God to help me, that He's yelling directions and I can't even hear Him."

"Well, quit yelling," Liz told her.

"I can't—I'm so scared," Tracey said. "He'll have to do like lifeguards and conk me over the head. And then when I wake up, it'll all be over, I'll be safe. I wouldn't mind."

"You mean, like get you in a car accident and make

you be paralyzed for life?" Liz asked. "Get your attention that way?"

"I hope not," Tracey said. "But if He had to—if that's what it takes for me to understand—I just hope He does it fast."

"Whoo, boy. I'll stay agnostic, thanks," Liz said.

"I had this dream the other night—" Tracey began.

Liz flopped down on the floor. "Whoa! A vision! Was it a vision?"

"No," Tracey said. "Never mind." She picked up her Bible.

"Oh, come on, Jac. I'm sorry. Tell me your dream," Liz said.

"It's not something to laugh at!" Tracey exclaimed.

Liz sat up on her knees and leaned closer so Tracey had to look her in the face. "I'm not laughing. What'd you dream?"

Tracey set the Bible aside again. "I was in these woods," she said. "I've been in them before once or twice—"

"You mean in real life?" Liz asked.

"No, only in dreams. But it always feels like the same woods. Anyway, I had my armor on—the sword and the shield and some kind of uniform or other. And I wasn't scared or anything, but I didn't know exactly where I was in the woods.

"Then I saw this little wooden hunting lodge kind of place. There was smoke coming from the chimney, so I went up to the door. I didn't even knock, I just walked in.

"There was this man sitting at a long table. It was a big wooden table on trestles. And all around the room, on shelves, there were bottles and bottles. All sizes, all shapes of bottles."

"Was he a sorcerer?" Liz asked.

"No, not those kind of bottles," Tracey said. "They were kind of cheerful and normal—like, some were mason jars and some were real fat bottles, and some were elegant. I think it was a kind of tavern."

Liz's eyes got big, but true to her promise, she didn't laugh or make a joke.

"So at last I just looked at him, and he said, 'Why not take off your sword and shield and sit with me a while until you have to leave again?'

"It sounds casual when I say it now," Tracey continued, "but when he said it, it was so nice, so kind and sincere. Like he really wanted me to come and sit with him. And I thought, well, maybe he can help me, so I took off the sword and shield and sat down.

"He told me all these stories—I don't remember now what they were—but they all had to do with things that happened on the other side of the lodge from where I'd come in. See, he had his back to another door, and that was the door that he'd used to come in. I wanted to go through that door, but he told me I couldn't. He said I had to leave soon, but before I left, he would let me drink anything that was in the house.

"So I looked around the room, but I kept remembering that Christians shouldn't drink. I was scared to pick out a bottle because I was afraid it might have something alcoholic in it. So I asked him to pick one for me.

"He reached down, took a bottle from alongside him, and poured it into a cup for me. He told me to drink it all at once. I told him again that I wasn't supposed to drink alcohol, and he told me to drink it all at once, so I did."

"Was it wine?" Liz asked.

Tracey shrugged. "When I set the cup down, he looked me in the face and said, 'Now you will forget everything.'

"And I jumped up and was scared, but he looked at me and said, 'I give you forgetfulness.'

"And I was kind of screaming and saying things like, 'Forget my parents? Forget who I am? Forget it all?' And he didn't answer me—you know, the way people don't answer you when you're saying the obvious. I knew it was true—like I was doomed to forget because of what I'd drunk. I got so scared that I woke up. I jumped out of bed and went running around the room looking for my sword and shield."

Liz was impressed. "I wish I had dreams like that."

"I don't think people who really believe the Bible are supposed to have dreams like that," Tracey said.

"Why?" Liz asked, startled. "What's it got to do with sex?"

In spite of her seriousness, Tracey laughed. "Nothing, Liz. It doesn't have a thing to do with sex. What kind of a question was that?"

"Well, then what was wrong with it as a dream—" Liz began, then stopped. "Do you mean, the man at the table was God or something?"

"I was thinking of Jesus," Tracey told her.

"You mean, like it was a vision?" Liz asked.

"I just can't get it out of my head," Tracey said. "I've never had a dream like that one."

"But Trace, you haven't forgotten anything," Liz

exclaimed. "You know me, you know this place—hey, what's your middle name?"

"Cool it, Liz, I know I haven't forgotten anything. I just—I don't know. Dreams are usually less real than things are when you're awake. But this one felt more real. Like I could have reached through it somehow and grabbed heaven itself. Like it was all in front of me, but my own stupidity kept me from seeing it. Does that make sense?"

"No," Liz said.

"I guess not," Tracey agreed.

THIRTEEN

Basketball enthusiasm at MoJoe mounted to a fever pitch as the Valkyries won the next two games. Sister Mary announced a poster contest to cheer the team on. Numerous cartoons and shield designs dotted the halls of the school and then multiplied as the team won again and came within two games of the play-offs.

Some of the posters were very badly done, but others showed all the talent and discipline that MoJoe could boast. The contest winner was a poster cut from heavy cardboard in the shape of a broad shield. It was white with a black ribbon slashed diagonally across it; in red letters on one half was the word *Strength* and on the other half *Truth.* Underneath, across the ribbon, was a black silhouette of a Valkyrie on a winged horse. The entire shield was topped with a cardboard basketball covered in orange latex and stippled somehow, to give it the look and texture of a real basketball. The center panel of the ball had been trimmed away to accommodate the words *Champions, 1976,* with room above to add either *Division* or *District.*

The team chose the winner, and the vote on the shield was almost unanimous. At the pep rally held in early February, many of the posters were paraded across the stage before the winner was announced. The blare of the red trumpets, the shouts of the girls, and the new clash of homemade swords and shields—that year's fad—nearly deafened Tracey. As alternate captain of the team, she was called upon to lead cheers, and the very idea filled her with a sudden shyness.

But Liz, who had done this sort of thing before, laughed at her nervousness. "Just get up there when it's your turn, Jac," she told her younger friend. "They love you already. They'll do all the yelling. Watch me."

She nimbly hopped up onto the stage, and the audience immediately responded with cheers, catcalls, and applause. Liz whirled her hand in the air and let out a piercing whistle, getting another cheer and more whistles in reply. "Rowdy!" she yelled, and instantly the cheer was taken up.

She glanced at Tracey with a slight smile as the entire crowd of girls beat out the cheer with their feet and hands, chanting the refrain.

Only slightly hampered by her uniform, Tracey leaped onto the stage alongside Liz to take the next cheer. "MoJoe Ho Ho!" she called, trying to look brave. The girls didn't notice her fear as they launched into one of their favorite cheers.

The "Ho Ho" was several stanzas long, and during the cheer, Tracey had a chance to control her nerves and evaluate the situation. The faces below her were eager, willing, and smiling. She realized with a slight jolt that she had become a kind of school hero, that there were girls who admired not only her ability with a basketball, but her strict—they thought—adherence to honesty and virtue and kindness. The humility the realization evoked nearly stunned her.

"One more! One more!" the crowd yelled as she prepared to jump off the stage.

"Give 'em one more!" Liz yelled to her.

Tracey opened her mouth and found that she couldn't think of a cheer. She drew a complete blank. For one instant, the idea of being a basketball hero, of having somehow reached this pinnacle at MoJoe, tore her with shock as she realized what she really was, or once had been—that lonely, quiet hanger-on who had smoked on the roof at home and hung around with other hangers-on like Jody and Alice.

Who was she, really? The pathetic Tracey flung down the stairs, or the Valkyrie with the sword and shield? She turned from the crowd and looked for Liz, suddenly confused.

The girls in the front realized that she'd gone blank. "What's your favorite cheer?" they yelled up to her. "We'll do your favorite."

She was tongue-tied until she saw Liz's face among the crowd of ballplayers off to the side, ready to come up on stage for the roll call that would end the rally. For a moment's Liz's face seemed to swim a little, but Liz was smiling. "What's your favorite, Jac?"

"The song," Tracey stammered.

"What?" they yelled up to her.

"The song! For strength the black!" she yelled back.

She realized, after she said it, that they might be disappointed to sing the oratorical school song, but they weren't. Within seconds, the crowd hushed, and the seniors in the front began it for her.

For strength the black, for truth the white,
Our colors we hold dear.
Let strength and truth abide in us
In every heart sincere.

Pure Valkyries and maidens fair,
We pledge our loyalty;
The shield we love, nor can it fail
As our hearts are true to thee.

O Mary and Joseph, school we hail,
Our bles't Sanctuary,
The shield we carry in our hearts
Is yours eternally.

The anthem rose with a solemn volume in the closed room, swelling greater and greater in Tracey's heart. She didn't know why, but tears came to her eyes and trickled down her cheeks until she had to jump off the stage so they wouldn't see her sob from being so overwhelmed. Liz jumped back up on the stage to take over.

Much later, after dinner and in the privacy of the room, she asked Liz about it.

"Why was I crying, Liz?"

"Well, what were you thinking about?" Liz asked in return.

"I got kind of scared for a minute, like I couldn't remember who I was."

Liz turned quickly.

"I didn't mean it that way," Tracey said. "I mean, who is Tracey Jacamuzzi?"

"You had to think of that at a pep rally?"

"Liz, they were cheering for me. Don't you know how much things have changed for me?" Tracey demanded. "Man, when I lived at home, I was nothing, nobody. I didn't have the energy or the drive—or the brains, either—of a hungry mouse. Now, all of a sudden I'm Miss Important or something."

"Times have been tough for you," Liz reminded her. "It was going to make you or break you, Jac. That's why I threw my hand in with yours—I thought maybe you would make it in the end."

"I'm really glad you became my friend, Liz," Tracey said. "I don't know what I would have done if you hadn't stepped in that night—"

"You'd have gone down fighting." Liz looked at Tracey with a rare expression of sensitivity and understanding. "But I know girls who know why you're here, and they admire you for holding out for your religion. And they know you don't cut Mary or St. Bernard no slack. I know you say too much sometimes, but you don't give in, and that's good." She assumed a more carefree look, but her words were as earnest as the first had been. "A lot of the seniors think you've done this place some good. They like you a lot. So, in my book, that's what you are, a Valkyrie."

"The Tracey who got slapped around and beat up was killed," Tracey added, more to herself than to Liz. "I keep forgetting that—killed in Christ and raised a new creation. The Valkyrie was born the day I got saved, but the Tracey part doesn't always stay dead."

"Jac?" Liz asked.

"Never mind," Tracey said. "It's something I'm still learning."

F O U R T E E N

M an, if this is how it feels to be a winner, I think I'll just be glad when it's over," Liz said across the back of the seat. Tracey shot her a glance before turning to look up at Maddie in the rearview mirror.

Tracey was sitting in the first seat behind the driver's chair, with Liz behind her in the second seat. Maddie looked up at the mirror and smiled briefly before returning her attention to the road. "You've been through this before, Liz," she said.

"Gets worse each time," Liz said with a little gulp. "If we don't do it tonight, it'll be too late for me, forever. This is my last year."

Tracey looked back at Liz, sympathetic and yet a little surprised at her unusual case of nerves. "We've never stopped to look back all season," she told Liz. "Tonight's no different. Lady of the Valley is ours this time."

Liz closed her eyes. "I hope so," she whispered, almost prayerfully. She kept her eyes closed and sank back in the seat, shutting them all out for the moment.

Tracey turned to look up at Maddie again in the mirror. Maddie could not spare her a look, but she said, looking out at the traffic, "And how are you feeling about the game tonight, Tracey?"

Tracey leaned forward in her seat, closer to the back of Maddie's head. "Don't talk basketball with me, Maddie," she said. "Tell me about the other things we talked about before." She realized too late that she had not even said please. Her tone must have betrayed her impatient desire to hear from Maddie more new things she had never heard before, new things that each day made her beliefs more clear.

But Maddie, normally a stickler for manners, didn't seem to notice Tracey's tone or rough words. "What shall I tell you, dear? Did you have a question?" she asked.

"Just go over it all again," Tracey begged, and remembered to add, "please. All about God knowing His people and putting us in Him, and adoption—all of it."

On their bus trips to and from the away games—whenever Maddie had been able to drive—Tracey had spent much of her time listening instead of talking. From Maddie, she had begun to understand the eternal sonship of Christ, a doctrine she had thought she understood until Maddie had explained its implications: Christ had brought her into Himself and given her a position in His sonship, a new position as a son of God that could never be altered.

That night, Maddie again reviewed the concept with Tracey and reminded her of the Bible verse references she could check. The other girls were busy talking with each other, and even CPR had been brought into conversation with some of the second-string girls.

No one noticed the earnestness with which Tracey hung on the Christian woman's impromptu lecture.

Too soon, the bus pulled into the parking lot of the municipal gym where the division championship would be played.

The second the brake was set, Liz leaped up, wide awake.

"Let's go!" she yelled, and the rest of the girls took up the shout. Tracey forgot her own conversation and jumped up too, her mind instantly switched to the adventure at hand. The sudden realization of the game's importance slammed into her for the first time.

"Let's go in singing!" she exclaimed.

"Conga line!" Liz yelled, and she put her hands on Tracey's shoulders. "We are the MoJoes, the mighty, mighty MoJoes! Everywhere we go, people wanna know—"

Tracey shot one glance at Maddie, who smiled and waved them on.

Tracey held up the first finger of each hand and led the swaying, singing line of girls toward the gym. Bright lights spilled out through the glass doors into the late afternoon dusk. Inside, the gym was already hot and noisy. The MoJoes hurried back to the dressing room to leave their things and get out on the floor for drills and warm-ups.

The Chickens of the Valley, as the MoJoes called them, already had their mascot out on the floor and had started their warmup. The Valley girls looked ready and willing, but as Tracey came bursting through the doors behind Liz, she felt as though her own strength, her own spirit, and her own will were all stronger. She felt very much like a Valkyrie.

The referees signaled. The Valkyries quickly disappeared back into the locker room, waiting behind the double doors while the other team performed its fanfare—a loud drum tattoo while the mascot promenaded and the girls ran out and took their positions. Then Sister Theresa gave a nod to her newly improved pep band of one additional trumpeter and two girls on trombones. They lifted their instruments in unison and blew the fanfare for the Valkyries.

Liz and Scooter burst through the doors with the banner, and Tracey came right behind them with the sword and shield. Maddie had taken her usual seat by the team bench, and Tracey faced her for the first bow. Then she clashed sword on shield. All of the MoJoes in the audience who had swords and shields did likewise, and she heard that year's new chant—harsh and hard and militant and glorious: "Mo-Joe! Mo-Joe! Mo-Joe!"

Tracey ran to take her place, and the rest of the team came running out and got into formation for the MoJoe song.

The gym was almost nauseatingly hot. As Tracey hurriedly shucked the armor and slid it toward some MoJoe girls in the audience, she wondered what the building custodian had been thinking. Already, the people in the audience had shed their coats, and some of the nonuniformed spectators had also thrown off pullover sweaters. Some of the MoJoe girls had already found enough nerve to "go slang" in their uniforms— rolling up their sleeves, unbuttoning their boleros, and pushing down their socks—in defiance of school rules.

After the song, the second-string hurried to the bench while the first-string came to center for a brief lecture from the head referee. Liz shot Tracey a look and held down two fingers: *Try for a fast break from the jump*. Tracey gave Liz a slight nod and passed the sign to Dibbles. Dibbles passed the sign to Scooter, and Tracey saw Scooter's brief look of understanding.

Tracey faded back and then stopped, unnoticed by the other team. The ref threw the ball, and Tracey raced toward the MoJoe basket. Liz slapped the ball to Scooter, who passed to Dibbles, and Dibbles threw furiously for the top of the key. Tracey leaped up, got the ball, took three more steps and shot, sinking the first basket of the game.

Thunderous applause greeted this exploit. The trumpets blared. Tracey wiped sweat from her eyes. The gym was so hot. *Why doesn't somebody turn the heat down?* she wondered. The ball changed hands, and she scurried back to defense.

The Lady of the Valley team that year had some good shooters—when they got close enough. CPR had drilled a strong defense into the Valkyries, warning them not to drift more than two paces from the key when under the basket, and not at all when at the top of the key. The Valley girls got most of their points from inside the key, and they were known to bait defense out in order to let themselves in.

Valley took several passes back and forth, and Tracey felt the nudge of temptation to jump out and intercept a pass. But CPR's warnings, scoldings, and admonitions were too fresh in her mind for her to risk what was normally a regular part of her tactics. The slow passes could be tricks to bring her out.

The whistle blew for the thirty-second violation, and the ball changed ownership again. The Valley coach called a time-out.

The Valkyries quickly retired to the sidelines, where CPR waved them in. "Just like that," she said quickly. "Keep the doors closed. Use the short post as soon as you get it down on offense."

They all nodded and ran back to the court.

The Valley team was ready for another try at a fast break, and they hurried into position to defend the MoJoe key. Dibbles and the other MoJoe guard brought the ball down unhindered. Liz came out to the top of the key, and Dibbles passed off to her quickly as she ran into the key. The Valley defense covered Liz too quickly, and Liz passed back to Dibbles as Tracey also came out by the basket.

But the sight of Dibbles in the middle of the key with the ball brought the Valley defense down on top of her. She shot in the direction they least expected— back out to Liz—before racing out of the key. Liz shot, unhampered, and sank the ball with a whoosh.

One of the Valley guards, perhaps prompted by desperation, made a long pass to her teammate just ahead of Tracey. Tracey saw the girl turn to get the ball, turned herself, leaped, and intercepted.

"Here!" Scooter yelled from across the key. Tracey passed to her, and Scooter took the ball down for two more points.

MoJoe ended the first quarter up by eight points, and CPR risked letting Peggy go in for a few minutes. The lead shortened by only two points. Peggy came back out, and Tracey switched with one of the second-string girls to take a short rest. So far, her shooting was tied with Liz's.

She gratefully sank down onto the bench and took the towel that one of her teammates handed her.

Hands came down on her shoulders with the half-rough, half-gentle massage customarily given by the schoolmates who sat behind the bench.

Tracey leaned back into it. "This gym is like an oven," she gasped, her eyes closed.

"I was wondering how it felt out there," a familiar voice said. Tracey opened her eyes and turned to see that Maddie was behind her.

"Don't you mind the sweat?" she asked, glancing down at her soaked uniform.

"We're all sweating anyway," Maddie said. "Turn round and let us finish. CPR will pop you back in at the next basket or time-out."

Tracey nodded and turned back around while Maddie and two of the other girls worked on her. Their hands were warm, and the gym was hot, and she was sticking to the bench. She held the clean white towel to her face and scrubbed herself with it, hard.

CPR did put her back in before two minutes of play had elapsed, and Scooter came out for a rest.

By halftime the Valkyries were up by a ten-point spread. Liz was jubilant, but the heat had become a sucking, stifling thing to Tracey. It pulled sweat from her slick body and dried out her eyes and mouth.

"Don't you get giddy with success!" CPR scolded the team back in the locker room. "I've seen teams a whole lot less experienced than Valley take a game like this and turn it around. They're desperate now. Desperate! They've got plays they haven't tried yet. They'll take more chances next half. But don't you take chances. I don't care if they offer you a pot of gold—stay on the key. Keep them out of the castle.

They got in the key enough last half to make me worry. We ought to have a twenty-point lead."

"What about this heat, coach?" Peggy asked. "Can't you get the custodian?"

"The thermostat is broken," CPR told them. "Drink up the water now, so it's assimilated better by the time third quarter starts. Don't you fret about that heat. This team is in better physical shape than any team in the league. The heat may save us if we can't save ourselves."

"We're winning by ten points, Coach!" Liz exclaimed.

"That's not enough! We usually win by ten points when I bring in the least experienced players, not the most. You get out there and play like a team, girls. Fast breaks are nice and showy, but that's not our game. Strategy. We'll gloat and glory when we have the trophy. Right now you tell yourselves the score is too low and we have to bump it up."

The second half started with both teams feeling desperate. CPR's brief scolding had gone to the heart of every girl, but especially the seniors. Scooter and Liz knew that this was their last chance to do it at MoJoe. There might be other victories in other places, but never this one again, never the sword and the shield, never the song for strength and truth, never the same people to love and to hate again.

Tracey felt the difference as Scooter got the long pass and put the ball in on MoJoe's typical jump-ball fast break. Scooter and Liz were going all out now. There was no showmanship in their moves, none of the stuff picked up from watching Sixers games. Everything was short, fast, and hard. The rhythm drew Tracey

110

in; this was her type of ball too—intense and demanding and a little dangerous.

She had thought that they had outplayed Valley very well in the first half. But now she realized that in the first half MoJoe had been testing the situation, more cautious than necessary. Now Liz and she and Scooter moved and passed the way the last two seasons had taught them, keeping the key alive and busy. They used their short post strategy less, and CPR did not insist that they rely on it.

The heat did come into play. By fourth quarter, Tracey saw that the Valley girls could not keep up the pace. They wasted motion in their play, and at last the extra efforts and excessive heat took their toll. MoJoe ran away with the ball and the game, and by the ten-second countdown, they were ahead by twenty-four points.

The MoJoes yelled the countdown from the bleachers, then flooded onto the court as the buzzer went off. Liz, wet as a fish, hugged Tracey and pulled her feet off the ground. They were swept up by the crowd of players, spectators, and even the sisters.

It was impossible to get to the Valley team even to shake hands. They were already leaving the floor in dismal failure, and the victorious MoJoe crowd was too thick to be navigated easily. It took a lot of gentle pushing and determined walking to get back to the locker room. Tracey wearily pulled on her sweats and coat, feeling the chill from the open back door.

She was glad to get back to the cool bus, to flop down on a seat near the front and near Maddie. She sank into a doze, exhausted by the biggest victory of her basketball career and the hottest game of her life.

FIFTEEN

Tracey became aware, by degrees, that Liz was carrying on a conversation with Maddie Murdoch. Even in her doze, she was able to feel some surprise at this fact. Liz had to be at least as tired and sucked out from that heat as she was.

Her thoughts would have faded again, but the bus slowed, and she felt the gears shift down. They were pulling into the school.

Some of the girls woke up enough to ask, "No McDonald's?"

"Father Williams wants us right away in his office," CPR told them. "He'll have something waiting for us, I'm sure."

The prospect of food was cheering, but most of the girls groaned at the thought of a long, dull meeting with the headmaster—when what they really wanted was to be celebrating in the halls or at their homes, the toast of friends and family.

Tracey gathered her things and filed out with her teammates. "See you next time, Maddie?" she asked.

"I wouldn't miss it, dear. You get some rest tonight, all right?"

"Sure. Thanks for driving."

She stumbled off the bus, followed by Liz.

"Jac," Liz said sharply, her voice annoyed.

"What?"

"You know, you could have stayed and talked with Maddie on the way home."

"I didn't know you didn't want to talk alone."

"I don't mean that!" Liz exclaimed. "Man, where's your consideration? You think Maddie wasn't as tired as anyone? She had to drive. She couldn't conk out."

"I'd have talked with her if she'd asked!" Tracey said with perfect honesty.

"Nobody should have to ask you. That's what friends do. Maddie would have done it for you."

"What are you getting mad for?" Tracey asked, feeling an overwhelming sense of helplessness in the face of Liz's reprimand. "Was I rude? Everyone else fell asleep."

"Not rude!" Liz exclaimed. "Just . . . just dumb—or something. Come on, we'll talk about it later." She led the way after the knot of girls.

"Are you mad at me?" Tracey called, running to catch up with her.

Liz shot her a glance of exasperation. "Tracey Jacamuzzi, when are you going to start seeing it all, babe? When's the whole picture going to hit you? The world doesn't revolve around you!"

Tracey still didn't understand, and Liz wouldn't say any more.

Father Williams was in his cluttered office. Some of his paraphernalia and debris had been pushed aside to make room for the team, and several boxes of pizza stood open on his desk.

"Eat up, Valkyries," he invited. He looked happy, more excited than Tracey had ever seen him. He was usually careful to stay calm and nonchalant, but that night there was an eagerness in his eyes that was almost boyish. He might have been a teammate himself, except for the gender difference.

"Ladies," he told them as they sat around on chairs or on the floor. He leaned against the desk. "I was very proud of you tonight. I know you want to get back to your friends and cheer and carry on, but I had to call you aside and commend you for your excellent playing tonight. Some of you know that there were scouts in the audience—"

"Were they the ones who turned up the heat?" Liz asked. Everyone laughed, including Father Williams.

"We'll have to look into that," he said. "But I want to tell you that everybody was impressed with the team. Some of you have opened the doors to college for yourselves, if you'll only walk through. There are some good schools who recruit women ballplayers."

Tracey's interest perked up. There had always been too many other things to think about in her life for college to claim any of her attention. But now, for the first time, she paid the idea some serious regard. She realized with a slight shock that her studying had grown from being an escape to being something she genuinely enjoyed. And she didn't want to stop next year. She wanted to discover the other secrets in books like Wylie's books.

With an effort, she returned her attention to Father Williams. The rest of his little speech was mostly about sportsmanship, team spirit, and being examples to the other girls.

"Above all," he said, "be examples. You know, nobody ever really took the Valkyrie mascot very seriously until this year. I want each of you to think about what a Valkyrie is: a shield maiden of heaven. Could we convert her to our faith, we would call her a shield maiden of the Lord of Hosts. That's quite a title, especially when you consider that many people believe that all of mythology is in some ways a reflection or shadow of the true order. If we are imitating something that we only dimly see through the veil of the material world, then each of you has taken upon yourself a serious and maybe a sacred emblem."

Tracey listened intently. Was this really Father Williams? He had never been so interesting, so sincere, and certainly never so persuasive. Tracey saw that her teammates were genuinely moved by his words.

"MoJoe has a reputation for toughness," he reminded them. "Even tonight we heard the other people calling us JDs. But you can change that."

"What's wrong with toughness, Father?" Scooter challenged. "It won us the division title."

"Susan, toughness combined with virtue is what I long to see in each of you," he told her. "We reach for strength and truth together. What I don't want is toughness for the sake of toughness. Now, while you have the power of influence on your classmates, live the lives of the shield maidens of the Lord of Hosts."

His speech left them sober and solemn. They finished eating and he dismissed them. As they climbed the stairs to their rooms, Peggy said to Tracey, "It was a good talk, I guess. But I notice he held it back until we became winners."

Tracey looked at her with sudden understanding. "You're right."

Peggy nodded. "He picks winners and sticks with them, Jac. Welcome to the real world."

"But what he said was true," Tracey told her.

"Oh, yeah—"

"Peggy!" Tracey exclaimed. Peggy looked at her, and Tracey realized that the last couple of years had taken away some of Peggy's bubbling happiness and good cheer. "When we were freshmen, you risked a lot to get me out of trouble. I know you did."

"Sure," Peggy said.

"If we bucked the system then, we can buck it now. We're ballplayers now. Who's going to hurt us? Scooter?"

"You're really high on what he said, aren't you?" Peggy asked.

"I hate this place most of all because it turns girls against each other. All the dumb, fat, and ugly kids end up on the bottom. Everybody does to each other what Mary or our parents did to us."

"What a philosopher!" Peggy exclaimed, half mocking and half tempted—by the look on her face—to listen to Tracey.

"My folks don't care about me. I never had what it took to please them," Tracey said. "My dad was slamming me around before I ever changed religions, and my mom didn't love any of us enough to be honest. And she's given up all of my brothers and sisters so she can get with some guy named Jim. You know all that's true."

"Everybody's got sad stories, Jac," Peggy said.

"Well, as long as I'm not on the bottom—now that I am somebody—I'm going to do what he said. No more calling freshmen 'freshman,' or pretending I don't see who's been pegged for being a narc. Maybe we'll lose district, but I'll always be a Valkyrie."

Liz had caught up with them by this time. She didn't say anything to Tracey's statement, but she didn't have to. Liz had never played by MoJoe's rules, so there was no need to ask her to stop. Tracey suddenly found herself blushing with shame.

Later, as they rummaged around for their shower things, Tracey remembered what Liz had said as they'd left the bus.

"You want to talk about all that business about Maddie?" Tracey asked her.

It was a Friday night, so there was no study time, but most of the girls were exhausted and in bad need of showers. From the staircase, they could hear the cheering and yelling of the other boarders who had gathered for an impromptu pep rally.

"It's just this," Liz said, busy with her things and not looking up. "It's like, now that you know Maddie likes you, you're all happy. Because somehow you got yourself all tied up in the fact that she's pure or holy or good or something—"

"She is," Tracey exclaimed.

"Yeah, I know she is!" Liz said. "And now that she likes you OK, you don't feel cheap or dirty anymore, I bet."

The words brought a second scarlet flush across Tracey's cheeks. Her confidences to Liz about feeling dirty and cheap had been delicately made. "So what?" she asked.

"You don't think about Maddie, or consider her, or even treat her like a real person, Trace!" Liz exclaimed. "She's just there to explain the Bible to you and make you feel like you're OK. Why don't you think about her for once? Why don't you treat people like real people for once and think about them?"

Tracey blinked. This heartfelt and loud rebuke from Liz was almost the equivalent of a slap in the face.

"I think about you, Liz," she said lamely.

"I've watched you learn to do it with me," Liz told her. "A step at a time. And that's OK. But other times, Tracey—you just don't know me at all."

"I'm your best friend!" Tracey exclaimed.

"Yeah, and you don't half know me!"

"Well, what can I do to know you better?" Tracey asked, hoping somehow to placate Liz's anger. She had no idea what Liz was talking about.

The older girl studied her a second and at last relented. "Nothing," she said, calming down.

"Just tell me, Liz. I'll change, I'll do anything," Tracey promised.

"No, kid. You are my best friend, and we have been through a lot together. I'm going to go get a shower. Don't take it too serious when I start yelling." She slung her towels over her shoulder, picked up her shower bucket, and left the room.

They didn't have much to say to each other for the rest of the night. Tracey felt as unseated as any Valkyrie that had ever been flipped from her saddle. She wondered how long Liz's disapproval had been growing.

The memory of Liz's rebuke kept stinging. After lights-out and the forbidden whispering—longer than

118

usual on this jubilant night—had quieted down, Tracey lay awake and wondered what she had done to offend her friend. That she had seriously offended Liz was without doubt.

She wondered what it was about herself that always alienated the people she loved best, the people who should have loved her best. Was it the same thing that had made her so repugnant to her father, or that had made it easy for her mother to abandon all of them? And now had this blind enemy to Tracey, sprouting from Tracey's own person, also driven her best friend away?

This question, and the fear of losing Liz's friendship, became worse as the night wore on. Tracey rolled into her pillow as she started to cry. *What is it about me that makes me be so alone all my life?*

She might have cried herself to sleep alone, but there was a rustle from Liz's bunk. Liz got up and came and sat on the floor by her bed. "Don't cry about it, Jac. It's nothing," Liz said.

"I'm all right," Tracey gasped. She knew that her silent tears could not have awakened Liz. She too had been awake all this time.

"Baby, you're the best friend I've ever had," Liz said. "I've never had a friend like you before, and I don't think I'll ever be lucky enough to have one again."

"I want to be a good friend," Tracey gasped, keeping her face in the pillow so she wouldn't wake anybody else.

"I know that when I say the word, Jac's by my side," Liz told her. "I know that. And I know I hide a lot of stuff. It's not fair to get mad when people can't read the things I hide."

"You aren't mad?" Tracey begged.

"No, babe. I'm glad we're friends. I couldn't have made it through this place without you. You never asked me to be nothing but what I am."

"What about Maddie?" Tracey asked.

"Jac—" Liz hesitated. Then she said, "Don't worry about Maddie. She's taken care of herself through a lousy husband and two lousy kids. I just want to make sure that . . . that she gets her share, maybe."

"Her share of what?" Tracey asked.

"Of whatever she's looking for," Liz said. "Or of whatever God's promised to her. That's how she would say it."

"She and I are friends now," Tracey reminded her. "I'd have stayed up on the bus if she'd asked me, Liz, I really would have."

Again Liz hesitated. Then she said, "Yeah, I know, kid. It's cool. I overreacted. You all right now?"

Tracey nodded and at last turned to look at Liz. "Yeah, I'm all right," she said. "I can go to sleep now."

"Good night, Jac."

"Good night, Liz."

SIXTEEN

Although MoJoe had already held one big pep rally, another was quickly scheduled for the Thursday night before the championship game. Alumni and former teachers were coming in for it, and the parents of the town students had been invited. Instead of being tagged on to the end of the school day like most pep rallies were, this one was to be held at seven o'clock.

In the glow of victory and the bright hopes for district championships, the Sanctuary of Mary and Joseph assumed another atmosphere. Instead of being the dismal refuge for girls who were discipline problems, it was again touted as an academic power player among prep schools. The newspapers ran several articles on MoJoe, praising its high academics and strict discipline.

MoJoe would be playing for the district title against a school three times its size: Villa Marie. And yet it was hard to pick a favorite to win, another feather in MoJoe's cap. Their diminutive size won them the reputation of being a David against a Goliath. Though the chances of victory were said to be even, MoJoe some-how won the favor of the little towns sprawled around its campus.

As team captain, Liz Lukas was interviewed. Under strict orders—and maybe threats—from both Sister Patricia Rose and Sister Mary, Liz gave a straight-forward interview to the newspaper people and the television reporter who came to the school to do a one-minute spot about the championships.

Clear-skinned, blonde-haired, with no makeup and a broad, strong smile, Liz was the picture of a Catholic high school basketball player. Or, she was the picture of what people hoped most Catholic high school ball-players were like. She had already talked with several college scouts about basketball scholarships, and her desire to go on to college was also a public relations plus for the team. After the interview, which was taped on Monday but not aired until Thursday, Liz actually gave in to the excitement enough to call her parents from the hall telephone and tell them what was going on.

The upshot, she told Tracey, was that her parents were coming to the game.

"What?" Tracey exclaimed, dismayed. "Yours too?" She got hold of herself. "I'm sorry, Liz. I didn't mean to sound so sad about it."

"Sad?" Liz asked. "You? What about me? My folks never cared about basketball at all until I told them I got on the news. Now it's hit them that this is big-time to everybody else. I should have kept my mouth shut."

Tracey wasn't fooled. "Come on, Liz. You knew if you told them about the interview that they would come."

Liz couldn't quite meet Tracey's eye. "Well . . . maybe I did. Maybe I hoped a little bit. If they don't get it by this time, they never will. It's my one chance to win out."

Tracey's regret faded. Certainly, if getting interviewed on television could have won her the love of her father, she would have done the exact same thing. "You're right. Maybe this'll wake them up a little," she agreed. "Get them hip to what's going on in the real world. So they're coming. When?"

"Thursday afternoon," Liz said with a slight smile.

"You're going to stay off campus with them?" Tracey asked, and Liz nodded. It was a great chance to get away from the school, to walk around the small town and be recognized by everybody.

"You come on out to dinner with us," Liz invited.

"You better let your folks know before you start asking people out with them," Tracey warned. "I'll be OK."

Inwardly, she was sharply disappointed. Peggy's family was coming for the event; Scooter's parents were coming; Dibbles's family would be there. And all of the town players, of course, would be having parties and going out. Only Tracey was left.

On Wednesday, she went down to the gym to practice a while in private. She accomplished this by simply not going to chorus class. With the championship at hand, Sister Theresa was beside herself. The chorus classes had been drafted into making cloth banners, and some of the girls were quickly sewing up uniforms for the small pep band, which had now grown to five with the discovery that Tina McCorkle could play the drums.

Tracey's absence would not be noticed by Sister Theresa, who was usually pretty distracted even on regular, peaceful days. If she did notice, she would never bring it up to anybody. Tracey's regular attendance had won her a certain immunity from suspicion.

The gym was empty, and Tracey got one of the balls and worked on shooting from the foul line. At least Maddie would be driving the team bus. But then she realized that with everybody's parents there, CPR might not require Maddie. Would Maddie come anyway?

Well, CPR did like the team to be together. She might insist that they all go together in the bus to ensure that they got to the gym on time. Yes, Tracey decided, that would be exactly like CPR. The poor woman was already uptight enough over this game. She wouldn't leave something as fundamental as attendance up to the girls when she could take care of it herself.

"Tracey Jacamuzzi!"

She turned at the sound of Father Bing's voice.

"Hi," she said.

He crossed the gym floor quickly. "What are you doing in here, dear?" he asked. "Why aren't you in class?"

She looked down. "I didn't want to go to class," she said.

"Tracey." His voice held reproof. "I never took you to be one who would take advantage of her position in order to cut class or break rules."

"Come on, Father," she said. "Everybody's partying up there anyway. What's wrong with coming down here to shoot baskets?"

"You belong in class," he reminded her. His voice was not nearly as severe as Mary's would have been.

"Look," Tracey told him, "everybody's all high over this game, Father. I'm just trying to get myself psyched up too, OK?"

"Aren't you psyched up for it?" he asked.

"No, I'm not psyched up for it!" she said, a little angrily. "Everybody else on the team is getting ready for a real big weekend, win or lose. And here I am, stuck in this place, win or lose. Every time something good happens, I miss it."

He let out a sigh, and his sternness faded. "Have you called your parents? Your mother, at least?" he asked.

"I wrote and told her after the last game that this was a big one coming up, but . . . it doesn't matter to her." She looked up at him. "I couldn't come out and ask. It would hurt too much when she said no."

"You're sure that she would have?" he asked.

"I wish you'd get the sun out of your eyes, Father," Tracey said. She felt her eyes filling up with tears. "Go call her yourself and ask her. She won't come. I'm so neatly out of the way here. She doesn't send money; she doesn't ask how I'm doing; she has no idea what my grades are—even though she gets a copy of my report card. The only time she ever came up here was to tell me she and my dad were divorcing and to make sure that I swallowed her cock-and-bull story enough so my dad wouldn't use me in court."

"I am going to call her and ask her to come," Father Bing told Tracey. "We'll see what happens."

"Can I stay and practice?" she asked.

He nodded. "Just this once."

As he walked away, Tracey thoughtfully dropped the ball and let it come back up to her hand. He really did have the sun in his eyes.

Dinner was a jubilant meal. Liz and Tracey sat together with Scooter and several other seniors. Among the congratulations of the other girls, especially the seniors, Tracey felt a little better.

Their talk, even this close to the championships, was on college. Scooter had been accepted at Cornell, and over Easter she was going up to see the campus and try to find a place to live.

"Scholarship?" one of the girls asked her.

"No way, let my parents pay for it," she exclaimed with a short laugh. "And pay they will. I intend to leave the life of a pauper behind me."

"That's the spirit!" one of the girls said. "What about you, Liz?"

"Just the opposite," Liz said. "I'm taking the best basketball scholarship I can get—I don't care which school it is or what I major in. I'm just waiting to rub my dad's nose in it that I got to college by being just what I am and not what he wanted me to be."

"That's right!" several of them exclaimed in admiration of her spirit.

"What about you, Jac?" Scooter asked her with startling friendliness. "Any of those scouts pick you out yet?"

"Not a one," Tracey said. "Got a call from Notre Dame, though. How's that for a laugh?"

"You didn't tell me that!" Liz exclaimed.

"Oh, St. Bernard took the message and told me I could call back on the office phone."

"You could do it at lunch tomorrow," Liz said.

Tracey gave her another glance. "Are you kidding? What am I going to do at Notre Dame? When I get out of here, baby, I'm never looking back at Catholic school."

"Well, you got a year to decide," Liz said with unusual hesitation.

"Nobody at Notre Dame's going to make you be anything," Scooter told her. "They're a good school, and they'd jump to get a good ballplayer who's a good student too."

"Whoa!" Tracey said, holding up both hands. "Nobody at any Catholic school's going to tell me anything, because I'm going to a non-Catholic college."

Talk turned to the colleges that the other girls had applied to, and Tracey listened carefully. You had to be accepted, then, at many of these places. It seemed that acceptance wasn't a guaranteed thing. She hoped her own grades were good enough. She had A's in everything but geometry and Algebra II. Both of those courses had been B's. She wondered how much that told against a person.

The night was a tense one in the halls, and nobody got much studying done. From seven until eight, the swish of gowns could be heard periodically as St. Bernard or CPR banged on doors and demanded silence. They interrupted a few parties among roommates and actually confiscated the fixings.

But after eight o'clock, they appeared to have given it up. In fact, St. Bernard even returned the tray of cupcakes she'd taken from Peggy's room.

"Next time have chocolate," she told them, trying to sound severe. "I don't like white cake very much."

"Come in and have another, Sister," Peggy invited

her. The girls in neighboring rooms cautiously popped their heads out into the hallway to gauge the situation.

"No, thank you, miss," St. Bernard said. "You just keep quiet in there while you eat—and shame on you for eating a cupcake on the night before the big game. What would Sister Patricia Rose say?"

"I only count ten here," Peggy said. "You took away twelve. So what did Sister Patricia Rose say?"

"She said, next time bring chocolate," St. Bernard told her. She turned to go back up the hall, and all the heads popped back inside. The doors closed.

S E V E N T E E N

The girls on the team were not given carte blanche to skip classes on Friday, the day of the big game. But they did have to leave school early in order to make the two-hour journey to the big college gym where they would play Villa Marie; eat a decent meal; and have a short rest before the game. So they were required to attend classes only until noon. As a further concession, their individual teachers could excuse them from morning classes if they saw fit.

Tracey's morning classes were English, Latin III, and Spanish I. On Thursday, she applied to each teacher and was granted the three excuses that promised her complete freedom the next day. That was some balm for her unhappiness over being left in the halls alone on the night before the championships.

All day Thursday, the whole school was in a fever over the big rally. Visitors strolled across the grounds, distracting the nuns as well as the girls. It was odd to see St. Bernard acting like any other person, hugging former students and chattering away in her happiness.

A new student council had been formed that year —admittedly not good for much—and the council members were called down to the gym to toil over the decorations. The business students were pressed into typing and mimeographing song sheets for all the cheers. The journalism class worked on saddle-stapling them into booklets.

Sister Theresa had a fit of nerves at lunchtime and called in the pep band to practice the fanfares one more time. Not long afterward, a note came around requesting that the basketball team go out to the hockey field to have their pictures taken.

It was an unusually mild day for late winter, and the girls were glad to get out and stroll around the grounds while they waited for the photographer. They eventually realized that the note had been a counterfeit. The nuns never discovered the prank, so the team had a free afternoon.

Late afternoon was also when the parents of team girls started showing up. They found their daughters out on the field and were saved from the bother of having to find the school office and request them.

Tracey met Peggy's parents, two round, middle-aged people who seemed very kindhearted and very proud of Peggy.

"So you're the Protestant!" Mr. Melsom exclaimed as he shook Tracey's hand.

"Daddy!" Peggy screamed.

Tracey smiled. "I guess I am, sir." She shot a wry smile at Peggy, imagining the contents of Peggy's letters home.

"And the Valkyrie," Mr. Melsom added.

"That too," Tracey told him. "But so is Peggy."

"We all are!" Liz exclaimed, throwing one arm across Tracey's shoulders and holding out her other to shake hands with the Melsoms.

Dibbles's parents had arrived too. They seemed as confused by Dibbles's odd humor as anybody else, and her sudden ascension to being a major player on a major high school ball team had apparently taken them off guard. Still looking a little confused, they shook hands with all of the girls and hurried away with Dibbles, eager—it seemed—to have the game, the rules, the positions, and her teammates all explained. They were happy to cheer her on, Tracey thought. They had just never expected such a thing. It was all pretty new to Dibbles too, but she showed her surprise less.

Liz's parents came after afternoon classes had ended. Knowing their way around, they came to the hall, and a note was sent up to Liz.

"Five-thirty!" Liz exclaimed, irritated. "See what I mean, Jac? We've got to be back here by six-thirty to dress for the pep rally."

"You got an hour," Tracey told her.

"Yeah, to get them checked in at a motel and get dinner and get back here. This is just like them. Never hurry for what's important to me—just get here in their own sweet time and in style."

Tracey had wanted very much to go down and meet Liz's parents, but she decided this wasn't the time.

"Look, CPR's down there, and she's edgy already," she reminded Liz. "On your way out, tell her you're going to dinner, and watch and see if she doesn't tell your folks herself to get you back here on time. She's not afraid to whip your parents into shape."

"Good idea. See you at the gym." And Liz ran out,

her school uniform on and her overnight case in her hand.

Feeling a little alone and unwanted, Tracey leaned against the wall. But she decided that moping might be dangerous to their chances of a victory. She had to snap out of it and put on as brave a face as possible at dinner. The other girls would be glad to have one ball-player there, anyway.

After dinner, Tracey hurried to get her basketball uniform together and go down to the gym and change. Like the rest of the girls, she had been wondering all day long how the gym would be decorated for the rally.

But even the team was not allowed into the gym itself. They were let in by the back door and allowed only as far as the locker room to change.

One by one, all of the stragglers drifted in.

"How was it?" Tracey asked Liz as the blonde girl strode in.

"Not bad; feels kind of good," Liz told her. "My old man's pretty impressed to know what some of the scouts have said. He's going to have a lot to think about."

"Your stomach OK?" Tracey asked.

"Good enough. I'm under a vow not to touch Tastykakes until after the game."

"Whoa!" Tracey exclaimed in admiration.

"Yeah, well, it was a shotgun promise. CPR made me take a holy oath when she found out that I was staying off campus tonight. And don't worry—I'll keep my troth." Her eyes looked a little distant as she said, "I can eat Tastykakes from tomorrow night until the kingdom comes, I guess."

"That's right. It's our last game together," Tracey

said. They looked at each other. Liz looked away first. She quickly walked over to the sink as though to wash her hands. Just then the door opened, and Maddie Murdoch walked in, looking a little out of place in her skirt and blouse and long, roomy coat.

"Hey! It's the mascot!" Liz yelled in greeting.

"No, scamp, only the bus driver," Maddie told her, smiling. Her eyes sought and found Tracey. "How are you, then, Tracey?"

"Good enough, I guess," Tracey said. "What's up?"

"Father Williams and I thought you might like to take a night off at my house," Maddie told her. "But he's made me promise to have you in bed by nine, and I have to have your solemn word on that."

"That's really nice of you," Tracey said.

"Oh, I'd love to have your company, if you'll only come."

"Sure. Thank you. And don't worry, I'll be in bed by nine." Tracey smiled at Maddie, but some inner urge made her ask, "He called my mom, didn't he?"

Maddie looked down and tried to sound casual, but she said, "Yes, I suppose he did." She looked at Tracey.

"I warned him," Tracey said, trying to get some pleasure out of having been right.

"I'll come get you after the rally," Maddie told her.

Tracey jerked her head toward the direction of the hall. "Up there, if you like. I'll have to get a few things together."

"All right, then. I'll be watching tonight. So look strong and brave for me."

"You bet!" Tracey called after her.

She looked at Liz, who had returned from the sink. "Was that all right? I wasn't rude, was I?"

133

"Jac, you're fine," Liz said. "Maddie really likes you, and I really like you too. Just forget that other stuff I said that night. Come on, let's get the banner and the sword and shield."

EIGHTEEN

The plan for the pep rally was for each class to present some type of skit or demonstration of school spirit. The basketball team was required to make an appearance at the very beginning and at the end. For the rest of the time, they had a front bench in the stands reserved for them.

They gathered at the locker room doors, each girl craning her neck to see out into the gym, which by then was falling silent.

"All I can see are curtains—black and white," Tracey whispered to the girls behind her.

"There's the whistle, get ready," Liz hissed to Scooter. Scooter nodded. They heard the trumpet fanfare and the roll of MoJoe's new drum. The whistle shrilled again, and Liz and Scooter ran out with the banner. Tracey waited a moment longer and then ran out after them.

The gym had been transformed. From ceiling to floor, drapes of white material hid the ugly walls, and black velvet bunting was draped against the white in regular, evenly spaced arcs. Hung between the black arcs were shields, white with a red slash, and with the silhouette of the Valkyrie on them. They looked like they were made of felt glued to heavy cardboard backing, and now Tracey realized why everybody had been so busy. Endless, tedious hours must have gone into finishing them on time.

The gym was bright and hot, flooded with electric light. Even before Liz and Scooter were in place, the cheering of the crowd seemed almost a material thing, breaking over them in waves. A lot of people from the town had come.

Tracey, waving the sword, ducked under the banner and saluted the audience. She ran up and down in front of the bleachers, waving the sword, while everybody cheered. Her part finished, she threw the armor onto the reserved bench and took her place on the floor. The rest of team came out to the blare of the trumpets and the driving, rolling beat of the drum.

They started off with a few favorite cheers, and then the senior class made its presentation, a parody of *The Wizard of Oz* depicting MoJoe's search for the district championships. Tracey gradually realized that the Dorothy character was supposed to be a typical MoJoe underclassman, but each of her companions was a member of the team. Short and stubby Toto, played by one of the girls on her knees, was Dibbles. The scarecrow, who had blonde hair sticking out all over, was Liz Lukas. The tin man was Scooter. The cowardly lion was Brenda, the other first-string guard. Then Glenda the good witch showed up with a Bible, and Tracey recognized herself. The wizard was CPR, and the wicked witch, according to the narrator of the skit, was the principal of a certain rival high school. But at the end of the skit, when the wicked witch was destroyed by putting her hand in a bucket of water and coming up with a mousetrap on her hand, the girls had little doubt as to who she was really supposed to be.

After that skit they did more cheers, and the junior class put on a gymnastics show. Only three juniors had ever taken gymnastics, so the demonstration wasn't very good, but the crowd was enthusiastic and gave them a big round of applause.

Still more cheers followed, and the rally ended with the sophomores and freshmen building a human pyramid. After they had cleared the floor, the lights went out and a small firecracker was tossed into the middle of the floor. It exploded with a small bang, and the lights came up for the crowd to see the team standing in formation. The pep band played another fanfare with the drum booming, and both sides of the gym competed to see who could cheer loudest.

Finally, all became silent, and the team began the school song. By request of Sister Theresa, the audience waited for the team to sing the first stanza alone before joining in. Tracey was surprised at how lovely and serene their voices sounded together, facing what to them was a huge crowd. As they finished the fourth line of the song, Sister Theresa signaled to the audience, and everybody joined in.

That ended the rally, and the team hurried back in single file to the locker room. Though most of the girls were ready to run back for refreshments and to mill around with the visitors, Tracey quickly gathered her things and went up to the hall.

Maddie did not waste any time either. Tracey had

not finished throwing things into her overnight case when there was a knock at the door.

"Come in," she called, and Maddie stepped inside.

"That was fast," Tracey said.

"I saw you had gone, and I was just as glad to get away. Things seem to be at fever pitch out there," Maddie said. She surveyed the room.

"Who knows how everybody's going to take it if we lose?" Tracey said, zipping up her bag. "I'm ready if you're ready."

Maddie had obviously prepared for Tracey's visit. One of the bedrooms—the one closest to the kitchen and living room—was newly vacuumed and dusted, and the covers on the bed were already turned down.

Tracey had never noticed the decor of the bedrooms on her two previous visits to Maddie's house. The room where she was to stay had been Beth Ann's room. The furniture was white, and the bedspread was made of a pink-and-white print, with ruffly edges. The curtains were also ruffly, and there were teddy bears here and there. The bed itself had an enormous mound of pillows on it, all in pink, white, or the print that matched the bedspread. There were even ruffles on one of the lampshades.

Tracey's own room at home had been a hodgepodge of Star Trek artifacts, paperback books, Scholastic posters, and other odds and ends that she had collected, including part of the vertebrae of a buck that her father had shot.

She set down her overnight case on the thick carpet.

"I hope you'll be comfortable here," Maddie said.

"It sure is a nice room," Tracey said, half to Maddie

and half to herself. "It's like being in a hotel or a story or something."

Then she wondered if it had been polite to say that, and she glanced at Maddie. Maddie had that look, which Tracey had seen before, of desperately hiding a smile.

"You can laugh," Tracey told her. "I don't mind."

Maddie did smile, but whatever had struck her as funny was already passing. "Would you like a little supper, dear?" she said. "I could make up some muffins while you change into your pajamas and robe."

"Sure, thanks," Tracey told her.

It was wonderful to be able to shower as long as she liked without having people yelling for her to hurry. But she realized, after she had toweled herself dry, that her nightgown and robe were both very old and very ripped. Their condition hardly mattered in the halls, but she realized that it would surprise Maddie very much indeed. Even at the games, Maddie's attire was always perfect, and her clothes never showed wear or stains.

True to Tracey's guess, Maddie did give her a quick head-to-toe glance when she appeared in the kitchen.

"I like my nightclothes well broken in," Tracey said with a little laugh.

"Oh, my dear, so do I. And just when they're soft enough and familiar enough, it seems it's time to get new ones. Come into the living room if you like. I've set the timer on these."

As Tracey went into the living room, Maddie went back and turned out the bathroom light and the hall light. For the first time, Tracey realized that when she went to bed that night, she would be perfectly alone in a perfectly dark place. Unexpectedly, the realization sent a slight thrill of fear over her. For a moment, she didn't want to be at Maddie's at all. She wanted to be back in the halls, with Liz nearby.

The ghastly inappropriateness of fearing the dark and missing her friend made her force these thoughts away. Maddie had been very kind to have her over. Even if she were back at the halls, Liz wouldn't be there.

Am I really afraid of the dark? she wondered. Right on top of that thought came the memory of some of her worst bad dreams.

Just then Maddie returned. "You know, dear, I hardly know your story," she said. She seated herself alongside Tracey on the sofa. "We've talked so much of doctrine and of the Lord that I've been remiss in asking you about yourself, haven't I?"

"Oh, there's not much to tell," Tracey said. "I guess you know the worst."

Maddie cocked her head. "I wasn't thinking of the worst, Tracey." She seemed to sense that Tracey was ill at ease about something, but she didn't pursue it. "But I wouldn't want you to think I'm not interested," she added. "It's sometimes so difficult to talk on the bus. Where have you come from, dear?"

"I thought Liz told you all that."

"A few things. She let me know that there was trouble in your family and that something had incensed some of the girls—and Sister Mary—against you. You seem to be doing very well, though."

Maddie smiled. In a gesture as natural and affectionate as those Tracey could barely remember receiving from her own mother during childhood, she used her hand to smooth Tracey's short, uneven bangs. The touch reminded Tracey of how she must look to Maddie: rail thin, her face gaunt from the constant running of basketball, her eyes too large for her thin face. Her body gave off a wiry intensity, a readiness to spring into action, even when she was trying to sit and rest. Her nightclothes were ragged, and her hair had been rather badly cut by one of her classmates. And Tracey knew that her story would be the topper to the image that she presented.

"I do OK," she said. "You see, when I was younger, I started noticing some things at home, and I got scared—I don't even know of what. I was just scared because both my parents were gone all the time. So I got on my bike one time, and I went to go see if my mom was really playing bingo at the place where she said she'd be. Only, she wasn't there."

So she began her story, a story she had thought was very short and straightforward. As she told it, though, she realized that it was rather long, and it had a lot of trailers.

Maddie ran to get the muffins when the buzzer went off, and in that short intermission, Tracey wondered if she had said too much. This time, she had held nothing back, not anything that her father had done, not anything that had been said. Part of her reasoning was the never-forgotten memory of Maddie catching her fighting. She had always wanted to make it clear to Maddie that the black eye she'd had when they first met at the train station had not been from brawling.

As Maddie hurried to shake the muffins into a basket and put some things on a tray, Tracey decided to let her off from the rest of the tale. Even Tracey realized that her personal history was as grueling as it was anything else.

But when Maddie returned, her eyes were wet. She had taken a paper napkin for herself, and she gave Tracey a cloth one.

"I can stop," Tracey offered.

"No, dear, don't mind me at all," Maddie said. And Tracey realized that Maddie was crying.

"Maybe I shouldn't have told you about getting knocked down the stairs like that," she ventured.

"Oh, my." Maddie's eyes became wetter. "It's the thought of you smoking and fighting so young, dear. You were nothing but a little girl. You're still so young. Go on, though. I'm all right."

So Tracey did, all the way up to her arrival at Mo-Joe. She stopped there because she had to eat and be in bed by nine, and the clock read eight forty-five. Maddie hurried to make her a belated cup of tea.

Tracey could tell that her personal history had been stunning to the woman. After Maddie returned with the tea, Tracey felt Maddie's eyes on her as Maddie practically waited on her hand and foot, holding the teacup for her, handing her the butter plate. Usually, being the object of such scrutiny would have been annoying to Tracey, but she realized that she was dealing with a person far more naive than a person ought to be, easily and deeply shocked by things, profoundly hurt over the injuries dealt out to others. It was an odd mix. This woman who had so easily hauled her and Scooter around by the ears was the same woman who had spoken so clearly about God's mercy. She had not only spoken clearly, but with a sweetness that showed she loved the doctrines she taught, loved the freedom

they would give to Tracey. And here she was again, believing in God's goodness and yet weeping for Tracey,
ever so quietly and with great restraint.

"Oh, dear," Maddie said as Tracey finished. "There
it is, nine o'clock."

"I'll stay true to my word," Tracey said. "To bed I
go. Say, would you mind if . . . if I left on the hall
light?"

With a smile, Maddie leaned closer and said, "I
have a better idea. We promised Father Williams to
get you into bed by nine, but there's no reason you
have to be asleep by then."

"No, I can sleep as late as you'll let me, tomorrow,"
Tracey said. "I got permission to cut my morning classes."

"I'll sit by you a while, dear, and we can continue
our conversation."

This was a tremendous relief. Tracey wondered if
Maddie suspected that she didn't want to sleep all by
herself in the dark. But she decided that such a thing
was unlikely. Why would anybody suspected a grown
girl of being afraid of the dark? She hurried to brush
her teeth and climb into bed. What to do with all the
pillows was something of a puzzle, but she decided finally to pile them on the floor, against the wall.

Maddie brought her Bible into the bedroom. She
pulled up a chair from the white desk and asked Tracey
to go on with her tale.

"MoJoe's a long, sad story, Maddie," Tracey told her
frankly. "And I better not go into it the night before
our big game." With a little flush she remembered her
first confrontation with Maddie, and she did not want
to go into that now. She did not want to remember
how hard her first year had been. Most of all, she did

not want to see that look of disapproval from Maddie about the fight.

"All right then, dear." That was all Maddie said. But her hand passed across Tracey's forehead for a moment. "I know it's been hard for you."

"It's not so bad, now," Tracey told her. "Nothing's as bad as it used to be."

"Oh, it's so tragic—such a tragedy," Maddie said quietly.

"What is?" Tracey asked.

"All the many parts."

"Any of us could get over any of it except that Sandra Kean is dead," Tracey added, then said in a much quieter voice, "but everybody's forgotten her by now."

Maddie leaned over her. "Nothing is ever forgotten," she said in a low voice. "Not by the one mind that knows and understands all of it."

"What about the things we want to forget?" Tracey asked suddenly.

"He will make us forget the things that bowed us down, darling," she said. "But then He remembers them for us. Our tears are in His bottle. He doesn't forget what grieved us."

She looked searchingly at Tracey, and Tracey heard herself saying, "I wish you had never seen that fight, Maddie. I wish it had never happened, but—" She remembered how desperate she had felt during those dark days. "It had to happen. It had to."

"Can't you tell me what Scooter did to you, Tracey?" Maddie asked kindly. "Can't you tell me that?"

"Who told you Scooter did anything?" Tracey asked warily.

"Darling, you were fighting with Scooter. And I

saw the change in you as soon as I pulled you up." She rested her hand against Tracey's forehead. "You were so reserved, so sad when I first saw you at the bus station. But when I saw you again on the hockey field, you were changed. At first I thought it was just from fighting. I thought that Scooter had attacked you: You were so white and ghostlike."

"Did Liz tell you the rest?" Tracey whispered.

"I never asked her, dear. She did tell me the others had started it—had provoked you until you had to strike back." Sensing Tracey's anxiety at the thought that Liz had told the story, she smiled reassuringly. But her look quickly turned to one of concern. "Oh, what did they do to you?" she asked. "Can you not tell me?"

Again, Tracey felt the urge to give in, to tell it. Almost of their own accord, her hands reached up, and Maddie took them in hers. And Tracey nearly told it. But she stopped short. To her, it was such a horrible thing that she was not sure what an adult would do if it came out—have Scooter expelled, break up the team. And then the consequences would be left for Tracey to face.

The moment passed. Tracey looked down and held on to her troubled silence.

Maddie said, "I knew by the time that Sister Mary started her lecture that something dreadful had happened to you. I was trying so hard to piece together what might have passed. I've never seen young ladies fight—especially not like that. Nothing made sense." Her eyes were distant at the memory, but then they returned to Tracey. "I'm sorry that, when you came to my house, I reproached you a second time with it," she said.

"You should have reproached me," Tracey told her.

"You're a grown-up. You're not supposed to approve of fighting."

"It was of no help to you when I did," Maddie reminded her. "Perhaps if I had listened first . . . It was perfectly clear that somebody had done something that had frightened you."

"Yes," Tracey said without thinking, her mind drawn back to those dreadful days.

"But you cannot tell me?" Maddie asked.

"No," she whispered.

"Have you forgiven Scooter?"

Tracey wasn't sure how to answer the question. She had never tried to avenge herself since that fight on the hockey field. She had assisted Scooter after Liz had hit her. "Maybe I have," she said after a moment. There was a tiredness and a finality in her voice that signaled an end to their conversation. She could not think all these things through on the night before the game.

Maddie sat back in her chair. By degrees their conversation became quieter and quieter and then trailed off into silence, until Tracey realized that Maddie had opened her Bible to read it.

Turned away from the lamp, Tracey at last fell asleep. Maddie must have dimmed the lights further, for as Tracey slowly emerged from her sound sleep, there was nothing pressing against her eyes, urging them to open. The room felt dark, and she kept her eyes closed.

And yet, she felt Maddie's hand on her forehead again, and it seemed that Maddie was speaking to her.

Tracey was full of sleep and a tremendous sense of well-being, so it puzzled but did not trouble her that

Maddie should still be talking. She gradually realized that the hand on her forehead was not exactly on her forehead, but it was rubbing the tiny hollow between her eyebrows. The sensation was very relaxing; it almost seemed calculated to keep a sleeping person asleep. So why, Tracey wondered in her unhurried puzzlement, was Maddie talking?

She could not pick out all of the words, just phrases here and there: *masterpiece, our God,* words that one would use in prayer.

These words, which seemed partly addressed to another person and partly addressed to her, rushed over Tracey with a particular and unexpected sweetness. She had never heard Maddie speak so solemnly and yet with so much gladness, so humbly and yet with so much authority. Though her inclination was to fall soundly asleep again, Tracey woke up more so she could make some answer to Maddie, perhaps thank her for such a prayer.

That was when she realized that the voice was not Maddie's voice. It was not a woman's voice, but a man's. *No,* Tracey thought, *not a man's, either.* The sweetness in it, the very gladness, did not belong to any human voice she had ever heard. She realized that Maddie was not in the room at all, and yet she was not alone; some other glad presence was with her.

As Tracey struggled to wake up, the sensation on her forehead stopped, and the glad voice was interrupted. With a tremendous effort she snapped her eyes open and let her gaze traverse the dark room. There was no fear in the darkness now—only wonder. And then she realized that there was still a hand on her head, its motionless finger touching that slight crevice between her eyes.

"Hey!" she yelled, and she sat up. It was her own hand. She glanced at it suspiciously as though it were newly attached to her arm.

No, she thought. *No way.* She looked around the dark room. It was dark indeed, but the silence still seemed to be ringing with gladness.

The hall light flipped on, sending into the room stark white rays that hurt her eyes for a moment. Next came Maddie, tying her robe.

"Are you all right, dear? Were you dreaming?" she asked, sitting down next to Tracey.

"Yes, I was dreaming," Tracey said, a little dazed.

"Shall I turn on the light?"

"No, no. It wasn't a bad dream, Maddie." Her awakening senses told her not to tell Maddie she'd been listening to angels. *In the morning,* she thought. *In the morning I can decide if it was a dream or not.*

"Would you like me to stay with you a while?" Maddie asked, attempting to sound offhand, probably so Tracey wouldn't think she suspected her of being afraid of the dark.

"Oh, no!" Tracey exclaimed. "Who could be scared now?"

Waking up at MoJoe, if a girl slept until the rising bell, always involved a sudden springing into action—the charge for the shower bucket and robe; the race down the hall; the anxious decision between stall or shower, knowing that whichever was second choice would mean a wait in line; the rush to blow-dry hair and curl it if necessary; the planning always in progress as to what books were needed and what homework had not been done; and the concern over what was for breakfast and if there would be seconds on good things.

At Maddie's, waking up occurred with the sound of Maddie's voice, and there was no rush for anything. Tracey took her time getting ready while the wonderful smell of real waffles and bacon drifted back to her room.

She gathered up her things, made up the bed as best as she could, hiding the flaws with the enormous pile of pillows, and came out to the kitchen.

Maddie, still wrapped in her quilted robe, suddenly

seemed a familiar, cozy accessory, and Tracey didn't feel shy at all as she gave her a good morning hug.

"Did you sleep all right?" Maddie asked with a smile. It was amazing how pleasant Maddie and everything at her house was.

Tracey nodded. "Can I help you?" she asked after a lame moment of silence.

"Oh, I think I've got it, dear. You might set out plates if you like." Setting the table was one thing Tracey could do at least passably well. Her mother had always thought her silverware was badly spaced, but since it was early morning, maybe Maddie wouldn't notice.

Breakfast was a pleasant meal. It began to dawn on Tracey that Maddie's sense of good manners went much deeper than anything Tracey had learned before, either at MoJoe or in her own home. To Maddie, being moody or silent was as unthinkable as pitching food all over the kitchen or chasing people with a rolling pin.

I wish I were that way, Tracey thought, *so easy with people and happy to see everybody.* But right on top of that wish came the realization that Maddie's ability stemmed from a sincere desire to make people at home —and that such a skill might require only discipline and a strong sense of the needs of other people.

The idea that being a good housekeeper and hostess might rest on moral grounds instead of on domestic skills was a new one to Tracey, and it was a vast relief. Why, that meant that even lousy cooks and housecleaners could be hospitable; they'd just have to take their guests out all the time or learn easy things to make.

"What are you thinking, dear?" Maddie asked.

Tracey started. "Oh, I didn't mean to get so quiet!"

150

she said with a laugh, wondering again if she had been rude. "I got my head all caught up in something. But it's gone now."

Maddie had to go to her office that day. They finished breakfast before seven, and she directed Tracey to throw a load of dark clothes in the washing machine, and to include her basketball uniform and warm-up suit with them. Tracey obeyed, getting the settings on the washer right.

She realized guiltily that she had left the living room the night before without offering to take her dishes out to the kitchen, leaving them for Maddie without even a *please* or a *thank-you*. So while Maddie went back to her own bathroom and bedroom to shower and dress, Tracey washed up their breakfast things, leaving only the waffle iron, which she was a little afraid of. But Maddie was pleased all the same when she came back out, dressed for work in a blue plaid jumper and blue tie.

"How nice to have such a helper in the kitchen," she exclaimed. Tracey smiled and made herself scarce, relieved that she had not messed up anything so far. Her hunt for something to do while the clothes were drying was rewarded when Liz telephoned.

"For you, Tracey," Maddie called.

Liz's voice on the line was loud and self-assured. "Ain't this the life, baby? Hey, I wonder what the other MoJoes are doing right now?"

"Getting packed up for first-hour class, I guess," Tracey said.

Liz let out a loud, happy laugh. "I guess so. You going up to the school soon?"

"Soon as my clothes get dry."

151

Liz was in no hurry to hang up, so Tracey stayed on with her until the clothes were done.

Maddie was ready for work. They folded up the school blouse, basketball uniform, and warm-up suit, and put Tracey's basketball shoes on top. But as they got into the car, Tracey exclaimed, "Hey, I left my other stuff inside!"

"Oh, we'll get them later," Maddie told her airily.

Tracey didn't want to hold her up, so she agreed. They drove in silence, and Maddie pulled up at the front door of the hall.

"See you at noon," she said. Tracey gathered her things and turned to her.

"Thanks a lot, Maddie," she said. For some reason, she remembered how unhappy Liz had been over the way she had treated Maddie. So she said, "I . . . I really like you. You know that, don't you?"

Maddie laughed. "Yes, dear." She kissed Tracey's cheek. "You run along and let me get to work, and I'll see you later."

"Sure."

There was work to be done, undraping the gym and cleaning up from the previous night. As Tracey had predicted, CPR mandated that every team member ride the bus to the game. Nobody minded. For Liz and Scooter, this was the last ride to a game. Win or lose, this would be the last game for them, the last everything.

Tracey had not thought much about the ending of her basketball partnership with Liz. As the whole team worked in the gym, pulling down banners and bunting and shields, she realized that Liz was purposely keeping herself nearby, not saying much.

"You nervous?" Tracey asked at last, and she was surprised to feel a new and unexpected strangeness with Liz.

"I guess," Liz said briefly, keeping her eyes on the white draping that she was trying to pull down from its nails.

Tracey stood there for a moment, letting the feeling of strangeness wash over her. She felt that she should be saying something to Liz, but she didn't know what. Liz stopped.

"You all right?" she asked.

"I tried to be polite to Maddie," Tracey said at last.

Liz nodded. "I knew you would."

"No, last night I didn't even think about it and just left her to wash up our dishes. What a dope. You were right about what you said that day, Liz. I just don't think about other people."

Liz dropped the curtain and turned around and looked at her.

"Do I treat other people as badly as I've treated Maddie?" Tracey asked.

Liz gave her a rueful smile. "You don't treat people bad, baby. I mean, people who treat people bad are people like the Deep Six, or like Mary. I was just uptight because sometimes you don't seem to think about other people."

"Not just Maddie, huh?" Tracey asked, with a growing sense of embarrassment.

Liz waved it away. "Doesn't matter now. It's just part of growing up, right? We've all made mistakes with other people."

"Just seems like I've made so many enemies," Tracey confessed to her. "Maybe there didn't have to be so many—"

"You treat your enemies OK," Liz said, dropping one hand on Tracey's shoulder. "I know you, Jac. Don't you be kicking yourself all through the afternoon and the game tonight. You never took a cheap shot on Scooter or Rita Jo or Mary or anybody. And you've got lots of friends—everybody on this team, and everybody in this school except the pushers. Now, quit worrying."

"I ought to sit up by Maddie on the bus, shouldn't I?" Tracey asked.

"It'd be nice," Liz told her. "It's a long drive."

"Will you sit up by me too, Liz?" she asked. "Please?" She realized that she had never asked Liz a favor before —not with an actual *please* attached to it, and not with the understanding that Liz might have something else she would prefer to do.

"Jac, I always sit by you—almost always!" Liz exclaimed with a slight laugh. "So, sure." But the difference in Tracey's tone must have sparked something in her, because her laugh stopped, and for a moment she regarded her younger friend with a look of tenderness and bittersweet sorrow that Tracey would never have guessed was hidden under her carefree exterior. Then Liz turned back to the drapery.

They worked in the gym until it was time to leave for the game. Curiously subdued, the girls got their things from the locker room and filed out to the bus in almost complete silence. For many of the girls, it was only nerves, but for the seniors on the team, a sudden notion of what this game might mean descended upon them. It was their last chance. Even Scooter was quiet.

The girls greeted Maddie as they climbed aboard. Tracey and Liz took the front seat behind the driver's chair.

"Well, and how are you, girls?" Maddie asked pleasantly.

"I'm OK, but Tracey's been awful sick all morning," Liz said loudly. "Something about eating waffles that were like bricks. Wasn't that what you told me, Jac?"

"Liz!" Tracey exclaimed. She looked quickly at Maddie. "You know that's not true, Maddie. I'm fine— I never—"

But Maddie only laughed at Liz's irreverent humor. "Go on, now. I'll give you bricks!" she replied as she swung the doors closed. "All aboard, girls?"

CPR gave her the high sign, and Maddie pulled out. As they passed the classrooms, everybody on the team came over to one side of the bus. Their schoolmates waved to them from the windows. Classes would be dismissed in another hour for the game.

They took their seats again, and Liz said, "I hope we do it for them this time."

"So do I," Tracey said.

Though they had sat up front to keep Maddie company, they both fell into silence. Tracey's mind returned to her request to Liz that morning. She wondered what kind of friend she had been to Liz. Certainly an obedient one. Seldom had she ever argued with the older girl, and never had she disobeyed her.

But Tracey couldn't take much credit for an absolute obedience that had only resulted in gain for herself. Under Liz's tutelage she had made the team, ascended in the ranks of the players until she was second only to Liz, and gained prestige until the toughest girl at MoJoe had been obliged to leave her alone. Liz had opened to her every friendship that Liz herself enjoyed—not only the casual friendships with everybody, but the deep and important ones too: Peggy, and through Peggy, Dibbles, and Maddie herself.

It shocked Tracey for a moment to remember that it had been Liz who had reintroduced her to Maddie and had pressured her into apologizing. Indeed, Liz—by example and by influence—had gradually overcome Tracey's reluctance to like this good woman. Liz had taught Tracey to listen to the people she distrusted and feared, and thereby to come to understand them.

With another startling realization, Tracey understood that Maddie was the type of person a loner like Liz might want to keep to herself—for Maddie was filled with compassion for the girls, and she was certainly generous. Unlike Liz's own parents, Maddie accepted all of them for exactly who they were. With Maddie, they were all free to be big and loud and Valkyries.

Tracey wondered why she had never realized all of these things before. Chalk it up to never thinking at all about other people. She had been so wrapped up in her own problems that she had never looked beyond them. And now, the view that this broader look presented was stunning.

"Girls, if you get much quieter, I'm bound to fall asleep," Maddie said. Tracey snapped out of her reverie, and Liz, whatever she had been thinking, also came alive again.

For the rest of the trip, they talked and joked and even sang a few songs to warm up for the game. But after the long ride was over, as they pulled into the parking lot of the gym where they would be playing, all of the girls, Liz and Tracey included, fell silent again.

The quick jog to the locker room, which they shared

with the Villa Marie team, the hurried change into their uniforms, the warm-up; all of these passed in a blur for Tracey. For a few blessed minutes she even forgot all of the new thoughts she had been thinking.

But when the time came, and they stood crowded behind the double doors waiting to make their entrance under the banner, she turned and looked at Liz, who—with Scooter—had her face glued to the glass panel on the door, watching intently for the signal to enter.

Liz must have sensed something, because she turned, saw Tracey watching her with a big-eyed stare, and smiled at her.

"Calm down, kid," she said in a low voice.

"Good . . . good luck, Liz," Tracey said, and Liz looked back at her, more solemnly.

"Good luck, Jac. Do me proud."

"There go the trumpets," Scooter said. "Let's go."

Tracey gave them a few seconds to burst through the doors and get a head start, and then she burst out after them.

Even that part was a blur. She was aware enough to realize that this was the biggest crowd she had ever imagined playing ball in front of—rows and rows of people all the way up to the roof, so many that she didn't know who was on MoJoe's side and who was on the other team's side. But her eyes at last fixed on Maddie, behind the Valkyrie team bench, and then she ran to her place. The drum boomed for the team as each girl ran and took her place.

Villa Marie also had a good fanfare. They had more drums, and their two trumpeters were very good. The girls on the team had no banner, but they ran out onto the floor in a straight line, each girl wearing a black scarf with eyeholes in it, like a bandit's mask. When they had taken their places, they pulled the scarves off and used them in a short but complicated dancelike routine of hard hand-claps, waving scarves, and fast twirls. It was very effective. Tracey thought their team must be called the Bandits, but after the ceremonies and singing were over, Liz told her that they were the Villa Marie Villains.

"Valkyries and Villains," Tracey said with a short laugh. "Well, if anybody should be rivals, it's our teams."

The entire gym subsided into an intense silence as they came to center. Liz gave Tracey the two-finger signal, and Tracey passed it to Dibbles. But as she did, she noticed a forward from the Villains watching her, then passing the same sign to the other Villain forward.

Tracey glanced sharply at Dibbles to warn her, but just then they jumped, and Liz slapped the ball.

There was nothing to do but hustle. Tracey raced for the basket, saw the ball coming out of the corner of her eye—too fast and too high for her to get it at the top of the key—and kept going to get under it. It seemed that the Villain forward was right on top of her. She frantically jumped, and more by instinct than reason hit the ball back up instead of trying to catch it with two enemy hands in the way. The ball popped up in an arc. They were so close to the basket that it hit the rim, skidded over it, hit the backboard, and went in.

An enormous uproar of applause, trumpets, and drums greeted this exploit. Tracey had no idea how good the play had looked to the audience. The only thing she realized was that Villa Marie was razor-sharp, possessing a rare and intense discipline like nothing MoJoe had played against all year. And the Villains seemed to know the MoJoe plays and signals.

She ran back and traded slaps of congratulations with her teammates, but she was aware of Liz's second glance at her. Liz saw the alarm and caution on Tracey's face and understood it.

As the Villain offense came up, they seemed cautious themselves. The MoJoes kept the key locked tight, and it took the Villains so long to shoot once one of them got inside that they were almost fouled for the thirty-second violation.

When they did shoot, Liz put up a great block, knocking the ball to Scooter while Tracey raced down the court again. Somehow there were girls all around her, and as the ball came sailing toward her, there were hands everywhere, blocking her vision, reaching for the ball. She jumped to get it, but the Villain center took it—almost out of her grasp.

Incredibly, two other MoJoe girls were by her at the half-court line, with Liz and Scooter on the way down. The entire MoJoe team frantically backpedaled to protect the Villain basket, but they were too late. The Villains sank the ball with a clear shot that whooshed through the net. Drums boomed. Trumpets blared. CPR called a time-out.

"Strategy, girls!" she exclaimed. "No more of these incredible passes. They're setting up a good half-court press."

"They know our plays and our signals," Tracey said.

"Use the short post," CPR told them. "Avoid the long passes. I don't care if they know the signals. You have enough skill to outplay them. Go back in there and do it."

They went back in. Dibbles and Brenda started down with the ball, and Tracey saw that almost nobody from the Villains was down at the defense key. They were all at half-court.

For a moment, the MoJoes didn't seem to know what to do. Then Tracey ran up through the Villains and stopped short in front of one of them. She caught the pass from Dibbles and took it around the girl, back toward their own basket, brushing the girl as she went.

The ref's whistle cut through the gym. "Offensive foul! 42!"

Tracey looked up, startled. Liz shot her a glance and said nothing. It looked like it was going to be that type of game.

A small flame of irritation went through Tracey. None of the MoJoes knew these refs, and it seemed a hard disadvantage to get called for something that had been acceptable all season. Still, they all knew the rules. They would have to adjust to a less physical game.

Her foul stood out in large relief to her, but in the next few minutes, she lost the shame of being the first and only one to foul. Liz fouled twice; Scooter fouled; Dibbles fouled. A couple of the Villains also fouled— once for traveling and once for three seconds. But the MoJoe fouls were all personal fouls. Any more would give the other team foul shots, and the Villains were already ahead by five.

CPR called another time-out.

"Those refs just come from the mountain?" Liz asked, irritated.

"We don't pick our referees," CPR snapped. "Play by the rules and you won't get fouled. You girls are doing a sloppy job of it out there! Now, get your act together. It takes a tenth of a second to see where your man is when you're breaking through a half-court press. Use your eyes."

She handed out some other directions to each of them, but they all knew the main thing was to quit fouling. They were well able to keep the Villains out of the key; it was the intercepted balls that were killing them—those, and the fouls. None of the MoJoes were used to playing against a half-court press.

"I don't think we're going to win," Tracey gasped to Liz as they went back out onto the court.

"Jac, just play ball with me," Liz told her. She quickly threw one arm across Tracey's wet shoulders. "Forget the championships, forget CPR. Play ball with me. That's all I want you to do."

"What about the game?" Tracey asked her.

"Lukas! Get to your position!" CPR bawled.

"When you and I play ball, we'll win the game," Liz promised, letting her go and running to her place. "If we can win at all," she added over her shoulder.

That's what it's always been, Tracey thought. *When it's Liz and me, it seems like we do OK.*

"Jac!" Liz yelled. Tracey leaped to catch a long pass —thrown in spite of CPR's veto—and brought it down the lane. She neatly dodged around one Villain, and her eyes roved for some sight of Liz.

Tracey came into the key at the top, and Liz was already getting under the basket.

"Fake shot!" Liz yelled. Tracey jumped up, aimed for the basket, and neatly arced the ball straight up and into Liz's hands while the Villains ran to guard the basket. Liz jumped and shot and sank it.

They ran back to defense, and Liz got close enough to tell her, "Get above the half-court line next time Dibs brings it down. Long-pass it to me down the lane if you can. I'll pass it back to you at the top of the key. Shoot or pass."

"That's long post!" Tracey exclaimed.

"Play what I say, Jac!"

"OK!"

They blocked the shot from the Villains and Scooter passed quickly to Dibbles, a short chest pass that the Villain guard almost intercepted. While she was off-balance and inadvertently blocking her own teammate, Dibbles passed to Tracey, and Tracey came down only far enough to get the ball to Liz in one long pass. The Villains raced to guard the basket again as Tracey came in more slowly to the top of the key, clear for a few seconds from a guard. Liz dribbled the few steps down to the basket, did a half-turn and passed back out to Tracey. Tracey jumped and shot, sinking the ball. The Villa Marie coach called a time-out.

"Here's where she tells them we've switched to long post," Liz said as they walked off the floor.

"And here's where CPR bawls us out for doing it," Tracey said.

"Well, we pulled the score up to one point," Liz exclaimed. "Let her get mad."

As it turned out, CPR didn't say anything. She only directed them to rinse out their mouths, which they did.

In the last minute of play they scored another basket,

and the first quarter ended with the Valkyries one point ahead.

"It's got to be man-on-man," Liz said in a low voice to Tracey and Scooter. CPR either heard her or guessed Liz's opinion.

"We can't win with man-on-man," she said. "We don't have the tall players for man-on-man!"

"We can't win with zone playing either!" Liz retorted.

"You'll kill yourselves with man-on-man!" CPR exclaimed. "That's just what they want—to tire you out. You can't play an entire game of man-on-man, and they can. They have a lot of height on us. There's nothing they'd like more than to run my three tall players right into the ground."

Liz looked down in mute testimony to CPR's correct assessment. "Then we can't win," she said.

"Just play ball with me, Liz," Tracey said quietly. "Isn't that what you wanted?"

"If you want us to die trying in this game, then I will, Jac," Liz said.

"I don't want that, Liz. I just want us to play a good game and have fun," Tracey said. Liz stood up as the refs came back onto the floor. She looked down at Tracey. Tracey realized that this was Liz's only chance to show her parents that she was important, that she could do something too. It would be impossible just to play to have fun. Once again, Tracey had missed the obvious in another person's life. This game meant everything to Liz.

She stood up. "I'll die trying in this game, Liz," she said. "Because maybe we can do it in the end."

The whistle blew, and they went back out on the floor. Tracey wondered at herself again. Liz had never said much about her parents, but it was obvious that their poor understanding of their tall, strapping daughter, their unwillingness to accommodate her tomboy tastes, their willingness to send her away to boarding schools when they had never sent her older brother away during his childhood—all of these things had made a great empty wound in Liz. She hid the wound, but suddenly Tracey realized that anybody who was really thinking about Liz at all, really concerned for her life and her happiness, would have seen and understood how such alienation must hurt.

At least I was sent away over religion, Tracey thought. *Maybe Dad didn't love me a lot, but I could have come home anytime I wanted to if I had given up the religion. But Liz can't give up being big and tall.*

She was amazed at herself for not having talked with Liz more about it, for not having worked harder to let Liz know that being big and tall was great. Though neither Liz nor Tracey were beautiful, Tracey's tallness was a thin and whipcord kind of tallness that, she realized, would have been less offensive than Liz's broad-shouldered, wide-handed tallness. Tracey had possessed the power to offer an outsider's approval of Liz, but she never had. She might have compared Liz to a Valkyrie, with her blonde hair and loud, carefree happiness. Certainly, if Liz were put into armor and seated on a horse, she would look like a shield maiden straight from mythology.

So why had Tracey never said anything? Why had she never sensed in Liz the pain of rejection that she herself had felt? With a slight shock at the ghastly inappropriateness of her behavior, she realized that she had made too much of her own parents' rejection. Liz had made too little of hers, but anybody who had cared would have seen it, identified it, entered it with her, and helped her through it. Maddie Murdoch had tried, and she had succeeded at times. Had not Liz called upon her after Sandra Kean's suicide?

Tracey felt a pang, not of jealousy, but of bitter regret. It was her own fault, not Liz's, that Liz had not turned to her in that darkest hour of remorse and guilt. For Liz had wisely guessed that Tracey was not mature enough to take such a burden on herself, to react with discretion and compassion. Only after months of watching Liz suffer had Tracey somehow learned to keep quiet and not to personally rebuke all the people she had felt were partially guilty for Sandra's death.

She might have continued in this new vein of self-discovery, but the demands of the game were upon them. She wanted to win for Liz's sake, so she pushed away all intrusive thoughts.

They entered the second quarter up by one point. The score teeter-tottered between the two teams.

Tracey felt—in that quarter, anyway—that the MoJoes were better shooters than their rivals. But they were also a lot better at picking up fouls. And each time they fouled, the Villains got one or two free shots.

The Villains' half-court press eventually forced the MoJoes into a game of running—running until they were running themselves into the ground. Nobody wanted to expressly disobey CPR's orders, but you couldn't stand where you were and watch Dibbles walk into a trap without at last running up to assist. So then you ended up running the whole way down, using pick-and-roll strategies and short—very short—passes.

Even with the extra stress of a new style of play, Liz,

Tracey, and Scooter were tall and skillful enough to keep up with their counterparts. In fact, Tracey felt that she and Liz were the two best players on the court. Sometimes, trapped right under the basket, they could set up a great rebounding strategy and score. They were able to trick the Villains a couple of times on long-post plays or on simple fakes.

The problem was the pace of the game. MoJoe had been known in its division for playing a fast game, but clearly, fast for the division was not nearly fast enough for the district. And the sad truth was that MoJoe's second-string was not nearly fast enough or tall enough to cope with Villa Marie's first- or second-string. Villa Marie had the luxury of more girls to choose from, and it showed.

At halftime the Valkyries were down by only two points, and several of the girls were talking about losing with honor. CPR made them be quiet.

"You're doing great," she said, and this was the worst sign of all—though only Liz and Tracey understood what it meant. "The long-post play is working well. And their half-court press is starting to fall apart."

She glanced at Tracey. "You're showing great dexterity in getting around those people. Just watch out for offensive fouls. Debbie, Brenda, pass to Jacamuzzi if you get trapped."

Tracey was stunned to hear such frank praise from CPR. In the two years since CPR had picked her for the team, her coach had never sent much praise Tracey's way, even though she would sometimes hand out compliments to the other players. Tracey suddenly wondered why. And she wondered why this nun, whom she had once admired so much, had become such a

166

stranger to her. She and CPR were always wary with each other. What had changed them?

But there was no time to think of that. She had enough on her mind. Here at halftime, there was a chance to return to her earlier thoughts. They were in the locker room for the first half of the break, most of them prone on benches, just glad to breathe and to rest while the second-string girls stood or helped them into knee braces, ankle braces, or clean socks.

Tracey glanced over at Liz. "It's some game," she said to the older girl. "You look good out there, Liz. Win or lose, you're still the best player on the floor."

"Let's go till we drop, Jac," Liz said with a smile. She seemed in better spirits. Maybe she thought they might actually win, or maybe, Liz-like, she had accepted her fate and was marching bravely to meet it, all regrets behind her.

They cleared out to let the other team have a turn in the locker room, and Tracey, upon standing, felt the red-hot needles racing through her shins, into her ankles, and even around her toes. The bottoms of her feet were blistered.

Limping slightly, the first-string ran back onto the floor. Some of the MoJoes clapped and whistled, and a few of the red horns blared.

They collapsed onto the team bench. CPR, suddenly at a loss, paced back and forth in front of them.

Dibbles, as easily and freely as though they had a twenty-point lead, turned and waved to her parents.

"They think this is a gas," she said to Tracey. "You think we'll win?"

Tracey almost said no, she didn't. But then she wondered if she ought to. "We'll have to do our best,"

167

she said instead. She had a slight stomachache from running so hard and so long. Hands from the bleachers behind her reached down to massage her shoulders, but she shook her head. She was afraid to relax any more, afraid to be at rest for fear that she wouldn't get wound up quite so tight again.

Maddie, who was among the people behind her, said nothing until the buzzer went off. As the first-string got up, she called out, "Good luck, girls!"

Both Liz and Tracey looked back and smiled. They slapped their hands together, looked at each other and laughed, and ran out on the floor.

"Well, we got good luck if we ain't got nothing else," Liz said as they came to the center.

Tracey felt a difference in the second half. Her reflexes weren't as good, and her body wasn't quite as able to obey what her mind was telling it. It was evident that the first-string of the Villains was also worn out. The problem was that the Villains' second-string seemed, to Tracey, just as good as the first-string had been. They came in one at a time, giving their players four minutes of rest apiece.

CPR also began switching people out. Dibbles took a break and Peggy came in for her.

"Peggy!" Tracey yelled in greeting, and play resumed.

MoJoe's best plays and most magnificent interceptions occurred in the second half. Tracey scored more points in the second half than in the first, and she and Liz even put together an impromptu alley-oop that brought cheers of admiration from both teams.

But the Villains had worked up their full head of steam. They were simply able to outshoot MoJoe. CPR pulled both Tracey and Liz at the end of the third quarter.

"Come on, Coach," Liz begged. "We've come this far. Let us back in."

"You staggered out there!" CPR exclaimed. "I saw you! You nearly fell down!"

"I caught my foot on something—"

"It was the floor, Miss Lukas!"

"Anybody can stub her toe! Come on, Coach! Let us back in!"

"Fourth quarter, we'll see," CPR said.

"Coach!" Tracey exclaimed. She rarely talked back to CPR anymore, mindful of their one historic clash of wills. And suddenly, today, she had the idea that CPR disliked her—had disliked her since she had joined the team. Well, she was a big mouth, and the one time she had made amends with CPR, she had embarrassed her half to death. There was no way to get CPR to like her in twenty seconds' time, but there was always the option of begging.

"This is her last game," Tracey said. "Let her play. Who cares if we all drop over after the game?"

"And you want to play too, I suppose," CPR said.

"I'll do whatever you want. I'll sit out the whole game. Just let Liz play," Tracey said.

CPR sighed heavily, rolled her eyes, and said, "Lukas and Jacamuzzi, go in."

They leaped from the bench and ran to the table to give their numbers.

By fourth quarter, the team's discipline had started to fall apart, and it was harder to hold the plays together when they got a chance to use them. They were down by six, and Liz yelled to Tracey, "Just get into the key when I do!"

In the end, Liz and Tracey came back to doing

what they had done at the very beginning, before Tracey had even made the team. They shot from either side of the basket and rebounded. If the knot of defense got too tight, Tracey or Liz would pass to the top of the key, to Scooter, and she could usually sink it from there. The score crept closer, and for one minute of play, Tracey actually wondered if they might just take the game.

The first-string of the Villains came back out then; their own discipline somewhat loosened. Everybody in the gym was screaming so loud, it was no longer like human voices, only waves and waves of noise, like the ocean hitting the sand. Tracey no longer felt her pain, and there were a few moments when she felt as though she were not running at all but floating, as though she never consciously tried to catch the ball; but it somehow floated to her, and they were all floating, first in one direction and then the other.

Twice in a row on offense, she caught long passes, wove her way, semiconsciously, through a knot of Villains, and jumped higher than she had yet jumped to tip the ball into the net.

The pulsating pounding of the crowd took on a distinguishable shape. "Jac! Jac! Jac!" And then, as she passed to Liz, "Lu-kas! Lu-kas! Lu-kas!"

And then, more gradually, the rhythm changed into words she knew but took a moment to recognize. It was the countdown: "Five, four, three, two, one!" and the harsh buzzer.

She looked at the scoreboard and saw that MoJoe had lost by three points.

She felt like dropping to her knees, but instead she walked in a circle and let the ball drop. Sweat came pouring in streams from her hairline and underarms, in sheets down her stomach and legs, in burning pools into her shoes. It was odd that, having just lost the championship, her first worry was that she had no dry appendage to wipe the sweat off her face.

A hand clapped her back. "High scorer this time, Jac," the voice of the team's scorekeeper said. "You outshot Liz by four points."

Reality set in, and Tracey burst out crying.

TWENTY

The locker room was silent. Liz sat alone on one of the wooden benches, and even Tracey dared not say anything to her. She had mastered her tears, and she wished she had the courage to say something kind and good to Liz.

She wondered what she could have said anyway. Even apart from the unhappy revelation that she had outshot Liz, she had been ready to fall apart with sorrow and regret. Everything had changed for her during the game, during this last horrible game when she'd realized so forcibly that this was the last time for her and Liz. Win or lose, she would have been overwhelmed with sorrow. Because now the truth that she should have been thinking about all year was on top of her: This was the last game with Liz, because it was the last year with Liz. And from now on, everything was going to be the last thing. The last Easter holiday; the last examination week; the last good-bye when Liz left at commencement, never to come back, and Tracey stayed.

They'd have to turn in their uniforms next week, and they'd never both be wearing them again.

I wonder if I ever really cared about winning? Tracey thought. *I always played hard because I loved my friends, not because I ever gave a rip about this game.*

Without a word, she gathered her things. CPR entered the locker room. "Does anybody need to take the bus back to school?" she asked, reminding them that they could all ride home with their parents or friends. Except for Tracey.

"Just me, Sister," Tracey said quietly. Liz looked up. Before Liz could break the silence by asking Tracey to come with her or by offering to ride with Tracey on the bus, CPR said, "Well, Maddie told me that your things are at her house. Father Williams said that you can go back with her in the school car. Father Williams will take the bus back himself. It's a very long ride for that bus. I don't think he wants the two of you alone on those country roads. Be back at the school by ten."

It was only seven-thirty. If they hurried in a regular car, they would make it back to Maddie's in time to get something to eat, and Tracey fervently hoped that Maddie would offer her something. She wanted Maddie's quiet company even more than she wanted food, and she wanted some time to recover herself before she went back to MoJoe as an ordinary person and not a basketball star.

Maddie gave Tracey a sympathetic smile and a big hug when Tracey came out of the locker room.

"Oh, you're my star player and my champion, Tracey," Maddie exclaimed. "And I was proud of you out there. You played with all the heart and the drive a person could have asked for."

Tracey shook her head. "Oh, Maddie," she said, and her eyes filled up with tears. She looked up at Maddie. "It's not the game. It's everything."

"It's all right, dear, we'll get you some good supper and peace and quiet." And Maddie, still under the impression that Tracey was grieving about the game, led her out. Tracey felt in no position to contradict her.

But once they were in the car and on their way, Tracey said again, "It's not the game, Maddie. It's what I realized during the game."

"What, dear?" Maddie asked.

"I don't know how to say it. My head's so full, I can't get it all in order," Tracey complained. "It's Liz and basketball and being a Valkyrie and everything."

"I don't follow you."

"I can't explain it yet—but it's like I'm seeing my-self for the first time, and there have been so many other times when I thought I was seeing myself for the first time. Just let me think it through a while."

Tracey didn't have the strength to be frank about all of her failings with anybody other than the Lord. But she had failed, and miserably. What kind of Valkyrie accepted every kind of favor from a friend, every comfort that Liz had given her, every help, and yet returned only obedience? She had hardly ever thought about Liz's griefs and Liz's sorrows, hardly ever attempted to pierce through that shield of loud laughter and open carelessness that she had known all along was false.

Was there ever a time when Liz had not felt the obligation of protecting Tracey, of shielding her from the Sister Marys, the suicides, the ragings of Scooter, the snubs of CPR? Liz had sacrificed her own relation-

ship with CPR, that favorite above all favorites, in order to stand by Tracey. She had risked the team's unity
by helping Tracey that first year.

And what had Tracey done? Gotten drunk when
Liz had needed her, more than ever, to urge sobriety
and dignity and to be brave for both of them. Become
enraged and left the team in spite of Liz's pleas for her
not to—and even then it had been CPR and not Liz who
had brought Tracey back. It should have been Liz. Tracey
ought to have rejoined the team as soon as Liz had
asked her.

Tracey had talked so loudly about bucking the system at MoJoe, but Liz had simply done it—no fanfare,
no policy statements, nothing but the quiet and sure
actions of a person who could not be brought to her
knees by lousy parents or Sister Mary or both.

"Would you like to talk about it, Tracey?" Maddie
asked. "Any part of it?"

"I guess," Tracey said, "that I'm not a very good
friend to Liz." She forced herself to change the subject.
"What about the game, Maddie? Was there ever any
hope for us?"

"It was well played," Maddie said. "Another minute
or so—the score may have gone the other way." She
hesitated and then said, "It was obvious, anyway, that
the other team had studied you out very carefully."

Tracey kept their conversation on the team and the
game and the season. But while they talked, other
parts of her mind were working on other things, listening, it seemed, to the first true version of all that had
passed in her life.

There had been a cheapness in her—a mouthiness,
a fear of being wrong or ridiculed—that had prompted

so much of what she had done, especially her first year. She had thought her mother cheap because of adultery, but now she realized that her own cheapness had prided itself on moral purity while making a hash of respect for elders and humility and simple friendship. Had she ever done anything that was not based on *looking* like a Christian? Had she ever done a kind act simply because she had genuinely loved another person? Had she ever forgotten herself for more than half a second?

The only thing she could think of was the secret money she had given to Peggy so she could eat at McDonald's. Tracey had honestly felt Peggy's unhappy situation and had kept her funding project quiet. But that didn't seem like much, not in a whole three years of professing to be different because of being a true Christian.

After a while, conversation lagged. Maddie and Tracey came home in silence, and Tracey went to her room to get her things together.

"It's only nine now," Maddie called to her. "I'll make us some supper, if you like."

Tracey put her head back out. "Sure, thanks."

It took only two minutes to get everything into her overnight case and bring it out to set by the door.

"It's shortbread and tea—is that all right?" Maddie asked.

Tracey had no idea what shortbread was. Hoping that it wasn't pig insides, which she thought were called some kind of bread, she said, "Sounds great."

"I'll be right in. Take a rest on the couch if you like."

Tracey did as she was told and sat down on the

couch. It was right here, just one night ago, that she had told Maddie all about herself. All about herself, except not really all about herself. For Maddie had been as kind to Tracey as Liz had been. And if there ever was a person that Tracey had misunderstood, and hurt, and liked only for the things she did for Tracey, it was Maddie Murdoch.

It was then that Tracey fully understood what Liz had told her weeks ago after the division title game. Now she saw how she had treated Maddie, even when she had been nice to her. To Tracey, Maddie had been a source of information, as warm and as comforting as Wylie, and just as one-dimensional.

Tracey had never thought much of Maddie's own feelings, except in respect to herself and to Maddie's regard for her. She had never stopped to contemplate this Christian woman whom she—and Tracey cringed at the thought—had hated at first for interfering, then had labeled as a goody-goody, and then had dismissed as too tenderhearted and too easily shocked. The stunning arrogance of her own opinions about Maddie nearly took her breath away. The truth was that Maddie possessed a profoundness of sense and sensitivity that only a vulgar idiot would laugh at or fail to comprehend.

Who in the world was Tracey Jacamuzzi to decide what people were like and what their faults were? Especially people who had done only good to her. True, she had forgiven Scooter, and she had passed lightly over the Murphys' desertion of her; yet those people who had been good to her, those were the ones she had treated badly. Liz herself had commented that Tracey treated her enemies very well. And now Tracey felt the stunning blow of why Liz had seemed so restrained when they had talked in the school gym. Because even then, at the dawning of Tracey's self-understanding, Liz had realized that Tracey did not know how she had failed her own friends, how little she had worked to understand the people who cared about her most.

For a moment, the image of Maddie as she had first met her rose in Tracey's mind: Maddie, awash in brilliant sunlight, tall and kind, offering her hand to Tracey, seeing through the makeup to the bruised person underneath, silently committing herself to be protective of her. Or Maddie, with the multicolored spangles from the stained-glass window falling on her hair, coming to the foot of the stairs in the main hall, beseeching Tracey for friendship between them. And Maddie, wrapping her coat around the two of them, drawing Tracey in from her grief, seeing—in spite of Tracey's camouflage—that Tracey doubted the Resurrection, doubted everything good about her faith. For that was Maddie as well, approachable and kind, willing to bear with Tracey, to listen and explain. A sudden longing for Maddie—her voice, her sureness, her humor, her warmth, everything about her—gripped Tracey's heart harder and more painfully than she had ever longed for her own mother or Jean or anybody else. With the longing came a realization that she would never get away from her worst self if Maddie did not help her.

"You'll be glad for this, won't you?" Maddie asked, coming into the living room with a tray. She set it down on the coffee table and hurried to arrange things.

Without a voice for a moment, Tracey watched

Maddie as she moved some shortbread biscuits from the tray onto a plate. The very actions of her hands filled Tracey with shame. *And now,* she reminded herself, *the last basketball game is over. I won't see Maddie again until next season.*

When we get to heaven, Tracey thought, *Maddie will be one of the highest ranks. She'll be a princess in heaven—no, a Valkyrie, a real one. And I'll be a garbage collector. What am I doing here?*

Maddie sat down on the couch and glanced at her. "Are you sure you're all right, Tracey?"

Tracey let out her breath, very slowly. "Maddie," she said, "how have you put up with me this long?"

"What?" Maddie asked.

"You're a . . . a . . . work, I mean, a masterpiece," Tracey said, blushing a little to be using such odd language, "of God's mercy. You're . . . everything I'm not—everything I wish I was. Maddie, I'm rude and selfish and stupid. I thought I told you the worst of me . . . but I never told you about . . . pride . . . and being a big mouth . . . and thinking badly of people who I don't have a right to . . . to even know at all."

Maddie became grave. The room was silent. She didn't say anything for a moment; then very quietly she said, "Tracey, haven't you and I made our peace?"

Tracey couldn't meet her eye, but she nodded. "I . . . I don't deserve you," she said at last. "And now that I know that I don't, Maddie, I wish that I did, or that someday I could. If only God would put me where I can't hurt anybody else—then at least I wouldn't be able to."

She keenly felt the loss as she forced the words out. Suddenly, more than anything, she wanted to have

Maddie's friendship, Maddie's selfless love, Maddie's gentle and articulate guidance. But she couldn't pretend to be better than what she was, and she couldn't rationalize her faults with some promise to herself to be better in the future. Maddie had to know the truth.

"Please forgive me for all my pride and selfishness, Maddie," she said. "You'd better take me back to the school now. I shouldn't stay here."

In reply, Maddie picked up the plate of shortbread cookies. "I know that you must be hungry," she said gently. She held the plate up to Tracey. "Please eat, darling."

The hospitable gesture was not the answer Tracey had expected. It startled her into meeting Maddie's eye.

"Maddie—" she began.

"Please, darling. You've got to eat something."

Maddie fixed her with a gaze of concern, but it was a concern that was resolved to have its way. She did not move the plate away, and Tracey realized that she would not—not until Tracey had eaten. Helpless in the face of such insistence, and realizing that Maddie was not going to take her to school or reply to her confession until she'd finished the simple meal, Tracey nodded and took a piece of the shortbread. She obediently ate, and Maddie served her, holding the plate with one hand and using the other to pass her the cup of tea. Nor would Maddie set the plate aside until, one by one, Tracey had eaten each piece of shortbread. It felt like the longest meal she had ever eaten, with Maddie right there watching her and serving her, and it was tremendously humbling.

"Do you feel better?" Maddie asked when Tracey had finished. Maddie set the plate and cup on the coffee table.

"I wanted to ask you to forgive me," Tracey said. "I'm sorry I haven't been good to you. All I've ever done is hurt people."

"And you want me to send you away for that?" Maddie asked.

"Yes," Tracey said. "So that I can't hurt you. So that I can't disappoint you—or God either—anymore."

"Darling, if you really believe that all you've done is hurt people," Maddie said, "then I need to keep you right here, right by me."

The answer was so unexpected that Tracey stopped and drew a blank. After a moment she asked, "Why?"

"To teach you how to love people. To love you," Maddie said. "And I'll answer for it to God if I do any other thing."

"What do you mean?" Tracey asked.

"Listen to me," Maddie said. She rested her hand on Tracey's shoulder, and she spoke gravely and deliberately. "I have to tell you something, and you must hear me out and respect what it is I have to say."

She was so grave that Tracey whispered, "Yes, Maddie."

Maddie's eyes held hers for a moment, and then Maddie said, "From the day I wrenched you up by one ear and saw that angry, honest face of yours, you have belonged to me. It didn't take me long to realize it." Maddie's eyes became more gentle, and her voice became a little distant and somehow more Irish. "Oooh, and that Sister Mary made you speak your faith to me, and you were ashamed for what you had done, but I loved you all at once. I never spoke a word to her of it, but I knew I would have you to myself."

"You did?" Tracey asked.

"Aye, and it was a long enough wait. You took your time coming, didn't you? But now I have you, and I'll not let you go." She drew Tracey close. For a moment, she looked at Tracey, and Tracey saw approval and certainty in her eyes. At last Maddie said, "Is it all right, then? Do you believe me? Do you know that you're mine?"

Tracey didn't know what to say, but something inside her made her speak before she could think about it. "Maddie, look at my arm," she heard herself say.

This was not the answer Maddie had expected. For the briefest moment she looked confused, and then she asked, "Your arm, Tracey?"

Tracey nodded down at her own arm. "There, under the sleeve. Push it up."

With a puzzled glance at Tracey, Maddie obediently pushed the sleeve of Tracey's blouse up past the elbow and looked. A thin, faint line still marked the skin, fading month by month, but not invisible yet.

Tracey had never shown the scar to anyone, and her own eyes were trained to avoid looking at it. As soon as Maddie touched her sleeve, she regretted her rash openness. But before she could change her mind, the sleeve was up, and Maddie's glance had fallen on the line. It was now only about two and a half inches long, much diminished from when it had circled the circumference of her arm.

"Is that a scar?" Maddie asked quietly.

"Oh, Maddie," Tracey said suddenly. Tears came into her eyes at the memory of Maddie's original scolding. "I had to fight. I really did. They did that to me."

Maddie seemed to have no voice for a moment. Tracey sensed that—whatever Maddie might have imagined—the woman had never suspected anything close to the real thing.

"What was done to you?" Maddie finally asked, her voice low and deadly serious.

"It was called Step One," Tracey told her, not meeting Maddie's eyes. "A kind of torture, and it left a mark so people would know that they'd got you. I think . . . I think it was piano wire wrapped around with cloth or leather or something."

Maddie's hand gently took hold of Tracey's chin, guiding her eyes back to Maddie's.

"When was this done?" she asked, not unkindly but a little sternly, as though determined to right the wrong.

"When I was a freshman," Tracey said. "More than two years ago. Just before you saw me fighting Scooter."

"Scooter did this to you?"

"There were six of them."

"But Scooter was one of them?"

Tracey nodded. "And that's what they did to Sandra Kean. They did it to her the night before they did it to me."

"Tracey, why did you never tell?" Maddie asked.

"Because of what they would do to me if I told," she said. "You couldn't fight them back then—not that way. It was Liz who found the way—through basketball."

Maddie was silent. She would have drawn Tracey closer, put her arms around her, perhaps with the idea of consoling her, but Tracey stopped her. "Maddie," Tracey said. "You've got to promise me that you won't tell. If it ever got out that I told you—even with me being so good at basketball—"

She had expected an argument, but to her surprise, Maddie said clearly, almost resolutely, "No, it's useless to tell now. They—" But she stopped herself. She rolled the sleeve down and buttoned the cuff. When she looked at Tracey, her voice became gentle again. "But I promised you that the Lord would bring you to a forgetfulness of all of that, Tracey, and He will. And I've told you that you're mine—truly my own." She framed Tracey's face in her hands.

"What does that mean?" Tracey asked.

"You'll have to let me show you, Tracey," Maddie told her. "I only want to know if you can believe any part of it now."

For a moment, Tracey didn't know what to say. But Maddie's eyes were on her, and Maddie's face was intent, concerned, and filled with an expression so tender, and yet so grave, that Tracey knew she had to believe her. She nodded.

"I believe you, Maddie," Tracey said. "But I'm afraid I'll hurt you because I've always been so selfish."

Maddie relaxed and smiled. "Don't you fear for me," she said. "You're my gift from God." And she brushed aside the loose hair—still damp—from Tracey's face.

They were both quiet, until at last Maddie said, "You've never let God prove His favor to you, Tracey. See if He doesn't prove Himself to you." She kissed Tracey's forehead.

Tracey didn't say anything. Somehow the entire conversation had gotten away from her. She wondered if admitting to being arrogant and a big mouth was really as horrible as it had seemed before she had done it. Because certainly, here was a whole world of genuine compassion and love that she had never guessed at.

Maddie reached down to the coffee table, picked up the phone, and used her thumb to punch in the number. Tracey realized that it had to be about time to be back at the hall.

"Hello, Father," Maddie said into the phone. "Yes, it is. Tracey and I have gotten back, and since tomorrow is Saturday, I was wondering if you'd mind if she stayed over." There was a pause. "Oh, yes, she's a little upset right now. Crying a little. We've both been crying." She looked at Tracey and smiled. No doubt Father Williams was asking from the viewpoint of the game. "Well, thank you, I appreciate it. Good-bye."

She hung up the phone and smiled down at Tracey. "I knew that driving that bus would win me some favors sometime. Would you like to stay over?"

"Yes," Tracey said.

"All right, then. Your room is ready. And I'll sit up with you a while."

Tracey looked up at her. "Maddie," she said, "thank you."

"Before you thank me," Maddie told her gently, "there's something I've got to say. There's something more you've got to do, Tracey."

"Yes, Maddie?" Tracey resolved to take whatever Maddie said humbly and obediently. Maybe it was time for Maddie to frankly discuss with her some of her faults and the ways she would have to mend them.

Maddie reached again for the tray on the coffee table and piled some more of the shortbread biscuits onto Tracey's plate. She held the plate up to Tracey again. "I think you should eat a little more. You haven't had anywhere near enough."

I t was nearly two in the afternoon when Tracey returned to the hall and her room.

"Jac," Liz said as Tracey entered, still a little wide-eyed from the way things had changed so much in twenty-four hours.

"Sorry I'm late," Tracey said. "Have your parents gone?"

"Yeah, right after breakfast." Liz stood up from the lower bunk. "How are you? They told me you were crying."

"I'm all right." Her eyes fixed on Liz, she set her things down and sat on her own lower bunk. Liz, sensing that some great change had been wrought in Tracey, also sat down again.

"What is it?" she asked.

"I hardly know where to start," Tracey said. "I feel like some of this is stuff I should have said a long time ago. All I wanted then was to fit in with you—"

"Nothing wrong with that," Liz said.

"Now I want to thank you . . . and . . . and treat you like I should have treated you all along."

"You've been a good friend, Jac. I've told you that," Liz said.

"Well, I've never stabbed you in the back," Tracey conceded. "But . . . when I think of everything you did for me—you made me somebody again, Liz. You didn't only save my life—you gave me a person I could be. I don't feel like I've done anywhere near that for you. Even though there were times I might have. I'm really sorry."

"I can look back with no regrets," Liz told her.

"None?" Tracey asked. Liz looked down.

"OK," she admitted after a pause. "I got a little out of patience—once. And maybe once or twice I wished I could have told you things, but then I stopped myself. I wanted to tell you I'd burned the film for a long time. But I knew the secret would kill you. I knew you'd have to face the decision to turn me in or not. Wasn't until you were already so torn apart with how I was acting that I finally told you—and then I figured, hey, maybe it would have been better just to tell you at the beginning."

Tracey shook her head, and they were both silent. At last Tracey said, "You were right. The decision would have killed me. I'm glad you spared me, at least until the next year."

"And yet you never told," Liz said.

Tracey opened her hands and gave a slight shrug. "Maybe I should have, maybe not. I just couldn't. You'd been punished enough. Besides, I think they know by now."

Liz raised her head, puzzled.

"It came to me last night," Tracey said. "After I was in bed at Maddie's. I was kind of thinking over all our times here, and I started wondering how you did it."

"You never did ask me," Liz said.

"It never even puzzled me until last night," Tracey told her. "And then I started thinking about it, and I remembered that you have the key to the gym. And then I remembered that the gym key opens CPR's little office in the gym. And she keeps her keys in her office in her desk. You had all the time in the world to get into her office, get her keys, and while she was at dinner, get the school's front office unlocked, and then return the keys and get to dinner yourself. Later on, you went back down to the unlocked school office, got the film, and locked the door behind you. There was kerosene from the shed to burn the film."

"That's about it," Liz admitted.

Tracey nodded. "So anyway, I figure they know perfectly well who did it. But they aren't saying either. And I always knew that if I did tell, Mary would never believe that I didn't have a part in it. So I figured, in such a crooked place, there's no real moral imperative to tell. I wasn't going to put myself through an inquisition, or you either." She raised her eyes to Liz's. "They had already exacted their punishment from Sandra Kean. I wouldn't let them do it again."

Liz's eyes dropped. "That was my fault. I should have admitted it after she did."

Tracey sighed. "Don't be fooled, Liz. Then Mary would have punished Sandra for lying and for the crime she lied about. It would have gone worse for her." Tracey shook her head. "You shouldn't have done it at all—which I think you know—but Sandra shouldn't have tried such a way-out scheme to get glory for herself and make friends."

She stood up. "I'm just sorry," she said, "that I've never been the friend to you that you've been to me. But I want you to know that I really am grateful to you, and I admire you a lot, Liz. And I think you're the best and bravest Valkyrie I know—except maybe for Maddie."

Liz looked up, and their eyes met. They were both silent. It felt almost like they were seeing each other for the first time. Tracey finally saw with perfect clarity her vulnerable friend to whom she owed so much. What Liz saw, Tracey never knew for sure.

After a moment, Tracey went to unpack her overnight case, and Liz said, "So how late did you stay up last night at Maddie's, soaking up her sympathy and chocolate chip cookies?"

"Shortbread cookies," Tracey corrected her, slinging her suitcase onto her bed. "Not real late. What'd you guys do?"

"Oh, me and my folks went to the motel, and they got a little put out with me for staying so glum. But when they brought me back this morning, lots of the girls hung out the windows and clapped for me. I was glad."

She looked at Tracey to hear her report of what she'd done.

"I found out a lot about myself yesterday," Tracey said.

"I could see you were doing some heavy thinking," Liz told her.

"And then—I guess you might say—God made me realize a lot of things." Tracey opened one of the top drawers to put her underwear away.

189

"Like what?"

"Like what a big mouth and a prig I can be, and lots of things." She stopped and looked up, but not at Liz. "But then He showed me how His mercy reaches deeper than we can think. He's making changes in us we don't guess until the change is done. One little yank is all we know of months of surgery."

"What?" Liz asked.

Tracey turned to her. "Just when I realized that I don't deserve you or Maddie, just when I confessed it all to Maddie, that's when she told me that I belong to her—like a daughter or something." Again, Tracey's eyes left Liz's. "That's when I realized that ever since I came to this prison, God was making me free. Through you, through Maddie—I was stupid when I came here. I was living for the moment, the feeling—whatever. I was a slave before I ever walked through the gate. But now I know how to love people. Now I know how to want to be pure and good, enough to cry for it. I can even be disgusted with myself and get the forgiveness of God. It's not so much that I'm free as that I'm alive —and I was dead for so long."

Liz stood up, much impressed with Tracey's words.

"And it's not just that," Tracey told her. "God showed me last night that He's never been angry with me—not since I've been saved. I can come to Him through Christ, Liz. God is really my Father."

"How did He prove that?" Liz asked.

"Because He made another Christian, Maddie, see all of my sins—even when I didn't see them. And she loved me anyway. And God told her that I would be-long to her, and she was glad. If one Christian can love me that much in the love of God, then I know that

God loves me. So now I'm not only alive, Liz. I'm free. Because now I know that God loves me. He's never left me alone in this place. I was just so pigheaded, I kept telling myself that He did."

She held out both hands, almost a gesture of helplessness. "But He was always with me. And now I know it. He did what He did to get me to where I got last night —all at the end of myself." She leaned back against the chest of drawers. "I came begging for bread, and God gave me a kingdom. Now I know that I belong to Christ in God, and everything He gives me, He gives me because He loves me, not because I love Him. Salvation comes from God, not man."

They looked at each other. Tracey's new eloquence, if not the content of her words, had obviously struck Liz.

"When I realized how much God must love me," Tracey concluded, "to have worked with me so hard— just to make me able to understand Maddie and love her myself, when I was so bigmouthed and prejudiced —that kind of realization, about how God really is concerned over me—that makes me feel really strong and brave inside. I feel like a real Valkyrie, then. When I know that God has a whole plan for my life and a separate calling just for me—to come and serve Him and sit at His table. Then I know that I'm a Valkyrie and a shield maiden of heaven."

Liz was quiet a moment and then gave a slow smile. "A Valkyrie, maybe," she said. "But what it really sounds like, Jac, is that you've become a Christian at last."

T W E N T Y - T W O

Maddie's request that Tracey work for her on Saturdays quickly received Father Williams's approval, and Tracey was able to go the very next Saturday.

She went through a long mental preparation for the cleaning at Maddie's. She desperately wanted to do a good job—not because she was afraid of angering Maddie or of displeasing her, but to show her that she wasn't just using her for a free morning in town, that she really did want to please her.

As it turned out, Maddie had the opposite concern. She seemed worried lest Tracey should think she had been drafted against her will.

They passed a rather awkward hour, with Tracey working as hard as she could and Maddie doing her best to slow her down, and at last Tracey admitted the truth. "I really stink at housework, Maddie. I always have. But if you'll just be patient with me, I know I'll get better."

"Dear, is it polite to say 'stink'?" Maddie asked gently.

"Well, it's true enough," Tracey told her. "The truest word that I know. But you only have to show me once, and then I'll be able to clean to suit you."

"You do a fine job of cleaning," Maddie protested. "Sometimes you're too hard on yourself. But see here. The floors aren't going anywhere, dear. There's some shortbread left. Would you like a snack?"

Tracey was always hungry, but her sense of duty made her say, after a slight hesitation, "I better clean. Maybe I'll get done in time to have some." And she went back to working industriously on the kitchen floor.

Only by degrees, as Maddie put off one chore after another, did Tracey realize that Maddie had brought her over more as a guest than as a worker from the school. She at last let herself be talked out of house-work and instead spent a half hour chatting, as Maddie called it. By that time, the floor was dry, and Maddie went to the kitchen to make them lunch.

While it was in the oven, she brought out "a few things picked up at a bargain sale, and some other odds and ends from Sears." The sight of several packages of underclothes, nightgowns, and a new robe brought a flush of humility to Tracey's face. But it was a humility without shame, accompanied only by a sense of wonder. She had already learned that pleasure, like pain, might come in a cup that simply had to be drained dry. That she did not deserve this generosity was clear to her, but that it was the will of God for her to accept it was also clear.

Maddie's promise that Tracey belonged to her obviously was going to include efforts to care for her. Tracey had not thought of that.

She was supposed to be back at the halls by one, so after a hurried lunch, they gathered her things together. Tracey regretted not having done more work.

"I feel like I'm taking a free ride from you," she told Maddie as she stood in the kitchen doorway, her hand holding the Sears bag, her eyes a little troubled as she surveyed the kitchen that she felt ought to have been cleaned.

Maddie regarded her with that look of tenderness, half smiling and half sad, that was uniquely Maddie's, especially when she was helping or comforting Tracey.

"Take a free ride," Maddie said. "As long as you like. Come and ride for free."

The direct invitation left Tracey blank for a moment. "I . . . I don't know what to say," she said at last. But she already knew what to do. She must accept it, be thankful for it, and wait to learn more of it. "There's nothing in this world like forgiveness," she said after a moment.

"It's all there really is, dear," Maddie whispered. "It's the only thing we really have to call our own." She hugged Tracey, her arms strong and sure.

Tracey most often thought of Maddie as gentle, elegant, and soft-spoken. But Maddie was a physically strong woman, tall and capable, and there was a possessive light that came into her eyes at the end of their visits, when she hugged Tracey. It was an expression both of longing and of satisfaction, a look that Tracey could take with her into the halls. It made her remember all over again that she had been given to Maddie and that Maddie missed her during the long week of school, even as she missed Maddie.

Over the next several weeks, Maddie worked more

changes in Tracey's wardrobe: a couple of new dresses to fit Tracey's unusual height, new high heels, and—so Tracey would not think Maddie was too formal—new running shoes. Maddie also provided her with soft new flannel sheets for her bed in the hall, new towels to replace her worn-out sets, a couple of lacy pillows that Liz laughed at for minutes on end, and countless other goodies.

"I sure am glad you're skinny, kid," Liz told her one day as they surveyed the wonderful larder of fruit tarts, brownies, cookies, and cupcakes that Maddie always sent along with Tracey when her so-called Saturday "work" was over.

"Only things in the world better than Tastykakes," Tracey told her, passing blueberry torte to Liz.

"I sure am glad it's working out," Liz said.

Tracey nodded. She had no idea how to explain to Liz the inexpressible comfort of having Maddie after the long years of solitude—and the comfort of knowing that after leaving MoJoe next year, she would not face an empty future but would have a real home. At night, she was no longer the prisoner of awful nightmares, but of happiness so intense that it sometimes woke her up just so she could think about it. Happiness like that had to be thought about for a while. Tracey felt completely forgiven and loved by God and by everything that belonged to God.

"Now," Liz said with a sly smile, "you owe me for all of this. I did bring you guys together your freshman year. So what do I get out of it?"

Tracey looked at her, thought for a moment, and then put her hand on Liz's shoulder. "Come and be my sister, Liz," she said seriously.

The reply startled Liz.

"Maddie won't turn you away, and you know it," Tracey told her. "She'll love you as much as she loves me."

"You really think you want to share?" Liz asked gently, but with a hint of shrewdness.

"Selfish people like me are full of fears and worries," Tracey admitted. "But I know I want you to be happy. Maddie's all that I have, and so she's all that I can share."

"I don't think anybody's ever offered me so much," Liz said after a moment. "I know you're happy, baby. I'm not going to horn in on it—not yet, anyway."

"You wouldn't be horning in, Liz," Tracey reproved her.

"Maybe not. But between the two of you, you guys will get me converted one way or another," Liz said.

Tracey sensed in her words the real reason for her refusal of Tracey's offer. But Liz's straightforward refusal could not hide from Tracey the momentary look of respect and even gratitude. Nor did it hide from Tracey the realization that Liz had come within a hair of accepting.

"B ing told me I'm getting the sportsmanship medal,"
Liz said. She tried to sound offhand, and in an effort at carelessness, she leaned over and checked the
bottles of cola they'd put into the stream.

It was too dark for Tracey to get a look at her
friend's face, but she didn't need to. For Liz's sake, she
also sounded offhand. "Was he hinting, or did he mean
it's been decided and you'll get it?"

"I'm getting it," Liz said.

In the darkness Tracey's mind flipped over to
Scooter, sensing her continued disappointment in seeing Liz once again being promoted. *Scooter could have
taken on any person in this school,* Tracey thought. *Even
me, because she's smarter. But the one person she couldn't
take on—that's the one she had to pick.* Out loud she said,
"Nobody deserves it more than you, Liz."

"Ah, lots of the girls are good sports," Liz replied.

"I know better than the rest of them how much you
deserve it. I can never thank you enough. I never knew

I could be so grateful. Because I never knew a person could be such a friend to me."

Liz was quiet for a moment. The sounds of crickets and peepers reminded them of the sweetness of being outside the dorms at midnight, on the night before graduation.

At last Tracey added, "I never knew one person could do so much for another person."

Liz said, "It was the smartest good turn I ever did, I guess. But you're grateful to Maddie too, right?"

"Of course. That's . . . that's a whole different kind," Tracey said.

They fell silent again. It was their last night as roommates, their last night as schoolmates.

Tracey had wondered about the rightness of sneaking out after bedtime; she had also worried that Sister Mary would be smart enough to figure out that this would be the last night for misdemeanors.

But Liz had guaranteed that Mary would not be counting heads. As usual, the acting principal had been seeing to all of the commencement arrangements herself, making sure that the greatest of the school's few public ceremonies would be perfect. She was in no shape to go out on patrol. All of the sisters were very tired: There had been report cards to finish, and each of the seniors was required to turn in a philosophy-of-life paper that would be graded and judged for an award to be handed out at commencement. Sister St. Gerard had been in charge of that project, and it was a sure thing that—even as Tracey and Liz sat out in the woods by the hockey field enjoying their colas—St. Gerard was sitting up somewhere inside the school, working her way through a belated pot of coffee and a stack of philosophy-of-life papers.

As for explaining this little outing to Maddie, Tracey planned to be honest. Maddie would not approve of it, might even lecture her, but somehow Tracey's drive to treasure every last hour with Liz made her willing to take the risk. She was aware that Maddie was slowly and gradually building up a certain authority over her, and so far Tracey had submitted to anything Maddie asked or even suggested. But Tracey also took pleasure in doing everything she wanted to do before giving in to Maddie. She keenly felt Maddie's generosity and kindness, and her sense of duty dictated that she be obedient in return. But in the interval while Maddie hesitated to push her authority to its limits, Tracey intended to enjoy herself.

"I think they're ready," Liz said, and she pulled two of the four bottles out of the stream. She deftly pried the caps off with the steel button of her jacket. Though June had come, the night was chilly. They would have preferred coffee, tea, or hot chocolate, but Pepsi had been a lot more convenient.

"Here's to the next team captain," Liz said as they raised their bottles in salute.

"Whoever she may be," Tracey added.

"Don't be a dope. It's you."

"Baby, you got the sun in your eyes," Tracey said. "Neither CPR nor Mary will stand by and let me be team captain."

"You were alternate this year. Alternate always becomes team captain."

"What'd Sister Madeleine tell us in vocabulary?" Tracey mused. "Sop, that's it. We'll call it a sop, thrown to me for my efforts. But I won't be captain—and besides, I don't care."

"Yes, you do."

"Think what you want if it will help you to swear off Roman Catholicism," Tracey said carelessly. "The fun's gone out of basketball now, and I don't care what Mary does. Basketball's just another chance to get off this campus and be with somebody who really loves me. I couldn't care less about the game."

"I almost think you mean that," Liz said.

Tracey paused. "I do," she said. "Nothing's the same any more. Christianity is like diving off a cliff—like the girl said at the end of *Love Story*, you know, falling over a waterfall in slow motion. But she was talking about dying, and this is like somehow becoming more alive."

Liz was silent, but in the dimness she turned and looked expectantly at Tracey. Though Liz had forbidden excessive talk of religion in the past, she did not interfere with it anymore.

"It's like a diving action because there's no going back," Tracey said, "but the further you go as you dive, and the longer the fall lasts, the deeper and deeper you go into something like glory. Glory after glory. Until you're going so fast you know you'll get killed as soon as you hit anything. But it doesn't matter anymore. Because you know it'll be just another transfiguring—something that's deeper and yet bigger and higher too."

"What's like the diving action?" Liz asked. "God? Or having someone who loves you?"

"I can't say because it's both the same thing for me. It came all together. When Maddie told me that I belonged to her, God told me in the same breath that He had done this to take away all the things that had made me so sad and alone. It's a whole new life—a whole new start. I feel like everything before that, everything sad and horrible—even my sins—were all leading up to that moment. When I became something else—when I was set free."

"So it won't bug you if Mary snookers you out of being team captain?"

"It might bug me for a little while—like an afternoon—but Mary can't break my heart anymore."

Liz took a long drink of her soda. After a suitable pause, their conversation turned to other things, to past games and to previous evenings. Long after the moon went down they sat and talked, huddled down into their jackets, savoring the privacy and the memories and the sweet smell of the woods. At last, at a quarter till three, stiff-legged from sitting so long and cold to the bone, they helped each other up and hobbled back up to the dorm. With very little difficulty, they climbed in through a bathroom window and went up to bed.

T W E N T Y - F O U R

Graduation day dawned hot and fair. Previous ceremonies had always seemed long to Tracey, but that morning—when part of her tried to hold on to each passing moment as though she could slow down time by her own concentration—the ceremony seemed especially brief. Liz's moment of triumph with the sportsmanship medal was a mere glimpse at the hard work and the years of patient training given to her teammates.

She and Liz had arranged to make their public goodbyes short. But after the ceremony had ended, all of the teammates grouped together around Liz and Scooter and the other seniors. Tracey desperately wanted to leave, and she knew that Liz did too. Liz would be embarrassed, and Tracey didn't like all of the crying. It had an insincere ring, and Tracey suspected that a lot of it was worked up merely to make a good show. Even Scooter insisted on throwing herself onto Liz's shoulder for a good cry and a long farewell, and before she got to Tracey to do the same thing, Tracey wanted to be gone.

To her relief, Maddie managed to slip through the crowd of parents and students. The Valkyries dropped back a little bit as she approached. They seemed to expect her to say a few words, a sort of formal good-bye.

"It's been a pleasure getting to know you, girls," she said to those who stood in white robes. "I'm going to miss you all."

They each hugged her in turn, but Liz was last. Tracey was surprised to see her friend's face cloud up for the first time.

"Good-bye, my dear," Maddie said, and Liz surprised even Maddie by putting her arms around Maddie's neck.

"Don't say good-bye to me," Liz said huskily. For a moment, scarcely more than a breath, she hugged herself into Maddie's shoulder. "Don't say good-bye to me, Maddie."

Liz's parents, weary of the wait, were edging closer, eager to end the emotional farewells. But Tracey was riveted by the change in Liz's emotions. For a moment she saw again the distressed, vulnerable girl, nearly overwhelmed with guilt and remorse and loneliness.

"Why, Liz," Maddie whispered as she reluctantly let the girl go.

"I want you always to love me," Liz said. The shock that hit Tracey at those words almost made her numb to the sudden pity that wrung her heart.

"I do, dear," Maddie said kindly. She set the strap of her purse on her shoulder, took Liz's face between her hands, and looked at Liz with an expression Tracey recognized: satisfaction and longing, both together. Liz looked at her and said nothing, her blue eyes large and—for once—vulnerable. "You must write to me and come to see me," Maddie said. "Come at Thanksgiving if you can't come sooner." As she kissed Liz's cheek, she passed a small wrapped bundle and a card from her purse into Liz's hands. Then she took Liz's face again and fixed her eyes with that look—that look that said some part of you must always belong to Maddie.

"Thank you," Liz gasped.

Liz's parents stepped up, impatient to be gone. The last Tracey saw of Liz that day was a stark tableau: the big blonde girl looking lost and alone, her hands clasping Maddie's small gift, her wet eyes following the two of them as they left the school grounds. In the background, Liz's parents were plucking at her gown, telling her it was time to go. Once again, Tracey wondered at how little she knew her own best friend.

In Maddie's car, they were both silent until Tracey said at last, "Just when I think Liz won't become a Christian, she acts like she almost will; but every time she seems about to do it, she stops and goes the other way."

"There's so much to Liz that she never shows," Maddie murmured. She glanced over at Tracey with a careful look, but for the moment Tracey couldn't offer any reassurance. She felt the devastation in Liz's last expression. She told herself, for perhaps the hundredth time since she had made the offer, that Liz should have accepted a bigger share in Maddie. And she knew that at that moment Liz herself felt the regret of not having done so.

After a long pause, Maddie said, "Liz will be all

right, dear. She's under God's care. We have been praying for her."

Tracey leaned back in the car seat and closed her eyes. For the first time she let the freedom of being with Maddie for the first week of summer flow over her. Liz's unhappiness reminded her of all that she had failed to do as Liz's friend, but it also reminded her of her own vast good fortune. And at last there was time: no homework, no projects, no Sister Mary keeping an eye on the curfew, no jangle of bells.

Tracey opened her eyes and looked at Maddie, who had her eyes on the road.

Again, in an action repeated too many times to count, Tracey appraised Maddie's features—her eyes, flecked with green highlights; her high cheekbones and broad, wide smile; the lift of her head that made her look a little like a heroine from an old-fashioned novel.

"I used to wonder if maybe you weren't some kind of angel," Tracey said at last. "Sometimes I used to think that in a place like this, and in a life like mine, you couldn't be a human being. And you look so much like a Valkyrie too. I used to wonder if maybe someday after you'd decided I could go on without you, I would wake up to find you gone. Back to heaven."

Maddie's sudden laughter surprised her. "Oh, Tracey!" she exclaimed. "The thoughts that come out of your head! You'll always be able to surprise me." She glanced slyly at Tracey for a second. "I almost think you might like me more if I were one of those Valkyries of yours."

"I don't think I could like you any better than I like you now," Tracey said. "Sometimes I just wonder— why me? Why did you love me best of all?"

"Because the Lord told me to," Maddie said. "And He saw to it."

Tracey lowered her eyes. She looked out her window at the countryside flashing past. "I can never repay you, Maddie," she said to the window. "I don't think I could ever be like you are, and I could never do for you all the things you've done for me. But I want God to repay you. He says He loves people who help other people. I hope He remembers you." Two tears rolled from her eyes. Her prayers for Maddie were the most sincere that she prayed. Fervent gratitude was entirely new to Tracey, but she did not resist it.

Maddie had to clear her throat twice before she said, "Thank you, dear."

Tracey's initiation to life with Maddie had been delightful so far. She was getting used to being liked—and not only liked, but welcomed—and to receiving clothing and other gifts that were thoughtfully chosen. Maddie, though careful of manners and courtesy, was not shy, and Tracey found herself getting used to good night kisses, to tugs on her hair, and to the hospitable way Maddie had of setting each dish before Tracey at mealtime, punctuating the setting down of a bowl or plate with a clasp of her hand on Tracey's shoulder or on the back of her neck. Such a gesture was completely foreign to Tracey, and the impression it gave her of being personally waited on never left her.

The entire initiation process gave rise to other emotions in Tracey. Maddie did not compare herself to Tracey's mother, and Tracey had never said much about her mother's treatment of her children. But it was becoming more and more clear every day that Tracey's mother had viewed her own children as things to be tended to, as duties, and sometimes as nuisances. Tracey had dressed as she had pleased, in jeans and sweatshirts or T-shirts, before her arrival at MoJoe. Nobody had taught her the nicer, finer methods of staying clean, smelling nice, caring for her hair, or making herself be pleasant company.

The long, quiet evenings with Maddie, never long enough or frequent enough during the school year, had never seemed to Tracey to be anything that mothers and daughters shared as a matter of course. She had always been alone. It had taken several months to realize, first, that Maddie had always spent most of her time with her children, and second, that Maddie's attendance upon her family was not unusual or amazing.

Gradually, Tracey realized that her mother's inattention at home, the absence of affection between mother and daughter, the weighty self-consciousness that Tracey felt before any tenderness or sorrow or emotional extreme, and her perception of herself as loud and too big and homely—they had all somehow been linked. But in the presence of Maddie's constant welcome, under the light touch of her hand, or caught in the approving gaze of her eyes, Tracey felt her self-consciousness fading away.

More and more, she had the feeling that she was at home, that she belonged. Once she had even remarked to Maddie that she felt as though her spirit had wandered all the time, going to and fro, especially at night, but that somehow Maddie had called it back and anchored it down in Tracey's body.

Unfortunately, Maddie's shock at such an analogy and all of the theological problems it entailed did much to quench Tracey's attempts to describe the changes she felt. In some instances, at least, it was better to enjoy the changes than to express them.

But now she had Maddie for a whole week, all to herself. And after putting her things away in the room that had become hers, she did exactly what she liked best: sat in the living room with Maddie, drank tea with her, and looked out the picture window at Maddie's garden—now in full bloom—and at the blue jays and starlings who swooped back and forth, crying and scolding.

"I'm going to try to get Peggy on first-string," she announced. "Peggy's staying over the summer."

"Did she ask you to coach her?"

"She really wants to start next season. She improved a lot this year," Tracey said.

"Do you think it will be another winning season?"

Tracey laughed a short laugh. "No, not without Liz. But we'll have a good time. Dibbles and Peggy and me on first-string."

"Father Williams told me that you could spend weekends here this summer," Maddie said. "Would you like that?"

"No curfew?" Tracey asked, looking up in such surprise that she nearly upset her teacup.

"Sunday night at five," Maddie told her. "But that's better than it's been. You'll be able to come to church with me in the mornings."

A tiny ripple of horror sent a brief crosscurrent through Tracey's happiness. She did not enjoy the idea of going to church. She almost said so, but then she checked herself. Christians had to go to church. That was the rule.

Maddie must have sensed some of her thoughts.

"You'll like church," she said, the faintest hint of reproof in her voice. "The sermons are very good, and the hymns will be helpful to you."

"I don't mind sermons and hymns," Tracey agreed. But that was all she said.

She knew that Maddie understood that she didn't want to meet the people. But hospitable Maddie could not understand Tracey's unusual shyness around church people, the people Maddie liked best. As she glanced down at Tracey again, the girl wondered if they were about to have their first disagreement. But she had already purposed to be obedient to Maddie. She would go to church. She just couldn't make herself like it.

But Maddie did not rebuke her. "Where have you been and where are you going, Tracey?" she asked, using her usual expression that signaled her inability to understand. After a pause she smiled—somewhat ruefully—and the conversation continued on safer subjects.

PART TWO

SENIOR YEAR

TWENTY-FIVE

"Look, Father, this working in the library all week every week, with no pay, isn't fair," Tracey demanded.

She and Father Williams sat opposite each other, separated by his vast and cluttered desk. He was leaned back in his chair, his empty pipe in his hands. He tapped it thoughtfully against the flat of one palm as she talked.

Tracey was forward in her chair, intent on driving home the point. "Nobody out in the real world makes a kid work all week for no pay."

"My dear, I sympathize with you," he said gently. "But remember, we are giving you room and board."

"Well, I checked with my mom, and she says my dad's paying you on a twelve-month plan," Tracey retorted. "In fact, I'm supposed to be allowed to take summer school if I want."

"Hmm, how awkward," he muttered, and his blue eyes looked up at her, always friendly. "Don't tell me you're going to start demanding back pay."

"I do deserve it," she said quietly.

"So much money would have to be sent to your father or your mother," he reminded her. "Even if I wanted to, I would never be allowed to hand over several hundred dollars to a teenager."

"Who's going to stop you?" she asked.

"I allow Sister Mary the power of the purse," he said. "Though I retain the right of veto. But even we answer to those higher up the chain than ourselves. Our books are audited, and a sudden remittance of several hundred dollars to a sixteen-year-old—"

"Seventeen," she corrected.

"Seventeen," he admitted, "would raise eyebrows. I don't think you want the money sent home, do you?"

"No," she said. "But if I worked as hard and as long in a department store, I would have the money, and nobody would care who raised eyebrows. It's only fair."

He gave a slight nod. "I can talk with Sister Mary—"

"Oh, come on, Father!"

"The only alternative to getting Sister Mary's agreement to pay you full minimum wage, Miss Jacamuzzi, is for you to allow me to do what I can do for you," he told her, and he smiled and shrugged. "Eighty dollars a week."

She let out her breath in a loud sigh of exasperation.

"You know, Father, after I graduate, I won't have a place to go. And I'm not making that up," she told him. "I want to start a bank account."

"I know you're not making it up, dear," he said, an unusual seriousness crossing his face. "I understand that your family has some problems—" He cut himself off for a moment as he puzzled it out. Up until that moment, he had been carrying on the conversation with an attitude of amusing himself while he dickered with her over wages. But now, as he looked absently at his marked and scarred desk blotter, he seemed genuinely deep in thought.

"How's this?" he said suddenly. "Eighty a week for the summer. When first semester comes, your schedule will be pretty full, but after Christmas, I think that your only required classes are English and Ethics. We'll see about getting you something in town."

Her eyes opened wide. "Really? During the school year?"

With a gracious incline of his head, Father Williams assented. "I think it's the only way for you to come up with some savings. In view of your father's feelings toward you and your mother's lack of . . . stability at this point, it might be the safest choice to make."

"Sister Mary's never going to go for it," she predicted gloomily.

"Leave Sister Mary to me and Mrs. Murdoch," he said cryptically. "I think, between the two of us, we'll bring her to my point of view. But not until the time is right."

Now that the glorious week of vacation with Maddie was over, Tracey had fallen back into the usual routine of summer, working from early morning until early afternoon, spending most of her free time on the court or in the gym.

She was surprised at how dedicated Peggy became. Up until that year, Peggy's commitment to basketball had been a lively interest, but no more than that. But from the day Tracey returned to campus from Maddie's house, she found her friend almost always willing to get out on the court with her and practice.

The days were at their longest, and Tracey and Peggy

worked all evening, every evening except on weekends, under the outside hoops. Sometimes Dibbles—who was staying for summer school—joined them, but most often it was just the two of them. On the weekends, Tracey went to Maddie's, but she knew that Peggy practiced alone.

As though gripped with the reality that it had to be this year or never, Peggy came at the game with a lot more intensity and a new, almost fierce, concentration. She desperately wanted to make first-string in the fall. There were a lot of hurdles to overcome—and not all of them were skill-oriented. Over the last year, Tracey had dimly sensed a slight difference between Peggy and most of the teammates. Sweet-tempered, obliging, homely, and poor, Peggy lacked the flash of Liz's boldness, Tracey's idealism, and Scooter's lawlessness. There was something about her that made people think she wasn't as good a basketball player as she was. Tracey had been disappointed last season when CPR had again put Peggy on second-string. Had the coach merely misjudged? Peggy had made some great rebounds and great shots every season that she'd played. Nobody ever seemed to remember them. The good-natured, agreeable, nonflashy Peggy was easy to forget, from the top of her unadorned head to the soles of her old-fashioned deck shoes.

With a great many exclamations over how much it cost these days to buy a pair of "sneakers," Maddie had nonetheless consulted carefully and had purchased a pair of Adidas basketball shoes for Tracey. Running shoes and basketball shoes were just becoming fashionable, and the expensive gift had surprised Tracey. She had begun her basketball playing career with nothing more extravagant than girls' Keds. Even Liz had used canvas shoes with rubber soles during her first two years on the team.

Peggy still played in old-fashioned gym shoes, and as they circled and looped around each other on the court, Tracey couldn't help but notice the faded blue canvas tops and the ugly band of white that marked the edge of the sole.

It was sadly true too, that Peggy's Valkyrie warm-up suit—purchased new the year before—did not fit her well. It was droopy and hung on her in folds. When she came out with the rest of the team, nobody seemed to notice. But when she stood alone in the outfit, she looked even less likely than ever to be on the first string of one of the best teams in New England. Her uniform was no better; the shorts came down almost to her knees, making her legs look short and thick.

Liz's legs had been heavy to look at, no matter what length her shorts, but as soon as she took off running, anybody could see the incredible muscle of her legs, propelling her down the court or lifting her for jumps. Tracey's own legs were long and thin like a runner's. Though not an attractive girl in her own estimation, she knew she looked every inch a basketball player.

She didn't know how to improve Peggy's image. New basketball shoes—real basketball shoes—would have helped. Perhaps a few skillful alterations to the uniform and warm-up suit would also have helped, but Tracey knew that Maddie would not alter the shorts. Maddie didn't approve of short shorts, not even for basketball uniforms. And altering the warm-up suit would require a lot of time. Besides, Tracey wasn't sure how effective it would be. Somehow it seemed that

Peggy would look a little dumpy no matter what she wore.

The next time Dibbles stopped by Tracey's room for coffee and some of Maddie's muffins, Tracey approached the subject with her. Dibbles herself was short and round—even after having shed ten pounds during the previous season—yet when she played hard and fast, she radiated power, compactness, and speed.

Dibbles listened to Tracey and then nodded with uncharacteristic seriousness. "It's her moves," she said, as she filled her mouth with a huge bite of muffin. She swallowed, smiled to acknowledge how good it was, and added, "Peggy doesn't run right, Jac. And when she's guarding, she doesn't guard right."

"Her hands stay up," Tracey protested.

Dibbles shrugged. "The rest of her body isn't right. Watch her when she's guarding the basket against me. She'll kind of sidle sideways—which is OK—but she'll lead with the right leg and almost drag her left foot. And when she ought to be leading with the left foot, she'll push off with the right and let the left go where it will, like her mind's not as attached to her left foot as it is to her right."

Tracey had never thought about how to move when she guarded or ran. Early in her basketball career, she had become aware of running with greater ease and fluidness down the court, but it had just happened that way. She had never worked on it. And after a few weeks of practice with Liz, her awkwardness at guarding Liz had also lessened, so that without thinking she had become almost like a shadow, practically on top of Liz every time she had tried to make a shot.

"Peggy's not graceful, Jac," Dibbles explained.

"She's not coordinated enough with her feet. And CPR's really coordinated. She likes to see the team moving and weaving in a good rhythm. That's why she never thinks very much of Peggy. But Peg's a real good shooter. The top of her body's real good for basketball. She can shoot and rebound, and she's smart about passing off."

"So she's never going to look good," Tracey said.

"Not unless you make her a shooter," Dibbles advised. "CPR wants a team that can run and play strategy —but really, the name of the game is sinking baskets. I bet if she sees Peggy make some hard shots, she'll move her up."

Tracey had never noticed that the campus was beautiful in the summer. When she sat on the step in front of the main hall, positioned at an angle so she couldn't see the retirees' wing and all that it signified, she could look out over the hockey field, past the gym, all the way down to the trees. A faint shimmer hung over the clipped grass, and an early summer scent of freshness sometimes reached her. Even the buildings, which she had once thought ugly and shabby and even stark, retained a certain dignity—weary perhaps, of all that had gone on in and around them, but not to be blamed for what they had witnessed. There was a warmth to their brownness, a familiarity between her eyes and the designs of the lines of mortar between the brownstones.

But maybe, she reflected, the campus only seemed beautiful because its hold on her was loosened. She sat now on the step, her overnight case at her feet, her ears waiting for the familiar sound of Maddie's car. Today was Friday, and she was going over to Maddie's house—

going home, she reminded herself. MoJoe had taken on the characteristics of a temporary place. It no longer could impoverish her; it no longer ruled her. Nor even could it dictate all of her actions. Maddie stood between Tracey and Sister Mary. Tracey would carry full details of every event on campus to Maddie, including any private interviews. She had already sensed that Mary disliked personal publicity. The presence—even the invisible presence—of another adult who lived outside the confines of the campus would do much to make Sister Mary more guarded in her actions.

For entire days on end—perhaps even for a week at a time here and there—Tracey had forgotten all about Sister Mary. Not forgotten the principal's person: That was impossible during the school year's routine of announcements and appearances. But she had forgotten to dread her, forgotten to suspect her of always being up to something. There were moments when Tracey could regard Sister Mary face-to-face, almost with absent-mindedness, as her mind scanned over homework assignments not yet attended to.

The faint crunch of a tire on gravel and the fainter whine of an automatic transmission shifting gears reached her ears. She stood up expectantly. The campus was a beautiful place, but it was most beautiful at five-thirty on a Friday night. Two days of freedom lay ahead, dimmed only by the faint apprehension she always felt about going to church with Maddie. But Sunday school and church lasted only about three hours all together. It was not a heavy price to pay for her weekend.

Tracey knew that Maddie wanted her to like church more. And she knew that her shyness at church, her absolute silence among those free, self-assured, Protestant people who knew the right words and the way to talk and greet each other, had surprised Maddie. Not even just surprised, but shocked her.

She had witnessed Maddie's silent struggle with herself over whether or not to talk to Tracey about a Christian's duty to like church. And Tracey was aware that her agreeableness about every other matter pertaining to God and Christianity—especially her frank gratitude to Maddie herself—had compelled Maddie to silence about church matters. Maddie did not doubt Tracey's Christianity, but she could not understand the girl's aversion to church. And Tracey knew it. But she also knew that it would be useless to explain her feelings. Maddie liked people, and she fit in with them. Her whole approach was different from Tracey's.

"There's my girl," Maddie greeted her as Tracey opened the car door and threw her overnight case into the back.

"Hi," Tracey said, and she smiled as she climbed in. She greeted Maddie with the customary kiss on the cheek, then buckled her seat belt. "Are we going to eat at home tonight, Maddie?"

"Did you have a preference?" Maddie asked, looking over with a friendly smile. Sometimes on Fridays they went to Friendlies, and every now and then they even managed a visit to a Chinese restaurant in town. Tracey had never eaten Chinese food until Maddie had introduced her to it.

"I'd like to eat at home if you don't mind cooking," she said. She had a lot to tell Maddie, and it was hard to talk at ease in a restaurant. Strictly speaking, she was supposed to be in uniform to eat out, and she had already taken the liberty of wearing street clothes for the drive to Maddie's house. With most of the sisters gone, it was easier to get by with outings out of uniform, but going right into town without it would be asking for a reprimand.

"No, I don't mind a bit." Maddie laughed. "I'll send out for pizza or Chinese." She guided the car down the drive and through the gates.

The comment made Tracey pause to remember Maddie's willingness to have her over and treat her as a welcome guest. She was about to comment on it, but Maddie spoke first.

"There's a teen outing tonight if you want to go. A scavenger hunt."

Tracey's heart sank. "What's a scavenger hunt?" she asked.

"The group breaks into four teams, and each team has to find a list of certain things," Maddie told her. "I think that it's clues this time. All of the clues lead to a meeting point somewhere outside of town. Whatever team arrives first wins. It lasts an hour or so, and then there's a party in the church basement." She glanced at Tracey. The hopefulness in her eyes was barely hidden, but she tried to sound casual. "Would you like to go, dear?"

"No," Tracey said honestly. "I want to spend tonight with you."

She saw that she'd disappointed Maddie, and she discerned a faint frustration as Maddie turned her eyes back to the road. The idea that maybe she got on Maddie's nerves nudged Tracey. Maybe Friday through Sunday evening was too long for them to be together. It didn't feel that way to her—but then, Maddie didn't need Tracey like Tracey needed Maddie.

"Do you want me to go?" she asked.

"I think it would be good for you to go—" Maddie began, but then she glanced at Tracey and changed her mind. Tracey's dread must have been apparent. "But then maybe not. We have so much catching up to do, and I hardly see you as it is." As they pulled up to one of the town's few red lights, she reached over and tugged on Tracey's bangs. "I'll keep you for myself tonight, dear. The youth group will have to do without."

"And you don't mind?" Tracey asked.

Maddie's smile was tender. "Not a bit. If it were up to me, I would keep you all summer for myself."

The light changed to green, and as Maddie pulled out and concentrated on the road, Tracey let out a silent breath of relief. Maddie had changed her mind this time about the youth outing, but it was obviously on her mind. And Tracey realized that Maddie wasn't trying to get her out of the house so much as she was trying to get her to like the church kids and be a part of them. All of her efforts were for Tracey's own good. And that made it worse. Sooner or later, they were going to be at cross-purposes, with Maddie wanting Tracey to at least try to fit in, and Tracey just as determinedly avoiding the church teens. She had already seen enough and heard enough to realize that she didn't understand them.

For one thing, there were boys in the youth group. Tracey didn't understand boys, and she didn't like this set of them. They had short hair like the men in the church, and most of them dressed in suits and ties of quiet colors. They even carried Bibles, but her expectations of them had been dashed the first morning she had seen them grouped into their clique in the church parking lot between Sunday school and the service. They bragged to each other, their uneven and cracked, sometimes shrill voices raised in argument as each one tried to outboast or outshout his fellow. But then, when a girl walked by, they all became hangdog and silent—or they smirked at each other and looked away, as though too stupid or too silly to make eye contact.

The consciousness of being Christian didn't seem to have much impact on them. But the girls liked them, and this also bothered Tracey. She wondered why she was the only person who thought that the boys were ignoble show-offs and unworthy of attention.

The girls didn't annoy Tracey like the boys did. But one look at the pastor's teenage daughter had warned her that whatever she did, she would have to keep quiet around the church girls. They knew how to dress, and she didn't. They knew how to wear makeup, and she didn't. Some of them wore dresses every day of the week. The entire church seemed to support the idea of girls' being very ladylike and sedate.

Tracey was sure she would annoy them. She had a loud voice and broad gestures, and she stood head and shoulders above any crowd she was in. Though Maddie dressed her in attractive clothing for church, Tracey knew that she lacked grace in wearing it. She knew that when she passed in front of people she didn't know—especially her peers—her attitude was indefinably different from that expected of a church girl.

At her best, Tracey was proud and far more resolute than any woman in the church, conscious at every moment of the importance of integrity, honor, and courage, but heedless of things like meekness and silence and small steps. At her worst, she was hangdog silent; the memories of her many fights, her desperate family circumstances, and the fact that she could play basketball better than any of the boys, despite their boasts, put up a wall so high and so thick that she could not get through it to the people around her—nor could they reach her.

She did not mean to fall into silence as they drove the rest of the way home, nor was she aware of Maddie's glance at her as she took her suitcase to her room. But when she came out again, unconsciously tense and a little unsure of herself while this issue remained unsettled, Maddie was already on the phone, ordering dinner.

She hung up as Tracey peeped around the kitchen doorway.

"Thirty minutes," she said pleasantly. "Can you wait that long?"

"I bet I can," Tracey said agreeably. "Just wave some pepperoni under my nose if I get faint."

"That would be a good way for me to lose a hand, or at least a finger," Maddie replied with a smile. She put her arms around Tracey. "I'm so glad you're here, Tracey. The house is far too quiet when you're gone." She kissed Tracey's cheek. Tracey hadn't realized she was tense until she felt herself relax. Maddie still loved her just as much as at the beginning. *Of course,* she told herself. *She'd never stop just because I don't like church.*

"Did you have a nice week?" Maddie asked. "Have you gotten your first paycheck?"

"Father made me promise I'd put it in the bank," Tracey told her. "Except he'll let me tithe it."

Maddie nodded. "We'll get your account started in the morning. The bank is open until noon." She brushed aside Tracey's bangs, and Tracey realized that everything was all right. Before the pizza even came, she felt at home again and was telling Maddie all about Peggy and what Dibbles had said.

L et's hear you pray, saint."
  "Let's hear you pray, saint."
"Let's hear you pray, saint."

It seemed to Tracey that the voices had been chanting for some time, yet only now were they becoming audible. She looked around, felt her hands tighten on some type of heavy pole that had been thrust into the ground, and saw with a slight start that Scooter and some other girls stood not far from her, each dressed in a basketball warm-up suit. Scooter looked different, and yet somehow familiar.

Over the seasons, Scooter had dropped her outright hostility toward Tracey. Sometimes she had harbored a defensive or tough look on her face, but Tracey had regarded the tough expression as Scooter's refuge against her unsureness with Tracey and Liz and their popularity.

But now, with another shock, Tracey saw Scooter again in all of her old hatefulness and scorn. And Liz was gone. Scooter was not alone: Rita, Missy, and the other members of the Deep Six stood with her now on a slight rise of barren ground, less than twenty feet away from Tracey. Rita slapped a leather thong against one open palm, and the significance of that gesture burned a hole of fear through Tracey's middle. In an instant she was the young, frightened freshman again, and they had her cornered. It was worse this time because she knew what was coming. To be overpowered and subdued and then tortured—the thought sent a chill down her, so severe that she was nearly sick.

"Let's hear you pray, saint," Scooter said again. "One last time before we get you again."

They were all laughing at her, and they were coming to get her—right out in the open this time.

Tracey understood in an instant how hopeless the situation was. Her hands tightened on the pole as though she might make it a fence between herself and them, but they were coming toward her now.

"Let's hear you pray," Scooter said.

"I go first," Rita exclaimed.

"Come on, Tracey, pray."

She hardly knew why she did it, but she suddenly wrenched the pole out of the ground, and as she did, she realized that it was not a pole but a spear. It didn't frighten them—after all, they outnumbered her six to one.

"Pray—come on, saint, pray!" Scooter said with a sneer.

"This is my prayer," Tracey gasped, and she felt the fear that had tightened her throat and reduced her voice to a whisper. She raised her voice to a yell, against the fear, not even knowing what she would say next: "Glory to God! Glory to God in the highest!"

And she flung the spear at them. It left her hand with such force that it nearly pulled her after it, as though her cry had suffused it with its own strength, and she fell forward so hard that she rolled onto her back, stunned as though struck.

For a long moment she lay on her back, gasping, all strength gone. The first thing she did was raise her eyes to see what had happened to the six on the hillock, but all she got was a glimpse of a few pairs of feet and legs flung onto the ground. She could not stand up yet to properly survey the field of their brief battle, but she realized that the single spear had either killed or stunned all six of them.

It's killed me too, she thought. But she was too weak and tired to regret dying. Her outcry still seemed to hang in the air, and now, as she listened, she realized that it was echoing back at her from far away, rolling over the hills like the sound of a bugle or trumpet. A moment later she realized that it was not an echo, but that someone far away had taken it up. And then she realized that whoever had taken it up was coming closer, but she did not have the strength to roll onto her side and watch for his arrival.

It was just as well. As she lay supine, she saw a speck in the opaque white sky above, and this speck grew as she watched it, until she realized that it was a person running toward her—a person all in white who ran with such sureness that she felt dizzy and disoriented. It was almost as though she were floating in the sky and he was running up a mountain to meet her at the summit. The optical illusion nearly made her nauseous, but the wonder she felt drove it away, and then her eyes adjusted.

As the person came closer, she thought it might be Maddie and then decided it wasn't her, all in an instant. The person was not necessarily male—in fact, his face had some of Maddie's aristocratic lines, and there was not a hint of stubble on his cheeks—but he was certainly of masculine gender. He emitted a living strength and activity that Tracey thought might kill her if he came too close.

Yet it seemed certain that his intentions toward her were kindly.

He called out to her, seemingly with encouragement, but a ground wind had come up, and she couldn't hear him.

He was cut off by the sudden appearance of three other sky creatures. They had the stature of big dogs, and yet their hands and feet were distinct. *A little like small wolfmen*, Tracey thought, and then they turned on the heavenly runner and buried their teeth in him. She watched in shock and horror.

The runner manifested only a grim dismay at this attack, though one of them had sunk its fangs into his chest. He raised a small sword and stabbed the creature, but its fangs did not unlock their hold.

Tracey felt the horror even more keenly, but she couldn't help noticing that the runner was not in the least frightened or even intimidated. Surely they would pull him apart—even in death, the huge teeth did not let go.

They're werewolves! she thought wildly, but before she could exclaim, the heavenly runner called, "Cry out your prayer that brought me!"

And Tracey felt new strength, and she cried out, "Glory to God in the highest! Glory to God in the highest!" even though her mind told her that this was ridiculous. If it was time to pray, then it was time to pray for help, not to offer praise.

But the cry was taken up. The white sky seemed to erupt with men in white, and Tracey felt a moment's dismay at herself for not realizing that the sky had always been ready with them—pregnant with heavenly soldiers eager to come forth and go to war. Even in the midst of the battle, she felt tremendously mortified by her own obtuseness.

"Glory to God!" They shouted it like thunder. "Glory to God in the highest!" With grim determination they went to help their fellow, and Tracey saw with new mortification that some of them were coming for her.

The sight brought a shudder of delight and horror. She did not know if she could bear to look into their faces up close, they were so filled with an emotion she had never seen before: some mixture of incredible tenderness and incredible determination. She knew that they would see into her the moment they looked into her eyes and face—they would see it all and would love her so that her sins would in one instant be apparent, forgiven, and destroyed. And she wasn't sure she would live through it. But they would surely look—it would be their first action, to know her.

The thunderous chorus rose around her, and the first of them touched down and ran toward her.

"You are ever with us!" the nearest one shouted.

"Glory to God in the highest!" the others shouted —their shout as terrible as it was wonderful, filling her with the dreadful delight of being seen and known by them.

She cried out, but she resolved to be known by these people and—if it killed her—to die under their eyes and understanding and wisdom.

She opened her eyes and called out again—not a prayer, only a loud outcry—and she found herself in the silent darkness of her room.

"Tracey! Tracey!" Maddie exclaimed. The light switched on.

"Turn it off!" Tracey cried, and Maddie did so, but the light from the hallway spilled into the room. Tracey realized that she was on her knees all the way at the foot of her bed, only inches from falling off onto the floor.

"Their eyes—the fight," Tracey said. "Something happened. It doesn't kill you, but they must be burning hot."

"Tracey—" Maddie began, and she looked a little more closely at Tracey's wide-eyed stare.

"I have to go outside," Tracey said. She got up onto her numbed legs and strode from the room.

"Take your robe—Tracey, wake up!" Maddie exclaimed and came after her. She got her arms around Tracey in the hallway under the light and stopped her.

"Tracey, you're dreaming. It's a dream," Maddie said. "Wake up, now!" At the tone of her voice, gentle yet firm, and just a little fearful, Tracey stopped and looked at her.

"Was that a dream?" Tracey asked. "How could that have been a dream? I have to see the sky, Maddie. I have to see if they're there. Come with me."

Without another word, Maddie threw Tracey's robe around her shoulders, and they passed through the living room, using the sliding glass door to leave the house and enter the garden.

The coolness penetrated Tracey's summer robe and thin nightgown, reviving her and returning her mind to her familiar surroundings. She heard the faithful peepers as they sang their rhythmic summer song of the cool evening and the waiting for sunrise. She smelled the familiar freshness of nighttime dew and a faint fragrance from Maddie's roses that lined the fence. In the clear sky above, a single plane flew high and silent, marked only by the twinkling of its wing lights. There were a few stars. The moon had gone down. But she still felt the expectation of the skies.

As she stood and surveyed the heavens, the sense of expectation dwindled. She knew it was there, but the feeling of immediacy waned so that she could co-exist with the heavens again.

Tracey drew a long breath, partly of relief and partly of regret. Assured by this sign of her return, Maddie asked, "Did you have a bad dream, dear?"

"Did anyone ever have a dream like that?" Tracey asked. "I shattered Goliath's spear, I think. It was David's trophy, but I'm the one who used it last."

"But the dream is over now," Maddie said.

"It wasn't a common dream," Tracey replied briefly. "I know who I am now." A great wave of tiredness went over her and made her shiver, and when she instinctively held out her arm to find Maddie, Maddie hugged her and then helped her into the robe properly and at last brought her back into the house.

"Can you sleep?"

"Yes, I can sleep," she said. "Thank you."

All the same, Maddie saw her into her bed and did not seem disposed to hurry away again. "You're sure you're all right?" she asked after Tracey was under the covers with her eyes already closing.

Tracey forced her eyes open and looked up at the silhouette of Maddie's face against the hall light. She realized again how good Maddie was—learned and brave and wise, yet homey and cheerful.

"I'll never be able to do some things or be some things," she said at last. "Some things that most other girls my age do."

Maddie only gave a brief nod, not comprehending.

Tracey went on, "And sometimes I think that some of the things that have happened to me have changed me forever—not for the bad; I know the Lord can take bad things away. I mean, just changed me. So that I'll never be like other people. Is that all right with you?"

"Whatever God makes you is fine with me," Maddie said, once more on familiar ground. "I don't expect you to be like other people."

"Then I'm all right, and I can sleep," Tracey said.

Eyes up! Eyes up! Eyes up!" Tracey chanted, each exclamation ending on a slightly higher note. She ran it all together, as Liz had done, so that it came out, "Eyesupeyesupeyesup!"

Peggy tried to roll around her, but Tracey nimbly blocked her and then let her go around the other way to make the shot. The basketball arced through the air and bounced off the rim, but Peggy beat Tracey on the rebound and pushed it up again. This time it went in.

"Nice job," Tracey said as the ball came down into her hands. "You're still dropping your eyes, though." She flipped the ball to her friend. "Drills."

With a sigh and a rueful smile, Peggy took the ball back up and brought it down while Tracey watched. The late afternoon breeze blew over the outside court. Both girls were sweating profusely. By school rules, they could not wear shorts except during gym classes and games, so they were clad in their sweatpants and T-shirts.

But at last the sun had started to drop, and the few

degrees of relief they could already feel were welcome. They had agreed to play up until the last minute allowable before supper, and they had about thirty minutes left.

Peggy was holding her eyes up better, a sign of her increasing familiarity and coordination with the ball. But she was no Liz Lukas; in fact, she was not even what Tracey had been by the end of her first year playing basketball.

Tracey realized that Dibbles had been right. You could improve Peggy's mobility, but you could never make her a mover, or a passer, or a receiver. She was a shooter. Unlike Tracey, who had to get one hand under the ball like a pedestal to shoot accurately, Peggy could shoot with her hands on either side of the ball. And unlike Tracey, who could not hook-shot at all except during practice, Peggy could hook-shot with a high percentage of success, even when Tracey was right on top of her.

Even so, there were problems. For one thing, Peggy was not good at jumping, so if she were blocked by a taller opponent, she would never get a shot off. Tracey rested her hands on her hips and watched as Peggy jogged back to the line and brought the ball down again.

It would mean that somebody would always have to be near her to save her and get the ball. They could keep Peggy outside and try to pass back out to her— but if she missed the passes—no, that wasn't it.

But Dibbles was good at moving and getting around. If Dibbles and Peggy played guard, then Dibbles would be outside too. She could bring the ball safely down and maybe make a nice wall for Peggy to shoot from. That strategy sounded safe. Dibbles could bring the ball down, then make a short pass off to Peggy at mid-court, then block her from the other team's defense long enough for Peggy either to make the shot or to give Tracey a chance to rebound it from the forward position.

If Peggy got blocked out, Dibbles herself was not a bad hand at shooting. She could bring it in a little closer and try a shot.

"Gonna be a whole new ball game," Tracey whispered to herself, and she keenly felt the regret. Gone forever were the days of tall girls dominating the team; the high jumping, aerial passes, and aerial shots were a thing of the past. She could jump as well as ever, but she was now a minority.

She doubted that the MoJoes would make finals this year. The very idea that such a high percentage of their shots would have to be outside shots boggled her mind. She was used to most of the shots coming from the forward zones or the middle of the key. Even when the guards had made shots from outside, it had always been when the forwards had pulled away the other team's defense, so the shots were pretty easy. But it looked like the upcoming season would be one of steady pressure for every player in every position.

She let Peggy finish the drill, and then they rebounded for a while until it was time to run for the showers. After they'd changed back to their school uniforms, they wandered over the grounds together toward the hall and their supper.

"I really appreciate your help," Peggy said. "You remind me a lot of Liz when you coach."

Tracey grinned briefly. "Thanks."

"You like coaching?"

"I guess."

"Will you follow in her footsteps next year and go into P.E.?"

The question surprised Tracey a little bit. "No," she said after a pause. "I guess not. I can't see myself teaching in a high school. When I get out of here, I'm never going to look back."

"Have you picked a major?" Peggy asked.

Tracey shrugged. "Not a major and not a college, really."

"You can get a scholarship to any good school," Peggy said, encouraging as always.

"I don't want to play basketball in college," Tracey told her. "Or—well, I don't mind playing ball; I just don't want to go to a secular school and have to major in P.E. A lot of the scholarships are strictly for P.E. And even the ones that aren't—I just don't know what I would major in."

"Major in anything you want," Peggy said.

"I want to go to a Christian college," Tracey told her. "They don't offer basketball scholarships. But I don't know how else I'll get to go to college. So I don't think about it much."

"You're going to go to college, aren't you?" Peggy asked.

"Yes, and if it has to be on a scholarship, that's how I'll do it," she admitted. "But maybe something else will turn up."

She didn't want to talk about it any more, and Peggy took the hint of her silence. As they entered the hall, she wisely changed the subject.

Letters from Liz had come with their usual regularity through the months of June and July, but with the coming of August they became more sporadic. Some-times Tracey would send off two in a row to her friend before hearing any answer back. She knew that Liz was busy, and that the upcoming move to college would be distracting her.

But as August passed and dwindled toward September, another huge wave of realization that Liz was gone washed over Tracey. She felt it most keenly during the last two weeks before school started. Every other year, these days had been her waiting period for her friend's return, but now more than ever she realized that Liz had really gone and that nothing could call her back.

Another realization that startled Tracey was that she had actually been happy during some of her time at MoJoe. She could look back to previous Augusts and Septembers and remember them with a fondness and a longing that she would not have expected of herself.

Peggy, always sensitive, suggested that they take more bicycle rides off campus while they had the chance. And Tracey went up and talked Mrs. Sladern into giving her the key to the bike barn. She and Peggy selected two old bicycles that were to their liking, and they pedaled off into the outside world.

Unlike Liz, Peggy actually liked to stop and point out old barns that struck her fancy, and she startled Tracey by suggesting that they park their bikes to ex-plore one of the abandoned two-story farmhouses that had become a kind of landmark in the area.

"Every time we've driven past this place on the bus, I've always wanted to look inside it," Peggy told her as they stood and rested in the entrance to the over-grown driveway. "I always wonder what's inside houses

—not the decor, but the rooms themselves and what they look like."

Tracey felt a lot of misgivings about going inside, but this was Peggy's last week of summer school. She would go home for ten days of vacation before returning for the fall semester. So this would be Peggy's only chance to explore the place.

"OK," Tracey said, and they explored it, much to Peggy's satisfaction. To Tracey, the house was just a collection of old, bare rooms. What wallpaper was left hung from the walls in long strips. The interior wasn't even dark, not even the attic. There were windows everywhere—glassless and framed with heavy wooden beams—and they let in enough daylight to light up the place.

The basement, though, was dark. Peggy was thrilled to find a huge fireplace in one wall—big enough for both of them to stand up in—and they discovered the empty shaft of a dumbwaiter.

By then it was past four in the afternoon, and Tracey suggested that they ought to leave. Peggy agreed, more satisfied and happy than Tracey had ever seen her. It made her want to tell Liz about it, and again she had to catch herself in the realization that Liz would not be back this year. She would have to write and tell her. And then she wondered if Liz would still care. This was no longer Liz's world.

TWENTY - NINE

After Peggy left, Tracey spent her afternoons riding in the country alone, reawakened to all that she had enjoyed on the quiet lanes away from the Sanctuary. It was true that much of the enjoyment had come from being with Liz, but Peggy had somehow taught her to appreciate it again for herself.

She liked to feel her own strength, dependable and steady, as she covered mile after mile on the old bicycle. And she liked the fresh, mild air of late August afternoons. The leaves were already preparing to change their colors, and the breezes had a hint of wildness in them, a forewarning of fall.

There was no doubt that Tracey did enjoy certain aspects of her exile. She had become familiar with it. Or maybe it was Maddie's touch that had taken so much of the regret and pain away from everything, giving her freedom to enjoy things more. Or maybe it was that she had left her fear behind. Somewhere along the way, she had come to regard Sister Mary and the entire system with less and less dread. Perhaps Liz's carelessness had set her the example. Perhaps her own realization that they could not expel her had made her realize that there would always be limits to what could be done to her. Perhaps the mousetrap trick and her glimpse of Sister Mary's utter shock and inability to strike back had given her a sense of humor about the whole place.

Tracey did not write to Liz about these subtle changes. But she did write about the rides in the country alone, the way that Peggy's skills had improved, everything Dibbles had said. She even wrote a detailed account of the exploration of the old house.

All the same, she did not hear again from Liz until the very first day of school, when the halls were filled with the sounds of people banging doors open and shut, and of suitcases being dragged up the threadbare carpets.

She and Peggy had piled Peggy's storage chest into the room next door to her own. Peggy and Dibbles would be roommates that year, right next door to Tracey. But Tracey—with a sense of owing something to posterity—had volunteered to have three freshmen in her room. Class sizes were down that year, so she was given two to look after.

While Tracey was directing the new girls on where to put their things and warning them about all of the meetings, meals, and services they were expected to attend that day and the next, the mail came for her: a letter from Liz.

As she ripped it open, she heard a voice out in the hall, loud and whiny and glad, calling for her. Dibbles had arrived. But Tracey took a moment to glance at the letter.

Dear Jac:

    You brought it all to life again for me in your last letter. I even cried a little. College can be almost as bad as

But just then Dibbles burst in, her small figure doing a parody of melodramatic gladness to see Tracey again.

"Can it be you? Can it be you?" she cried.

Tracey played along and clasped her hands together. "Darling, yes!"

They staged an embrace and Dibbles exclaimed, "Dare we kiss?"

Tracey didn't know what to say until she felt the side of her face mashed by the side of Dibbles's face, and then she started to laugh in spite of herself. Dibbles was imitating the way the lovers in *Green Dolphin Street* had "kissed." Instead of meeting lip-to-lip, or even of kissing lip-to-cheek, the man and woman had looked into each other's eyes and then had merely pushed the sides of their faces together, in lieu of a kiss.

"Oh, that was wonderful!" Dibbles exclaimed. "Let my sister become a nun! As long as I have you!"

"Then she'd be Sister Sister, I guess," Tracey quipped.

"Let's do it the other way!" Dibbles exclaimed, and they smashed the other sides of their faces together. The two freshmen, anxious and worried up to that moment, collapsed with laughter onto the lower bunks. They had never seen *Green Dolphin Street*, but the parody of an old movie was evident, and Dibbles's humor was infectious.

"Meet the kids," Tracey said when she and Dibbles had finished their joke. "This is Sheila and that's Diane."

"Charmed, I'm sure, ladies," Dibbles said, offering each of them a limp and ladylike hand. "We'll have to have you over for tea, as soon as we check your credit histories and social liaisons."

"Real D.A.R.'s, the both of them," Tracey assured her. "And Junior League, to boot."

"Ah, but can they play basketball?" Dibbles asked, raising her eyebrows like Groucho Marx.

"They claim not to," Tracey said, and both girls shook their heads in agreement. Sheila was small like Dibbles, but cute in a slender, almost childlike way. And Diane, though nearly as tall as Tracey, was barred from sports and phys ed because of petit mal. Tracey did not know much about epilepsy, and there had not been much time to talk with Diane about her medication, except to receive her assurances that her seizures were rare and usually not serious. But Tracey had already guessed that Sister Madeleine had put Diane in this room purposefully, knowing that Tracey's domain would be both safe and impregnable. Unlike most of the boarders, Diane seemed to want to be at MoJoe, heedless of its reputation as the last place before juvenile hall. She had already talked with admiration about the high academics, and there was a hint of pride in her voice when she spoke about being able to live away from home, her illness under control.

"I brought Tastykakes with me," Dibbles said.

"Let's get together and talk after supper," Tracey suggested. "Is Peggy back yet?"

"She's back in town, I think. But they're shopping. She'll put off coming in until the last minute."

245

"If you get to her first, invite her over."

"Sure thing," Dibbles agreed. "Well, girls, see you later."

Sheila and Diane were both too new to understand the positions that Tracey and Dibbles held among the students. They were suitably impressed with Tracey for being a senior, and she thought it would be a better idea to let the other girls clue them in on the importance of basketball at MoJoe. Soon enough, they would grasp Tracey's position in the hierarchy and their own advantages in being her roommates. Tracey's task for the moment was to get them moved in, settle them down, and give them the ground rules. Then she would have to hurry to scout all of the new students and see who would be likely prospects for the team.

But even Tracey had not fully reckoned the importance of her own position. She had no privacy that afternoon. Returning seniors and some of the juniors knocked on the door every few minutes, welcoming her back, reporting on their room locations. Lisa, one of Tracey's roommates from her freshman year, had graduated. But Amy was back, and her room was just down the hall. Toni and Nikki were back, in different rooms, of course. They were juniors. Ingrid, Barbara, and Regina—who didn't mind when she called them Ingy, Bingy, and Ringy—were seniors now, scattered throughout the halls, each with her own room to look after and boss around.

The influence of Liz Lukas was still plain. There was much less talk of putting freshmen in their place, and in front of Tracey, Sheila and Diane were addressed by their given first names instead of by their last names or by the ignominious title, "Freshman."

Tracey introduced them as friends, and nobody's eyebrows went up. In fact, Regina had always been something of a mother hen—when Liz had let her—and she supplied the thorough questioning about Diane's petit mal that Tracey had neglected.

Tracey had a lot to think about. For one thing, the pleasant surprise that she was now somebody, even without Liz, invited all kinds of thought and reflection. But the idea that there had been changes worked at MoJoe, and that she could further those changes, demanded even more attention and careful thought. The basketball team was no longer what it once had been. With herself, Dibbles, and probably Peggy all on first-string that year, it would be like a whole new administration. And if Tracey could only be made captain, there was no telling what she could do to change the system. On that thought, Tracey stopped herself. If she knew Sister Mary at all, she knew that Mary would never allow her to be team captain.

Her busy thoughts, along with all the interruptions, drove the memory of Liz's letter out of her mind until only a few minutes remained before supper. While everybody scurried to clean up and change, she had a minute to sit down on a lower bunk and read the letter in its entirety.

Dear Jac:

You brought it all to life again for me in your last letter. I even cried a little. College can be almost as bad as MoJoe, the first day. The girls on the team are OK, except they all know each other except for about three of us who are new. I'll never get on first-string this year. It's hard to play second fiddle.

College is so different too. But your letter brought me back to MoJoe with you. I almost felt like I was there. I've never been homesick for home, how could I be homesick for that place? It seemed like hell (sorry) or at least purgatory (but we don't believe in that), and yet now I wish I was just back there, practicing with you and getting ready for the new season. Have you heard the new song "Ride 'em Cowboy"? Be like the cowboy this year, don't let them throw you down. Neither will I. But Jac, the letter was so real. Please write me more long letters about everything you see and do. Don't leave the details out. You made me feel like I was there. I could see all the best parts in my mind for as long as the letter lasted. . . .

Tracey read on to the end of the letter. Typical of Liz, it filled both sides of one sheet of paper. But her plea stuck in Tracey's mind. Tracey's letters, short and more concerned with jokes and conversations about herself, had never been remarkable before, but suddenly —when she had become a narrator—she had struck the chord in Liz that she had always wanted to strike: the chord of responsiveness, gratitude, and openness.

She felt curiously humbled, and she wasn't sure why. But there would be plenty of things going on throughout the month of September. She could repeat what she had done before: Keep track of all that had passed, and describe the things worth remembering to Liz in accurate detail. The only trick Tracey had used in the previous letter had been to try to see it all so that she could re-create it for Liz's understanding. She had filled her mind with Liz's way of talking, listening, and observing, and she had narrated accordingly, concentrating on Liz and not herself.

T H I R T Y

M elsom, I want you to try the guard position this scrimmage," CPR said.

Inwardly, Tracey nodded in assent and relief, and she made a mental note to record this practice for Liz. This was the crucial moment, when CPR realized that Peggy would be better as a guard than as a forward.

"Dibbley, you play the other guard. Jacamuzzi, center for the white team. Trish Roberts, forward, and— you, freshman, what's your name?"

"Stetson," the freshman said.

"First name, and say 'Sister,'" CPR said curtly.

"Hilary Stetson, Sister," the freshman said. Tracey and Peggy exchanged glances. The blonde freshman was very good, as everybody had quickly realized. And she knew it. She was also pretty, although a certain boldness in her face had instantly recalled Scooter, Susan, and the Deep Six to Tracey's mind.

There was no doubt at this point that the white team in the scrimmage was CPR's first stab at picking the first-string. She quickly assembled the red team.

Up in the balcony of the gym, several of the sisters filed in.

Tracey and one of the freshman hopefuls jumped for the ball, and Tracey let her take it away so CPR could see if she was any good or not. She was pretty good, slapping the ball right to one of the other red team members.

Dibbles intervened and took it away while Tracey ran up under the white basket, arms up to get the pass. She nearly crashed into Hilary Stetson and barely had time to push the younger girl out of the way. "Get to your zone!" she barked. She jumped, got the ball, and came down running with it, aware that Hilary was still with her like a shadow. Was the idiotic freshman trying to steal the ball from her own teammate?

Exasperated, Tracey shot from the top of the key, sank it, and glared at her.

"Get back to your zone, forward!" she exclaimed.

"I thought you might miss with the ball," Hilary told her.

"You wish!" Tracey retorted. "Stay out from under my feet when I'm playing!"

"Stetson, watch your zone!" CPR barked. "Red team, let's go!"

There was no way, Tracey thought, that this team was going anywhere near the finals this year. The red team, made up of second-string hopefuls, ambled down the court with the ball.

"Get the anvils out of your pants!" CPR yelled. Tracey had never heard that one before.

With the same smoothness and unbroken rhythm, Dibbles glided around the red guard, took the ball, and long-passed all the way up the court to Trish Roberts.

251

Trish barely caught it, but she easily dribbled it up the key and did a successful layup. CPR shrilled on the whistle.

"Trish has come a long way," Tracey said to Dibbles as they came off the floor to get chewed out.

"I thought she was pretty good last year," Dibbles replied in her singsong voice. "She knows all the plays now—she just gets so nervous."

Instead of chewing them out, CPR simply redivided the two scrimmage teams. Tracey wondered why their coach had nothing more to say about the slowness of the second-string, nor about Hilary Stetson's disregard for zones.

She and Dibbles were on the red team this time, with three of the prospective second-stringers. She jumped for the ball against Hilary, and this time, instead of graciously letting her have a try with it, Tracey popped it up and over to Dibbles. She caught the look of surprise, resentment, and respect in the freshman's eye before they both ran down toward the red basket.

Hilary ran up to get under the basket and protect it, but Tracey slowed down as she came into the key, and Dibbles passed back to her. She shot from the top of the key and sank the ball with a satisfying whoosh.

When Peggy brought the ball down with the white team, her new abilities were much more apparent. She moved better today than she had moved at the end of the summer, suddenly wired from having an audience. And she wasn't afraid to pass off to some of the girls who were not as good as she. Tracey again made a mental note to report on this to Liz. Peggy's kindness and sense of fairness seemed inexhaustible.

By silent agreement, Tracey and Dibbles kept the

white team's forwards and center too well blocked for them to shoot. Hilary tried and missed under Tracey's blocking, and she almost missed catching the rebound, except that Tracey let her get it. At last—after violating the three-second rule, which CPR had not enforced—Hilary passed back out to Peggy, who instantly shot and sank the ball.

Tracey and Dibbles worked hard to make Peggy look good as a guard, and CPR was not slow to see Peggy's improvement. The girls had been through many practices so far that month, and CPR had praised Peggy often for her good shots and better handling of the ball.

It was also clear to Tracey that Dibbles herself had become a better player. She was faster and a lot more aggressive, getting into tight places and shooting or passing as she saw fit. She'd learned to run up against the person with the ball as though to block her, and then—just when it looked like Dibbles was ready to step across her path and cut her off—Dibbles would steal the ball instead. Even Tracey could not see how she was timing the quick theft.

Trish Roberts, a junior who had made the second-string the previous year, was quieter and less certain, but she religiously stuck to the plays and the strategy. She sometimes managed to be right where the person with the ball needed her to be, and she seemed to understand when it was best to pass off or risk a shot.

And then there was Hilary. Better, Tracey realized with a slight twinge of bitterness, than Tracey had been her sophomore year, better even than Scooter had been during Scooter's junior year.

But then Tracey had to correct herself. When she stood on the sidelines and watched Hilary shoot, pass, dribble, or do any of the drills, she saw that Hilary moved well and never fumbled or took a misstep. But when they scrimmaged, it was always Hilary who was getting in the way, taking lousy shots from bad positions, or fouling too much. During her first year on the team, Tracey had never taken risks; she had considered getting in the way to be one of the stupidest things a person could do, and her own mortification whenever she did mess up made her cautious and tenderly aware of where her teammates were at all times. And she had listened, listened, listened—always listened to Liz, and always with her own mouth shut. She had even listened to Scooter, the few times Scooter had given her advice or offered constructive criticism. But Hilary would not listen to anyone. Tracey wondered why CPR didn't take the freshman over to the side and pin back her ears.

Tracey had taught Dibbles, and Tracey had taught Peggy, and she knew that everybody needed criticism. And everybody needed to obey. That made a good team. Along with all of their skills and dexterity, there had to be humility and obedience. Tracey had never answered back to Liz, had never argued with her advice, and had never ignored her. Hilary ignored every player on the team who told her anything about staying in her zone.

"I just don't get it," Tracey said that night before supper. They had just come from practice and the showers, and she, Dibbles, and Peggy were enjoying an appetizer of Tastykakes and coffee. Because Dibbles and Peggy were both guards, their room had been christened the guard room, and it was becoming a meeting place for the older girls who knew each other. With the final cuts list coming out the next morning, the three of them were eager to finish up the Tastykakes before their training diet became mandatory.

"CPR would have been down our throats the first scrimmage if we had bungled our positions like that Stetson kid is doing," Tracey lamented. "What gives?"

"You've already bawled her out at every scrimmage," Dibbles pointed out.

"What difference does that make?" Tracey protested. "I'm not a nun!"

"Not by a long shot," Peggy added with a smile.

"You're team captain," Dibbles told her. "CPR will let you handle it. Just like she always let Liz handle you."

"She did?" Tracey asked.

"Sure. Liz always got to you first and said what needed to be said. And you always listened."

"Well, guess what? Hila-bomb isn't listening. And besides, I'm not team captain. Nobody's team captain. We won't know who the captain is until the list comes out tomorrow."

"Oh, Jac, you're the captain," Peggy said, leaning back onto the floor on her elbows.

"You guys still don't know how the game is played—"

"Is that why CPR told you to get down to the gym at seven and help her get the banner and sword and shield ready?" Dibbles asked. "Because you're not captain?"

"Maybe being in charge of the sword and shield had something to do with it," Tracey said dryly.

"Well, we'll all see tomorrow," Peggy said. She closed her eyes. "Man, I hope I make first-string this time."

"You did great—" Tracey began, but just then there was a knock at the door. Dibbles wearily got up to get it.

"If it's Trish, be extra nice," Tracey said in a low voice. "She needs confidence."

It was Trish. The shy junior looked a little uneasy, but hopeful, as she stood in the doorway. "Hi, I just got ready and I thought maybe I'd walk down to supper with you if you didn't mind—" she said.

"Hey, come on in!" Peggy called as Dibbles stepped aside.

"Look who it is!" Tracey exclaimed. "Pull up for some Tastykakes. Guaranteed to help dull the taste of supper tonight, whatever it is."

Assured by this welcome, Trish entered and sat down on the floor with them. They had time to gobble down the last of the cupcakes before it was time to go. Though Trish would have to sit with the juniors at supper, they walked down together, and Tracey was able to forget some of her concerns about the team.

It was still a surprising pleasure to be recognized apart from Liz, to have every upperclassman in the school greet her, to hear them talk in quiet voices about her ability as a ballplayer. She wondered if she was conceited to enjoy it, but the knowledge that her popularity would help her carry out her own plans made her even more eager to see how far she could go in the affections of her classmates. Liz had already warned her: Her position would not last past high school. If she was ever going to do anything with it, it would have to be now. In fact, it would have to happen before the rest of the school realized that the team would get nowhere near the championships this year.

As usual, she and Dibbles and Peggy were greeted loudly at their table, and when the prayer had been said and they were seated, everyone looked at them to open up the conversation. All Dibbles ever needed was an audience, and Peggy was good as her straight man. The two of them began a retelling of the day's practice. Tracey industriously ate. With the return of the basketball team and all of her social obligations at the start of the new year, she had sorely depleted Maddie's stock of goodies. And now that classes were in session, she was no longer allowed to spend entire weekends at Maddie's, only Saturday afternoons. So she was more obliged to rely on the school cafeteria to satisfy her appetite—which, as she herself admitted, was huge. She was now as tall as Maddie, and she had not yet stopped growing. And even though Liz had been the stockier of the two of them, Tracey had always been able to eat more than her blonde friend.

As the mealtime ended, a ripple of murmurs went through the tables, and Tracey looked up to see Sister Mary enter the dining room. She felt the old, familiar sinking feeling, but this time she checked it. Though she felt sure that Mary had come for no reason other than to call her in, she reminded herself that this was no time for dread or fear or even conflict. It was time to be cool and collected, as Liz had taught her.

After the bell, when they were all quiet, with their eyes fixed on Sister Mary, the acting principal said, "Good evening, girls." Her greeting was formally returned. "Is Tracey Jacamuzzi in tonight?" she asked. "Tracey Jacamuzzi?"

Tracey knew that Mary had seen her upon entering, but she raised her hand. Nonetheless, Mary squinted around the room as though blind. "I can't see you, dear, please stand."

Oh, here we go again, Tracey thought, and she stood up. She would stay standing until Mary permitted her to sit.

But as she stood up, she heard a piercing whistle and then a loud round of applause. The applause was taken up, and several other vociferous whistles of approval joined in.

Tracey glanced down at Dibbles, who had been the first to whistle and who was now clapping and banging her feet against the chair legs. Dibbles grinned up at her. Neither of them had expected last year's fame and glory to still be on anybody's mind. Nor was Tracey aware of how keenly so many of the students had watched her whenever she had practiced outside. She had not divided the glory with Liz upon Liz's departure, nor had she—as she had thought up to that moment—been given a chance to accrue her own glory. Instead she had inherited all of the glory that she and Liz and Scooter had once shared. And suddenly she realized the startling truth: The unpracticed student body thought that she would carry the team to a victory this year.

The applause did not subside, partly due to the efforts of the basketball team to keep it going, so Tracey looked around and then smiled and bowed a little. The applause swelled, there were more whistles, and then it gradually died away. She and Sister Mary looked at each other across the silent, expectant tables.

"I will see you in my office after supper. You are all dismissed," Mary said evenly, though a little out of breath, Tracey thought.

THIRTY - ONE

Sister Mary made no reference to the applause of the boarders for Tracey. Instead, she greeted Tracey with a short lecture on having a sweet and submissive spirit.

"Yes, Sister," Tracey said when she'd finished. "Thank you, Sister."

"You will not take that tone with me!" Mary snapped.

There had been a sound of triumph in Tracey's voice. Tracey snuffed it out as she said, "I'm sorry, Sister."

"You are still a rebel, miss. A megalomaniac rebel!" Mary exclaimed. "I ask you again, will you attend Mass this year? And you had better answer wisely."

This was new. Tracey had nearly forgotten their old clash over going to Mass. She wondered if the departure of Liz Lukas had also meant the departure of a certain wall of protection.

"I will not go to Mass, Sister," she said gravely.

"I warn you, Miss Jacamuzzi, if you refuse to conform to the dictates of this school, the consequences will be dire. Dire indeed."

She's going to pull me from the team, Tracey thought. But she said, "I cannot go to Mass, Sister."

"You have such plans, don't you?" Mary demanded, coming around the desk to stand with her face right in Tracey's. Tracey felt the violation of her personal space, but she also felt a certain satisfaction in being taller than Sister Mary. "You want to go to college, don't you? And you need a good recommendation if you're going to get a scholarship, miss! You'll need to say you held school offices! That you proved yourself responsible! Think about that!"

"At the end of my life, I'd like to tell God I obeyed Him," Tracey said.

"Can God get you a scholarship?" Mary challenged her. "Or has He put that in the hands of others?"

"God could make the stones shout hosanna," Tracey told her. "He'll get me to college."

"How dare you! You impudent, brazen girl!"

Only then did it strike Tracey that her choice of analogy had been unwise. Mary had taken it as a reference to the applause in the dining room.

"You will hold no office in this school!" Mary told her. "You will not be selected for Who's Who, or for any other organization of recognition. You will not even be put on the honor roll, do you hear me?"

"Yes, Sister."

"I mean it, Miss Jacamuzzi. I have been very tolerant of you in order to help you along, but I will make this year miserable for you—"

Tracey, mindful of Maddie Murdoch and of the vast fields of happiness and joy that Maddie had brought to her, looked down at Sister Mary in wonder. Did she really think, Tracey wondered, that taking it all away from her, even taking away basketball itself, could diminish her happiness one bit? *Somebody loves me at last,* Tracey told herself, as she had told herself many times over. Maddie was one thing Sister Mary could never take away from her, and Maddie was the only thing that really mattered to her.

Sister Mary, mistaking Tracey's look of wonder for a look of horror, repeated herself. "Yes, I mean it, Miss Jacamuzzi. I will make this year miserable for you—"

"I'd like to see you try!" Tracey exclaimed with a laugh of derision.

Sister Mary slapped her.

Tracey felt the shock and the imprint of the blow on her face, and she turned with it. The sudden shame drove deeply into her like a knife, but she faced Sister Mary eye-to-eye.

"You will look down!" Sister Mary exclaimed.

"Go on, slap me again," Tracey taunted. "Maybe it'll make you feel better, you—" She stopped herself. Anger nearly blinded her, anger and the sudden desire to hit back. But the idea of hitting back also horrified her. She did not believe in hitting teachers or adults. Tears had sprung into her eyes, but the anger drove them away.

Mary retreated back behind her desk. She did not repeat the command for Tracey to look down. She and Tracey stared at each other.

"What are you waiting for?" Mary suddenly exclaimed. "You heard me—no office, no awards. You will not be the captain of the team. Now, get out of my sight."

Tracey turned and strode to the door, but as she opened it, she turned around. She could still distinctly feel the imprint of the hand on her face. "Thank you, Sister," she said. And she walked out.

Upstairs, she had barely walked into her room when Peggy and Dibbles rushed over. Tracey's expression must have shown some of her anger and humiliation, and the handprint on her face was still there, made more clear by the fact that she had gone very pale.

"Tracey!" Peggy exclaimed, forgoing the usual nickname.

"It's all right, it's all right," Tracey exclaimed, and she found them suddenly on either side of her, with Sheila and Diane very close. Her vision blurred over from tears, but at the realization that they were all so concerned, the tears went away again—and with them, some of the sting to her ego.

Everybody had been curious about what Mary had wanted, and when Tracey looked up, she saw some of the girls from across the hall in the doorway.

"I'm all right," she said. "Mary gave me a slap. That's all. It's over now."

Peggy surprised her by letting out a string of profanity, all of it directed against Sister Mary. Diane unceremoniously shut the door, affording them more privacy.

"Easy does it, Peggy," Tracey said. "Don't give her the satisfaction."

"No way," Dibbles agreed, pulling Tracey's coffeepot down and reaching for the coffee. "She only did it because she didn't know what else to do." She glanced at Tracey with some admiration. "How'd you do it, Jac? What theological question did you hand her?"

Tracey sank down to the floor and sat with her back against the lower bunk. Silently, looking almost frightened, Diane and Sheila hunted up the odds and ends of Tastykakes and pastries from Maddie. Peggy sat down by Tracey, upset, Tracey realized. It took a lot to shake Peggy out of her normally kindhearted and easy-going manner, and this had done it.

"Look, you guys, I did talk back to her," Tracey said. "I laughed in her face—"

Peggy jumped up, ran to the door, and swung it open. "Hey, you guys, she laughed in Mary's face!" she bawled. Tracey heard several other doors pop open in response.

"Peggy, shut that door and get back here!" Tracey exclaimed.

Peggy unwillingly did so.

Tracey sighed in exasperation. She had been wrong, and she already could imagine the tremendous scolding that Maddie would give her—if Maddie ever found out about this. Maddie, Tracey realized suddenly, would make her apologize to Sister Mary. Mothers like Maddie were always marching their kids up to front doors to make them apologize.

Her roommates and friends quickly arranged everything for a short consolation meeting before study time started, but Tracey had barely sipped her coffee and started on the pastry when there was a knock and the doorknob turned. The cakes were whisked out of sight. CPR poked her head inside.

"Jacamuzzi, down to the gym in five minutes," she said. "We've got to organize the equipment."

"Right, Sister," Tracey said. "I'm sorry I thought I was going down at seven."

"All right, seven, then. Finish your cupcakes." She gave them all a wry look before she left.

"Wonder if she's seen Mary," Peggy mumbled.

"Don't worry about it," Tracey told her. "CPR's never been keen on me, even without Mary's advice. The nicest thing she's ever done for me was when she asked me to try out for the team. That was my first day of school. It's been downhill ever since."

"CPR doesn't dislike you, Jac," Dibbles said, but Tracey remembered that Dibbles had always been a favorite of CPR.

Surprisingly, Dibbles must have read the thought, but she didn't get angry. "I mean it," she said. "CPR helped me a lot because I was so short compared to everybody else, but she was always telling me to ask you for your help. She kept telling me that you had good moves and could work with me on getting around."

Tracey cocked an eyebrow. "It doesn't really matter," she said. "Mary's already put the kibosh on my holding any office at all in the school. I can't be team captain. Maybe that's what CPR's going to tell me."

"I don't know—" Dibbles said in her singsong voice.

"Get your sweats on, anyway," Peggy said. "She might need you to do some work down there."

THIRTY - TWO

The spears and the banner had been rolled together and thrust in straight behind the trampoline in the gym's storeroom. As Tracey and CPR levered the spears out from the tangle of volleyball netting that had fallen back there, Tracey kept up a running narration in her head, listing every detail for Liz: the smell of the dust and of the old and weathered rubber from the assorted basketballs, soccer balls, and volleyballs. She glanced over and noted the field hockey sticks, each blade worn smooth with time and practice, their storage bag slightly torn. The storage room was a few degrees cooler than the rest of the gym.

"What a mess!" CPR exclaimed in disgust. "These were put back here in a hurry. The banner's ripped to pieces in the middle, and look at this spear—oh, look at both of them! Falling apart."

They unfurled the banner and looked at the ruin of what had once been their glory. One of the spears had been wet by rainwater that had leaked in. The cardboard blade fell away as they lifted the spear up, and its head was a sodden mess. The other spear simply looked old and unwieldy and very badly made.

"We can get new ones made," Tracey said.

CPR glanced at her.

"Maybe one of the town girls could get her dad to turn one on a lathe for us," Tracey suggested. "See how it looks. If we varnished it, we could say good-bye to these papier-mâché things forever."

"Maybe it is time for a new look," CPR said. "Those Bandits last year outdid us with that welcome routine of theirs."

"Villains," Tracey corrected.

"Villains," she agreed.

"But we won't be running into them this year, I don't think," Tracey said.

CPR glanced at her sharply. "You don't think so?"

"No, Sister, I don't." Tracey hoped another confrontation wasn't on the way.

But CPR offered her only a grim smile. She picked up a basketball. "Come out on the court with me."

CPR was still wearing her sweat suit from their earlier practice. Her hair was drawn back from her face in a ponytail, with only her dark bangs showing up front.

"Go on, block the basket," she directed.

Tracey went down and CPR brought the ball in. "Don't you dare foul me, miss. I'm still your teacher," the nun warned as she came into Tracey and Tracey gave with her, but just barely.

"Purposeful fouls are a sin," Tracey agreed briefly, intent on the moves of her coach. CPR tried to side-step around her and then tried a roll around the other side, but Tracey was too fast for her.

At last, desperate, the coach went back toward the

top of the key, turned, and shot. They both ran after the rebound. Tracey managed to block her out of the way while she got it herself. She came down and rolled around CPR, then outraced her down the court and shot from halfway up the key. She sank the ball.

"Bring it down, hotshot." CPR tossed it to her, and Tracey obediently came down the court with it. Before she got to the key, while CPR's guarding was more relaxed than it should have been, she managed to pull away and shoot. She sank it with a *whoosh*.

CPR ran after the ball to bring it in. They played for about fifteen minutes, until Tracey felt warmed up and able, and then past that, until both of them were nearly breathless, able to laugh, and able to make fun of each other and call each other lucky for the baskets they made. At last—and Tracey realized that CPR was tiring—they both jumped on a close shot that Tracey was making, right up by the basket. CPR's fingers pushed vainly against the ball, trying to keep it from going in, but Tracey's fingers pushed it past CPR's hand, and it rolled up to the rim and over it.

They landed almost on top of each other. The ball bounced away. Both of them leaned against the wall, panting for breath. Tracey had never come so close to dunking it, less than half a hand. She would have to write to Liz about how it felt—that ultimate stretching and reaching, so intent on outdoing the coach.

CPR, right alongside her on the wall, watched the ball as it rolled away. "Whoever plays like that has a good chance at the championships," she said. "Believe it, and it's yours."

She looked up at Tracey, and suddenly she had never

seemed so accessible, so human, so nearly like any other person you might meet.

"Why have you never liked me?" Tracey asked.

The smile and good-natured chagrin left CPR's face. For a moment she looked dismayed, and then she turned serious. "I've always liked you," she said. "Come back to the storeroom. Get the ball, please."

Tracey obeyed and brought the ball in, not dribbling it, only carrying it. She came in and set the ball on the ball rack. CPR came out of her office, her breath regained. She held out one hand, and Tracey automatically opened her hand to take whatever the coach was handing her.

"Here is the key to the storeroom and office," CPR said. "I expect you to make sure that the spear—or spears—the banner, the sword and shield, and the stats book all get to the games, every game. No captain has ever failed once in doing that, and I'm leaving it up to you to see that you get it done for every game this season. I know you won't ruin a perfect record of responsibility and faithfulness."

"I can't be team captain, Sister," Tracey told her.

"Why not?" CPR asked. She looked up at Tracey with a look of sorrow that seemed genuine. "Do you really think I don't like you, Tracey?"

"Well, I did," Tracey told her. "But that's not it. Sister Mary has told me I can't be team captain."

"But, dear, you are team captain," CPR said. "You have the key. As long as you have the key, you are the captain."

Tracey put the key in her pocket.

"And here is a whistle that Liz left for you," CPR

said. "She used it sometimes when she was helping me run drills."

Tracey took the whistle with a sense of reverence. "Does this get passed on too?" she asked.

"No, dear. It's yours," CPR told her. "Liz knew she wouldn't be here for this, but she took a generous amount of credit for it, so she wanted to leave a memento."

Tracey smiled, remembering her friend.

"I'm sorry I've seemed curt," CPR told her, and Tracey lost the smile. "I wish . . . I wish now that I had done things differently." She put her hand on Tracey's shoulder and almost grasped it, but she didn't.

"Well, I had a big mouth," Tracey conceded. "I'm just glad you let me play."

"You never seemed to have a big mouth to me," CPR said. "But I do like you, and I want you to be team captain. You deserve it."

"I'll be a good captain for you, Sister," she promised.

For a moment they regarded each other, and then CPR said, "Come on, let's work out what to do about these spears."

"I'm glad the sword and shield are OK," Tracey said.

When Tracey came back to the hall that night, she was full of a secret, and not about her captaincy. She knew that this was no time to crow over that. She would have to wait and see what Mary did. She returned to her room and stayed there until after study time, then ran down to Trish's room.

"CPR wants us to get some money together for Peggy to get shoes," she whispered to Trish. "Father Williams said he would match whatever donations we make, so we figure twenty-five dollars will be enough."

Trish nodded and hunted through her purse for her money. Tracey had only been able to put in two dollars, and that had been pretty dear, but Trish came up with five.

As captain, Tracey was in charge of the money, but all she had to do was slip the envelope under CPR's door each night. Trish did not ask how Tracey had come to be the collector for the money. So far, her appointment as captain was a secret. The girls would find out in the morning when the list was posted. Tracey already knew that she was captain and Dibbles was alternate. She also knew that Peggy was the other first-string guard. Trish and Hilary Stetson would be the forwards, and Tracey would be playing center. But she was sworn to silence until the list came out.

It was her responsibility to bequeath the sword and shield to someone else now that she was captain. This choice was hard. Trish was as kindhearted as Peggy, though not—as far as the sword and shield were concerned—brave enough. The real choice lay between Peggy and Dibbles. Both of them had shrugged off all of the pressures to play games with their popularity. They were both too decent to go along with the system of tormenting narcs and of forcibly maintaining the status quo. And they had both worked hard for their positions on the team. They were honest, they were straight, and they were loyal.

But, Tracey realized, Dibbles already had the title of alternate captain, and she owed that position to Peggy. Peggy had been the one to continually encourage Dibbles to try out for the team and to practice, and

Peggy had introduced her to all of the other players before Dibbles had even been on the team.

And it was Peggy, long ago, Tracey remembered, who had first toasted Tracey with a salute "to all good Valkyries and true," as though somewhere in Peggy there also lay that necessary respect and reverence for the idea of the Valkyrie.

But more than that, the memory that settled the matter on Peggy's behalf was of an incident even longer ago, when Peggy had risked her own safety as a neutral and ignorant freshman to warn Tracey about the Deep Six. Now, in retrospect, Tracey wondered how she had dared to do it. All Tracey had been back then was trouble, sheer trouble with no guarantee of being anything but trouble. But Liz had wisely chosen Peggy to carry the warning. It now seemed wisest to let her carry the sword and shield.

Breakfast the next morning was lively as the girls waited for seven-fifteen to come so they could run down to the gym and see the list. Even Tracey felt a certain anxiety. A lot could happen between evening and morning. Suppose they got down there to find that somebody else was team captain? Suppose CPR came to her during first hour to take the key back?

She joined the crowd running down the hill to the gym, but the list read exactly as CPR had told her the previous night. Tracey's name appeared at the top, starred, with Dibbles's right below her. And right below Dibbles's name was Peggy's.

"I did it! I did it!" Peggy yelled. "First-string!" She jumped up and came down on both Tracey and Dibbles.

"Don't start the season by breaking our arms!" Tracey yelped, and the three of them ran back up the hill together, tangled up in backslapping, laughing, and yelling.

It feels so good (she wrote to Liz) to be a member of a group of friends, as long as the friends are good friends, friends like Valkyries. Sometimes I think, why aren't you here, Liz? But then, Dibbles and Peggy and you and I all played together last season, too. Why didn't I appreciate it then? Being friends with you has always been great, but why did I just wake up now to seeing how much Peggy has done for me, and how much fun Dibbles can be? If you were here, it would be perfect, but now I'll tell you about the plan to get Peggy some good basketball shoes. . . .

One other surprise about Tracey's senior year was that some of her classes were not nearly as difficult as they had been. Her English class was almost entirely a review of grammar, though it included a research paper next semester. Latin IV was mostly translation work, but the class was organized around group projects and cross-checking. There was very little outside work, except for brushing up on vocabulary and some of the less commonly used rules. But Tracey had always been good in Latin, and she was familiar with the rules and vocabulary.

Her ethics class required a series of short papers, and St. Bernard had a book list for them to read, but Tracey looked forward to the work in that class. She had an idea that she might have to call upon Maddie and Maddie's pastor for help, but she also knew that St. Bernard would be keenly interested in her papers. She and St. Bernard might clash over plain doctrine, but they each enjoyed the other's applications of her beliefs.

Tracey's absolute worst classes would be chemistry

and calculus. Liz had promised her that calculus was not nearly as hard as geometry had been, but then, Liz was good at math. People who were good at math were always pooh-poohing the fears of people who weren't.

Tracey was also in her fourth year of Spanish, and that course included outside readings in Spanish. They would be tackling part of *Don Quixote*. Several of the girls had already listened to *Man of La Mancha* in preparation, and several others had read the translation of the book.

The classes that morning were buzzing with the news of who had made the team. Tracey saw several freshmen grouped around Hilary Stetson. She felt a slight twinge of apprehension. "I'm Scooter squared," Liz had once boasted to her. In the sense of skill, that had been true. But Hilary really seemed to be Scooter squared—bold, aggressive, and probably cruel. Tracey felt no guilt for making such an assessment so early. There was something about the set of Hilary's eyes and lips: a look of brazen ambition and willfulness that Tracey had never seen on a freshman's face. Even when she had seen it in the faces of older girls like Rita Jo and Susan, it had only been when they were plotting something especially mean and vicious.

Hilary's instant promotion to the first-string had probably done her more harm than good, and it would do harm to every freshman.

"Hey, I hear you're captain!" Hilary suddenly called out to her, noticing Tracey's preoccupied stare.

"Yeah," Tracey said, and she walked away. Deliberately. Let the other freshmen see that she was not impressed with Hilary and that she would not back Hilary in any schemes.

She had not yet told Liz much about Hilary, nor had she said anything to Maddie. There were other matters to take up her thoughts.

At lunchtime, Tracey, Dibbles, and Peggy all sat together, their persons now sacrosanct. But Tracey waved Amy and Regina over when she saw them. Trish Roberts, hesitant at being a pink blouse among so many yellow blouses, hung back until Peggy called out to her.

"There's our new forward," Tracey greeted her.

"And our new captain!" Trish exclaimed.

"So much for the prognostications of Sister Mary!" Dibbles sang. "She must have cracked her crystal ball when she looked into it!"

"But it sure does surprise me, all the same," Tracey said. "She's never made an empty threat before—usually what she says, goes."

Amy looked up suddenly but then went back to her eating.

"I heard the spears are pretty messed up," Peggy ventured.

Tracey nodded. "One of the senior town girls said her dad can make us a real nice wooden spear and paint it and all for us. So we're going to give it a try."

"Only one?" Peggy asked.

Tracey nodded. "CPR wants to try one and use a cloth banner on it, a smaller one. She and Sister Theresa have got some new routine worked out."

"Who carries the sword and shield?" Amy asked. She was scribbling something into her memo book.

"That's for Tracey to know and the team to find out," Dibbles told her.

"Have the team come up to my room tonight," Tracey ordered. "I'll pass it on after supper."

There were no more questions after that. But as they stood up to leave, Tracey saw that someone had dropped a note onto her tray. She put it into her pocket, and after she had left the dining hall, she stopped to read it.

I heard something in the classroom last night. I want to tell you first.

Amy

Amy still worked as Sister Madeleine's helper, grading papers and doing some cleaning in the classrooms. It earned her pocket money and had been extremely useful for spying and gossiping purposes. She had contributed vital information to the team before, as well as numerous tidbits of information that had fueled many rumors. Small, serious, and industrious, Amy gave adults the impression that they could speak freely in front of her. They never suspected that she would have the imagination to carry tales back to the girls.

Tracey's classes ended at three o'clock that day. She went to the gym to practice before the official practice began, and she also retrieved the sword and shield to take to her room that night.

The team's official practice was another scrimmage, as CPR introduced all of the girls to the strategies they would be using. To Tracey's surprise, the coach pulled out more of the first-string players than second-string, and she spent most of her time showing the second-string girls ways to improve their dribbling, shooting, and passing. It was almost like a cuts practice instead of a team practice.

But then, so many of the second-string girls were brand-new, Tracey realized. She noticed that Father Williams had come in and gone up to the balcony. CPR put all of the first-string back in and divided them up with second-string girls to make the red team and white team. They played for about eight minutes, and even Tracey was satisfied to see that the second-string did seem to be improving. It was just such a different game this year. Again and again, as she watched Peggy shooting from way outside the key, she felt a familiar tenseness before she jumped to rebound. But Peggy sank most of her shots.

Tracey could also shoot and sink from outside the key, but her form was closer to the textbook style than Peggy's, closer to the standard for basketball players. Peggy shot almost as though she were chest-passing. But she could score. And she could do hook shots if she could get to the right spot on the floor. Tracey had never dared try a hook shot in a real game.

They ended practice a half hour before dinner. After a hurried shower, Tracey went down to Amy's room.

"I thought you might show up," Amy greeted her.

"Come on down to my room," Tracey said. She still had her robe on and had to change. "Or is this a secret conference?"

"No big secret." Amy followed her out.

"I was cleaning one of the classrooms last night," she began as Tracey hurried to put on navy blue socks, a slip, and the yellow blouse. "And Sister St. Gerard was in there, you know, grading papers or doing her rolls or something. Then she looked up at the door and hurried out. So I thought maybe something had come up about your meeting with Sister Mary. I still hadn't washed the blackboards, so I got the sponge and bucket and did that, and that put me right by the door—"

"What a trickster!" Tracey exclaimed in admiration.

"Well, it was CPR, not Sister Mary," Amy said. "And she sounded upset—talking real fast and low."

"Could you hear words?"

"Yes, some. She said something about 'did it anyway,' and 'she has the key now.' And then St. Gerard said it was CPR's decision and nobody else's, and it was a reflection of skill, and skill only. Then CPR asked her what might happen next, and St. Bernard was telling her not to worry. They talked about maybe somebody getting into trouble, but St. Gerard kept saying that everybody expected this. She said it was only fair, and she mentioned Father Williams."

"They never mentioned my name?" Tracey asked. She reached for her skirt.

"No, but I bet it was the whole thing over who would be team captain," Amy told her. "I think CPR started to cry."

"Oh, come on, Amy. Why would CPR cry?"

Amy shook her head and flushed a little under Tracey's scorn, but she stuck to her story. "I think she started to cry. I'm serious. I heard St. Gerard's voice get real soft and sympathetic, and it seemed like CPR was choked up—like she couldn't keep talking."

But Tracey dismissed the idea. "I know that St. Bernard and Mary don't get along," she said. "Anyway, I've suspected it for a long time. Maybe St. Bernard used this whole mess to get CPR on her side against Mary."

"What could CPR have done if you weren't team

captain?" Amy asked. "All of the girls would have been mad at her."

Tracey's mind went back to the night when she and CPR had argued in front of the team. The team, so quick to find hypocrisy in a teacher, had shunned CPR immediately. They had not noticed that Tracey herself had acted like a big baby, Tracey remembered.

The only other likely candidates for captain that year would have been Peggy and Dibbles, and both of them, Tracey was sure, would have refused the captaincy. After all, she had trained both of them herself, and they were loyal to her and smart enough to see through Mary's politics. No, it would have been a big mess if CPR had not picked her as team captain, and St. Bernard had probably driven that point home, whatever her motives.

Besides, Tracey realized, all of the teachers wanted the team to do well. MoJoe was unusual in that the faculty as well as the students were truly involved with basketball. Though it was a matter of discretion never to mention it, Tracey knew perfectly well that Father Williams bet on the Valkyries at every game, wagering against the headmasters or principals of the other schools. That was how he had afforded the pizza party last year, and that was probably how he would pay for his half of Peggy's shoes. Tracey knew the priest would never wager huge sums of money, but the friendly betting that went on symbolized the sense of pride that all of these men had in their respective teams.

Had anything upset the team this season, it would have been public and apparent, not only to Father Williams, but to the headmasters and principals of the other schools as well. And Father Williams would never have permitted such a disruption to continue. His own honor and reputation were tied up in the Valkyries somehow. If CPR had not picked Tracey as captain, and if the seniors on the team had complained to Father Williams, she was pretty sure he would have overruled CPR to save the morale of the team.

"I guess," she said at last as she pulled on her bolero and checked the pockets, "that it was for the best that CPR did what she did—even for CPR's best. I never thought much about how she gets caught in the middle."

Amy didn't know enough about the inner workings of the team to comment. Tracey nodded that she was ready, and they went down to supper together.

That Saturday, at Maddie's, Tracey was uncomfortable and restless. She had told Maddie about the team, and Maddie had seemed pleased at the news. After their lunch, she and Tracey worked on polishing the silver together, a time that they normally used to talk, and that Tracey liked better than most chores.

At last Maddie said, "Tracey, is something on your mind?"

"Yeah," Tracey said, and she sighed. It was hard to have to tell Maddie the bad things about herself. Maddie looked at her expectantly. Tracey said, "I've sinned, Maddie. I got punished for it, but I did sin, and I guess I should tell you."

"All right, then," Maddie said seriously.

"I laughed at Sister Mary," Tracey told her. "Right to her face. I just laughed at her and talked back to her."

"Oh, Tracey, what did you say?" Maddie asked.

"She told me I was a megalomaniac—what does that mean, anyway?—and she said that she could make the school year miserable for me, and then I laughed at her and told her to go ahead and try."

Maddie made a sound of surprise, but her eyes looked thoughtful. "Did you apologize to her?" she asked.

Tracey's cheeks burned at the suggestion. "No, of course not," she said.

"Well, you've got to, dear."

"But, Maddie, she slapped me. Wasn't that enough?"

Maddie looked startled at that, but she quickly said, "No, it's not enough at all. Whatever Sister Mary does to you must not affect your respect for her position as an adult. I don't think the slap was right, dear. If it's corporal punishment she wants, it needs to be done on your backside and not your face. But you must make your disrespect right with her, and be respectful."

S ister Mary?" Tracey asked, walking slowly and hesitantly into the office.

Though Mary had responded to her knock on the heavy door with a call to come in, she looked stunned at Tracey's appearance. Her surprise was quickly replaced with a look of disfavor.

"I have no time for you now."

"It won't take long, Sister," Tracey promised.

"What is it?"

Tracey drew in her breath and said, "I am very sorry for having talked back to you. It was disrespectful, and I am sorry."

"Very well. Leave at once," Mary said, and she went back to whatever she was working on at her desk. Tracey slipped out. Mary's curtness was humiliating, but overall her response was much more mild than Tracey had expected.

Long ago, during her summer residences, Tracey had gathered various bits of plunder left behind by the other boarders. She had boxes filled with mixtures of various brands of laundry powder, plastic bottles brim-ful with multicolored shampoo leftovers all mixed together, endless assortments of half-used toothpaste tubes, and various other odds and ends that she had scavenged when her money from home had dwindled. She could also have had innumerable stale cigarettes, matchbooks, and other less legal paraphernalia, but she had settled on hoarding only what was proper and expected.

Among her treasures were several white candles, left over from a power failure long ago and forgotten in a storage box up in one of the rooms where she had catalogued books. These now came in handy. She had envisioned making the passing of the sword and shield mysterious, lovely, and secret. If she'd had her way, they would all have enacted the ceremony hooded or dressed in white, but nothing could be perfect. She settled on turning her roommates out until study time, making the room as dark as possible, and mounting the candles in empty pop bottles.

She pushed back one of the bunkbeds to make more room in the center of the floor. When she lit the candles, their glow lent a secretive, mysterious air to the room. The flames were reflected in the sword and shield, which leaned against the built-in dresser.

Tracey heard her teammates congregating out in the hall. Dibbles had strict orders not to let them in until exactly 6:30, and there were suppressed whispers outside as they waited to come in.

No doubt the other students would be watching them with a mixture of enjoyment and envy, and this was exactly what Tracey wanted. In previous years, the team had used its influence to bully people into obeying them and falling into line, but she had already decided that she would pull the school after the team through sheer desire and admiration.

At last everything was ready, and the clock read 6:30. Dibbles tentatively knocked. Tracey put on the shield and took up the sword, and she called, "Come in, and come in quietly."

The girls on the team silently entered—most of them, anyway. They looked around at the dark room with the candles lit, and Tracey standing in her black warm-up suit with the sword and shield. One of the second-string girls silently shut the door.

"Where are the others?" Tracey asked. "The freshmen?" There was a boarding freshman who was a second-stringer, and Hilary, of course, was first-string. The three town girls on the team were not present, but they were not expected to be.

"We don't know," Dibbles said. "We told them we were having a meeting. I thought they would be here."

"This is something freshmen don't understand," Tracey said grimly. "It's time to pass on the sword and shield, and all of you know that the school left that up to me. Now it's my turn to leave it to somebody else. Whoever is chosen will wear this into the games, and she's expected to be the example of the Valkyrie to the rest of the team."

Everybody nodded. It was a solemn moment, but all of them were enjoying it mightily. Nobody was in a hurry.

"I had a hard time making the decision, but I think that I've made my choice based strictly on what I was told to do. Both Debbie Dibbley and I owe our positions on the team to this person, and I can remember my freshman year, how she promised me she would never laugh at me or ridicule me if it turned out that I couldn't play ball well."

Dibbles nodded slightly, recognizing Tracey's choice and consenting to it. For once, the short girl had no humorous comment to make, and Tracey saw that she was genuinely glad for her friend.

"This person never has ridiculed any student to my knowledge, never has hung back from doing the right thing, never has been afraid, even when we were losing on the court. Peggy, the sword and shield belong to you." She tapped Peggy on the front of the shoulder with the sword. "You know better than most people where I've failed, but it's my duty to encourage you not to fail. At the end of this school year, you will pass these on to the next worthy person on the team—second-string or first-string, it doesn't matter."

Peggy nodded her head in agreement. Tracey handed her the sword, hilt first, and then took the shield off and gave it to her. Peggy fitted the shield over her arm and looked at the rest of the team, her face slightly flushed.

"Come on, girls, let's let the others know our choice!" Tracey exclaimed. "Trish, get her other side!"

The girls cheered. She and Trish would have picked Peggy up, but just then there was a pounding on the door, and Amy's voice: "Tracey! Tracey!"

Those nearest the door threw it open and switched the lights on.

"They've got some freshman down in the john—" Amy began, her face white as ashes.

"Someone blow out these candles. And come with me," Tracey ordered. "I know who it'll be down there!"

285

She burst out of the room and ran down to the bathroom. None of the sisters were up on the hall. Some smart freshman had figured out that they usually lingered over their coffee or work until they had to come up to enforce study time at seven.

Seven members of the basketball team running down the hall was enough to make doors pop open. A sophomore with an ugly, acne-scarred face and a tough expression stood at the bathroom door. She had been directing people to use other bathrooms, but she started up when she saw the group of predominantly upper-classmen bearing down on her.

"Hanger-on!" Tracey exclaimed. "Just like Susan with Scooter!" Only Peggy would have understood the reference, but they all understood when Tracey grabbed the girl by both shoulders and pushed her out of the way.

"You'd better learn who to really be afraid of in this school!" Tracey said before she went in.

Tracey threw the door back. It hit the countertop with a crash and sprang back, but her arm was in the way, blocking it, as she and the others charged in.

"They're in the far stall!" Dibbles exclaimed as they all stopped for a second to scan the showers and stalls.

Tracey reached it in two strides, pulled the door outward, and plucked out the first two freshmen her hands found: Hilary and another girl. She hauled them out bodily. It was as though electricity were flowing through her. She didn't know if anger had made her stronger, or if she had just never realized how strong she was.

"Shut the bathroom door!" she exclaimed to Trish

as she pulled the two girls out. "Don't let them out of here!" Trish obediently closed the bathroom door all the way and stood against it.

One more girl was kneeling by the toilet, forcing the head of another girl inside.

Tracey pulled the captor out with the same wrenching motion. She flung her toward the rest of the team, recognizing the girl as the freshman on second-string. "And don't let her out, either!" she exclaimed.

"Oh, let me go! Let me go!" the girl inside pleaded with Tracey. "What did I do? What did I do?"

Her hair and face were dripping wet. How many times she had been held under, Tracey did not know. Most girls who were given "swirlys" came out red-faced from the cold water, but this girl's face was as white as a fish.

"I won't hurt you," Tracey said. "Come out. Can you stand up?"

She shook her head and burst out crying.

"Come on, we'll go to my room," Tracey said.

"Why? What for?"

"Come on," she said again, and when she got her arms under the girl's armpits, the freshman let her help her up.

On standing, the girl regained some of her composure and some of her color. "What are you doing?" she asked Tracey.

"I'm going to make a deal with you," Tracey said, putting an arm around the girl's shoulders. "And from now on, anybody who's after you will have to be after me too."

She helped the girl out of the stall.

Peggy's face was white, and Dibbles also looked

startled and a little angry. They glanced at Tracey for direction.

"Well, freshmen," Tracey said to the three she had pulled out. "Seven of us against three of you. What do you think of these odds?"

"Why don't you mind your own business?" Hilary snapped.

Though Peggy and Debbie looked as disgusted and angry as Tracey, most of the second-string girls who had come down with the team looked frightened. Tracey wasn't sure that they would obey her.

"Who will give these three a taste of their own medicine?" she asked.

"I will," Peggy said.

"I will," Dibbles said.

Trish and another girl nodded.

"If the rest of you are afraid, then just block the door," Tracey told them. "But hazing is over now. Nobody picks on anybody else in these halls. Do it," she ordered. "Just once for each. We won't be as bad to them as they were to her."

Dibbles and Peggy both grabbed Hilary and went into a stall with her. What she said before her face went into the water could not be printed in a letter to Liz, Tracey decided. But the other two freshmen stood mutely and without struggle, overcome by the importance and sheer numbers of their upperclassman adversaries— and perhaps demoralized by the quick defeat of their leader. Tracey, Dibbles, and Peggy had somehow known without a word to each other or to Hilary that she was the leader.

The toilet flushed, and then Hilary was flung out of the stall and the next girl pushed in. A moment later

288

there was another flush, and she was pushed out. The last went in, tears on her face by this time from the shame of the punishment, and she too was quickly dealt with.

"Now, throw them out of here!" Tracey exclaimed.

They opened the bathroom door and pushed each one out into the hall. Amy was out there, waiting to see what happened, and other girls stood in their doorways, watching.

The ignominious ejection of three freshmen, each one dripping wet down to the shoulders, produced laughs of appreciation and a few words of derision.

"All clear," Peggy whispered back to Tracey, and Tracey nodded that the team should leave. Peggy had come with the sword and shield, setting them on the bathroom countertop as things had escalated. She retrieved them, and Tracey said, "Peggy, lead the way back to my room, will you?"

So she did. Their silent walk back to Tracey's room, which was at the very end of the hall, by the back stairs, was answered by silence from the girls in their doorways. Tracey held onto the arm of the freshman they had rescued—an acquaintance of Diane's, she now realized—and she fixed her eyes and face with a look of grim determination. The lines had been drawn. She was resolved to pick up the fight she had begun as a freshman, and to finish it.

Now look, I'm not grilling you or interrogating you to hurt you," Tracey said in the privacy of her room. "I just want to know—has Sister Mary ever called you into her office?"

"Never!" Diane exclaimed on her friend's behalf.

"Diane," Tracey said.

"Never, honest, never!" the girl exclaimed. Her name was Elizabeth.

"They just say she's weird!" Diane added.

"Diane!" Tracey exclaimed. "Would you let her talk?"

Elizabeth started to cry again. "They just thought it would be funny," she said. "But I told them I would tell, and then they called me a narc and got mad at me—" She cried harder, too hard to talk any more, and when she could talk, she exclaimed, "I want to go back home! I hate this place!"

"Take it easy," Tracey said, standing up. Sheila and Diane glanced at her, startled by the tone of her voice. "Tomorrow after the team practice, I want you to meet me at the outside hoop."

"I can't play basketball!" Elizabeth cried. "Look at me!"

"I didn't say you were going to try out for the team," Tracey told her. "Haven't you ever played PIG or POISON?"

"Well, yeah," Elizabeth said, looking up at her.

"Then come play with me. And Dibbles and Peggy. Wear your blouse and skirt if you want. We won't break a sweat, just toss the ball around."

"Are we allowed to?" Elizabeth asked.

"I got the key to the storeroom. As long as I got the key, we can do it," Tracey promised.

"Just you guys and Elizabeth?" Sheila asked.

"Us guys and any freshmen who want to," Tracey said. "You two ought to come too. We'll have a good time."

Peggy and Dibbles were not quite as enthusiastic about the idea as the three freshmen were, but they agreed to shower quickly after practice and stand around under the hoops to play some rounds of PIG with the freshmen who wanted to.

"This is PR," Tracey told them. "Public relations. And any freshman who has a problem can come tell us on the court."

"If you say so, Jac," Dibbles exclaimed ruefully. "Up with Utopia!"

"Not Utopia—Valhalla," Tracey corrected her.

Her next letter to Liz burgeoned with the story of all that had happened. She could feel that same white-hot electricity passing through her as she wrote: anger, indignation, decision, strength. She knew now what it was to be so angry that she was in perfect control of herself, so angry that each muscle interaction func-

291

tioned better than normal, with power and strength radiating out from her solar plexus, pounding strength and sureness into her arms and hands and mind.

I'll make these halls the halls of Valhalla. It will begin in my room and radiate out until we make the girls like Hilary afraid to overstep themselves. Peggy and Debbie Dibbley are sick of all the cliques and trouble and hazing too. For just one year, I'd like to see everybody free to be herself without having to answer to the new Scooters, Susans, Rita Jos, etc.

Liz's speedy reply, which came an amazing six days later, cooled Tracey slightly and gave her back a touch of reality.

You'll never be more savage than a savage. Anyway, I hope not. You can't beat them at their own game. I roared when I read what you did in the bathroom, it was so funny, but you won't win that way. Sounds to me like Hilary will stoop lower than you will. I'm afraid you'll have to rely on your Christianity. Sounds funny, me telling you that, but Jesus is on my side. He's the One who said to love your enemies. You did it with Scooter, by the end. Don't stop now.

Liz was right. Again, it amazed Tracey that this girl of supposedly no religious convictions could reason with her so effectively from what Tracey herself knew to be true.

Still, what can I do? she asked the Lord. *Didn't You command Jehu to throw down Jezebel and kill the prophets of Baal? How can I fight people who use violence without using violence myself? How can I win against them without humiliating them? It's the only thing that makes them respect me.*

But she realized that no authority had been given to her to do what she had done. It had been one gang against the other in the bathroom that night. Her only real authority lay in having the key to the storeroom and the freedom to play PIG and POISON with the freshmen. It hardly seemed like enough. There would always be cruel people eager to find ways to get around her, as soon as they figured she would not use all the means and tactics open to her.

Only You can change people's hearts, she prayed. *I can't make them leave the younger and smaller and uglier kids alone unless You change hearts—or unless You make them behave through fear of You, if not through love of You.*

* * *

The spear and the cloth banner were finished in time for the first game. CPR brought it into the gym after practice one day and unwrapped it. All of the girls crowded around to admire the handiwork of the new emblem.

Like the old spears, it was taller than any of them, taller even than Tracey. The spearhead itself was merely a carved part of the whole, but the man who had made it for them had designed it to look as though it fit into grooves on the top of the spear, and he had wrapped a leather thong around it for effect. It was adorned with scrollwork and runic work down one side, and it had several painted bands around it, done to look like metal. He had also adorned it with black and white ribbons, some straight and flowing, and others curling in long ringlets.

"It's beautiful," Tracey said amid the *ooh's* and *aah's* of the Valkyries. CPR handed it to her. She passed it around for all of them to admire. Even Hilary did not disdain to stand among them and finger the runes carved into it.

"And here's the banner," CPR said, unfolding the long triangle of felt. It had a white background with black trim, and it bore the familiar silhouette of a Valkyrie on horseback against a scarlet shield.

"You'll have to come out waving it and twirling it," CPR told her. "Some of the girls here have been cheer-leaders—some of them do cheers for the boys' prep schools around here. Get them to show you a good way to bring it in."

"Uh-oh, Tracey's going to be a cheerleader!" Dibbles exclaimed. Everybody laughed.

Tracey actually felt herself blushing, but she grinned and said, "Not on your life. As long as there's drums and trumpets, I think I'll do just fine with some basic twirls and waves. And then I stand with it diago-nally, right? So the girls can run under the lower point of the banner?"

"Sounds good," CPR told her. "Peggy will run out right after you and stand alongside you."

"Then me, then me!" Dibbles exclaimed. Every-body laughed again.

"Then you, show-off," CPR said affectionately.

"Well, it's about time for some PIG," Tracey said with a glance at her watch. "Anybody else coming to play?"

"PIG for the pigs," Hilary muttered.

Dibbles and Peggy had looked ready to make excuses and get out of it, but at Hilary's remark they both nodded, and Trish said, "I'd like to come along if you don't mind, Jac."

"Sure, come on. Why should I mind?" Tracey asked.

"Well, it kind of looks like seniors and freshmen only out there."

"We'll get that straightened out today, then, when you show up!"

It was fastest and most convenient for them to get cleaned up and back into uniforms right away, before PIG or POISON. It was always cool right before dinner, and the games were not strenuous. Tracey spent most of her time showing the freshman girls how to shoot, or she clowned around with the basketball when it was her turn. They played only on Tuesdays and Thursdays, and so far the games had been a success. Tracey worked on recruiting new girls to come and play, and it was hard for them to turn down such a good social opportunity. Playing basketball with a senior who was captain of the team—as well as with her upperclassman friends—was a chance to leave the troubles and pressure of the hall behind.

Peggy and Dibbles became bored with the project at times, but Trish seemed interested. She often advised Tracey on whom to ask along, though she had never played herself until that day.

The game always lasted for about twenty minutes, and then everyone went to supper, while Tracey ran back to put the ball away and raced up to the halls to be on time.

Her humiliation of Hilary had also set a very good

example, and Tracey began to doubt her need to have repented so much from that one judicious act of violence. Hilary gave her a wide berth, and the sight of Tracey or of the upperclassmen on the basketball team did a great deal to cheer up most of the freshmen, a sign to Tracey that many quiet little initiations had been stopped by her quick actions.

Tracey went where she pleased in the halls, using the same brisk breeziness that Liz had taught her. Her religious beliefs were well-known, and she sensed that most of the girls admired her, if only for being a nonconformist who had successfully bucked the system. She recalled marveling at how the girls had repeated stories about Liz, but now she realized that they were repeating stories about her—stories that revealed their admiration. The tale of how Mary had slapped her had gotten around in several different versions, all of them indicting Mary as the villain. And rumor had it that Tracey had conspired with Liz on the historic mousetrap trick, although she hadn't. She tried to convince some of the students that she'd known nothing about it, but it was of no use.

One thing was gratifying to Tracey: The other students believed that she truly was a Christian. The fact that some of her previous behavior had been entirely against Christian practice either went unnoticed or did not bother them, and any confessions she made only made them respect her more. They compared the sisters to her and found them wanting; they talked about the politics in the school, in the Vatican, and in the Roman Catholic Church, but they said that Tracey was genuine.

Tracey knew how ungenuine she had been, how

many times she had failed, but she couldn't make any answer to these claims on her behalf. To deny them, she feared, would be to deny her faith. To accept them would be dishonest. The best thing she could think to do was turn the conversation back to God Himself, and such a technique—disappointingly—usually ended the conversation. Unless the Lord had some plan to strike down Sister Mary, nobody was much interested in Him.

Hey, Maddie, look at the new spear!" Tracey called, running over the grass with the spear to show her.

"My, what a lovely job!" Maddie exclaimed, running her hand up the scrollwork.

"And this is for you!" Tracey hugged her hello.

"Oh, that was nice."

The other girls streamed past, greeting Maddie as they went.

"I hope you've got the stats book and other things, Miss Jacamuzzi," CPR said.

"Dibbles has the stats book, and Peggy has the sword and shield," Tracey assured her. "Here are the spear and banner."

"Well, get them on board, then."

"Can we get pizza this Saturday?" Tracey asked Maddie.

"Oh, I was counting on it," Maddie said with a smile, another brief hug, and a tug for luck on Tracey's bangs. Tracey climbed aboard, barely aware that Hilary had been watching this transaction.

She stored the spear safely across the last two seats, then came up to the front of the bus to join her teammates.

"Us against St. Bede's," she exclaimed happily. "I feel lucky tonight."

"Here we go, MoJoe, here we go," Peggy sang.

The others joined in, "Here we go, MoJoe, here we go!"

There followed a complicated clapping routine, and then the beat changed. "Go, go, go Mo-Joe! Wahoo! Go, go, go Mo-Joe!"

Tracey got up and danced down the aisle, stamping her feet hard and clapping. They sang the whole round again, and then Dibbles came down. Peggy followed, and the rest of the team went down the aisle one by one.

When they had finished, breathless and cheered up, they sang some of the older songs and cheers from previous years. At last, Tracey went up to the very front to sit behind Maddie and keep her company.

"It's been a busy week, Maddie," she said.

"Has it, dear? Was it pleasant?"

"Was yours pleasant?" Tracey asked.

"Hmm, nice enough. I missed you, how's that?" She glanced at Tracey in the rearview mirror.

"Maddie, I apologized to Sister Mary, but she wasn't very impressed," Tracey said.

"Well, we can't change Sister Mary," Maddie told her. "But you've still got to do your part."

Tracey leaned forward. "Even if I got into trouble, though, you'd still have me over and everything, wouldn't you?"

"Yes," Maddie said. "You belong to me now."

"And you'd never slap me, would you?"

Maddie's eyes widened and darted up to the mirror. "Merciful heaven, what put that into your head?"

"I just want to know if you would ever hit me," Tracey said. "Did you hit your children?"

"Not nearly enough, I'm afraid," Maddie said gravely, her eyes fixed on the road. "I spoiled them."

"Spanking, you mean," Tracey said.

"Yes, dear, spanking. I hope I would never slap anybody," Maddie said.

"But you did spank, sometimes," Tracey added.

"Yes," Maddie said with a nod. She glanced up at the mirror.

"When did you stop spanking them?" Tracey asked.

"Too early," Maddie said again, very ruefully.

"This sounds like I've stepped into your life at a great time," Tracey told her. "Just when you decide that kids need more spankings. I think I've been hit enough. I don't like it."

Startled, Maddie looked up again. "Why would I spank you? Oh, a great girl of sixteen—"

"Seventeen," Tracey corrected.

"No, dear, I'd not spank you. You're too old."

"Well, what would you do?" Tracey asked.

"Tracey," Maddie said, sounding slightly exasperated, "I'd never send you away. And I expect that the sisters would punish you for anything you've done on campus."

"OK," Tracey said. Then she asked, "Are you mad at me?"

Maddie let out a loud breath, but after a pause she started to laugh and raised her hand. Tracey leaned forward so Maddie could tug on her bangs. "You're driving me mad, scamp, but I'm not angry. Give me the song you love to sing."

Tracey did enjoy the hymns sung at Maddie's church. They were more formal than the few she could remember from her first Baptist church, and she thought them prettier than most of the Catholic hymns. While the girls on the bus were chattering away, it was easy and safe to quietly sing a few of the church songs with Maddie, to learn them better or just to enjoy them.

My song is love unknown,
My Savior's love to me;
Love to the loveless shown,
That they might lovely be.
O who am I, that for my sake
My Lord should take frail flesh and die?

Tracey normally sang the hymns in a very low voice so that only Maddie could hear her, and sometimes Maddie would sing along or hum the harmony. But that night Peggy crept closer, so quietly that Tracey didn't hear her until she had finished singing.

"I've heard you sing that before, Jac," Peggy said. "I wish you'd teach it to me, it's so pretty."

Peggy could pick out chords on a guitar, a talent of inestimable worth in Tracey's eyes.

"Sure," Tracey said. "But it's Protestant."

"Oh, I don't care. I'd just like to be able to sing it."

The trip to St. Bede's was not a long one, and soon the bus was pulling in. It was a night game, and there were several familiar cars parked together in a cluster on one side of the building. From the open doorway, the strains of trumpet music spilled out into the dimness.

301

"Everybody help with gear!" Tracey called as they leaped off the bus. Two girls took the water cooler, another the first-aid kit. Dibbles grabbed the stats book, and Tracey and Peggy brought the fanfare equipment.

They had little time to warm up. Tracey had one fleeting memory of Liz, from the first game against St. Bede's long ago in the MoJoe gym, and she felt a sudden, regretful wish that her best friend were with her again. Things had changed so quickly, and she had worked many of the changes herself.

Then they were back behind the double doors, two of the second-string girls at either door, everybody else crowded behind Tracey—the spear held in both her hands, gripped diagonally across her body.

The trumpets and trombones began the fanfare from *Rocky*, a tune the pep band had copied and perfected while Sister Theresa—blissfully unaware that it had been plagiarized from a current movie—had admired the tune and learned to play it herself.

Tracey burst out through the doors and into the hot, bright gym. The roar of approval greeted her, the drumming on the bleachers, waves and waves of hands, and the blare of the red trumpets. The pep band's big drum hammered out a welcome.

She almost forgot the routine that she had so painstakingly learned with the spear, but then she snapped into it—weaving the spear with its banner and ribbons in figure eights as she had seen the men in kung fu movies do it, then twirling with it herself, and finally waving it back and forth in the air like a standard—before she came to a stop in the middle of the floor and held it in front of her, the butt planted on the floor by her left shoe, the banner hanging way past her right shoulder so the girls could run under it.

Peggy came up behind her, clashing sword on shield. She was answered by the girls who had made their own copies of her equipment. The trumpet fanfare began again. Dibbles raced out and, to everyone's shock, came up between Peggy and Tracey with a cartwheel. She did another cartwheel and came up standing before the audience like Nadia Comaneci, the Olympic gymnast, arms up and hands open. With an effort, Tracey tried not to look shocked. Dibbles ran to her corner of the floor.

The other girls ran out as expected. Tracey came to center with the spear, but Peggy ran to the side to throw off her armor. The St. Bede's girls came out in formation. This year they sang their school song, and after they had finished—although protocol dictated that MoJoe should have sung theirs first—the girls from the Sanctuary sang theirs. The effect, as usual, was lovely and emotional.

Tracey ran to the MoJoe half of the court, and everybody crowded around to get their hands on the spear.

When they had all grasped it, she started the cheer, "He-e-e-y, let's go! Let's fight! Let's win!"

They all yelled, and she slid the spear over to the stats table, where Maddie was keeping time for them. Maddie smiled at her.

St. Bede's, if they had improved, had improved only marginally. But Tracey was surprised—pleasantly so—that CPR kept the first-string in for the entire first quarter. Dibbles and Peggy worked well together as guards, and Dibbles's timing was as great as always. If

Peggy was tied up, she was unfailingly able to get clear to pass to Tracey, and Tracey could usually jump from where she caught the pass and put the ball in. If not, Trish Roberts usually got close enough to rebound, and even Hilary did better at playing her zone or at switching off under the basket. Tracey knew that CPR had talked sternly with the freshman after she had made the comment about "PIG for pigs." CPR's rebukes could be galling, and Tracey sensed that such a rebuke, coming right on top of Hilary's humiliation in the bathroom, had cooled off the freshman's ambitions for the moment.

The team's biggest problem was that Dibbles was not able to shoot as much as she had in previous games. She had to stay out for Peggy's sake, getting the ball back to her and keeping control in the outer zone, instead of coming in to switch off for the long-post and short-post strategies.

Still, it was a thing of beauty to watch Dibbles move up the court. There was a humorous aspect to it—the pumping legs, red face, and basic comic air that Dibbles could not seem to lose. But she simply snaked around people, and it was amazing.

Dibbles even threw some flare into the game, popping the ball in a high arc ahead of Tracey, so Tracey had to run for it, come up under it, and give it a second high pop to put it in the basket. Such a stunt was a real crowd pleaser, but they could do it only when the zone was clear. And Tracey wasn't sure that CPR wouldn't bawl them out for it when they got back to the bench. They did it twice in the first quarter, and the crowd roared its approval each time.

CPR did switch them out for the next quarter, but

she told them they would play again. In the meantime, the second-string did well enough on its own, maintaining the huge lead.

"Where'd you get that cartwheel idea from?" Tracey whispered to Dibbles.

"Weren't you impressed?" Dibbles asked in her singsongy voice. "I have all kinds of talent you know nothing about."

"Dibbles, you looked like a clown," Tracey told her.

"I look like a clown all the time," Dibbles whined pleasantly. "Didn't you like it?"

"We're supposed to look martial and able when we run out there."

"Hmm. Martial and able, martial and able," Dibbles murmured to herself. "I'll see what I can manage."

After the required stop at McDonald's, the bus rumbled pleasantly on its trip back to the campus. McDonald's was actually about two miles out of their way, but since they had won the game, CPR felt that the girls deserved the treat.

Hamburgers, shakes, and fries had hastily been downed, and now the girls—most of them—drowsed in their seats. A familiar coziness settled around Tracey as she sat in the front seat and talked quietly to Maddie, every now and then passing her a French fry, and sometimes singing a stanza or two of a song from church.

"Zion stands by hills surrounded, Zion, kept by power divine," she sang. "Is that right, Maddie? How's the rest of it go?"

"Oh, dear, that's not a common one. We only sang it that one Sunday," Maddie said quietly. "How did you remember it?"

"Just stuck in my head, I guess. I liked it, though." Tracey leaned forward, putting her face almost alongside Maddie. She felt happy and safe. They had won the game, the fanfare had gone well, and Maddie would love her regardless of the things she so hastily did sometimes.

At last they pulled up before the main hall. CPR would take the stats book back to the office herself, and some of the second-string girls volunteered to lug everything else back. Tracey gave Maddie a hug good-bye outside the bus.

"See you Saturday," she said, closing her eyes for a second to hang onto the warmth, the kindness, and the sweet smell that all made up Maddie.

"And you stay out of trouble," Maddie said, half laughing but meaning it.

"I'll try," Tracey promised. She let her go and started back up to the hall with her friends. But she looked back. "Bye," she called.

"Good-bye, dear," Maddie called back.

Peggy and Dibbles were half asleep, and nobody said anything. To Tracey's surprise, Hilary dropped back and fell into step with her.

"Tell me something," the younger girl said. Her voice was not unfriendly.

"Yeah?" Tracey asked.

"How'd you get in so good with Murdoch?"

Tracey glanced at her. "In good?"

"Yeah—gettin' to go over to her house, and havin' her buy your dinner and all that."

So, Hilary had been asking questions, her curiosity piqued by this advantageous friendship that Tracey enjoyed with Maddie.

"I didn't get in good with Maddie," Tracey said.

"Oh, of course not. Well, do you ever share the wealth?" Then Tracey realized that Hilary was saying it all to try to threaten her in some way. She was perfectly aware that Tracey considered the friendship a real friendship but was letting her know that she would move in if she could, for whatever reason she chose.

"Hilary, you pea brain!" Tracey exclaimed. Peggy and Dibbles looked back at them. "Make friends with Maddie yourself. I don't care. And I'll tell you something else—she would give you anything you needed, knowing you were just trying to get it out of her. And you'd think you were being so smart and so cool. While the whole time she would be feeling sorry for you for being so selfish and stupid! But she'll never stop being friends with me. She doesn't work that way. She doesn't switch off on her friendships."

Peggy shook her head. "You really can be a dope, Hilary."

"You guys are really high on each other and on Murdoch," Hilary said derisively. "Some dumb divorcée whose husband and kids ran out on her! That's what I've found out!"

"What about her kids?" Tracey asked.

"Sure—wouldn't you like to know?" Hilary exclaimed, triumphant for a moment. "And I'll tell you something else—she cracked up a few years ago. So think twice about how great she is!"

Tracey shook off her irritation. "All I know is that she loves me. That's all I care about." They entered the hall. She looked at Hilary. "I hated Maddie my first year here, and I treated her pretty badly. So do what you want. Things work out her way. All the time."

She started up the stairs, with Peggy and then Dibbles behind her. "Give it up, Hilary," Dibbles said as she passed Hilary. "Mrs. Murdoch would see right through you. And we're all on her side."

Hilary, instead of answering, threw another look at Tracey: smug, assured, and triumphant.

After her shower, Tracey peeped out of her room to see if any of the sisters were patrolling the halls. The way being clear, she slipped out, sidled down the few paces to the guard room, and slipped inside without knocking.

Peggy and Dibbles, already cleaned up and in their robes, looked up in surprise. Their roommates, seated at the desks, also turned around, but at a glance from Tracey they went back—or pretended to go back—to their homework.

"You're running some risks, aren't you?" Peggy asked. Since the start of the school year, Tracey had been religiously careful to obey all of the rules that she and Liz had once been so careless of. Maddie's influence had made her more aware of her responsibilities, even as an unwilling boarder at MoJoe.

"This is important," Tracey said. "What did Hilary mean about Maddie's kids?"

"Oh, to get you uptight, that's what she meant," Peggy said airily. She was seated in the middle of the floor with Dibbles. They had been playing Fish with a faded deck of cards.

"That stuff's so old," Dibbles added, picking through her cards. "Give me all your eights, Peg." Then she added, "Like it's all Maddie's fault. She married a jerk."

Tracey started, and she noticed the quick nudge that Peggy gave to Dibbles.

"Ouch!" Dibbles glanced sharply at Peggy. "Your eights, your eights! And quit hitting me!"

"I don't have any eights; oh, here's one." But she gave it to Debbie with a jab, as though desperately trying to warn her to be quiet.

"What stuff's so old?" Tracey asked.

"About her kids."

"What?" Tracey demanded. Dibbles looked up at her in surprise, and Peggy looked down in chagrin, defeated in her attempt to keep some secret.

"You know about her kids," Dibbles said.

"No, I don't, Dibbles," Tracey told her.

"It's just Mary-talk, Jac!" Peggy exclaimed. "Who else would tell stories about someone?"

"Tell me," Tracey said, and she sat down by them.

Dibbles shrugged. "Oh, it's been going around since I got on the team's first-string. You know, her husband took the kids, and she couldn't get them back."

"Well, who told you that?" Tracey demanded.

"I don't know." This once, Dibbles's singsongy tone annoyed Tracey. "Let's see, I think it was Scooter— yeah, or a couple of the girls were talking about it one night on the bus when you and Liz were up front with Maddie."

"So what's the story?" Tracey asked.

"The story's right out of Mary's mouth," Peggy snapped. "Something she invented when Maddie got too popular."

"Why didn't I ever hear it?" Tracey asked.

"Who was going to tell you and Liz?" Peggy asked in turn.

"Well, tell me now."

"Look, Jac—"

"Oh, for crying out loud," Dibbles said. "It's your turn, Peggy. The story is that Maddie's husband divorced her for some younger woman, and everybody thought that Maddie flipped out. She got real religious all of a sudden and wouldn't let the girls go to the dances anymore or to the movies. They moved out on her, back with him. One of them went off to college, really far away, and he moved out to California with his new wife and the other daughter. Both girls are in college now, but they never come home to Maddie." Dibbles looked at Tracey with frank curiosity. "Has Maddie ever mentioned them?"

"Sure," Tracey said, a little breathless from this account of Maddie's life.

Peggy glanced at her. "It's bull, Tracey, it's all bull."

Tracey looked down and shrugged.

"Maddie never flipped out," Dibbles said airily. "She made it through MoJoe—she can make it anywhere."

"No, she never flipped out," Tracey agreed. "But her daughters never do come home, and she's never talked about that—their not coming home—ever."

"Does she ever talk with them?" Peggy asked her. "Like on the phone?"

"I always thought so," Tracey said, then hesitated. "Well, I just assumed it."

"Has she got pictures of them up?" Dibbles asked, her attention at last diverted from the card game.

"Mostly in her room. I noticed them one day when I was vacuuming. But she keeps their two rooms all nice and neat and—the same, I guess you might say." Indeed, Maddie had talked about keeping the beds "fresh," and that task had required changing all of the sheets in all of the rooms every week, as though keeping the rooms in preparation, waiting. It suddenly seemed sad, even pathetic, and Tracey decided not to mention it to her friends.

THIRTY-EIGHT

For once, Maddie had a real list of chores to do when Tracey arrived on Saturday. As though in harmony with how unsettled Tracey had suddenly found her new world, Maddie seemed genuinely flustered that morning. It reminded Tracey that, although Maddie had saved her from so much, Maddie was still only human, subject to weaknesses, and perhaps had faults not yet apparent. The realization sent a pang of disappointment through Tracey, but she resolved to face it all—the real Maddie and not just the good Maddie—and stick with her if possible.

Accordingly, she immediately fell to work and followed all of Maddie's directions, vacuuming out the bedrooms, dusting, and changing the sheets, while Maddie cleaned the bathrooms, did laundry, and worked in the kitchen. As usual, Tracey did the housework with some tension and in a preoccupied silence. Normally, Maddie tried to lighten Tracey's mood and drive away her apprehension about doing things wrong, but that morning Maddie herself was preoccupied.

"Oh, dear, why did I forget that I had already invited the Wilsons over when I asked the Franklins to dinner tomorrow?" she lamented as Tracey entered the kitchen with an armload of towels from the clothes hamper. "Eleven people! And when I invited the Wilsons I knew that five would be a lot, and then when I invited the Franklins I knew that six would really be too much, and that was when I remembered I had invited the Wilsons, and it was too late, so now there are eleven people coming." She glanced helplessly around the kitchen. "Where will I put them?"

"We'll have to get the boards out of the attic," Tracey said, answering as best as she knew how. "Won't the dining room table seat a lot with two boards in it?"

"Yes," Maddie said absently, and Tracey realized that table space had not been the problem. Five, six, or eleven people seemed too many to Tracey, and she had no idea which parts of the intricacies of hostessing, cooking, and serving were worrying Maddie just then. So she made no other suggestions.

A few minutes later, Maddie asked her to go up and get the boards, which she did.

The morning passed quickly, and Tracey realized that there wouldn't be much time to talk that day. She wondered, now that the newness of "belonging" to Maddie was wearing off, if Maddie would find it more convenient at times like these to skip their Saturday afternoon visits. Tracey hoped not, but it seemed obvious that sooner or later affection had to wear off—the affection of a busy adult for a teenager, anyway.

She didn't want to be bothered by this realization. Something had warned her a long time ago not to make demands on Maddie, not to raise her own hopes

314

yet again, only to have time break them apart again. But she found that without her consent, her hopes and expectations had risen and had fastened on Maddie.

But as she came down from the attic with the table pads, Maddie's voice floated up from below. "Lunchtime, Tracey. Shall we eat in the living room?"

"If you like," Tracey called down as she eased the big pads down the stairs.

She pulled the dining room table apart, got the boards in, and dusted off the assembled table before putting the pads on. She washed her hands and came into the living room to find Maddie setting out Tracey's favorite lunch of finger sandwiches and hot tea.

"When did you have time to do this?" Tracey asked.

"Oh, a little careful planning," Maddie said with a smile as Tracey came and sat by her. "I made enough for you and for some appetizers for tomorrow."

This thoughtfulness was typical of Maddie, but Tracey felt especially grateful for it that day. Maddie must have noticed some of Tracey's new thoughts, because she reached over to clear aside her bangs. "What a big help you were, dear," she said.

"I know you love me," Tracey said unexpectedly, surprising even herself. "But do you ever love me as much as you did—that first time, when you told me you loved me and I belonged to you? Not all the time, but sometimes?"

"Why," Maddie seemed taken aback for only a moment, "I love you more—not just sometimes but all the time."

"More?" Tracey asked.

"Well, of course. I know you more now."

"Oh." Tracey nodded. The answer was so unexpected

that she only looked at Maddie for a moment and then returned to her lunch.

But after they were finished, and Maddie seemed much more relaxed and disposed to rest than to work, Tracey took a measure of the situation.

"How's it look for tomorrow?" she asked.

"Oh, I'll manage," Maddie said with a rueful smile. "The cleaning's done, and I've got most of the preparations ready, as much as possible. I'll set out the table tonight."

Tracey was leaned forward over her tea, while Maddie rested all the way back onto the couch. Tracey looked back at her.

"Can I ask you something?"

"Anything, dear."

"What about your daughters?" Tracey asked.

Maddie glanced at her. "What about them, dear?"

"Will they come home from college this summer?" Tracey asked. It was an innocent enough question, one that might likely raise her concern since she used Beth Ann's room.

"I'm not sure," Maddie said, then after a pause, "I expect not."

Tracey felt herself to be on thin ice, but she wanted to know how things were, the reasons—if there were several reasons—that Maddie had come to love her, and how she compared with Maddie's children. And besides all of that, she wondered how Maddie would be enduring isolation from her children. Maddie never spoke of them without regret and without blaming herself for whatever had happened.

"Can I ask you about them?" Tracey said.

"Yes, dear," Maddie told her, but she was more sober

now, and even Tracey could see a faint light of apprehension in her eyes—apprehension, or a certain sorriness.

Tracey was not good at initiating affection, nor had she ever had much experience in comforting people. But she leaned closer to Maddie. "Aren't they ever coming back?" she asked quietly. She felt keenly anxious at asking the question, but she also felt sorrow for Maddie.

"They say they won't," Maddie said quietly. After a long pause, she added, "I told you that I was foolish, and now I'm paying for it. My religion was just one more new idea to them, one more movement for me to join."

Tracey nodded and lowered her eyes.

"I drew the cords too tight, too fast," Maddie said. "But the girls were being pulled too fast into terrible things. I was afraid of what I had made them. But it must have been shocking—to them and to those people who had been our friends—when I made such drastic changes in what I allowed the girls to do."

"You don't have to say anything else," Tracey told her. "Debbie Dibbley told me about it—about the girls going away to your husband."

Maddie must have been accustomed to the gossip that losing her children had raised, for in that small town, and in that time, divorced women always kept their children unless something was horribly amiss. But she did ask, still in a soft voice, "How did Debbie know?"

"Scooter knew somehow. I think she told the team. Nobody ever told me until this week. Hilary was the person who mentioned it to me." She caught herself, suddenly aware that this revelation might shock Maddie. "I mean, it's not like people talk about it a lot. But

Scooter did tell the team. And Hilary likes to find out things about people."

Maddie nodded briefly, accepting the report. "I hurt my daughters, Tracey. I'm sure that losing my husband the way I did had its effect on me. But I was still responsible. I tried to control them at every step—to dominate them. There were shouting matches between us. I'm sure that it disgusted them. In the end, I taught them to hate my religion."

"Do you still love them?" Tracey asked.

"Of course," she said.

"Do they ever call you?"

"Yes—now and again. I've asked them to forgive me. I write them each week."

"And they write back?"

"Now and again. They each have a whole new life now." She glanced at Tracey. "I ought to tell you that the year my husband left, and I lost the girls, I had to go into hospital for three months. That's the rest of it, darling. But it came to me while I was in there, having lost everything that had made up my life, that either God is, or He isn't. He delivers, or He fails us. So I came out again and began the real study of His Word, the real discipling of my spirit and soul."

Genuine sorrow for Maddie made Tracey lean close again. "I wish I were beautiful, Maddie. I wish I could be beautiful and funny and remind you of them," she said. "I'd do what they would do. It could be like it was for you then."

"Oh, no," Maddie said, half with a laugh and half with a small sob. "No, that's not what I want." She put her arms around Tracey and pulled her in with a surprising strength and earnestness. "No, I want you the way you are: wild and sweet and crammed with all your ideals and notions. You are beautiful, Tracey. I wouldn't change you. I wouldn't change anything. Not a thing. This is what God wants. Everything, just as it is."

"What about them?" Tracey said. "They're your daughters."

"And you're my daughter," Maddie told her. "In His time, God will give them wisdom and bring them back to me. I never cease to pray for them. But the time is now—this moment." She stroked back Tracey's hair. "This daughter that God has sent me."

The statement sent an odd thrill of longing and happiness through Tracey, but she said, a little shocked, "I mean in real life, Maddie."

"Whatever God does is as real as real can be," Maddie said. "You don't doubt that you're my daughter, do you? That's what I meant when I said you belonged to me. I thought you knew that."

"No, because I knew you would have to love them more," Tracey said.

"More than you?" Maddie asked.

"Well, yes. I always thought so."

"I long for them," Maddie said. "I miss them. A day doesn't go by that I don't remember them." She took an instant to more deliberately brush Tracey's bangs aside and pass her hand across Tracey's forehead. "But I know full well that when I long for them, I'm longing for what they used to be, before their father and I taught them to be cynics and skeptics and irreligious. If they came back right now—right at this instant—it would be as strangers, antagonistic to what I've become, no matter how kindly I behave toward them. I would love them. I do love them. But if I pray for God to do a work in them, to at least reconcile us as mother and daughters, then I must give Him the time to do His work in them."

She stroked Tracey's forehead again. "And even as I pray for them and wait, God in His sovereign will would have me fulfill His work. He's working in you, and I have my part in that. I see Him pouring out His grace to you, Tracey. I see the love of God evident in you. We've hoped in God together. And there's a transparency in you that's beautiful."

"What's that mean?" Tracey asked.

"*Transparent* means being what you are, dear. Sweet."

Though Maddie had called her that before, Tracey still didn't quite know what being sweet meant, except that it was some way of being nice or pleasant. She would simply add *transparent* to her list of unfamiliar words.

"I fell into this world's illusions and undid myself," Maddie told her. "For I told myself that I had to maintain what had been given to me, hold onto it, fight for it, even fight against it to keep it for myself. God had to show me that all I can ever really possess is what He gives me. And what He gives me comes to me in His time, so that at this moment, right now, the mercy that He extends to me is the mercy I am to cherish, and the mercy for which I praise Him. There will be other mercies and other works of praise. But as long as I surrender them back to God and receive them anew from Him with thanksgiving, I lose nothing. And I gain everything. Everything good becomes mine. But in God's time." She lifted Tracey's chin. "Do you understand? You are an evidence of God's mercy. Given to me, Tracey, directly from the hand of God."

The answer was so unexpected and so weighty with Maddie's confidence in God's mercy that Tracey lost her voice for a moment. "Yes, Maddie," she whispered. She put her arm around Maddie's neck with a new confidence in her right to do so.

Maddie smiled. "You're my gift from God." Again, she clung to Tracey with surprising strength for a moment. "Given to me in mercy, so that we can praise God. The only thing we have is the graciousness of God."

"All right." They were still for a moment, and then Tracey went back to her tea. She found herself not inclined to say or ask anything else. The details that Hilary had suggested no longer mattered.

"Tracey," Maddie said after a moment, "you should know that I did find out that God is, that He delivers, that He keeps us."

"But the things from the past still hurt me," Tracey said, keeping her eyes on her cup of tea. "Even though I'm happy now."

"Yes, dear. Because even in the enjoyment of His mercy, we know that we need His mercy. He fulfills our expectations, and yet we always have expectations and needs for Him to fill. We experience the joy of heaven and the sorrows of earth—both at once."

For a moment, a vision of her sister Jean rose up before Tracey, and she understood. She wondered who Jean was now, and if she were all right, and the image of her younger sister pained her. But she entertained no thoughts of going back—not yet, not for a long time. A deep-seated belief that she must wait, and wait a long time, to rejoin her siblings had been born in her even before her parents divorced. Early in her exile, she had learned that she would drive herself crazy if she mulled over her family's separation every day. Instead, she had gradually learned to thrust aside her memories of her family, and she had come to believe that she would be able to rejoin them only when they were all adults, no longer under either her father's or her mother's rule.

Tracey thrust aside the memories again, and instead of continuing to think about her family, she finished her lunch and helped Maddie clean up and wash the dishes. They were quieter than usual as they worked. But if their silence had elements of pain in it, each of them was keenly aware that the other was nearby. And they both sensed the truth Maddie had spoken of—that of a wisdom and mercy constantly at work. It was a weighty understanding, and yet it was comforting as well. And neither of them was alone.

THIRTY - NINE

T racey was prepared for a much harder game when
the Valkyries next played, this time against
St. Agnes. It was a home game, one that Maddie was
not able to attend. The gym was positively crammed
with spectators—not just MoJoes, but girls from other
teams, and even spectators from town. It was only an
afternoon game, but the bleachers were packed.

"H-o-o-ot stuff!" Dibbles sang as she peeked out
through the double doors.

"Yeah, really hot stuff," Peggy added. "That's the
opposition out there in the stands, sizing us up."

"The only reason we don't size them up when they
play is that we're already smart enough to know how
they play," Tracey told her. "But the Villains' coach is
up there. See her? She's in a skirt and blouse, third row
from the top."

"Glory be," Dibbles sang. "I hope we give her her
money's worth. They must be pretty sure we'll get to
play-offs if they're scouting us this early."

"Since admission is free, I guess it wasn't hard to

get in the doors." Tracey unfurled the banner from the spear. "Come on, girls, line up!"

"Don't let all those people make you nervous, Jacamuzzi," Hilary sniped.

"Just stay out from underfoot," Tracey told her. "And keep cool."

"'Cause we have ways to make you cool!" Dibbles sang out, then exploded into laughter at her joke. "We don't want to see you flushed with defeat, right?" She shrieked with laughter again.

Hilary abruptly looked down as Peggy and Trish laughed. Tracey, mindful of Liz's brief lecture, tried hard not to laugh, but even though Dibbles' comments were not very kind, her tone was so funny it was hard to resist.

The trumpets saved her. "Let's go!" she exclaimed, and led the way out.

The game, to her surprise, was almost exactly like the St. Bede's game. CPR's only change was to play the second-string as much as possible, popping people in as soon as the first-string got the score up by six or more points. If the score held, she put more and more second-stringers in. But she warned the first-string to stay ready to go back in.

To Tracey's amazement, the first-string had very little trouble establishing an early lead. Though it was a full-court game, the Valkyries—thanks to Dibbles's and Peggy's skills—passed frequently: short passes back and forth, deceptive passes, trick passes. Trish was usually right where she needed to be, and Tracey herself could get into almost any position she picked to get a good shot. Dibbles and Peggy could send the ball to her once she got into place.

The score made it look like a close game: 78-72 in the Valkyries' favor. But the close numbers really reflected how much CPR had used the second-string, giving them practice against a good team.

After dinner that night, when it was customary to get together for mutual congratulations, Tracey went up to the guard room to find Peggy and Dibbles and a few other girls from the team grouped together. Peggy had her guitar.

"Let's try that song," Peggy said as Tracey entered. They had apparently been singing some Peter, Paul, and Mary. Tracey was a little surprised at this change of tone, but she nodded, and she and Peggy sang the hymn that was Tracey's favorite:

> My song is love unknown,
> My Savior's love to me;
> Love to the loveless shown,
> That they might lovely be.
> O who am I, that for my sake
> My Lord should take frail flesh and die?

Tracey was surprised when Dibbles joined in but not very surprised to see Trish trying to pick out the harmony and sing, or at least hum, along.

Peggy looked down at the fret board of the guitar as they finished. "Let's try it again," she said. "Maddie will like it if we can all sing it, won't she?"

They tried it again, with more of the girls joining in.

"That's so pretty," Peggy said when they'd finished.

"It's awful true," Tracey added, half to herself. Everybody looked at her, and she felt a little surprised when she realized that they would have listened to her if she had said anything else. But for once, she was not prepared to say anything else. It was all true. That said it all.

"Well, pick another one," Peggy told her, "before we call it a night."

"'Holy, Holy, Holy,'" Tracey said. It was one that all the girls knew because they sang it at Mass.

Holy, holy, holy, Lord God Almighty!
Early in the morning our song shall rise to Thee;
Holy, Holy, Holy! Merciful and mighty!
God in three persons, blessed Trinity!

They all joined in and sang, and as they did, Tracey remembered what Sister James and Sister Lucy had said so long ago about holiness. She understood now. Holiness was not darkness and stained-glass windows and incense, though they could suggest it to the senses. Rather, it was something that suffused the most ordinary of elements and by its own virtues raised them to grandeur. It was all crimson and silvery, roses that burned and transformed human hands, resurrections in deserted places. If God was cloaked in mystery, it was a mystery so wonderful, so filled with pleasures that humans could not define, that it made their feeble attempts to create auras of holiness vulgar—shocking, in fact—by contrast.

"Do the next," Peggy said in a subdued voice, and they all continued,

Holy, holy, holy! All the saints adore Thee,
Casting down their golden crowns around the
    glassy sea;

Cherubim and seraphim falling down before Thee,
Which wert, and art, and evermore shalt be.

For a moment, the thought held Tracey, that in falling down before Him, something came back. He could catch all human weakness and by that strengthen His own worshiper. And for an instant, the notion of falling before God, of surrendering will and self to God—if He were interested in those things—seemed to Tracey more alluring, more inviting, than any rest or pleasure or love she had ever known.

The room had gone very still and quiet. The sunset, in its momentary ripeness, sent long shafts of orange and pink onto the plain, pale walls. The strings of Peggy's guitar were black, and cast black shadows across the rose-tinted surface of the guitar's amber wood.

Tracey turned and saw CPR standing in the doorway.

All of the girls who were standing moved back a little, and though their action might have been attributed to simple politeness in giving the nun room to enter, it seemed to accent the fact that she was intruding on their meeting. The momentary hush descended into normal expectation.

"That was very beautiful," CPR said to Tracey. "I thought I should come up and speak to you all about our next game, but I won't interrupt your singing."

"We've finished, Sister," Peggy said, laying the guitar aside, out of the ray of sunset light that had transformed it for a moment.

They quickly turned to the subject of basketball. There were more difficult games ahead, and the team's reliance on only one or two people to make most of the shots made CPR nervous. It made all of the more experienced players nervous, including Tracey. Without meaning to, she had begun to hope that they would play in the championships again. And she knew that if any one person on the team became exclusively a shooter, or a passer, or a rebounder, the superior numbers of the Villains would enable them to tire out that person. Both the first- and second-strings had to become very good, and each person had to play well with all the others.

"It sounds like a corny old saying," CPR told them as she concluded their talk, "but we've got to be a team—think like a team, play like a team, act like a team—" She cut herself short. "Where's Hilary?" She looked again at Tracey, and Tracey could only shrug.

"Hilary does what she pleases," she said. "I haven't seen her since the game. She doesn't hang out with the team."

Coach and captain looked at each other for a moment, and then CPR looked down and said, "Well, it's time for study. You'd better put the guitar away and go to your rooms, girls."

"Let's get together and sing again tomorrow," Peggy said as she laid the guitar in its case. The others nodded, and the meeting broke up.

FORTY

It was just after lunch the next Monday that Sister St. Gerard, with an unreadable expression, handed Tracey a note to see Sister Mary at once. Tracey decided against asking St. Bernard any questions. She took the note and went to Mary's private office in the main hall.

The door was open, and she entered to see Sister Mary and Maddie Murdoch both inside. Maddie's glance at Tracey was concerned. Tracey looked at Sister Mary.

"Come in, Miss Jacamuzzi," Sister Mary said. "We have been discussing you. Mrs. Murdoch has raised an objection to my decision to restrict you to the campus on weekends."

"Restrict me to the campus?" Tracey asked. "What for? What did I do?"

"I thought perhaps I should bring you in here so that we could hammer out exactly what you have done," Sister Mary told her coldly. "Otherwise, it is not my practice to consult the boarders about their own discipline."

Sister Mary glanced at Maddie. "I feel that I have given Miss Jacamuzzi ample opportunity to explore her new faith, Mrs. Murdoch. Against my better judgment, I have adopted a laissez-faire attitude, to determine if she is genuine in following this radical fundamentalist calling of hers. So I have let you have an increasing influence over her. But the time has come to warn you that she is only using your generosity to her own advantage."

"What's going on?" Tracey demanded.

"Tracey," Maddie said gently, a warning to be quiet. But Maddie looked at Sister Mary and spoke on Tracey's behalf. "Well, tell me what has she done, then. I appreciate your wanting to have us both here before discussing it further, but I have doubts that restricting her from my house will help Tracey."

Sister Mary shot a look of triumph at Tracey, so open a look that Tracey was surprised she didn't realize how silly it made her look.

"Tell Mrs. Murdoch why I was forced to discipline you at the start of the season," Sister Mary said.

"When did you discipline me?" Tracey asked.

"Please do not pretend ignorance, Miss Jacamuzzi."

"Do you mean when you slapped me?" Tracey asked. "I already told her about that. She's the one who made me apologize to you."

For just the barest moment, Mary's mouth opened in surprise. Tracey felt a rush of relief. Was this all it was?

But Sister Mary quickly regained herself. "And no doubt that story was weighted to favor the slap and not the unbearable arrogance of the comments that provoked it," she insisted.

"Tracey was very clear in telling me that she was rude to you, Sister," Maddie said softly. "I was shocked and saddened by her behavior."

Sister Mary's eyes blazed behind her glasses. Her hand fumbled on the desktop behind her, reaching for a pencil and not finding one.

"And did she tell you," she asked again, "how she initiated three freshman basketball players onto the team?" She looked very deliberately at Tracey, and Tracey knew that her own face gave away her shock. *How could Sister Mary know about what had happened in the upstairs bathroom?*

"That was no initiation," Tracey said. "They were doing it to another student."

"Tracey Jacamuzzi physically overwhelmed three freshman girls in order to dunk their heads and faces into the toilets upstairs," Sister Mary said. "She held their faces under the water."

Maddie looked stunned.

Sister Mary looked back at Tracey. "Didn't you?"

A rush of protests, explanations, and counteraccusations flooded Tracey for a moment. But then she looked at Maddie's face, looked into her eyes, large and solemn, already grieved and a little sickened at this accusation, and Tracey said clearly, "Yes, Maddie, I did."

"Oh, Tracey," Maddie said. "Why?"

"They were tormenting another girl—" Tracey began.

"I never heard that!" Sister Mary exclaimed.

"And somebody came to get me to ask my help. I ran down with some of my friends and stopped them from what they were doing. We got the girl out, and then I ordered my friends to do it to the three girls who had done it to her—once each."

331

"Tracey," Maddie said in a low voice.

"How else could I have stopped them?" Tracey asked her.

"You will be restricted to this campus," Sister Mary told her. "And sent up for reflection and meditation—"

"No," Maddie Murdoch said softly. Then to Tracey, "Tracey, you must step out now. Sister Mary and I have to talk."

Sister Mary turned to Maddie, but Maddie looked at Tracey. "Go, Tracey," Maddie said. "But don't go far."

Tracey stepped out and closed the door behind her. She knew it was terribly wrong and dishonorable to listen, but she desperately wanted to hear this clash between Sister Mary and Maddie Murdoch. Unfortunately, the door was heavy, thick oak, and it was completely closed. Bits of words and phrases came out to her. She heard Maddie's voice, sharper than she had ever heard it, and the clear words, "—seventeen! She needs to make—" and then the rest was lost to her. This muted but apparently heated discussion went on for nearly fifteen minutes, but then the door was unexpectedly flung open by Maddie, who seemed in possession of herself, but very strong with seething anger. In the background, Sister Mary was furiously punching up the intercom on her desk, saying, "Father? Father, I need you down in my office!"

"Tracey," Maddie said in a voice so calm that it frightened Tracey, "you must go back to class now."

"Can you forgive me for what I did?" Tracey asked.

"You can't stay in these halls anymore," Maddie said in a strained whisper. "I can't let this be done to you. Go to class now and wait for me."

Tracey didn't know if this was an answer or not, but

the look on Maddie's face frightened her. "Yes, Maddie," she said. She hurried away.

Every face looked up as she hurried into English class and slid into her seat. Peggy, across the aisle, greeted her with a smile, but at the sight of Tracey's face, she whispered, "What's wrong?"

Sister Madeleine's eyes were on Tracey, so Tracey shook her head at Peggy. As soon as the bell rang, she said to her, "Somebody told Mary about what we did in the bathroom."

"What'd she do?"

"Mary called up Maddie Murdoch to tell her I'm on restriction, and Maddie came in to argue with her about it. That's when Mary told her what I did."

"We did it too," Peggy said.

"I didn't tell them who was with me," Tracey said. "I told you to do it, and you did it because I'm team captain. I'm responsible."

"No, we're responsible too, and I don't care if we get into trouble for it," Peggy said. "If Mary knows all about it, how come Hilary and her friends aren't in trouble for starting it? And they dunked that girl five or six times."

"I don't know, but Maddie's really upset. I've never seen her like this," Tracey said.

"Jac, she's not mad at you?" Peggy asked, alarmed.

"I'm not sure what she's mad at," Tracey said. "She told me to wait for her."

"We'll all go to Maddie," Peggy said. "We'll all tell her the whole story."

"I think she believes me," Tracey said. "But she's awfully upset."

There was no word from Maddie for the rest of that day. When Tracey came out of class, Maddie's station wagon was gone from the parking lot. Sister Mary did not appear again throughout the afternoon and evening. There were no announcements after the evening meal.

"Man, where could she be?" Tracey asked nobody in particular as she and Peggy and Dibbles walked up the steps after supper.

"You can be sure that whatever she's doing, she's looking out for you," Peggy told her.

But Tracey could still recall the horror in Maddie's eyes. Her actions had been repulsive to Maddie. "Of course," Tracey ventured, "she wouldn't give up on me."

"No!" Peggy and Dibbles both exclaimed.

"If she's trying to be a wall between you and Mary, you can bet it's going to take her some time," Peggy said. "Have a little faith."

Tracey was a little surprised that Peggy and Dibbles didn't ask her into the guard room for coffee. Instead, they disappeared quickly into the room and shut the door. Feeling a little left out and alone, Tracey went into her own room.

"Study hard, Jacamuzzi," a voice said before she could close the door behind her. Hilary was standing in the hall.

Tracey glanced back out at the freshman. "What do you want?"

"Heard that Mary's going to restrict you. What a shame."

"She hasn't restricted me," Tracey said shortly, and she closed the door. Then she leaned against it. Nobody could know what had passed in that office today—nobody, except the person who told Mary. What an irony that Hilary picked on the narcs and yet was one herself.

"Are you all right?" Sheila asked her. "You look pale, Jac."

"Yeah, I just had some trouble with Mary. She dragged Maddie into it." She forced herself over to the desk and sat down. There was a Latin translation test to study for, so she opened her textbook and tried to see the words, but her mind was far away.

The slow evening ticked by. Just as study time ended, Tracey went out into the hallway. She was just in time to see Dibbles and Peggy hurrying up the hall.

"Where have you guys been?" she asked suspiciously.

"Nowhere," Peggy said.

"You called Maddie, didn't you?" Tracey asked.

They both looked so guilty that she knew it was true, even though Peggy said, "No." Then Peggy and Dibbles glanced at each other.

"She wasn't home," Dibbles said.

"We wanted to tell her that we were the ones who were in the bathroom," Peggy told her.

Tracey didn't say anything, either of thanks or rebuke. She wondered where Maddie could be.

"We could go tell Mary that we were in on it," Dibbles said. "I mean, if she knows you were there, she must know we were there too. But we could insist that she include us in any punishment."

"Yeah, and we could insist that she nail those freshmen too," Peggy added. "I wonder who told?"

"Hilary told," Tracey said. "But you guys don't need to tell Mary. Maddie told me to wait, so I ought to just wait."

"Maybe Bing knows what's up," Peggy suggested.

"No. Or if he does, he's got to be on the school's side," Tracey said. "I don't want to go to him."

The endless night passed into another seemingly endless day. Tracey kept expecting to be called out of class, but nothing interrupted school. It was Tuesday, the day they usually played PIG outside, and she didn't want to do it, but she had to. Dibbles and Peggy were absent from the court, but Trish Roberts helped.

At last it was over, and Tracey hurried up to the halls to change for supper. She thought that maybe she would call Maddie after the evening meal. But there was no need to. Tracey pushed open the door to her room, and there was Maddie.

Tracey was so surprised and so relieved that she didn't say anything for a moment.

"Tracey," Maddie said gravely, "you must change. We've got to go see Sister Mary and Father Williams."

"All right," Tracey told her, and without another word she hurried into her school uniform. Maddie re-

mained silent until Tracey was tying on the saddle ox-
fords. As she straightened up, Maddie reached over
and fixed her collar for her.

"Is everything all right?" Tracey asked.

"It will be."

"Can you forgive me for what I did?"

"Yes, Tracey." But there was no smile from Maddie,
no assurances. Tracey looked down. She willed herself
to accept that she was in disgrace, but then Maddie
said, "I appreciate that you didn't know what else to
do, Tracey. But there were other things you might have
done."

"What?" Tracey asked.

"Simply stopped them and told them to leave," she
said. "You had the authority to simply chase them out.
And you'd have accomplished more by your example
of restraint and dignity than by avenging anybody. I
suppose that the girls you punished must hate you
now."

"I guess that at least one of them does," Tracey admitted.

"And they will hate what you represent. It was not
pleasing to God for you to punish those girls. You don't
have that authority over them."

"I'm sorry, Maddie. I'll do what it takes to make it
right," Tracey said humbly. "When it all happened, I
wasn't even thinking about what I could have done. I
was just determined to punish them and make them
leave people alone."

"This pattern is just going to keep repeating itself,"
Maddie said quietly. "There will be hazing, and you have
not learned to face it without fear and anger. You cannot
conquer it until your own feelings are behind you."

"Yes, Maddie," Tracey said.

"That's why you have to leave the hall," Maddie told her.

"But where will I go?" Tracey asked. The thought that Maddie—for the sake of righteousness—might allow her to be sent back to her mother suddenly occurred to her. "Not home?" she exclaimed.

"No, of course not. You'll live with me." Maddie glanced at her watch. "We've got an appointment in about two minutes. You'll have to miss dinner, but I'll get you something after. Come on, then."

Numb with surprise, Tracey followed her out of the room.

FORTY-TWO

Sister Mary was waiting for them in her office. Maddie closed the door behind them and said, "Is Father Williams not here yet?"

"He has been detained," Sister Mary said. "But he has instructed me to remind you that Tracey's father is paying her way here, and he has dictated that she be kept in the hall. His wishes are still clear: He wants us to encourage her to return to her faith."

Maddie had been fishing in her purse for something, and now she produced a piece of paper, which she held as though keeping it in reserve.

"Tracey is now seventeen," Maddie said. "She is nearly past her minority. It is time to consider her young adult life and what she will need."

"That is the concern of her parents," Mary retorted. "It is not our business."

"That is the concern of you and of me," Maddie replied. "If her parents will not provide for her future, then it certainly falls to us to do so." Her voice did not really increase in volume, but it did increase in its intensity.

Sister Mary met Maddie's eye, but Mary seemed surprised and sharply disturbed by this claim on her moral responsibilities. "I fail to see how I have become a guardian of any student after she leaves this school," she said.

"Her parents have abdicated their rule over her to a considerable degree," Maddie reminded her. "Her father has made it quite clear that when she turns eighteen, he is no longer responsible for her and will not assist her in any way. You cannot simply put her out on the street."

"But for right now, he has legal control over her, and we will obey his wishes. She will stay in the halls." Sister Mary returned Maddie's even and steady gaze with eyes blazing. "He has remitted her to our care, and that is the law."

"I don't think that a court of law would support you," Maddie said. "I am taking Tracey with me. Tonight. She will live with me and attend classes here according to the wishes of her father."

"We'll see you in a court of law before you take her off this campus ever again," Sister Mary said sharply. "She will certainly not be placed in your custody."

"Tracey, you must excuse us now," Maddie said, and Tracey realized with a sinking heart that once again she would not be allowed to witness this conflict of wills. Her own happiness seemed to be hanging on Maddie's ability to win this argument, and she did not want to leave.

Sister Mary turned to her. "Stay right there," she ordered. Then she glared at Maddie. "I know perfectly well that she will run after you, Mrs. Murdoch; that if I let her out of my sight, she'll be gone. She's as headstrong now as she was when she first came here."

Just then, Father Williams entered the room. He looked from Sister Mary to Maddie.

"If you think I have come here to ask your permission to take Tracey with me, you're sadly misled," Maddie said. "For I have not. I have come to notify you that I am doing the same." She put the paper down on Mary's desk. "This is a written and signed permission from Tracey's mother that Tracey may come and live with me. And that is all I need to offer you." She turned to Tracey. "Go get your things. We're leaving."

Father Williams made a move as though to say something, but Sister Mary picked up the phone. "She is under her father's care as well," Sister Mary insisted. "I will have the police in on this matter if I need to."

"I don't think—" Father Williams began.

"Oh, call them indeed," Maddie exclaimed. And now her voice rose as sharply as Sister Mary's. "For I myself wondered if I should disrupt the lives of these girls by doing the same, but I'll let you spare me the decision if you like. And when the police come, and we go to the legal system, you can then explain to a judge why it was that you stood by and let six upperclassmen beat and torture Sandra Kean, and why you let them beat and torture Tracey. For it's plain that you knew what happened."

Tracey gasped at this information, but Maddie went on.

"And we'll bring it out that Sandra Kean committed suicide a week before returning here. And then there's that solitary confinement that you use, and I don't doubt, when I have brought back Liz Lukas and several other graduates of recent years, that they can supply much more information of things I never dreamed of. For those girls are adults now, and I think that their words would carry weight."

Speechless for a moment, Mary set the phone down. She seemed to rally her thoughts, and might have spoken, but Father Williams made an abrupt gesture that silenced her. "Mrs. Murdoch," he said, "things happen at a school. We all know that. But you cannot deny that in the last few years, the Sanctuary has come back from a sharp spiritual decline and a decline in morale. Dragging us through the court system would only put us back where we were. The very best girls would be pulled out, and the other students—who cannot be policed every moment—would be under the control of the lowest elements of the student body."

"It's not my wish to destabilize this school," Maddie told him, her voice back to its normal tone and cadence. "I graduated from here myself, and I know, even now, that it's a better place for some of these girls than other places where they might be sent."

"Then tell me what you do want," he said.

"I want Tracey with me. She has been beaten here, and she has been accused of insanity over and over again by this woman. She is a God-fearing girl, but she has not learned the habits of a God-fearing woman." Maddie's voice became more strident, more intense. "I'll not have her ruined by the system here. She can learn what she's missed and be a better person for it. But she must come with me!"

"They are both megalomaniacs," Mary said. "And

that one was institutionalized." Tracey started at this, stunned to hear Maddie so accused. Father Williams shot another sharp glance toward Sister Mary to tell her to be quiet. He looked again at Maddie and didn't seem to know what to say.

For a moment, he and Maddie only looked at each other, and Tracey realized that the headmaster really was at a loss. Maddie turned again to Tracey. "Go get your things," she said in a low voice. "I'll be up to help you shortly."

This time, Sister Mary did not contradict her, and Tracey hurried out.

FORTY-THREE

Supper was over by the time Tracey hurried up the stairs to her room. Dibbles and Peggy were both waiting at her door.

"Come inside," Tracey said briefly, and they followed her in.

She hurried to pull out her suitcases, mindful that Maddie would be in a hurry to leave once she got away from Mary and Father Williams. It had been two days of nervousness for Tracey, but now a new nervousness was edging the other nervousness away. She wondered what life would be like away from the familiar halls. She would be starting all over again—again. And though she had felt familiar and at home with Maddie up until now, a new strangeness was creeping over her.

"Peggy—" she began.

"Maddie's taking you away," Peggy said. Peggy's voice and eyes betrayed the same new sense of strangeness. They were used to considering Maddie more as one of them—or at least as a person sympathetic with them—than as one of the sisters, but this sudden, decisive move on her part was startling. Maddie had not asked Tracey about it; she was simply doing it.

"Are you leaving the school?" Dibbles asked, for once not smiling and not even thinking about the funny side of things.

"No, just the halls," Tracey told them. She pulled open a drawer and lifted a jumble of clothes out of it. Peggy flipped the largest suitcase open for her.

Tracey was glad to see that they were sharing her feelings, but she decided not to act nervous or frightened. It would do no good, for she certainly had to go with Maddie now. And it would be a very bad start with Maddie to meet her brimming over with tears. "Somebody has to move in here to take my place," Tracey said. "I don't want Mary assigning Sheila and Diane to just anybody. Diane's got that health problem—"

"I'll get my stuff in here as soon as you go," Peggy promised, picking up Tracey's businesslike tone.

"Thanks, Peg, that's a relief."

"Well, we might as well give you a hand," Dibbles said.

They were silent as they worked. Just before they finished, Maddie knocked and entered, and the bell rang for study time. Sheila and Diane hurried in with their books.

"Almost ready, Maddie," Tracey said. Her mouth felt dry.

"You have all the time in the world, dear," Maddie said kindly. The stern, strident Maddie from the office had been left down there. This was the familiar, soft-spoken Maddie. "Can I help you?"

"It's almost finished," Peggy said cheerfully. Sheila and Diane looked confused and scared. They didn't say anything, but they stood where they were without moving.

Tracey zipped up the last suitcase. She looked at Peggy and Dibbles. Maddie's calm and cheerful entrance had restored a brief sense of normalcy to the situation, but now that the moment had come to march down those stairs, all the strangeness came back.

Tracey broke the awkward silence with a laugh. "Come on, you guys," she said. "I'll be right back here tomorrow morning."

"Oh, sure!" Dibbles said, and laughed too. "And now you can bring Maddie's cupcakes straight to us! It will be so much more convenient that way!"

Tracey looked at her two freshman roommates. "Peggy's going to move in with you guys," she said.

"You'll be back in school?" Diane asked.

"Yes," Tracey said.

Peggy and Dibbles seemed to forget to offer to help carry the suitcases down. They said good-bye, then stood and watched Tracey go as she and Maddie carried out the two suitcases and few small bags that held all of Tracey's possessions.

Without a word, she and Maddie stowed her gear in the back of the station wagon, and they got into the car and closed the doors. Neither of them said anything until they had pulled down the long drive and come to the open road.

Tracey took a long breath and let it out.

"Are you all right?" Maddie asked.

"Yes, Maddie. Are you?" she asked.

"Fine," Maddie said. "I regret having to say some of what I said before you, Tracey. But I cannot regret saying it."

Tracey knew that Maddie was a stickler for respect to authority; she would not have brought her accusations against Sister Mary in front of Tracey except for Mary's insistence that Tracey stay in the room.

"Can you still drive for the team?" Tracey asked.

"No," Maddie said. "No, they have terminated my ministries here, dear."

"Oh, Maddie," Tracey said. "All because of what I did. I am sorry."

"Oh, don't you believe it. What you did was very wrong, and it shocked me to think of you taking such revenge, Tracey. But if it weren't this, it would have been something else. I couldn't abide your being here. I couldn't stand having to send you back every Sunday night."

"How did you get my mother's permission?" Tracey asked.

"I went to see her," Maddie said.

The information stunned Tracey. It was a night of stunning surprises, but this was the topper. "You did? When?"

"I left last night," Maddie said. "I called her and drove down, and visited with her this morning."

"I can't believe she gave you her permission," Tracey said with some admiration.

"Aye, well, it wasn't easy at first. But you know, I sympathized with her over losing her children, and I told her to some degree how I had lost mine," Maddie explained. "And we talked about you, though of course I kept all your confidences. She believes that I am concerned for you. But I had to make concessions to her, dear. She wants you home at Christmas, and I agreed that you would be there."

"Maddie!" Tracey exclaimed.

"Tracey, it is right," Maddie said emphatically but not unkindly. "She is your mother, no matter what she's done. You owe her a certain duty."

"I thought that in Christ we don't have to be under things like duty and obligation," Tracey protested.

"We aren't enslaved to them," Maddie told her. "We follow them out of love for Him, not for love of duty." Her tone became coaxing, almost pleading. "Tracey, minister to your mother out of love for Christ."

Tracey didn't argue after that. She knew Maddie was right, but it was a bitter thought.

"When we get home, dear, I want you to unpack as quickly as you can," Maddie said. "You may as well change into your nightclothes and put your things in the laundry. We'll give them a good wash before we pack them away."

"Yes, Maddie." Tracey tried to sound willing and obedient. She wanted to be obedient to Maddie, but the thought of living under her care was a little intimidating. There had been a certain anonymity in the hall, a certain freedom from exposure. Now Maddie was going to know her—really know her. Not a detail could be hidden.

She didn't understand why she had never felt self-conscious before about living with somebody. She had roomed with Liz for nearly three years without thinking twice about it. And yet now she felt somewhat shy and self-conscious with Maddie. It was a little like getting to know Maddie all over again—the secret anxiety, the sense of Maddie being a stranger. What if Maddie ultimately tired of her, or couldn't keep her, or was disappointed in her?

At the house, they unloaded Tracey's things, and Tracey hurried to sort out what needed to be laundered and what should be put where. There wasn't time for a proper unpacking, but she hurriedly did what she could and then scrambled into her nightgown and robe so Maddie would not be kept waiting. The nightgown and robe she wore now were thick and long and comfortable—early gifts from Maddie. The feel of them comforted Tracey. So far, nothing had deterred Maddie from keeping her promises to her.

Tracey cautiously came out into the living room.

"Come and sit down, dear," Maddie invited her from the sofa. "Come and sit by me."

In spite of the sense of strangeness, Tracey was glad to. It was a familiar invitation from hospitable Maddie. But this time, Maddie opened her arms, and Tracey gladly came into them.

She had once been shy and self-conscious about being close to people, and she had learned over the last few months to enjoy the happy pleasure of being hugged by Maddie. But tonight she suddenly buried her face into Maddie's shoulder and neck, and was glad and relieved to feel Maddie's kiss on her cheek.

"Oh, you're trembling. It's all over now." And Maddie waited, her breathing calm, until Tracey calmed herself. "I'm glad you're here," Maddie whispered.

"You really are, Maddie?" Tracey asked, looking up at her from the shelter of her neck. "Do you still think the mercy of God gave me to you?"

"Of course I do. You could lay money on it, if I allowed it," Maddie said.

"I want to be good and obedient," Tracey said

anxiously, straightening up. "I really do. I don't ever want to make you mad—or sorry that I'm here."

"Oh, what nonsense," Maddie said with a smile. "Who could be sorry? Why, Sister Mary and I had to fight over who could keep you—and I won."

Tracey forced a smile at Maddie's way of putting it. But she could not really joke about it. "If you'll just always tell me, Maddie, what I need to do—" she began.

"Aye, that would be hard," Maddie said gently. She became very serious. "I want you to listen to me a moment, and think very hard over what I'm about to say."

"All right."

Maddie held Tracey's face by the chin and looked at her. "Obedience cannot be blind, Tracey," she said. "Oh, I suppose it can be, but that's how we get things like concentration camps and massacres, isn't it? For a Christian, obedience is never blind. In fact, it is the most profound statement of faith and knowledge that we can make."

"What does that mean?" Tracey asked. "Obedience is just doing the right thing."

"Yes, that's true enough. But sometimes we can fool ourselves about the right thing," Maddie said. She brushed aside Tracey's bangs with her hand and said, "Obedience is the giving up of ourselves, Tracey. It means taking our hands off our own selves and letting other hands remake us. Sometimes it means standing by and not doing what we would choose to do because we know that there's a Love and a Goodness doing its own work in us."

"God," said Tracey.

"Yes, darling, God. But also God's appointed agents. Sometimes His agents don't even love us. He's ready to

350

use them for our good and then throw them away, isn't He?" she asked, and Tracey nodded. She had heard enough sermons on the Philistines to know that God had raised them up to drive the children of Israel back from apostasy, time and time again.

"So much for them," Maddie said, seeing that Tracey understood. "It is hard to render obedience to those types—especially for a young Christian. Sometimes when somebody who doesn't love either us or God has the rule over us, we cannot see that it is still God who is working through that person."

"You mean like Sister Mary," Tracey said, lowering her eyes.

Maddie nodded, but her gaze became even more gentle as she said, "But then there are the people sent from God who love us, and He sends them because He loves us and them."

"You," Tracey said.

Maddie smiled. "You have that right." Her eyes became serious again as she regarded Tracey. "I want you to try to let go of your life, Tracey. And let me put my hands on it, and my reins."

Tracey slowly nodded, resolved to do whatever she asked.

Maddie smiled at her serious nod, but she became grave again, though her words were spoken with such an earnest tenderness that Tracey never doubted them. "You have mourned, I know, about some of the walls that have been torn down in your life. It looks to me like you have been trying to rebuild them, somehow trying to change the effect that the violence and the early knowledge of carnal things has had on you."

Maddie looked at her searchingly, but Tracey

couldn't nod, because she couldn't move. It was the most personal thing anybody had ever said to her, and it was exactly true. And Maddie knew it was so.

"But you can't rebuild those walls that adults tore down, Tracey," Maddie said. "Or if you could, it would take you years and years to do it."

A lump came up in Tracey's throat. So Maddie had seen her greatest fear and known it to be true. She could never be what she might have been. The violence of her past had scarred her forever, and it was manifesting itself everywhere in her life, in spite of her beliefs. And Maddie had seen it from the very beginning. Tracey did manage a slight nod, but she looked down, unable to meet Maddie's eyes.

Maddie's voice was sober, but still kind: "But I can rebuild those walls for you, Tracey, and return to you a good measure of the innocence and freshness of life that was torn down. And I believe it is what the Lord would have me to do. But you will have to step aside and let me do it."

Tracey looked up at her, her own eyes so sober and still that even Maddie could not have known the thoughts behind them. But Maddie's voice and expression were sure. "Obedience is not made up of obedient actions, Tracey. Obedience is surrender—surrender to God, and surrender to the authority of those He puts over your care."

"Maddie, I want to so much!" Tracey exclaimed. "If you would only help me and remind me of these things. I'm afraid I'll forget."

"I'm here to remind you," Maddie whispered, and she kissed Tracey's forehead and cheek. "I'm here to help you on your way. And I want you to remember that every authority over us—from the Lord on down —can be appealed to. Godly rule is easily entreated, easily moved to mercy and kindness."

Tears filled Tracey's eyes and spilled down her cheeks. "I know that you'll be good to me, Maddie. You're always good. And I'll be obedient to you," she promised.

"I know you will. Come here, darling." Tracey came into her arms again. Maddie's hand stroked Tracey's cheek and brushed away her tears.

It had shaken Tracey to hear her own deepest feelings described out loud, to know that the truest, most personal analysis of her character was known by another person. For a moment, despite Maddie's kind welcome, Tracey felt exposed and vulnerable.

"Darling," Maddie whispered, "has no one ever cherished you?"

"What?" Tracey asked.

"Has nobody ever taken you in her arms and told you how precious you are?" With the back of her hand, Maddie brushed Tracey's hair from her eyes. "You're a gift from God: sweet, and wild, and strong, and gentle —all at once. Has nobody had the sense to tell you so?"

Tracey looked up at her. "No," she said after a moment.

"It must be for me to do, then. My good girl. I'm so proud of you." Maddie held Tracey's face with one long hand and looked into her eyes. "All that you've endured. All that you've given. All that you will give. Was there ever a heart and soul that loved her friends so fiercely?" She kissed Tracey's forehead again and guided her head back to her shoulder. "Was there ever a heart so true to God, even when in gravest doubt?"

"You," Tracey whispered. "You just described your-self, Maddie."

"You," Maddie whispered. "Rest here in my arms. You're mine now. All mine. It was a fair fight. And, God be thanked, I won."

Tracey obeyed and nestled against her. As Maddie stroked her head and whispered to her, the last of Tracey's self-consciousness faded away, and a great peace and quietness settled over her. Deep inside, the understanding began to grow in Tracey's heart that obedience was not just a sacred calling, but an actual privilege—a language between people who loved each other, the evidence of having been chosen and accept-ing the choice. Truly, Maddie could expect obedience from nobody else but Tracey, and Tracey alone could return obedience to her. It was all that Maddie had said, and more. And now Tracey, not for her own self, resolved to worship God by her willingness to listen and be taught, to live again as an obedient member of a loving home.

Hilary, I want you to know that I realize that I wronged you when I dunked you like that in the bathroom," Tracey said. She had saved the most difficult apology until last. Already, she had found the two other freshmen whom she had ordered punished, and had apologized to them, or—as Maddie called it— "sought their forgiveness."

Hilary, leaning against one of the sets of drawers in her bedroom, eyed Tracey with disfavor. "So what am I supposed to do, kiss your feet for talking to me?" she asked.

"No," Tracey said. "I would like to ask you to forgive me, because what I did was very wrong."

Hilary gave a laugh of contempt, as though understanding something for the first time. "Mary's got you running scared now."

"Well," Tracey said, "no, not exactly." Maddie had impressed upon her that she must not be defensive when she talked to the three freshman girls. She must not be proud. She must not remind them that what they had been doing was also wrong. She must simply confess her wrong to them and get their forgiveness, if she could. Oddly enough, Tracey had thought she would be free at least to think all kinds of rotten things right back at Hilary, but now that she was in the act of obedience, her purpose seemed very clear, and no quick retorts even came to mind.

"I don't know what your plan is, Jacamuzzi, but you know where you and your forgiveness can go. I'll never make friends with you," Hilary said.

That was a stumper. Tracey had no desire whatsoever to be friends with Hilary, either—she had simply wanted to make peace with her. But she could not phrase it that way. She hesitated and then said, "We don't have to be friends, but I would like to know that we aren't enemies."

"We're teammates," Hilary said. "And that's it."

"All right," Tracey told her. Then she added, with an effort, "Thanks for that much." She exited the room.

The interviews with the two other girls had been much easier. One of them had tried to behave as though she'd been very wronged, but she had haughtily granted Tracey forgiveness. The other one, to Tracey's surprise, had poured out so much emotion—remorse, horror at herself for what she'd been talked into doing, grief over having made herself an enemy to most of the team, fear of Hilary—that Tracey had spent the better part of a free hour talking with her, consoling her, and promising her the friendship of the others.

She hurried from Hilary's room to the guard room to report to Peggy and Debbie the results of her pilgrimage of forgiveness. Neither Peggy nor Dibbles had much liked Tracey's decision to obediently seek forgiveness for her wrongs. But when she knocked on their door and entered, Dibbles hurriedly got up to make coffee, and Peggy said cheerfully, "Well, here she is, back from the lions! I see you're still in one piece!"

"Sit down, Jac," Dibbles sang out. "But don't start talking until I get back with the water!"

They made themselves comfortable, and Tracey started with the story that had worked out the best. "That freshman girl, Laura," she said. "She's all upset about what she did. She told me that she's sorry. And she's really scared of Hilary."

"Yeah, old Hilary is really taking over the freshman class," Dibbles agreed, then added in singsong, "Of course, now we can't do anything to stop her, because we believe in . . . *loooove*."

Peggy couldn't help laughing, and Tracey smiled too. "Well, you can stop Hilary from bothering Laura," she said. "I told Laura that we'd be glad to be friends with her—the ball team has always been close, and we want her to come to us."

"I don't think we can stop Hilary from being nasty," Peggy said. "But I'll do my best to make friends with Laura." She glanced at Dibbles. "If Laura's sorry—I mean, anybody can make a mistake. There's no point in ignoring her."

"Oh, I know, I know," Dibbles sang. "I'll be good to her. But do you think she's going to go back to the girl she dunked and apologize?"

"I bet she will," Tracey said. "I'll ask her to."

"Well, what about the other two?" Peggy asked.

"DeAnn said that she forgave me—" Tracey began.

"And what about what she did?" Dibbles exclaimed.

"We didn't talk about that."

357

"What about Hilary?" Peggy asked. Tracey shook her head. Peggy voiced what Tracey was thinking, "She's the Deep Six all rolled into one."

"That would make her pretty fat," Dibbles observed.

"I think," Tracey said, "that Hilary thinks I tried to set things right out of some sort of fear of being punished."

"Oh, sure!" Dibbles exclaimed. "Now Hila-bomb thinks she's got the team captain running scared just because she's got Mary wrapped around her little finger!"

Tracey shook her head in wonder at Hilary's scheming. "Even Hilary's not smart enough to get Mary wrapped around her little finger," she said. "In the end, it's Hilary who's going to be around Mary's finger."

"Whichever way it goes, the two of them make a fine matched set," Peggy grumbled. She started to pour the coffee around. Tracey watched her for a moment.

"Maddie said that Mary knew what the Deep Six did to Sandra Kean—and to me," Tracey said at last. "Is that true? Do you two know what they did, as well?"

Dibbles looked down, but Peggy said hesitantly, "There were rumors—we knew that they tortured you and Sandra. Anybody could have seen it for themselves."

"Could they have really known?" Tracey asked, meaning the sisters. "And not done anything?"

"I guess," Dibbles said, her voice still singsong but not as much, "it depends on what you mean by 'know,' Jac. I think that all the sisters knew you had become afraid of something; maybe they never asked questions past that. As for Mary—"

"Nothing happens that Mary doesn't know something about," Peggy said. "Oh, I know that Liz pulled off that mousetrap trick pretty well, and Mary fell for it without a second thought. But the Deep Six must have bragged about what they did to other girls. And I bet Sandra Kean may have told her own roommates—"

"And told Mary?" Tracey asked. "And Mary didn't help her?"

"She would have been too afraid to have told Mary," Peggy said. "But of course Mary would have known something had happened; suddenly her narc turned white as a ghost and couldn't—wouldn't—have those little sessions with Mary."

"Of course," Tracey whispered. It suddenly dawned on her that Sandra Kean, as one of Mary's own narcs, would have been very inexpert in hiding what had been done.

She was suddenly, starkly silent.

"Don't let it bother you anymore," Peggy urged her.

"Drink your coffee, Jac," Dibbles said. "What time is Maddie coming to pick you up?"

"Oh! Maddie!" And Tracey threw a quick glance at her watch. "Five minutes ago! I gotta go!" She scooped up her books and ran out the door. "Thanks for the coffee!" she called back, then hurried down the steps. Despite Maddie's tender and earnest talk with her the night before, and despite the enormous celebratory breakfast she had made for Tracey that morning, Tracey still felt the need to be on her very best behavior. Being five minutes late for pickup was not what she wanted.

Tracey thought her mind was a blank as she raced down the middle steps and bolted out the front doors of the main hall, intent only on getting to the drive as quickly as possible. But suddenly, when she saw Maddie outside, standing by the station wagon and looking around for her, something inside her abruptly came to the surface.

She ran to Maddie, who caught her happily in a hug and exclaimed, "Well, hello, scamp! Have you been playing truant?"

"Oh, Maddie," Tracey gasped, and burst out crying. "Why didn't they do anything if they knew? If they knew? Why didn't they stop them? Why did they let them do it to me?"

Maddie had been about to let her go so they could climb into the car, but she stopped and gave Tracey her full attention. "Oh, darling," she whispered.

Tracey sobbed three or four hard sobs of grief and anguish in her arms, then just as abruptly said, "No!" She pulled away, furious and breathless. "I wouldn't give in then! I won't now! I won, Maddie! I beat them!" She tried to jerk open the car door, but Maddie's gentle hands caught the books in Tracey's arm, and by putting one hand lightly on the open car door, she stopped Tracey from getting in.

"Yes, you did win," she said. "But not by being angry." She took the books and put them on the front seat. "Show me where they did it," Maddie said. "Do you think you can do that?"

"Yes," Tracey told her. Without a word, she led Maddie off the front drive and around to the side of the building. At first she still felt the defiant anger, and the long-held grief that she had so rarely shown. But the cool air of the late November afternoon was quiet and calming, and as they walked around the side of the building, the hush suddenly seemed almost chapel-like in its stillness, privacy, and solemnity. Tracey drew closer and closer to Maddie as they walked around to the side doors, and Maddie slipped an arm around her.

Tracey pointed to the hedge near the doors. "In there," she said.

"You don't know exactly where?" Maddie asked.

"Yes. Look there at that branch in the hedge that's twisted like an S. That's where Rita Jo was. I was down on the ground there, in front of her."

Maddie slipped both arms around Tracey. Tracey felt that she could bear this detailed revelation of what had passed, so long as Maddie was with her, and so long as they were alone.

Maddie was silent for a long time—and Tracey began to wonder why she would want to stand there so long—until at last she said, very thoughtfully, "So this was where my Tracey was laid down as a girl and raised up as a Valkyrie."

"What?" Tracey asked, her voice taking on some of Maddie's solemnity.

"At some point in the Christian life," Maddie said softly, "we begin to see what it might cost us. And in spite of it all, we go on. Because what is in us is not of man, but of God."

A lump came up into Tracey's throat. "But, Maddie," she quavered, "I failed so much after that. I fought—I hated you—"

"And yet you persevered," Maddie whispered. "And did it not all come right?" she asked. "You learned not to fight. You learned to love me. But first there had to be the laying-down place—that place where we are carried where we would not go. And yet we go. And by God's power, we return."

"You think God wanted them to do that to me?" Tracey whispered.

Maddie's eyes were large and solemn. "I do, my darling. But it does not excuse the ones who did it, and God did not enjoy your grief. Oh, He'll charge them for it. But He brought you up out of it—like a Valkyrie, all strong and cheerful and brave."

"So then all the rest was His will too," Tracey said. "What my father did, my mother—it's like He was somehow driving me here, driving me to this place—"

"Driving you to me, in the end," Maddie said. "For He sets the solitary in families. Yes. Everything in your life has been purposed and ordered by God. To conform you to the image of His Son, to give you the Water of Life that never runs dry."

For a long moment, Tracey didn't say anything. Not only had Maddie's words taken the harsh sting out of the day's revelations, they had opened up a wonderful balm, a line of reasoning that comforted her even more than Maddie's voice or her presence. At last she said, "It sounds too good to be true. I mean, that God did everything to make me a Valkyrie, to make me especially His."

"This is the resurrected life," Maddie said with a smile. "The life too good to be true for earthly creatures, but the only life fit for heavenly beings. Which is what we are, my Valkyrie."

They stood together a few seconds longer, and then Tracey said, "I could go home now, Maddie." And they walked arm in arm through the chapel-like stillness and back to the station wagon.

"Can I ask you something?" Tracey said quietly.

"Certainly."

"You told me once that you had to learn not to fight for what you wanted. But you did fight Sister Mary to get me to live with you. And I'm glad you did." Tracey's voice was genuinely puzzled. "But how did you work it out?"

"We usually do fight for things when we oughtn't, Tracey," Maddie said. "I think that knowing our weakness to fight presumptuously is what held me back. I've wanted you with me—oh, for a long time now. But I worried that trying to make a claim and force it was contrary to what God would have me do by faith." They reached the car and she fished her keys out, but they made no move to open the doors.

"But then, when Sister Mary said you would be separated from me, against your will and contrary to what was good for you," and Maddie laid emphasis on this last word, "then I understood that the time had come. Not to fight for myself, though I surely did want you with me. But to fight for what God has been doing in your life. To fight out of a belief in His grace at work in you." She glanced at Tracey. "Christian warfare at any level is always victorious. But we must assure our hearts that what we fight for really is to His glory, so that His purposes will be furthered."

Tracey nodded. "I understand. And it really was a different sort of fight than what I've done up in the halls."

"Oh, and it was grand too, wasn't it?" Maddie tugged on her bangs, and for a moment she fixed Tracey with eyes as delighted and joyful as any look of secret glee Tracey had ever gotten from Liz or Dibbles or Peggy. And then she was sensible Maddie again. "Let's go home, then. You'll be wanting your supper."

W ell, this is really it," Peggy said, coming up the middle aisle of the silent bus and sitting next to Tracey. Tracey glanced up at the back of CPR's head. CPR had driven to every away game since Maddie had been released from doing it.

Peggy sat in the seat behind Tracey. "Think we'll do it?"

"Seems like we can, doesn't it?" Tracey replied. "After the way we beat Chickens of the Valley and St. Agnes."

The season had flown by. The team had never lost, not once. They had never even had an agonizingly close game. Their passing was great; the second-string could hold its own against some tough competition. But of course, no competition was as tough as the Villains.

"Do you have the guitar tuned?" Tracey asked.

"Yeah." Peggy picked it up and called back, "Come on, you guys." The other girls came up. CPR glanced up at them in the rearview mirror, then looked out again at the dark road.

"First our favorite," Peggy said. "'My Song Is Love Unknown.'" She strummed the guitar to get the chords right, and they sang the song together. In the back of the bus, Hilary and one of her friends sat and talked, rather self-consciously, to judge by their expressions.

Tracey was aware of the expressions of most of her teammates. Their eyes were on her and Peggy and Dibbles, but mostly on her. This was the last game, the last chance for the team. More than that, it was the last time that she and Dibbles and Peggy would play together.

"Let's do 'Holy, Holy, Holy,'" Tracey said.

After their singing, they looked at Tracey expectantly. She pulled an index card out of her uniform pocket and read from it to them:

Behold, a king shall reign in righteousness, and princes shall rule in judgment. And a man shall be as an hiding place from the wind, and a covert from the tempest; as rivers of water in a dry place, as the shadow of a great rock in a weary land. And the eyes of them that see shall not be dim, and the ears of them that hear shall hearken. The heart also of the rash shall understand knowledge, and the tongue of the stammerers shall be ready to speak plainly.

When Tracey had finished, she slipped the card back into her pocket. It had become her habit to share a verse or two with the team at games and at practices. As long as she added nothing to what she read from Scripture, CPR permitted it. But suddenly from the driver's seat, without turning around, CPR said, "Who is the man, Tracey? The man who is the hiding place?"

"Christ," Tracey said. "This is an Old Testament prophecy of Him."

CPR nodded and said nothing more.

After the short devotional, several of the girls wandered back to their places. But Peggy and Dibbles stayed with her.

"I wanted to tell you something," Peggy said. "Well, first, thanks for having us over this past Sunday. Maddie's a great cook."

"She'll be at the game," Tracey said with a smile. "You can tell her yourself. She was glad you guys could come over again."

"Tracey," Peggy said, "my folks came up last night. You know that they'll be at the game too. I meant to wait because I didn't want to upset them right before the game, but it couldn't wait."

Tracey glanced at her, puzzled.

"I've decided that I can't attend a Catholic church anymore in good conscience, Tracey," Peggy said. Next to her, Dibbles nodded.

"I don't know if your church would be right for me either," Peggy added. "But I want to worship God the right way. I want to be a Christian—inwardly, I mean."

"We've both been reading the gospels of John that Maddie gave you to give us," Dibbles said.

"I just couldn't resist," Peggy said, and she looked troubled in spite of the greatness of what she was confessing. "I confessed it to God—I can't possibly be good enough to be a Christian. I want God to work through me like He worked through you all these years, somehow bringing you through. I asked Him to save me. But I don't know—I don't know that what you did would be right for me . . ." Her voice trailed off. Dibbles also looked troubled.

Heedless of being caught eavesdropping, a few of the girls hung over the seat behind the two seniors, listening. Trish Roberts looked especially intense.

"I'm sure that a lot of what I did was the wrong thing to do, Peggy," Tracey told her.

"Then what do we do?" Dibbles asked, and Tracey realized that both girls were serious about their faith in Christ.

"If it's Christ, and Christ alone," Tracey told them, "and we know that it is, then you have to turn to Him and to His Word. I think if you read the Bible carefully, and seek out books written by people who are good scholars and who believe the Bible, you will find the way. But most of all, you have to seek Christ—still in prayer, still asking for help. He has a way of working out things for our good."

Both girls nodded and leaned back, satisfied. The other girls nodded too. Tracey had answered well. And her own life had proved the truth of her words.

"Maddie's throwing that big bash for us tomorrow," Tracey reminded them. "You can check the books she's got. She would lend some to you to read."

Peggy and Dibbles nodded. With their parents in town over the weekend for the big game, they would be free to go where they pleased. Everybody's parents were here, and it was a sure thing that most of the girls would be dropping in for the party—whether it would be a victory party or a consolation party was yet to be determined. In either case, Maddie's contributions would be appreciated.

Maddie had made herself felt by the team, in spite

of having to end her work at the school. There were still occasional approved outings when she could host Tracey's friends, and she had attended nearly all of the games. And Maddie's care packages, even with Tracey out of the hall, managed to find their way pretty steadily into Dibbles's or Peggy's room, to be shared with the others.

Peggy strummed the guitar and sang to herself:

> For strength the black, for truth the white,
> Our colors we hold dear.
> Let strength and truth abide us
> In every heart sincere.

She let it trail off. Nervousness was building. The last game. The last shot for the championships. And Tracey felt—though she knew she shouldn't—that it was her last chance: her last chance at MoJoe to somehow be vindicated. She knew that she should not equate basketball skill with moral uprightness and goodness, but the equation was already there. Many of the girls did believe that because Tracey was a Christian she had somehow been given the gift to play basketball.

She remembered how Liz, no matter what she did, always ended up being held high in the estimation of the other girls. They had thought her brave, fearless, wonderfully reckless, and carefree. And now, similarly, they regarded Tracey as being fearlessly upright in her beliefs—and somehow, her ability in basketball was all tied up with that in their minds. It had been her best season so far, but like any player, she had blown points, missed shots, and fouled out. It didn't matter. They never noticed those things. When she raced out onto the court, tall and straight, with the spear in her hands, they cheered for her. When she played PIG or POISON with the underclassmen, they brought their disputes to her, and she adjudicated for them. They listened to her.

To end in defeat tonight would be the best thing for her own pride, Tracey thought. She always had to fight herself and her pride, and it seemed that winning this game might undo a lot that had been painstakingly won in her life. But then again, to disappoint their expectations and hopes for her, to prove at the end that she was just another girl—

She sighed. She was just another girl. *And yet I'm not*, she thought. She was His. He had given her everything. It would be wonderful to prove it on the court. But she shook her head at herself. She had proved it, but on another court.

"Are you OK, Jac?" Peggy asked.

"Yeah," she said, and offered a quick smile.

They were pulling into the gym. "Wanna pray?" Dibbles asked.

Tracey was too nervous to want to pray aloud. And she had been praying off and on the whole trip, so praying out loud was almost an interruption. But she obediently closed her eyes. Only Peggy and Dibbles were close by. She hesitated, searching for words. To her own surprise, Tracey said out loud, "Let strength and truth abide in us. Amen."

The gym blazed with light in the early spring night. As the girls clambered off the bus, carrying their equipment, they could hear the pep band's drums pounding. A huge bass drum had been added, and it dominated every game with its booming.

A new wave of nervousness rolled over all of them as they came one by one down the steps of the bus and surveyed the lights spilling out of the doors and windows. CPR came last.

"Every year it's them, and every year it's us," Peggy said.

"Yeah, but this year it's really us," Tracey replied. She felt her courage rising under the nervousness. Determination began to replace her fear. "You guys remember all the new signals, right?" she asked.

"We got 'em!" Dibbles exclaimed in her singsong voice. Tracey and Peggy and Dibbles looked at each other and laughed out loud.

"Then let's go!" Tracey exclaimed. "Bring the spears!"

They had modified many things for this last game. Though Tracey still carried the huge team spear, each of the girls had her own spear to carry. In fact, spears this season had replaced the fad of swords and shields from last season. Most of the girls had been able to cobble together broomsticks and rake handles into spears and lances, and the girls in the audience loved to brandish them and hold them high whenever somebody scored during the games. Tracey herself had used art class time to fashion an elaborate and long spear to give Maddie for this one game. Sister Madeleine had helped her on the intricate parts.

And they had modified their signals. The Villains had scouted the MoJoes from the very beginning, and Tracey's countermove had been to suggest signal changes that would be hard to detect or interpret.

So instead of hand signals, they would use yells to communicate plays back and forth. Two short yells for long post, three for short post, an Indian whoop to signal the wings to move out. Tracey had introduced the concept to CPR at the last practice before this big game, and CPR had approved it. They had practiced their cries for an hour and a half, and the new system worked well.

"Go get dressed, girls," CPR told them. "I'll see you in a few minutes."

There was a silent steadiness in all of them as they zipped up their warm-up suits and laced their basketball shoes. Tracey heard Dibbles, normally the first to regain and keep her comical composure, let out her breath in a hard sigh.

"It's just another game," Tracey said as she tied her shoe and double-bowed the knot.

"They're always so tough," Peggy said. She went to the walkway that led into the locker room from the gym. There was no door; rather, the narrow entrance hallway twisted around several corners before opening into the gym itself.

She came back to say, "There's got to be twice as many of them in the crowd as there are of us. I can tell from all those school uniforms."

"Yeah, but a lot of the other spectators are rooting for us," Tracey said. "After they did that spot on the news for us again, we got most of the town on our side."

"I saw Liz up there," Peggy said. "I'm glad she could come."

"Yeah, she's staying with Maddie and me," Tracey replied. "She came down for the weekend." There had been only enough time for her and Liz to hug each other and laugh and tease a little, and then Tracey had been hurried off into the team bus. But she had seen the changes in Liz—short, curled hair; makeup; nail polish; and the faintest suggestion of other things. She couldn't go to college without learning a lot of new things, and Tracey had felt some misgivings about seeing Liz. Yet Liz seemed delighted to see her again, and she was both polite and tenderly considerate in talking to Maddie. Her old flippancy was gone.

"There are scouts too," Peggy said absentmindedly. She was probably good enough now to be a serious contender for a scholarship.

"Are you sure you won't change your mind about that scholarship, Tracey?" Dibbles asked.

"I'm sure," she said. "I'm going to a Christian college. It doesn't have scholarships, but it costs less, anyway. I'm going to write books someday about church history—books that will be easy to read. And I'm going to teach it too. Where's the spear?"

"Over here." Dibbles handed her the team's spear.

"You guys got the routine down?" Tracey asked. "Come on, Peg. Let me help you." She fitted the shield over Peggy's arm and handed her the sword. "Let's get ready."

"Last time," Peggy said.

"And the best," Tracey added. "Follow me."

She led them through the twisting passageway and stood just inside the doorway. CPR hurried up. "Everybody ready?"

"We're ready," Tracey said.

People were clearing off the gym floor, making for the bleachers. The lights dimmed for a moment and came back up, and then the floodlights came on. By then the floor was empty. Tracey saw Maddie, sitting in the front row of the bleachers, directly across the gym from her. The spear that Tracey had made for her was in her hand, upright alongside her, its tip pointed at the high, domed ceiling. Tracey, standing with the team spear, her body at rest and yet as ready as a coil to spring into action, caught Maddie's glance. Maddie smiled. And Tracey smiled.

The pep band began its fanfare, except for the big drum. With a loud shout, she ran onto the gym floor, spear aloft, and the MoJoe spectators greeted her with shouts, spears waving. She ran to her place on the floor, and the music stopped. *One, two, three,* she counted to herself, then lifted the spear and pounded the butt of it on the gym floor. The big drum boomed once. She lifted the spear again and struck it down again, in time with the drum's boom. A third time, with the loud boom of the drum, she struck the spear on the floor. On that signal, the rest of the team rushed out, Peggy first. They held up their spears and shouted as they ran— long, drawn-out yells. They raced in a circle around the gym floor, spears raised, while the crowd yelled with them and the drum boomed a welcome. At last they fell into a formation behind Tracey, who had stayed standing.

The Villains came out next, repeating their routine from last year, wearing bandit masks and then twirling them and clapping, but after the bloodcurdling cries of the Valkyries, their routine fell a little flat. And nothing could compare with that huge drum.

The school songs were sung, and everybody cleared the court for the final instructions from their coaches. Both teams hastily cast off the warm-up suits that covered their basketball uniforms. Tracey held out the spear, and her teammates rallied to it, each of them gripping it.

"He-e-e-e-y, let's go! Let's fight! Let's win! Valhalla!" they cried.

Tracey ran to Maddie and gave her the team spear to take care of.

"Do well, dear!"

"I will, Maddie!"

All fear gone, Tracey centered in the middle with her opponent. The ref held the ball ready, the whistle in her mouth, and looked at the two of them as they both fixed their eyes on the place just above the ball. She tossed it up. Tracey let out a loud yell and came up under it, knocking it to Dibbles. The outcry startled the Villains center.

"Aaaah-ha!" Dibbles yelled, racing down the court with it.

The rest of the school suddenly got the idea, and they took up Dibbles's shout. Dibbles passed off to Tracey, and Tracey found herself surrounded by Villains. Rather than pass back out, she dodged between two of them, the ball going exactly where she willed it to go. She had not seen Liz yet in the stands, but now she thought she heard her, her voice carrying through the uproar of the crowd. "That's the way, Jac!"

As soon as Tracey got clear, she popped the ball high to Peggy, who was at the top of the key. Tracey raced into the key to rebound, but Peggy sank it with a *whoosh*.

The drum boomed, the girls hammered on the bleachers. Spears waved.

The sounds broke in waves over them. Tracey could see that the Villains were not following the MoJoe plays nearly as well as they had last year, and the yelling puzzled and even intimidated them. At one point, she found herself face-to-face with the Villains center, who was determined to block her as she tried to pass forward to Trish, who had come under the basket for short post.

Tracey's yell produced nothing but a sneer from the Villains center, until Tracey, looking like she would pass forward, grinned at the girl, yelled again, and dropped the ball back behind her, where short Dibbles caught it. Tracey turned and made herself a wall, and Dibbles shot unhampered and sank it. The drum boomed. The MoJoes screamed in delight.

But the Villains had lost none of their tight playing and half-court press. They were two or three times better than any other team that MoJoe ever played. Time and again, they faked out the Valkyrie defense. They had long shooters too this year, and Tracey was a grim witness when the Villains center sank a shot from almost back at the half-court line.

The first quarter ended with the Valkyries up by two points. At the bench, all of them practically buried their faces into the plastic cups of lemon water that CPR and Liz Lukas handed out to them.

"Baby, you really got 'em spooked," Liz said, and Tracey felt the rub of Liz's forearm across her head, for good luck.

"I think we might do it," Tracey whispered. Her

voice was gone. She looked down the long rows of people until she saw Maddie and smiled at her.

"You girls cannot keep up intensity like this through four quarters," CPR said.

"I can," Tracey whispered. "I know I can."

"We'll see. It's no use ruining your voice just for a trophy," CPR told her.

"What about that offense of theirs?" Peggy asked. "They're shooting from farther away this year."

"They may not be as good at long passes as we are," CPR said. "Try some interceptions. We're all so scared of losing our zone work that we might be letting them take advantage of us."

Tracey nodded. They had been hanging back on defense, waiting for the enemy to come to them.

"Let's take it to them!" she exclaimed in a hoarse whisper.

The buzzer called them back in. Play resumed. It took the MoJoes a few minutes to get their interception game down well, and the score tipped back in the Villains' favor. But their center got too cocky and threw a long pass way up the floor. Tracey ran in from the lane, jumped high, and brought it down. And there was Trish Roberts, exactly where she needed to be, at the top of the Valkyries' key. Tracey passed to her, and Trish took it in unhampered for a layup.

The first-string of the Villains came back in. They begrudged the Valkyries' every point, every step. Again and again, Tracey found herself surrounded by their blue uniforms, hedged in. She had lost her speaking voice, but she kept up the yelling—no longer signaling plays, but using every chance to break their concentration and to rally her teammates. She passed through the Villains' legs when she could, or dropped the ball over her shoulder for Dibbles to get from behind, but many times she just faked them out and found a way through. Once she popped the ball high, like a jump ball, and came up under it as everybody scrambled, and then she slammed it to Peggy.

The drum boomed, the crowd kept up its yells, the lights blazed down. Blisters sprouted on Tracey's feet. By the second half they had torn away from the skin, and her feet became soaked with sweat and blood. They burned on the bottom, but for the moment it was a good feeling.

The game pounded on—hard-driving defense against them, high jumps, good passes, control of the ball while dribbling. Dibbles came through on a great alley-oop with Peggy while Tracey rested on the bench for two minutes in the third quarter. The MoJoes went wild.

Maddie came over to the bench and sat by Tracey. Up until then, she had avoided doing anything that would look like she was forcing her reinstatement. Such tricks were beneath her. But Tracey was glad that she had suspended her own rule that night.

"I think we can win," Tracey whispered, not a shred of speaking voice left.

"You've got to outlast them," Maddie said.

"I can outlast them," she whispered.

Tracey had to recognize that Hilary was also doing brilliantly. For tonight, at least, she was following directions, and she played with a lot of grace and awareness. She looked better than Tracey had looked her sophomore year, and she looked better than Scooter had ever looked. She was more trim and graceful than Peggy, but the older girl still possessed more experience and that subtle knowledge of her teammates that came from years of play together.

Tracey realized with a slight jolt that once she graduated, taking Peggy and Dibbles with her, the team would be left to Hilary. Maybe Trish Roberts could stand against her, but Trish would be graduating next year. And then the team, the school—they were going to slip back. Every organizational rule was still in place to maintain the old system. Once Tracey was gone, with Maddie gone too, there would be nothing in place to save the changes that had been worked.

CPR put Tracey back in. The Villains were up by two again. With a bold yell, she raced out onto the floor, her feet burning. The ball came in, and she leaped between the two Villains guards to take it, then passed off to Dibbles, who was right in place to receive it. Dibbles scurried to the basket, shot, and scored.

The floating feeling—which Tracey had forgotten about since last year's game—returned. She did not feel her feet hitting the floor, nor the ball hitting her hand as she dribbled and moved. Her eyes saw the ways she had to turn and twist to roll around the Villains forward, but her body didn't feel it when she did it. The crowd began to sound far away, roaring, with a steady boom-booming in its throat, deep in its throat.

Without making the decision consciously, she blocked the Villains guard and turned, letting Dibbles roll around her with the ball. The guard went after Dibbles, but Dibbles passed back to Tracey, and Tracey charged into the key with the ball. She saw three blue uniforms stacked up against her, and without thinking she jumped up to free her hands from the tangle of their arms, shot, and made the basket.

The break before the fourth quarter was filled with CPR speaking earnestly, her face intense. The words rolled over Tracey like the roar of the crowd, but she didn't hear what they said. She knew what had to be done.

Out in the haze of the game, she noticed that the floor was very wet. The ball was wet in places. A huge blue uniform came up like a wall and hit her. She heard the breath get knocked out of her, but she hardly felt it, nor did she feel the floor when she hit it. The whistle shrilled. The crowd booed at the girl who had fouled. Tracey got up, unharmed, and took and made her foul shots.

They were running away with the game and she didn't know it. She heard the crowd, like ocean waves pounding, saw their exultant faces, wondered why they felt so sure of themselves this soon in the fourth quarter, and passed to Dibbles, who ran up and did a successful layup, then a cartwheel.

The lights seemed too bright. There were rings of brightness around them. They were reflected in brilliant but streaky pools on the gym floor. The ball went out-of-bounds with both teams scrambling for it, and they had to jump for it. As she waited for Peggy and the Villains girl who had last touched it to get ready and jump, she saw Maddie, very close by, looking at her from the bleachers. Pools of the light were at her feet and blazing down on her head. She had one spear upright in her hand, the other alongside her, leaning against the bench. Tracey's own warm-up suit lay spread across her knees, the red emblem of the Valkyrie bold and visible. Peggy jumped and slapped the ball to Hilary, who raced for the basket. Tracey got ahead of her, and

Hilary passed forward to her to keep it out of the reach of the Villains. And Tracey saw herself, as she ran down for the basket, reflected in the glass doors that led from the school into the gym. The light surrounded her with its rings, shone off her face and arms and legs, pooled around her feet. She jumped and shot, unable to escape the illumination of the lights.

It seemed like hours later when she heard the crowd's voice take a different note, but she could not hear it distinctly. A tremendous roaring in her ears was making it hard to hear anything distinctly. The Villains seemed desperate now. Their faces looked earnest, but their moves were suddenly halfhearted. And then she realized that it was the countdown. Determined to make it one last time, she raced down the length of the court, avoiding the blue uniforms, and she heard Dibbles and Peggy and Trish and the others shouting for her to get there. She leaped up and threw from the top of the key just as the buzzer sounded, and the ball whisked through the net.

Suddenly there were people everywhere, all around her. Spears were being flung into the air. She heard the drum. She looked at the scoreboard. The Valkyries had won by sixteen points.

Liz came up under her arm, talking fast and smiling, and then Tracey felt Maddie's sure arms helping her off the floor, and Maddie was smiling.

What brought Tracey back was Dibbles throwing a splash of the lemon water over her. The coolness raced down her hot skin and revived her. But she couldn't catch her breath, and her throat was too dry.

"Water," she said.

Then everybody was very concerned, and a sudden,

confused hush went through the people around her, and they made her drink a cup of the lemon water slowly. It restored her vision and her hearing, though suddenly her feet hurt so much she didn't know how she was going to walk. "I'm all right," she said. "Just let me sit here."

The other girls hoisted CPR up into the air with loud cheers. They called Liz over to join them, and she did.

Maddie at once took charge of Tracey. "We'll have to get you home," she said, wrapping her arms around her. "Oh, you are a sight. There's blood on your shoes and socks." But she hugged Tracey.

"Oh, Maddie, I'm all sweaty! Be careful."

Maddie ignored the warning. Her eyes were alight. "Oh, it was well-played. It almost wasn't basketball anymore." She looked into Tracey's eyes and smiled. "I'm proud of you. Do you want more water?"

"No, but I don't think I can move yet," Tracey said ruefully. She felt so sore and so tired that she wondered how she was going to stand. Her returning sensibilities were letting off alarm after alarm at the state her feet were in, the tearing feeling of shinsplints, and the desperate cry of her bloodstream for nutrition.

"Just stay right here for a second or two," Maddie said. "We'll send Liz in to get your things and then help you out to the car." She held Tracey's head to her shoulder for a moment, and she gleefully whispered, so nobody else would hear, "Oh, you should have seen Sister Mary's face. She'll be praying for graduation now."

This type of crowing was so unlike Maddie that Tracey looked up at her in surprise.

"I know, I know," Maddie whispered, trying to be contrite. But her eyes danced. "Oh, what a sad day it was for her when she set herself to make you miserable. God has exalted you."

Liz hurried back from the crowd of players. "Tough play, Jac!" she exclaimed in admiration. "Just about did you in!" She looked at Tracey with a smile. "If this had to be the end, I'm glad you went out with such a bang."

Tracey suddenly looked up at her. "It's not the end, not for me."

"I meant about being a Valkyrie," Liz said. She grinned again, sympathetic with the punishment Tracey had taken on the court. "Let me go get your gym bag," she said. "I'll be right back."

Maddie moved down and lifted Tracey's right foot up onto the bleachers, then her left foot. She began to unlace the basketball shoes for Tracey. "There are clean socks in your bag, dear. We ought to see to your poor feet."

Tracey looked at Maddie. "I don't think being a Valkyrie ends with basketball," she whispered.

"Of course not," Maddie told her. She glanced up as she loosened the laces, and her eyes were confident and happy. "Basketball was just the preparation. So long as there is a heaven and a kingdom, I suppose that the Lord will make for Himself a few shield maidens to go out and conquer in His name."